The Scene of the Crime

Kyrie. Tom's human mind identified her a second before his reptilian self, startled, scared, surprised, would have opened his mouth and let out with a jet of flame.

He tried to shape her name, but the reptilian throat didn't lend itself to it.

She was looking into his eyes, horrified. He tried to shape an apology but what came out was a semigrowling hiss.

"Tom," she said, her voice raspy and hoarse, her eyes frightened and . . . pitying? "Tom, you killed someone."

Killed? He was sure he hadn't. He stopped on a breath, then tasted in his mouth the metallic and—to his dragon senses—bright and delicious symphony of flavors that was blood.

Blood? Human blood?

The shock of it seemed to wake him. He looked down to see a corpse between his paws. His paws were smeared with blood. The corpse was a bundle, indistinct, neither male nor female, neither young nor old. It smelled dead. Freshly dead.

Had he killed someone?

He tried to remember and he couldn't. The dragon . . .

He took his hand to his forehead, felt the clamminess of blood on his skin, and realized he was human again. Human, smeared with blood, standing by a corpse.

And Kyrie had seen him kill someone.

"No," he said, not sure to whom he spoke. "Oh, please, no."

Baen Books by Sarah A. Hoyt

Draw One in the Dark

Gentleman Takes a Chance (forthcoming)

Draw One
in the Dark

Sarah A. Hoyt

DRAW ONE IN THE DARK

Copyright © 2006 by Sarah A. Hoyt

A Baen Book

Baen Publishing Enterprises
P.O. Box 1403
Riverdale, NY 10471
www.baen.com

ISBN 10: 1-4165-5542-0
ISBN 13: 978-1-4165-5542-1

Cover art by Dave Seely

First Baen paperback printing, May 2008

Distributed by Simon & Schuster
1230 Avenue of the Americas
New York, NY 10020

Library of Congress Cataloging-in-Publication Data: 2006023926
Printed in the United States of America

10 9 8 7 6 5 4 3 2 1

Pages by
Frank Aguirre at Hypertext Book and Journal Services
hypertext1@gmail.com

DEDICATION

One of the amazing side benefits of becoming a professional writer is to be able to personally meet and become friends with people you've read and admired from afar.

I'd like to dedicate this book to David Drake, whose friendship, by itself, is enough to compensate for all the tribulations, sweat, and tears of a career in writing.

ACKNOWLEDGMENTS

I would like to thank Sofie Skapski, Kate Paulk, Pam Uphoff, and Lee McGregor for proofing and doing occasional continuity interventions. Without them, this story would be very difficult to follow. And I'd like to thank my husband, Dan Hoyt, who at a crucial point in the story came up and told me how much I was playing with his emotions and how he needed the rest of the story right then. It made finishing the book much more fun.

The July night sprawled, warm and deep blue over Goldport, Colorado. In the distance the mountains were little more than suspicions of deeper darkness, a jagged outline where no stars appeared.

Most of Goldport was equally dark, from its slumbering suburbs to the blind silence of its downtown shops. Only the streetlights shone, at intervals, piercing the velvet blackness like so many stars.

At the edge of the western suburbs that climbed—square block after square block—into the lower slopes of the Rockies, the neon sign outside a Chinese restaurant flickered. *Three Luck Dragon* flared, faded, then flared again, and finally turned off completely.

A hand with nails that were, perhaps, just a little too long turned over a sign that hung on the window, so that the word "closed" faced the parking lot.

After a while, a sound broke the silence. A flapping noise, as though of sheets unfurling in the silent night. Or perhaps of large wings beating.

Descending.

Had anyone been awake, he'd have seen a large, dark creature—serpentine and thin—with vast unfolding wings

1

descend from the night sky till his huge taloned feet met the asphalt. It closed its wings about itself and waited.

It did not wait long. From alleys and darkened streets, people emerged: teenagers, in tight jeans and T-shirts, looking nervous, sidling out of the shadows, glancing over their shoulders as if afraid of being followed. From yet other alleys . . . *creatures* emerged: long, sinuous, in moist glistening colors between green and blue. They slid, monstrous heads low to the ground, curved fangs like daggers unsheathed in the moonlight. And sometimes dragons seemed to shift to naked teenagers and back again. In and out of the shadows, knit with walls and garbage bins, slithering along the hot cement of the pavement came young men who were dragons and dragons who were nervous young men.

They gathered in front of the Great Sky Dragon. And waited.

At length the dragon spoke, in a voice like pearls rolling upon old gold. "Where is it?" he asked. "Did you get it back?"

The amorphous crowd of humans and dragons moved. There was the impression of someone pushed forward. A rustle of cloth and wings. A murmur of speech.

The young man pushed forward was slender, though there was a suggestion of muscles beneath his leg-molding jeans and of a substantial chest straining the fabric of the white T-shirt. His bare arm displayed a tattoo of a large, green, glistening dragon and his eyes had an oriental fold, though it was clear from his light brown hair, his pale skin that he was not wholly Asian.

He was, however, completely scared. He stood trembling in front of the monster, who brought a vast golden eye to fix on him. "Yesss?" the dragon said. "You have something to report? You've found the Pearl of Heaven?"

The young man shook his head, his straight, lank hair swinging from side to side.

"No?" the dragon asked. Light glimmered on its fangs as he spoke, and his golden eye came very close to the boy, as if to examine him better.

"It wasn't there," the youth said, rapidly, his English not so much accented as retaining the lilt of someone who'd grown up in a community full of Chinese speakers. "We looked all over his apartment. It wasn't there."

The golden eye blinked, vein-laced green skin obstructing it for just a moment. Then the huge head pulled back a little and tilted. "We do not," it said, fangs glimmering, "tolerate failure."

It darted forward, so quickly the movement seemed to leave a green trail in the air like an afterimage. The fangs glistened. A delicate tongue came forth.

The boy's scream echoed a second too late, like bad special effects. It still hung in the air as the youth, feet and hands flailing, was lifted high into the night by the great dragon head.

A crunching sound. A brief glimmer. Two halves of the boy tumbling, in a shower of blood, toward the parking lot.

A scurry of cloth and wings followed, as men and dragons scrambled away.

The great golden eyes turned to them. The green muzzle was stained red. "We do not tolerate failure," it said. "Find the Pearl of Heaven. Kill the thief."

It opened its wings and, still looking intently at the crowd, flapped their great green length, till it rose into the dark, dark sky.

In the parking lot below no one moved till the last vestiges of the sinuous green and gold body had disappeared from view.

Kyrie was worried about Tom. Which was strange, because Tom was not one of her friends. Nor would *she* have thought she could care less if he stopped showing up at work altogether.

But now he was late and she was worried. . . .

She tapped her foot impatiently as she stared out at the window of the Athens, the Greek diner on Fairfax Avenue where she'd worked for the last year. Her wavy hair, dyed in multicolored layers, gave the effect of a tapestry. It went well with her honey-dark skin, her exotic features, and the bright red feather earring dangling from her ear, but it looked oddly out of place with the much-washed full-length red apron with "Athens" blazoned in green across the chest.

Outside everything appeared normal—the winding serpentine road between tall brick buildings, the darkened facade of the used CD store across the street, the occasional lone passing car.

She looked away, disgusted, from the windows splashed with bright, hand-scrawled advertisements for specials "—souvlaki and fries—$3.99, clam chowder—99¢, fresh rice pudding—" and at the large plastic clock high on the wall.

Midnight. And Tom should have come in at nine. Tom had never been late before. Oh, she'd had her doubts when Frank hired the young street tough with the unkempt dark curls, the leather jacket and boots, and the track marks up both of his arms, clear as day. But he had always come in on time, and he was polite to the customers, and he never seemed to be out of it. Not during work time.

"Kyrie," Frank said, from behind her. Kyrie turned to see him, behind the counter—a short, dark, middle-aged man, who looked Greek but seemed to be a mix of Italian and French and Greek and whatever else had fallen in the melting pot. He was testy today. The woman he'd been dating—or at least was sweet on, as she often walked with him to work, or after work—hadn't come in.

He gave Kyrie a dark look from beneath his bushy eyebrows. "Table seven," he said.

She looked at table seven, the broad table by the front window. And that was a problem, because the moon was full on the table, bathing it. It didn't seem to bother the gaggle of students sitting at it, talking and laughing and eating a never-ending jumble of slices of pie, dolmades, rice pudding dishes, and olives, all of it washed down with coffee.

Of course, there was no reason it should bother them, Kyrie reminded herself. Probably not. Moonlight only bothered her. Only her . . .

No. She wouldn't let moonlight do anything. She wouldn't give in to it. She had it under control. It had been months. She was not going to lose control now.

The students needed warm-ups for their coffee. And heaven knew they might very well have decided they needed more olives. Or pie.

She lifted the walk-through portion of the counter and ducked behind for the carafe, then back again, walking briskly toward the table.

Her hand stretched, with the pot's plastic handle firmly grasped in manicured fingers, nails adorned with violet-blue fingernail polish. One cup refilled, two, and a young man probably two or three years younger than Kyrie stretched his cup for a warm-up. The cup glistened, glazed porcelain under the full moonlight of August.

Kyrie's hand entered the pool of moonlight, brighter than the fluorescent lights in the distant ceiling. She felt it like a sting upon the skin, like bathwater just a little too hot for touch. For a disturbing second, she felt as if her fingernails lengthened.

She bit the inside of her cheek, and told herself no, but it didn't help, because part of her mind, some part way at the back and mostly submerged, gave her memories of a hot and wet jungle, of walking amid the lush foliage. Memories of soft mulch beneath her paws. Memories of creatures scurrying in the dark undergrowth. Creatures who were scared of her.

Moonlight felt like wine on her lips, like a touch of fever. She felt as if an unheard rhythm pounded through her veins and presently—

"Could we have another piece of pie, too?" a redheaded girl with a Southern drawl asked, snapping Kyrie out of her trance.

Fingernails—Kyrie checked—were the right length. Was it her imagination that the polish seemed a little cracked and crazed? Probably.

She could still feel the need for a jungle, for greenery— she who'd grown up in foster homes in several cement-and-metal jungles. The biggest woods she'd ever seen were city parks. Or the miles of greenery from the windows of the Greyhound that had brought her to Colorado.

These memories, these thoughts, were just illusions, nothing more. She remembered those times she had surrendered to the madness.

"One piece of pie," she said, taking the small notebook from her apron pocket and concentrating gratefully on its solidity. Paper that rustled, a pencil that was growing far too blunt and required lots of pressure on the page.

"And some olives," one of the young men said.

"Oh, and more rice pudding," one of the others said, setting off a lengthy order, paper being scratched by pencil and nails that, Kyrie told herself, were not growing any longer. Not at all.

Still she felt tension leave her as she turned her back on the table and walked out of the moonlit area. Passing into the shadow felt as if some inner pressure receded, as though something she'd been fighting with all her will and mind had now been withdrawn.

While she was drawing a breath of relief, she heard the sound—like wings unfolding, or like a very large blanket flapping. It came, she thought, from the back of the diner, from the parking lot that abutted warehouses and the blind wall at the back of a bed-and-breakfast.

Kyrie wanted to go look, but people were waiting for their food, so she set about getting the pie and the olives and the rice pudding—all of it preprepared—from the refrigerator behind the counter. Next to it, Frank was peeling and cutting potatoes for the Athens's famous "fresh made fries, never frozen," which were also advertised on the facade, somewhere.

While she worked, some of the regulars came in. A tall blond man who carried a journal in which he wrote obsessively every night between midnight and four in the morning. And a heavyset, dark-haired woman who came in for a pastry on her way to her job at one of the warehouses.

Kyrie looked again at the clock. Half an hour, and still no Tom. She took the newcomers' orders.

On one of her trips behind the counter, for the carafe of coffee, she told Frank, "Tom is late."

But Frank only shrugged and grunted, which was pretty odd behavior for the guy who had brought Tom in out of nowhere, hired him with no work history while Tom was, admittedly, living in the homeless shelter down the street.

As Kyrie returned the carafe to its rest, after the round of warm-ups, she heard the scream. It was a lone scream, at first, startled and cut short. It too came from the parking lot at the back.

She told herself it was nothing to do with her. There were all sorts of people out there at night. Goldport didn't exactly have a large population of homeless, but it had some, and some of them were crazy enough to scream for no reason.

Swallowing hard, she told herself it meant nothing, absolutely nothing. It was just a sound, one of the random sounds of night in the city. It wasn't anything to worry about. It—

The scream echoed again, intense, frightened, a wail of distress in the night. Looking around her, Kyrie could tell no one else had heard it. Or at least, if Frank's shoulders were a little tenser than normal, as he dropped fries into a huge vat of oil, it was the tenseness of expectation, as if he were listening for Tom.

It wasn't the look of someone who'd heard a death scream. In fact, the only person who might have heard it was the blond guy, who had stopped writing on his journal and was staring up, into mid-air. But Kyrie was not about to ask a man who wrote half the night what exactly he had heard or hadn't. Besides the guy—nicknamed "The Poet" by the diner staff—always gave the impression of being on edge and ready to lose all self-control, from the tips of his long, nervous fingers to the ends of his tennis shoes.

And yet . . .

And yet she couldn't pretend nothing had happened. She knew she had heard the scream. With that type of scream, someone or something was in trouble bad. Back there. In the parking lot. At this time of night most of the clientele of the Athens came in on foot, from the nearby apartment complexes or from the college dorms just a couple of blocks away. It could be hours before anyone went out to the parking lot.

Kyrie didn't want to go out there, either. But she could not ignore it. She had the crazy feeling that whatever was happening out there involved Tom, and, what the heck, she might not like the man, but neither did she want him dead.

She gave a last round of warm-ups, looked toward the counter where Frank was still seemingly absorbed in his frying, and edged out toward the hallway that led to the back.

It curved past the bathrooms so, if Frank saw her, he would think she was going to the bathroom. She was not sure why she didn't want him to know she was going to the parking lot. Except that—as she got to the glass door at the back—when she saw the parking lot bathed in the moonlight, she thought that something might happen out there, something . . . Something she didn't want her employer to know about her.

Not that it could happen. There was nothing that could happen, she thought, as she turned the key. Nothing had happened in months. She wasn't sure what she thought had happened back then hadn't all been a dream.

The key hadn't been turned in some time and it stuck, but finally the resistence gave way, and she opened the door, and plunged into the burning moonlight.

Feeling of jungle, need for undergrowth and vegetation, her heart beating madly in her eardrums, and she was holding it together, barely holding it together, hoping . . .

She jumped out onto the parking lot and called out, "Tom—"

Something not quite a roar answered her. She stopped.

And then the smell hit her. Fresh blood. Spilled blood. She trembled and tried to stop. Tried to think.

But her nose scented blood and her mouth filled with saliva, and her hands curved and her nails grew. Somehow, with clumsy claws, she unbuttoned her uniform. She never knew how. As the last piece of clothing fell to the ground, she felt a spasm contort her whole body.

And a large, black jungle cat ran swiftly across the parking lot. Toward the smell of blood.

Soft pads on asphalt. Asphalt. The word appeared alien to Kyrie's mind, locked in the great loping body, feeling the movement, the agility, and not quite believing it.

Strange feeling on pads. Hard, scratchy.

Muscles coiling and uncoiling like darkness flowing in moonlit patches. Bright moonlight like a river of fire and joy. Running. Smelling with a sense that no human ever possessed.

And the feline stopped, alert, head thrown back, sniffing. A soft growl made its way up a throat that Kyrie could only just believe was her own.

Smell—a rich, spicy, flowing smell, like cinnamon on a cold winter night in Kyrie's human memory, like rich molten chocolate, like freshly picked apples to that dwindling part of herself who thought with human memories.

She took a deep breath and felt her mouth fill and overflow with drool, while her paws moved, step on step, toward the smell, soft pads on asphalt, growl rising from throat.

What was it? What could it be? Her human mind could not identify the smell that came at her with depth and meaning that humans did not seem capable of perceiving.

She felt drool drop through her half-open mouth, onto the asphalt, as she looked around for the possible source of the wondrous scent.

There were . . . cars—she had to force herself to remember the word, to realize these were man-made and not some natural plant or animal in a jungle she'd never seen but that was all this body knew and wanted to remember.

Cars. She shook her great head. Her own small, battered Ford, and two big vans that belonged to Frank and which he used for the daily shopping.

Around the edge of the vehicles she followed the scent. It was coming from right there, behind the vans, from dark liquid flowing along the asphalt, between the wheels of the van. She padded around the vans. Liquid looked black and glistened under moonlight, and she was about to take an experimental lap when the shadow startled her.

At first it was just that. A shadow, formless, moving on the asphalt. Something with wings. Something.

Her hackles rising, she jumped back, cowering, head lifted, growling. And saw it.

A . . . lizard. No. No lizard had ever been this size. A . . . creature, green and scaly and immense, with wings that stretched between the earth and the sky.

The feline Kyrie dropped to her belly, paws stretched out in front of her, a low growl rising, while her hair stood on end, trying to make the already large jungle cat look bigger.

The human Kyrie, torpid and half-dormant, a passenger in her own brain that had been taken over by this dream of moonlight and forest, looked at the beast and thought, *Dragon.*

Not the slender, convoluted form of the Chinese dragons with their huge, bewhiskered faces. No. Nordic. A sturdy Nordic dragon, stout of body, with the sort of wings that truly seemed like they could devour the icy blue sky of the Norsemen and not notice.

Huge, feral, it stood before Kyrie, fangs bared, both wings extended, tip to tip probably a good twelve feet. Its muzzle was stained a dark red, and—as Kyrie knit her belly to the concrete—it hissed, a threatening hiss.

It will flame me next, Kyrie thought. But she couldn't get the big cat to move. Bewildered by something that the now dominant part of her couldn't comprehend, she lay on her belly and growled.

And the Kyrie part of her mind, the human part, looked bewildered at the dragon wings, which were a fantastic construction of bones and translucent glittering skin that faded from green to gold. And she thought that dragons weren't supposed to look that beautiful.

Particularly not a dragon whose muzzle was stained with blood.

And on that, on the one word, she identified the enticing smell. Blood. Fresh blood. She remembered smelling it before the shape-shift. But it smelled nothing like blood through the big cat's senses.

With the feline's sharp eyes, she could see, beneath the paws of the dragon, a dark bundle that looked like a human body.

Human blood. And she'd almost lapped it.

Shock and revulsion did what her fear couldn't. They broke the human Kyrie out of the prison at the back of her own mind. Free, she pushed the animal back.

Push and push and push, she told herself she must be Kyrie. She must be human. Kyrie was smart enough to run away before the dragon let out with fire.

And never mind that the dragon might run her down, kill her. At least she would be able to think with a human mind.

All of a sudden, the animal gave, and she felt the spasms that contorted her body back to two human legs, two human arms, the solidity of a human body, lying on the concrete, hands on the ground, toes supporting her lower body.

She started to rise to run, but the dragon made a sudden, startled movement.

It was not a spring to attack nor a cowering in fear. Either of those she could have accepted as normal for the beast. It was a vague, startled jump. A familiar, startled jump.

Like coming on Tom around the corner of the hallway leading to the bathroom and meeting him coming out of it. Tom jumped that way, startled, not quite scared, and she always thought he'd been shooting up in there—must have been shooting up in there.

Now the same guilty jump from the dragon, and the massive head swung down to her prone body, to look at her with huge, startled blue eyes. Tom's eyes.

Kyrie. His human mind identified her a second before his reptilian self, startled, scared, surprised, would have opened his mouth and let out with a jet of flame.

His mouth opened, he just managed to control the flame. He tried to shape her name, but the reptilian throat didn't lend itself to it.

Tom felt his nictitating eyelids blink, sideways, before his normal eyelids, the eyelids he was used to, blinked up and down.

She stood up, slowly, shivering. She was honey-colored all over. Both sets of his eyelids blinked again. He'd always thought that she had a tan. No lines. And her breasts were much fuller than they looked beneath the uniform and apron—heavy, rounded forms miraculously, perfectly horizontal in defiance of gravity.

He realized he was staring and looked up to see her looking into his eyes, horrified. He tried to shape an apology but what came out was a semigrowling hiss.

"Tom," she said, her voice raspy and hoarse, her eyes frightened and . . . pitying? "Tom, you killed someone."

Killed? He was sure he hadn't. He stopped on a breath, then tasted in his mouth the metallic and—to his dragon senses—bright and delicious symphony of flavors that was blood.

Blood? Human blood?

The shock of it seemed to wake him. He looked down to see a corpse between his paws. His paws were smeared with blood. The corpse was a bundle, indistinct, neither male nor female, neither young nor old. It smelled dead. Freshly dead.

Had he run someone down? Killed him? Had he?

He tried to remember and he couldn't. The dragon . . .

He took his hand to his forehead, felt the clamminess of blood on his skin, and realized he was human again. Human, smeared with blood, standing by a corpse.

And Kyrie had seen him kill someone.

"No," he said, not sure to whom he spoke. "Oh, please, no."

❖   ❖   ❖

Tom's voice was low at the best of times. Now it came out growly and raspy, like gravel dragging around on a river bottom. His transformation, much faster than hers, had been so fast that she'd hardly seen it.

He stood by the corpse. Broad shoulders, small waist, muscular legs, powerful arms. A body that, except for his being all of five-six, and for the track marks on his arms, could have graced the cover of bodybuilding magazines. Only his muscles weren't developed to the grotesque level the field demanded.

And above it all was a face that managed to make him look like a frightened little boy.

His hair had come loose from the rubber band he used to confine it in a ponytail. Loose, it just touched his arms, in a rumple of irregular curls. His skin was pale, very pale all over. Not exactly vampire white. More like aged ivory, even and smooth. And his eyes were a deep, dark, and yet somehow brilliant blue.

They now opened in total horror, as he stared at her and rasped, "I didn't. Kill."

Her first reaction was to snap out that of course he had. She'd seen him by the corpse, his muzzle stained by blood. Then she remembered she'd almost lapped the blood herself. Lapped. And she'd known what it was before shifting too.

She shuddered, and remembered what the blood smelled like to the jungle cat. The beast, as she'd learned to call it years ago, when she'd first turned into it. Or hallucinated turning into it, as she'd convinced herself had happened over time. That theory might have to be discarded now, unless she was hallucinating Tom's shifting, too.

"I don't remember chasing," he said. "Killing."

A look down at the corpse told her nothing, save that it had been mauled. But wouldn't Tom . . . the dragon have mauled it anyway? Whether he'd killed it or not?

Tom was looking down, horrified, trembling. Shock. He was in shock. If she left him here, he would stay like that. Till they were caught.

She reached for his arm. His skin felt skin cold, clammy to the touch. Was it being the dragon? Or being naked in the night? Or the shock? She had to do something about the shock. No. She had to do something, period.

"Come," she said. "Come."

He obeyed. Like a child, he allowed her to pull him all the way to the back door of the diner.

She stooped to pick up her clothes, trying not to get blood on them.

✦   ✦   ✦

Tom stumbled after Kyrie, confused. The parking lot was cold. He felt it on his wet skin. Wet. He looked down and saw patches of blood on his body. Human blood.

"You're shaking like a leaf," Kyrie whispered. She opened the back door of the Athens and looked in, along the corridor that curved gently toward the bathroom. She said, "Go in. Quickly. Get into the women's bathroom. Don't lock it. I'll come."

He rushed forward, obeying. In his current state, he couldn't think of doing anything but obeying. But a part of his brain, moving fast beneath the sluggish surface of his shocked mind, wondered, *Why the women's bathroom?* Then he realized the women's bathroom was just one large room and locked, while in the men's restroom they'd managed to cram the stall and a row of urinals. And the outer door didn't lock.

Yeah, there would be more room in the women's bathroom to clean up, he thought, even as he skidded into the door to the bathroom, on damp, bare feet.

"Why didn't you turn the light on?" Kyrie said, coming in after him, turning the light on.

She went to the sink and started washing herself, making use of the paper towels and the water. Considering where she'd been, she had very little blood on her. Not like Tom. He tasted blood on his tongue.

And now he was shaking again.

"Stop that," Kyrie said. She was clean now, and putting her clothes back on. How had she managed to get out of her clothes before shifting?

He tried to remember his own clothes, and where he'd left them, but his memory was fogged and confused, intercut by the bright golden blur of the dragon's thoughts.

"Are you going to clean yourself or am I going to have to?" Kyrie asked. She'd somehow got fully dressed before he could notice. She stood there, looking proper, in her apron. She'd even put the earring back on her ear. She'd remembered to take that off. What was she? Some kind of machine?

Tom pulled his hair back from his face. "I'm naked," he said.

"I've noticed," she said, but she wasn't looking. And now she had the expression back on her face—the expression she'd shown Tom since the first day he'd arrived at the Athens and Frank had offered him a job. The expression that meant he was no good, he was possibly dangerous, and that Frank was crazy to trust him.

He knew she would glare at his track marks next and, damn it all, he hadn't shot up since he'd got— Well, since he'd got the job. He stopped the thoughts of whatever else he'd got forcefully. You really never knew what the other dragons could hear. He didn't think they were telepathic. He thought they were just watching him really closely. But he wasn't about to bet on it. No way. He wasn't about to let his guard down. He'd seen what they could do, way back when—

He shook his head and took deep breaths to drive away his memory—which could force him to become a dragon as fast as the shine of the moon or the smell of blood. He concentrated on the thought that it was nearby. It. The treasure he'd stolen. The magic that helped him stay himself.

A wet and cold paper towel touched his chest and he jumped. Kyrie's glance at him held a challenge. "I'll do it if I have to," she said.

He shook his head and pulled the towel from her hand, rubbing it briskly on his shoulders, his arms, his chest. He discarded it in the trash can, thinking about DNA evidence and trying not to. Telling himself he couldn't have done it, he couldn't have killed anyone. He couldn't. He just couldn't. That was something he couldn't live with—knowing for sure he'd killed anyone.

But the police would think— The police—

He started shaking again and took deep breaths to control it. He folded another mass of paper towels and wet it and ran it on his face, his hands. The face looking back at him from the mirror looked more red than white, smeared with blood.

Whose blood? Who had that person been, out in the parking lot? Tom didn't remember anything. Nothing, before opening his eyes, staring at the dead body, and seeing Kyrie. And that wasn't right. It had been like that at first, but it had given him more control and he was supposed to know what he'd done while in dragon form. He was supposed to remember.

Kyrie was looking at him, attentively, cautiously, like a bomb expert trying to decide which wire to cut in a peculiar homemade contraption.

Tom bit his tongue and managed a good imitation of his normal, gruff tone. "It's all right," he said. "I'm fine."

She cocked her head to one side, managing to convey wordlessly that there were about a million interpretations of *fine* and none of them applied to him. But aloud she said, "I'm going out for just a second. Lock up after me.

When I come back I will knock once. Only once. Let me in when I do."

Tom locked the door behind her, obediently. He wondered where she was going, but it wasn't like he had any room left to argue about what she might want to do. He should count himself lucky she hadn't screamed bloody murder when she'd found him in the parking lot. Perhaps she should have screamed bloody murder. Wasn't that the name for what he'd done? No— He hadn't— He couldn't—

A muffled knock. He realized that not only had Kyrie been gone for a while, but also that he'd somehow managed to remove most of the red stains from his hands and face. His hair was a drying, sticky mass that he didn't want to investigate, much less clean.

"That will do," she said. "You can wear these." She extended to him, at the end of a stiff arm—like a person feeding a wild animal—what looked like a red jogging suit.

"It's mine," she said, as though mistaking his hesitation for a belief that she'd mugged a vagrant for the clothes. Or taken them from the corpse. "I usually jog in the morning before going home. Safer here. It's a main street."

He swallowed hard, trying not to think of what street would be less safe than Fairfax. But then if she lived nearby—as he did—in the interlacing warren of downtown streets, there would be many less safe. Well, not less safe in reality—the crime rate in Goldport was never that high and most deaths were crimes committed by and between gang members. But on the side streets, dotted with tiny houses, or with huge Victorian mansions long since turned into tiny apartments, a woman jogging alone in the wee hours of the morning would not be seen.

And that, perhaps, meant she wouldn't be safe—because she could disappear and not be noticed for hours.

A thought that whoever tried to attack this woman would be far from safe himself crossed Tom's mind and he beat it down. Perhaps that was what she was afraid of. Of being mugged in the dark street and killing—

He grabbed the jogging suit. It felt too cold to his hands, and too distant—as if it weren't real fabric but some fabriclike illusion that his senses refused to acknowledge fully. As if he weren't really here. As if this were all a dream and he would, shortly, wake up back in the safety of his teenage room, in his father's house, with his stereo, his TV, his game system, all those things he'd needed when life itself wasn't exciting enough.

The clothes fit. Of course they would fit. Kyrie was his height, just about, and while his shoulders were much broader, and his chest far more muscular, she had other . . . endowments. A memory of her in the parking lot swept like a wave over him, and he felt a warm blush climb his cheeks and adjusted his—her—jogging pants and prayed that she wasn't focusing there just now.

But he might have been too late, because she frowned as if she were about to ask if blood turned him on. She didn't, though. Just said, "Wait for me. By the back door."

"The back?" he said. His voice came out too low and raspy. "But—"

"You can't walk through the diner like that. It's clear your hair is caked with blood. Someone might notice and say something. Later. When . . . someone asks."

The police. But neither of them mentioned it.

"I'm going to tell Frank I'm going out for a moment," she said.

He nodded. She was efficient. She was determined. And she was helping him. It was more than he could have hoped for. And certainly no fault at all of hers if it made him feel helpless and out of control.

As he hadn't been in six months.

Kyrie wasn't sure what she was going to tell Frank. She had some idea he'd already be on simmer from what he would see as her sudden disappearance. In the ten steps between the bathroom and the diner proper, she ran her options through her mind—she could tell him she felt ill. She felt ill enough after the mess in the parking lot and the more specific mess in the bathroom. And the last thing any greasy-spoon owner wanted was to have a sick employee—visibly sick—tending to tables. On the other hand, if she did that, she was going to be some hours short this month. Because there was no way she could come back again tonight. And there was rent to pay.

She didn't know what she going to say at all until she emerged from the corridor into the yellowish light of the diner and said, "Frank, I need a few minutes, to go to Tom's." Which made perfect sense as she said it. A few minutes should suffice to go to Tom's house, because Tom walked here, and if Tom walked here, he couldn't live very far away. That meant a couple of minutes would also see him back to his home with no problem at all. And her back here, pretending she'd just dropped by his place.

Frank was attending to the students' table and had the sort of look on his face that meant he was trying very hard not to explode. Kyrie had worked for him for a year and she'd been a reliable employee, never late, rarely sick, and trustworthy enough to be left alone with the register on occasion. None of which were easy to come by in a college town in Colorado for the late-night shift and considering what Frank was willing to pay.

He looked over his shoulder at Kyrie, and his brows beetled together, nonetheless, and he managed, "What? More minutes?"

"Tom is sick," she said. "He called me." Let Frank wonder why and how she'd given Tom her cell-phone number. "He wants me to buy him some stuff at the pharmacy and drop it by. Over-the-counter stuff," she added, thinking that most of what Tom probably took was not over-the-counter.

Frank looked like he was going to say something like that, for just a moment, but he gave it up. Probably he couldn't imagine Kyrie buying illegal drugs. And in that he would be right. She got enough lawlessness in her everyday life, enough to hide and disguise, that she did not need any more adrenaline.

So Frank shrugged, which might be taken for agreement, and Kyrie rushed back down the hallway, hoping to find Tom, hoping Tom hadn't shifted, hoping that for once things would go well. For just this once.

Tom was where she expected him—at the back of the diner, facing the door to the parking lot. He was pale and had started trembling again, and there wasn't much she could say or do for that. She wondered if he'd killed the man. She didn't want to think about it. It didn't matter. If he had, could she blame him? She knew the confusion of mind, the prevalence of the beast-self over every civilized learning, every instinct, even. How could she accuse someone else who'd given in perhaps further?

Of course she could, a deeper voice said, because she didn't give in. She'd fought her—as she'd thought—hallucinations tooth and nail and she'd held onto a normal life of sorts. No friends, no family, no one who might discover what she'd thought was her hideous madness, but she made her own money, she lived her own life.

She managed a weak smile at Tom by way of reassurance, as she turned the key and opened the door.

She took a deep breath to steel herself against the smell of blood, the light of the moon. She must stay in control. She must.

But she wasn't ready for the other smell—the hot, musky and definitely male smell that invaded her nostrils as she stepped onto the parking lot.

Dizziness and her mouth went dry and her whole body started fluttering on the verge of shifting shape, and she told herself no. No. Regained control just in time to see it, at the edge of the parking lot, under one of the lights.

Not it. Him. The smell was clear as a hallelujah chorus in her head. He was at the edge of the parking lot, and he was tawny and huge and muscular.

A lion. He was a lion. Was he a lion like she was a panther and Tom was a dragon, or . . .

Or what? An invader from the vast Colorado savannah outside Goldport? Where lions and zebras chased each other under the hot tropical sun?

She shook her head at her own silliness.

Behind her, Tom drew breath, noisily. "Is it?" he asked.

"Yes," she said.

"But—" He drew breath again and something—something about the movement of his feet against the asphalt, something about his breathing, perhaps something about his smell (since when could she smell people this way?) made her think he was about to run.

She put out a hand to his arm. "Do not run," she said. "Walk steadily."

His arm felt cold and smooth under her hand. Light sprinkling of hair. Very little of it for a male. Perhaps being a dragon . . . She didn't want to think of that. She didn't want to think of Tom, muzzle deep in blood.

Which of course meant the lion could smell them. Smell the blood on them. "You mustn't run," she said. "We . . . Cats are triggered by motion. If you run he will give chase. Walk slowly and steadily toward my car. The small white one. Come."

They made their way slowly, steadily, across the parking lot, in the reek of blood. Perhaps the lion wouldn't be able to smell Tom in the overwhelming smell.

Perhaps they could make it to the car. Perhaps . . . perhaps the moon was made of green cheese and it would rain pea soup tomorrow.

He smelled powerful, musky. She could hear him draw breath, was aware of the touch of paw pads on the asphalt. She felt those movements as if they were her own, her heart accelerating and seeming to beat at her throat, suffocating her.

Paw touching asphalt, and paw touching asphalt, and paw touching asphalt. Measured steps. Not a run. Please don't let it be a run.

And her movements matched his—slow, measured, trying to appear unconcerned, escorting Tom to the car, guiding him.

Tom walked like a wooden puppet. Was he that terrified of the lion? Didn't he know in his dragon form he was as big? Bigger? Stronger? Why was he afraid?

But her rational self understood. He was afraid because he was in human form. And every human at the back of his mind feared the large felines who lurked in the shadows and who could eat him in two bites.

Kyrie herself was sweating and cold by degrees, and felt as if her legs were made of water, as she concentrated on following the beast's movements by sound.

They hit the moonlight, out of the shadow of the diner and into the fully illuminated parking lot. The heat of it felt like fire playing over Kyrie's skin and she kept her head lowered. She took deep breaths. Her heartbeat echoed some old jungle rhythm but she told herself she would not, she would not, she could not shift.

And the smell of him—of the lion—enveloped her, stronger than ever. Her senses, sharpened from wanting to transform, gave her data about him that a mere nose should not be able to gather. That he was young. That he was healthy. That he was virile.

She pulled Tom forward, and the lion followed them at a distance—step, step, step, unhurried, unafraid. She prayed he wouldn't start running. She prayed he wouldn't leap. And inside, deep inside, she felt as if he was toying with her. Playing. Like a cat with a mouse.

She was not a mouse.

Sweat formed on her scalp, dripped toward her eyes, made her blink. The car loomed in front of her, white and looking much bigger than it usually did. Looking like safety.

Kyrie pushed her key-fob button to unlock it, and felt as if her fingers slipped on the smooth plastic, as though she had claws and unwieldy paws.

No. She must not. She must remain human. She must.

Breathing deeply and only managing to inhale more unabashed male musk, she shoved Tom, slightly, and said, "Go around to the passenger side. Get in."

Go, give him a divided target. Go, but for the love of all that's holy, don't stop. Don't stop. Don't let him catch you. She didn't know which she feared most. The idea of being attacked or the idea of seeing Tom attacked, of seeing Tom torn to pieces. Of shifting. Of joining in.

She shuddered as her too-clumsy fingers struggled with the car handle. She saw Tom open the door on the other side. Get in. She struggled with the handle.

And the lion was twenty steps away, crouching in the full light of the moon, augmented by the light of a parking-lot lamp above her. He was crouching, front down low and hindquarters high.

Hindquarters trembling. Legs bunching.

Jump. He was going to—

He jumped, clearing the space between them, and she leaned hard against her car, her heart hammering in her chest, her body divided and dividing her mind. Her human body, her human mind, wanted to scream, to hide. Her human body knew that the huge body would hit her, claws would rend her. That she was about to die.

But her other mind . . . Her other mind practically died in the ecstatic smell of healthy young male. Her other mind thought the lion knew her, guessed her, smelled her for an equal. That the lion wanted— Not to eat her.

She realized she'd closed her eyes, when she felt him landing near her—landing with all four paws on the asphalt. Not on her, but so close to her she felt the breeze of his falling, and smelled him, smelled him hot and strong and oh, so impossibly male.

She felt her body spasm, wish to shift. She fought it. She struggled to stay herself.

Through half-open eyes, she saw a lion's face turned toward her, its golden eyes glowing, its whole expression betraying . . . smugness?

Then it opened its mouth, the fangs glowing in the light and a soft growl started at the back of its throat. She didn't know if it was threatening her or . . .

Something to the growl—something to the sound crept along her nerves like a tingle on the verge of aching. If she stayed— If she stayed . . .

The car door opened, shoving her. She leapt aside, to avoid being pushed into the lion. A hand reached out of the car, dragged her. She fell onto her seat. Blinked. Tom. Tom had pulled her into the car.

"Drive," Tom said. "Drive."

He reached across her, as he spoke and slammed the door. From outside, the lion made a rumbling sound that might have been amusement.

She didn't remember turning the ignition. She didn't remember stepping on the gas. But she realized she was driving down Fairfax. Tall, silent apartment houses succeeded each other on either side of the road, lighted by sporadic white pools of light from the street lamps.

"Where do you live?" she managed, glancing at Tom. Part of her wanted to tell him she hadn't been afraid, she hadn't been . . .

But she wasn't even sure she could explain what she'd been. She had been afraid. That was a huge beast. But also, at some level, she was afraid she would end up shifting, cavorting with him. Over a half-devoured human carcass.

"Two blocks down," Tom said, and swallowed, as if he'd had the same thought at the same time. "Audubon Apartments. On the left."

She remembered the place. Not one of the graceful Victorian remnants, but half a dozen rectangular red-brick boxes sharing a parking lot. During the day there were any number of kids playing in the parking lot, and usually one or two men working on cars or drinking beer.

Now, in the dark of night, it was silent and ill lit. As she pulled into the parking lot, Tom asked, "It was one of us, wasn't it?"

"Pardon?" she said. She knew what he meant. She knew all too well. He was asking if the lion was like them. If the lion too had a human form and one not so human. But Kyrie had managed until very recently to convince herself she only had one form and that everything else was hallucination. Mental illness.

Now this whole thing felt like mental illness. She parked the car, turned the engine off.

"You know . . ." Tom said. His blue eyes were earnest, and he plucked at her sleeve like a little kid seeking reassurance. "You know, a shape-shifter. Like us."

She shrugged. "Seems unlikely it escaped from a zoo," she said. "Someone would have given the alarm, wouldn't they?"

Tom nodded, as if considering this. "What . . . what did it want?"

Kyrie shrugged. She wanted to say *he* wanted everything but all she had to go on was the smell. And she didn't wish to discuss her response to the smell with Tom.

"Do you think it killed the . . . person?"

Did you? Kyrie thought, but only shrugged. How did you ask someone who looked as bewildered and shocked as Tom if he'd committed murder? And was she really feeling sorry for Tom? *Must be going soft in the head.*

Tom got out of the car, patted down where the pockets would be in normal pants, and Kyrie realized he wouldn't have keys.

But he turned around and said, "Thank you for driving me," and pushed the door as if to close it.

"Wait, do you have keys?"

He shrugged. "The neighbor usually keeps them," he said. "For me. I keep his."

His? For some reason it had never occurred to Kyrie that someone like Tom could entrust his key—or anything else—to a male. If she'd thought of his social life outside work at all, she imagined a never-ending succession of sweet things across his mattress. But now she realized she was probably wrong. It was unlikely there was anyone on his mattress. He had come from a homeless shelter. And he was a dragon.

"Keith keeps my key and I keep his. . . . So if we lose it while we're out," Tom said, an edge of impatience in his voice. "He's a college student. They lose their keys." He hesitated a minute. "Gets stinking drunk too." He said it as if he, himself, never took any mind-altering substances.

And out of nowhere, an altruistic impulse, or perhaps the thought that he'd saved her—from what?—with the lion in the parking lot, made her get out. "I'll come with you," she said. "To make sure you get in okay."

She had a feeling, a strange feeling something was wrong. Wrong with this parking lot, with this entire area. There was a feeling of being watched and not in a friendly manner, but she wasn't sure by whom, or how. Any other day, any other time, she would have shrugged it off. But now . . . Well . . . perhaps she was picking up smell or something. Something was definitely wrong.

She got out of the car, unsteady on her legs, glad that the moonlight was hidden by the shadows of the buildings. The pressure of the full moonlight was all she needed now. At the same time, she felt as if the buildings themselves were looming shapes waiting to jump her.

It wasn't possible, was it? For the buildings to be shifters? With a human form? What was this? How many people did it afflict? And why was she afraid?

She wasn't sure of anything anymore. Sweat trickled down her back and her legs felt like water while she followed Tom to the steps outside the door of the nearest building.

"Keith might not be home," Tom said, pressing the button. Actually, it was damn bloody sure that Keith Vorpal would not be home. Keith was a film student at Goldport College and somewhat of a ladies' man. One or the other tended to keep him out of the house on warm summer nights. He always assumed Tom had the same sort of life and only seemed somewhat amused that Tom managed to come home naked so often. He took Tom's mutters of "some good beer" or a "glass too many" and asked no questions. Which in itself would be worrisome, except that Keith's own life was such a mess of perils and odd adventures that he probably took it for granted everyone else's life was that crazy. And no worse.

Their arrangement with the keys rested on a vague hope that one of them might be home when the other needed a key. So far it had worked out, more or less. But there was always the chance . . .

Tom rang again. A buzz he recognized as Keith's voice came through the loudspeaker. He couldn't actually understand what Keith said, but he could guess. "It's Tom, man," Tom said. "Lost my key, somehow . . ."

Another buzz that Tom—with long practice—understood to mean that he should ring Keith's door and Keith would give him the key. Then the front door clicked open.

"Sorry there's no elevator, but—" Tom started, and shut up. Most apartment buildings in Goldport, much less most apartment buildings in downtown Goldport, didn't have elevators. He must be having flashbacks to his childhood in an upscale NY condo.

As it was, the Audubon was more upscale than the places he'd lived in the last five years even when he'd been out of the shelter. There were no rats. The cement stairs covered in worn carpet were clean enough and didn't smell of piss. And if, now and then, like on the third floor, you could hear a baby cry through the thin door of an apartment, you could be sure the little tyke had just awakened and needed to nurse, and not that he was being beaten within an inch of his life.

These were solid working-class apartments, where people scrimped and saved to get by and might wear clothes from thrift-shop racks, but where most families had two parents and both parents worked, and where kids went to school and played, instead of doing drugs. Or selling them.

Yeah, it could be much, much worse. Tom rubbed his hand across his face as he climbed, fast as his feet could carry him, up to the third floor. He hated shifting shape—particularly shifting shape when he didn't mean to and staying shifted for . . . hours, he guessed, as his last memory was from when the moon first appeared in the sky, around maybe nine. He wondered what he'd been doing. It had been months since shifting had come with such total memory loss.

If he could find his clothes, he would know what had happened, but right now he only had a memory of fear—of fleeing. And then nothing at all until he'd come to himself in that parking lot, with Kyrie staring at him and the bloodied corpse at his feet.

They'd reached the landing on the third floor and he lurched to Keith's door on the left, and pushed the doorbell. Despite his having called, he didn't expect a fast response and didn't get it. From inside came Keith's voice and a higher, clearly female voice, and then the sound of footsteps, something falling, more footsteps.

Tom smiled despite himself, guessing that Keith had still been explaining to his visitor why the doorbell had rung from downstairs, when it rang again up here.

When the door opened, Keith looked disheveled and sleepy. He was a young kid—although to be honest he might be older than Tom. Tom just perceived him as much younger than himself—perhaps because Keith didn't shift. Keith was blond and generally good-looking. Right then, he was blinking, his blue eyes displaying the curiously naked look of the eyes of people who normally wore glasses and suddenly found themselves without.

His hair was a mess and he looked confused, but he was grinning as he handed Tom a set of keys. Though the student held the door almost closed, Tom glimpsed a redheaded girl behind Keith. He felt a little envious. It had been years since he'd even dreamed of sharing his bed with anyone. He could never guarantee he wouldn't shift and scare a date halfway to death. Or worse.

Then he realized Keith was looking enviously at him. Tom followed the direction of Keith's gaze, and saw Kyrie standing just behind him, hands on hips, as though daring Keith to make a comment. And Tom felt at the same time ridiculously pleased that Keith thought he could be involved with someone like Kyrie and a little jealous of Keith's admiration for her. Keith didn't even know her. He didn't even know who she was. He didn't know that she shifted as well.

"Thanks," Tom said, a little more dryly than he should. He snatched the key from Keith's hand and started up the stairs at a faster clip than he should, considering how he felt.

Keith grinned. "No problem. But I have to go back. This girl is something else. She swears she saw a dragon flying over the building. A dragon." He shook his head.

A dragon. Tom managed a noncommittal sound of empathy. Probably Tom. But Tom didn't dare ask questions about what he'd been doing or what direction he'd been flying. Instead, he turned and started up the stairs. Up and up and up, to his fifth-floor landing, Kyrie's steady gait keeping pace with his.

His door was . . . locked. He let out a breath he hadn't been aware of holding in. After all, he did not know how or when he'd shifted and all he had was the memory of fear, of running away. It was possible *they* had found him in his apartment. It was possible . . . If they'd figured out his name, and they must have by now, it would have been easy.

But the door was locked, his doormat looked untouched. Everything was as it should be. No light came under his door. Everything was normal at least to human senses and he didn't want to use his dragon senses. He didn't want to reach for that other self, for fear it would bring them. And for fear of what he might do. He swallowed hard, thinking of the corpse.

There could be nothing odd in his apartment. The only reason his hand trembled was because of his being so tired. And the corpse and everything.

He slid the key in and turned it.

In the moment before Tom opened the door Kyrie had a wild surge of panic. She wanted to tell him to wait, but she couldn't speak. And she didn't know why he should wait. She just had a feeling—added up from rustling, from sounds she could not possibly have heard, from an odd smell, from a weird tingle up her spine—that something was wrong, very wrong.

Perhaps Tom was going to drag her into his apartment and— And what? Imagination failed her. She had seen him in that bathroom, so slow and confused he didn't even seem to know how to wipe away blood from himself. She had seen him standing there, helpless. She could hardly believe he would now turn around and rape her.

On the other hand, didn't they sacrifice virgins to dragons in the Middle Ages? She almost smiled at the thought of Tom as virgin-despoiler. The way he looked, he'd have trouble beating away the ones who threw themselves at him. Kyrie managed to calm herself completely, when Tom reached in and turned on the light.

The light revealed an unprepossessing living room, with the type of dark brown carpet that landlords slapped down when they didn't expect to rent to the upper echelons of society. But the rest . . .

The furniture, what there was of it—splinters of bookcase, remnants of couches with ugly brown polyester covering—seemed to have been piled up in the middle of the room as if someone had been getting ready to light a bonfire. And the window—the huge picture window opposite—was broken. A thousand splinters littered the carpet. Books and pieces of books fluttered all over.

Tom made a sound of distress and stepped into the room, and Kyrie stepped in behind him. He knelt by a pile of something on the carpet, and Kyrie focused on it, noticing shreds of denim, and what might or might not once have been a white T-shirt. And over it all, a torn purple rag, with the Athens logo. The Athens sent the aprons home with the employees to get laundered at employee expense.

That meant that Tom had been ready to go to work when . . . The tingle in her spine grew stronger and the feeling that something was wrong, very wrong overwhelmed her. It was like a scream both soundless and so loud that it took over her whole thought, overcame her whole mind, reverberated from her whole being.

"Tom," she said, putting a hand on his shoulder. "Tom, we'd best—"

She never had time to finish. Someone or something, moving soundlessly behind them, had closed the door.

Kyrie heard the bolt slide home and turned, skin prickling, hair standing on end, to stare openmouthed at three men who stood between them and the door.

Men was dignifying them with a name they didn't quite deserve. They were boys, maybe nineteen or twenty, just at the edge of manhood. Oriental, dressed all in black, they clearly had watched one too many ninja movies. The middle one wore exquisitely groomed, slightly too long hair, the bangs arranged so they fell to perfection and didn't move. He must have spent a fortune on product.

The ones on either side were not so stylishly groomed, but one sported a tattoo of a Chinese letter in the middle of his forehead, while the other had a tattoo of a red dragon on the back of each hand—those clearly visible and he was clenching his fists and holding them up in a gesture more reminiscent of boxing than karate.

The far one shouted something, and Kyrie grabbed hold of Tom's arm, and shoved him behind her. He'd gone wooden puppet again.

The pretty boy in the middle laughed and said something—Kyrie presumed in Chinese—to his friend. Then added in English, "He only speaks English." But when he turned to Tom all traces of laughter had vanished from his expression, as he said, "You know what we want. You foiled the first fool who came looking, but, you see, we returned for you. Now give it to us, and we might not kill you or your pretty girlfriend."

Pretty girlfriend? Kyrie registered as if from a long way away that they were talking about her. Truth was, very few people ever had called her pretty. She was too . . . striking, and proud to be called that. Also at some level people must always have sensed what she was, because since she'd turned fifteen and the panther had made its first appearance, few men had made taunting comments in her presence. Hell, few men even addressed her in any way.

But if there was an instinct for self-protection, this trio was lacking it. The little one with the two dragons on the backs of his hands started laughing.

At least, he threw his head back and Kyrie thought he was laughing, a high-pitched, hysterical laughter. And then she realized what the laughter really was as his outlines blurred and he started to shift. Wings, and curving neck. All of it in lovely tones of red and gold, like all those Chinese paintings. But the features—which in paintings had always made Kyrie think of a naughty cat— looked malevolent. He hissed, between lips wholly unprepared for speech, "Give us the pearl."

Pearl? A pearl seemed like a very odd thing for Tom to steal. Was it some form of drug? Kyrie glanced behind her, to see Tom shaking his head violently. The fact that he was the approximate color of curdled milk, his normally pale skin looking downright unhealthy and grey, did not reassure her that by his shaking his head he meant he'd never heard of such a thing as a pearl.

"Tom?" she said.

He only shook his head again.

"Right," the middle one said. "You want to play rough, rough it is."

And suddenly a golden dragon took up most of the small brown room. And there were claws reaching for Kyrie. No. Talons. And someone's fangs were close to her face, a smell like a thousand long-forgotten sushi dinners invading her nostrils. A forked tongue licked her ear and through the lips not fashioned for speech, through the accent that he showed even in English, she nonetheless understood the young man's words as he said, "We're going to have so much fun."

She'd never shifted when she was scared. The few times she'd shifted it had been just the moon and usually summer calling to her, the feeling of jungle in her mind, at the back of her brain.

But as her fear closed upon her throat, making breathing almost impossible, as her heart pounded seemingly in her ears, as her blood seemed to race away from her leaving her cold as ice, she felt something . . .

She wasn't sure what was happening until she heard the growl erupt from her throat. A full growl, fashioned from melodies of the jungle.

Lizards. Uppity lizards, at that. They dared challenge her? Try to grab her?

Turning around, she swiped a giant paw across the tender underflesh of a clawed foot holding her. And then she leapt for the throat of the giant beast who was trying to claw her down.

It was—the part of her that remained human, deep in the mists of consciousness thought—like the armada and the English ships. The Spanish armada's huge, slow ships might be stronger and better armored. But they had no hope against the small English ships that could sail around them, landing shots where they wished till the giant ship was crippled.

Kyrie grabbed the beast by the throat, hanging on, till she tasted blood—and what blood. It was like drinking the finest champagne straight from the bottle.

The beast yelled and reached for her with its claws. It managed to scrape her flank, in a bright slash of pain. But she jumped out of the way before the creature could grab her, and she was on top of his head, as both his friends converged, trying to grab her. And she leapt at the soft underbelly of the red one—Two Dragons, the human Kyrie thought—in a mad dance of claws sinking into soft, unarmored flesh.

And then up again, and leaping at the eye of the next dragon.

That there were three of them was not an advantage. After all, three large, slower-moving beings only helped each other get hopelessly entangled while Kyrie danced upon them like a deadly firefly, in a frenzy of wounding, a joy of blood.

She was vaguely aware that she too was bleeding, that there were punctures on her hide and that, somehow, one of them had managed to sink his fangs into her front leg— her right arm. But she didn't care. Right then, allowed the madness she'd long denied, she jumped at the dragon's eyes, swiping her claws across them and relishing the dragon's shriek of pain, the bright blood jumping from the right eye. She jumped and leapt, possessed of fierce anger, of maddened, repressed rage.

But while the beast exulted in the carnage, while the feline gyrated in mayhem, a small trickling feeling formed at the back of Kyrie's mind. It was like the first melting tip of an icicle, dropping cold reason on her hot madness. The feeling, at first, was no more than that—just a trickling cold, protesting, demanding—she wasn't sure what. The beast, in its frenzy, ignored it.

Until slowly, slowly, the feeling became words and the words became panic in Kyrie's mind. She was fighting all three dragons. She was keeping all three dragons at bay— just. But there were three of them, there was one of her, and the beast's muscles were starting to hurt and . . . How could she get out of here?

There was no way of reaching the door. All the dragons were between her and the door and none of her sorties had brought her close to escaping.

Blood in her nostrils, mad fury in the beast's brain, what remained of the human Kyrie tried to think and came up with nothing but an insistent, white surge of panic. And she couldn't let it slow her down. She couldn't. If she did, all would be lost. But she couldn't fight forever.

In a twirl, claws sinking into the nearest dragon's hide, she thought of Tom. But the corner into which he'd shrunk when she'd shifted was vacant.

The coward had run out the door behind her back, hadn't he?

She felt a horrible sense of betrayal, a letdown at this, and her extended paw faltered, and the dragon above her reared.

It was the center dragon—who in human form had artificially smooth and immovable hair. In dragon form he had a tall crest, red and gold. Well, it had been red and gold, it was now much darker red in spots, thanks to Kyrie's claws. And blood ran down its cheek from one of its eyes. But the other eye was unblinking fixed hatred as it opened its jaws wide, wide, fangs glistening.

Kyrie needed to jump. She needed to. But her muscles felt powerless, spent. Stretched elastic that would not spring again.

So this is how it ends . . .

The big head descended to devour her, teeth ready to break her neck. And a taloned paw grabbed her roughly around the middle, swept her back.

She turned. She turned with her remnant of strength, her very last drop of fury, to snarl at the dragon behind her.

She snarled at him, Tom thought—amazed he could think clearly in dragon form. He'd willed himself into being a dragon. Willed himself into it.

He desired it and pushed. He knew she was going to have problems leaving. He knew she couldn't fly.

And he knew she was an idiot for even fighting. They had no chance. But then, neither could he leave her to die alone. She had taken care of him, when she'd found him in suspicious circumstances. She'd shown him more kindness than his own father had. And she was a shifter like him. They were family: bonded deeper than any shared genes, any joint upbringing.

He shifted suddenly, unexpectedly, leaping in the air, and out of his corner so quickly the other dragons didn't seem to register it. He had only the time to see that she was cowering, that the dragon above her would finish her. And then he was reaching for her, grabbing her, jumping out the open window, even as she turned to snarl at him.

But the snarl—lip pulled back from vicious fangs— faltered as she recognized him.

He held her as gently and firmly as he could. He mustn't drop her. But neither must he hurt her. He could smell blood from her. He could smell fear.

He unfurled his wings—huge parachutes. Above him, the other dragons hadn't appeared yet. Perhaps she'd done more damage than he'd thought. Perhaps they had a few minutes. A very few minutes.

Down in the parking lot, her car was a small abandoned toy. Her keys would be in his apartment, he thought, and shook his huge head, amazed at the clarity of the human thought in beast form. Normally he didn't even remember what he'd done as a dragon. Perhaps because he was responsible for another? He'd never been responsible for anyone but himself.

But they must run. They must get out of here very fast. And as beasts, he could not explain to her what danger they were in. He couldn't even think, clearly think, of where to run.

The dragon wished to crawl under a rock, preferably by a river, and hide.

But Goldport was not so big on rivers. There was Panner's Creek, which in the summer became a mere trickle winding amid sun-parched boulders.

He flew her down to the parking lot, slowly, landed by the car, and wished to shift. He didn't dare reach for the strength of the talisman to allow himself to shift. No. The dragons would sense that.

Instead, setting Kyrie down carefully, he *willed* himself to shift. He thought himself human, and shivered, as his body spasmed in painful change.

He was naked. Naked, sitting on the warm asphalt of the parking lot, next to Kyrie's car and a panther. No. Next to Kyrie. In the next minute, she also shifted, and appeared as a naked, bloodied young woman, lying on the pavement next to him.

"The car," he rasped at her, his voice hesitant, difficult, like a long-neglected instrument. "We must leave. Soon. They will pursue."

She looked at him with confused, tired eyes. Her chin was scratched, and there was too much blood on her everywhere. He wondered how much of it was hers. Did they need to go to the hospital? They healed very quickly. At least Tom did. But what if these wounds were too serious? How could they go to the hospital? How could they explain anything?

"I don't have keys," she said, and patted her hips as though looking for keys in pockets that were no longer there.

Tom nodded. He got up, feeling about a hundred years old after two shifts in such a short time. His legs hurt, as did his arms, and his whole body felt as though someone had belabored him with sticks.

But he was human now and he could think. He remembered.

One eye on the window of his apartment, wondering how long he had, he said, "I'm sorry. I'll pay." Then he grabbed one of the stones on the flower bed nearby—a stone-bed, to tell the truth, since he'd never seen flowers there. He smashed the window with the stone, reached in, unlocked the door.

Sweeping the crumbs of glass from the seat, he smashed the key holder, reached down to the floor, and grabbed a screwdriver he'd noticed there while Kyrie was driving him. "Remembered you had this here," he said, turning to see her bewildered expression as her car started. And then, "Get in. I'll pay for the damage. Just get in."

Was it his imagination, or had he seen the shadow of a wing in the window above?

He reached across to unlock the passenger door, as she jumped in.

She fumbled with the seat belt as he tore out of the parking lot in a screech of rubber. Sweat was dripping from his forehead into his eyes. He was sure he was sitting on a chunk of glass. It had been years since he'd driven and he found the turns odd and difficult. The car his father had given him as a sixteenth-birthday gift handled much better than this. Good thing there was almost no traffic on the roads at this time.

He tore around the corner of Fairfax, turning into a narrower street and hoping he was only imagining the noise of wings above. He tried to choose tree-lined streets, knowing well enough that it was harder to see into them from above. The vision of dragons seemed to focus naturally on moving things. In a street of trees, shaken by the wind, in which shadows shifted and shook, it would be harder to see them.

Some of these streets were narrow enough—and the trees above them well over a hundred years old—that it made it impossible to see the streets at all, except as a green canopy. He took one street, then another, then yet another, tearing down quiet residential streets like a madman and probably causing the families snug in their brick ranches to wonder what was happening out there.

They passed two people walking, male and female, he tall and she much shorter, leaning into him. Shorts, T-shirts, a swirling white skirt, a vision of normalcy and a relationship that he couldn't aspire to, and Tom bit his lip and thumped the side of the wheel with his hand, bringing a startled glance from Kyrie.

He'd gone a good ten minutes and was starting to think they'd lost their pursuers, when he thought of Kyrie. He turned to her, wanting to explain he really would pay and that she should not—

Her dark eyes gazed into his, unwavering. "How many cars have you stolen?" she asked.

The way he'd hot-wired the car, quickly—she swore it had taken him less than a few seconds—had chilled Kyrie to the bone.

She supposed she should have known someone with a drug problem, working minimum-wage jobs had to supplement with crime, but all of a sudden she realized he was more dangerous—more out of control than she'd thought.

More out of control than the other dragons?

And yet, after he'd driven like a madman for a while, he looked at her with a devastatingly scared expression in his pale face. Despite chiseled features and the now all-too-obvious dark shadow of unshaven beard, he managed to look about five and worried he'd be put in time-out.

"How many cars have you stolen?" she asked, before she knew she was going to say it.

His expression closed. She would not be able to describe it any other way. The eager, almost childish panic vanished, leaving in its place a dark, unreadable glare, his eyebrows low over his dark blue eyes. He turned away, looking forward, and shrugged, a calculated shrug from his broad shoulders. One quarter inch up, one quarter inch down.

"I used to go joy riding," he said. "When I was a kid. I got bored." And when she didn't answer that, he added. "Look, I've told you. I'll pay you for the damage." And again, at her continued silence. "I couldn't let us be caught. If they'd caught us, they'd have killed us."

At this, he stopped. He stopped long enough for her to gather her thoughts. She felt so tired that if she weren't in pain, she would have fallen asleep. But she hurt. Her shoulder felt as if it had been dislocated in the fight. There was a slash across her torso that she prayed wouldn't need stitches, and a broad swath of her buttock felt scraped, as though it had rubbed hard against a scaly hide. Which it probably had, though she didn't remember.

"Who are they?" she finally asked. "Why are they after you?"

"They're a Chinese triad," he said. "They're members of a . . . crime syndicate. Asian."

"Admirably described," she said, and heard the hint of sarcasm in her own voice, and was surprised she still had the strength for it. "But what do they want with you?"

He hesitated. For just a moment he glanced at her, and the scared little boy was back, with wide-open eyes, and slightly parted lips.

He looked back at the road in time to take them, tightly, around a corner, tires squealing, car tilting. "They think I stole something from them," he said, with the defensive tone of a child explaining it really, really, really wasn't him who put the clamp on the cat's tail.

Something. Kyrie was not so naive that she didn't know Chinese crime syndicates—like most crime syndicates—dealt mostly in various drugs. "A drug deal gone bad?" she asked.

He had the nerve to tighten his lips, and shake his head. "I don't deal drugs," he said.

Whee. There was one form of criminality he didn't stoop to. Who would have thunk it? "So . . ."

"I didn't steal it, okay?" he said. "I didn't steal anything. They think I did, and they're trying to get it back."

"Sounds ugly," she said. Somehow she felt he was lying but also not lying. There was an edge to his tone as if he weren't quite so sure how he'd got himself into this type of situation.

"It is," he said. "They've been after me for months." He shrugged. "Only they've just figured out my name, I think. Now they can follow me, wherever I live. They're shifters. Dragons."

"I gathered."

"They worship the Great Sky Dragon. . . ."

"Uh?" She had never heard of any shifter divinity. But then again, she'd never heard of any other shifters. All of a sudden, vertiginously, as though standing at the edge of a precipice and seeing a whole world open before her, she wondered if there was a whole culture, a whole society she didn't know about. Some place she belonged, whole families of shifters. Perhaps the only reason she'd never known about it because she'd been abandoned at birth and she didn't know her own birth family. "Shifters have their own gods?"

Tom shrugged. "I think he was a Chinese divinity. Or one of their sacred animals, or something."

"Did you get involved with them because you . . . shift? Into a dragon? Is your family . . . does your family shift?"

Tom shook his head. "My father doesn't. . . . No."

"Then how did you get involved with the triad?"

He looked confused, then shrugged—not a precise shrug. "I don't know," he said. He seemed on the verge of saying something, but shook his head, as if to his own thoughts. "My father—" He stopped dead, as though something in him had halted not just the words but the train of thought as well.

They were driving down a narrow, tree-bordered street. Ahead of them loomed the dark expanse of the Castle—officially known as Chateau D'Aubigerne, a castle imported from the Loire, stone by stone, by a man enriched in the gold rush. It now stood smack dab in the center of Goldport, abandoned and empty, surrounded by gardens gone to seed and an eight-foot-high iron fence like massed spears. Now and then there was talk of someone buying it, restoring it, and making it into a hotel, a mall, a resort, or just a monument for tourists to gawk at. But all those projects seemed nonstarters, perhaps because the Castle was well away from all the hotels and convention centers, on a street of tiny, workmen's brick ranches, with cars on blocks and broken plastic toys in the front yards.

Tom slowed down till he was going a normal speed and said, "Where can I take you?"

"Beg your pardon?"

He grinned at her, a fugitive grin that transformed his features and gave her a startling glimpse of what might lurk underneath the troubled young man's aggression—humor? Joy? "Where can I drop you off? Where do you live?" He smiled at her, a less naughty smile this time, more that of a patient adult facing a stupid child. "You can't go to work like that, can you?"

She shook her head, panicked. Gee. Frank was going to be mad. She might already have lost her job. A surge of anger at Tom came up, but then vanished again. Someone had once told Kyrie that if you lost a job making less than ten dollars and hour you could find another one within the day. In her experience this was true. And besides, it wasn't like Tom had asked her for help.

She'd just jumped in and helped him. Hell, she thought she'd learned not to do that years ago.

"My place," she said. "It's down the next street. Turn right. Third house on the left."

"House?"

"Rental. It's smaller than an apartment, really. I just . . . I don't like people around."

He nodded and maneuvered through the turn and up to her house, at a speed that could only be considered sedate after his early high jinks.

The house was tiny—eight hundred square feet and one bedroom, but it had a driveway—a narrow strip of concrete that led right up to the back door and from which a narrow walking path led to the front door. This late at night—or early in the morning—all of Kyrie's neighbors would be asleep and she was grateful for that.

As Tom pulled up to the back door, she had only two steps to go, stark naked. And she always left the key under a rock in the nearby flower bed. She hated to be locked out of her house and didn't know anyone in town she could trust with a key. It was one of the side effects of moving around so much.

As she started to open the door, she looked at Tom. He was sitting behind the wheel, the engine still going, looking forward. The car was hers, but she could hardly tell him to leave it and run off naked into the night. On the other hand—where was he going to go even with the car?

She had to invite him in. She didn't really want to, but she saw nothing else she could do. Nothing else a decent human being could do. She tapped him on the arm. "Turn that off. Come inside. Have a shower. I'll grab another jogging suit for you."

He looked surprised. Dumbfounded as if she'd offered him a fortune. "Are you sure?"

"Where would you go otherwise?"

He shrugged. "I'll figure . . . I'll figure something. I always do." For just a second a dangerous liquid quality crept into his voice, but he only shook his head and swallowed. "Look, it's not safe to be around me."

"I've noticed. But you have nowhere else to go. Come inside. I'll make coffee."

He took a few seconds, then grabbed the screwdriver and turned it. And nodded at her. "Can I come out through your side?" he said. "Less—"

"Exposure, yes," she said. "And don't break anything. I have a key."

She dove out the door and retrieved her key from its hiding place.

Later Tom would think he might never have agreed to go to Kyrie's house, except for the chunk of glass slowly working its way into his buttock.

It was clear she didn't really want him around, and he wasn't sure he could blame her. After all, he wasn't sure he wanted himself around most of the time. And she'd seen him at one of his most dangerous moments.

It would probably be a kindness for him to leave. But then he came up on the fact that he was naked, he was shaking with exhaustion, and there was a big glass chunk becoming a permanent part of his behind.

He turned off the car and waited till she was out and had opened the door before he dove out of the car after her. And stepped into a cozy kitchen—cozy and homey and like no place he'd ever been before.

His father's condo had been huge. This entire house would probably fit in the kitchen. And the kitchen of that house had been white and chrome, imported Italian marble and mosaic floors. But it was the domain of Mrs. Lopez, their cook. Never the family kitchen. Never a place where the family gathered for meals.

Of course no family could really gather in this kitchen either. Not unless they were all unusually close. It was barely big enough to contain both of them, a card table, two folding chairs, a refrigerator, stove, and a tiny counter with sink. Above the table, on the wall, hung a painting of an old-fashioned bicycle done in shades of red and pink on black, the front wheel dwarfing the rest.

Kyrie closed the door behind him. "This way," she said, as she led him out of the kitchen via the interior door, and into a hallway. She opened another door and turned the light on. "The bathroom. I'll go get you something to wear."

He stepped into the bathroom, where there was just enough space for himself between tub, sink, and toilet.

Kyrie returned almost immediately and knocked, and he hid himself behind the door as he opened it. It seemed silly when they'd been together, naked for most of the evening. But then Kyrie had put on a robe—a fluffy, pink robe that made her look young and feminine.

She handed him a bundle of clothes and said, "There's plenty of water. Outsized water heater, so don't worry too much. But I'd like to shower after you, so don't use more than you have to."

He nodded, took the clothes, set them on the toilet tank, and started the shower. Plunging under the water, he felt it like a warm caress. He tried not to notice that it ran red-stained down the drain. The corpse . . .

The corpse seemed wholly unreal in this white-tiled shower that smelled of lavender and a subtle hint of Kyrie's perfume. Tom had never noticed her perfume before, but it was definitely her smell. Something spicy and soft that he'd caught before as an undertone at work.

He removed the glass chunk from his backside, by touch, then soaped himself vigorously. He had no right to intrude on her life, nor to bring his own messes into her house. He had no right to endanger her. He should leave as soon as possible.

Guiltily, he used her shampoo, which was some designer brand and smelled of vanilla. His hair, too, yielded quantities of red bloodstained water.

What would the police think? Would the police track him? And Kyrie? He'd tell them she was innocent. He was the murderer.

Was he the murderer?

He couldn't think about it. Stepping out of the tub, he heard Kyrie knock at the door. She then opened it a sliver, and held out a towel. "Sorry. Forgot to give them earlier," she said.

And she was being kind to him. Far kinder than anyone had been in a long time. He thanked her, dried himself, combed his hair with his fingers, the thick black curls falling into their natural unruliness, and dressed in her jogging suit.

Coming out the door, he had his words ready. About how he would be going now, no time to chat, really, best thing would be to get out of her hair as soon as possible, and then—

And then she was waiting at the door and smiled at him. "I made coffee. It's in the kitchen. Do you drink coffee? I won't be a minute."

And she went past him into the steam-filled bathroom.

He couldn't exactly leave when she was being so friendly, so he went into the kitchen, where she'd run the coffeemaker, and set cups, sugar, and cream out. He didn't know whether to laugh or cry that one of the cups was embossed with a dragon, but he took it anyway.

Kyrie showered quickly, wondering what was wrong with her. Didn't she want him out of the house? Now? Yesterday?

But she'd never talked with another of her kind. And perhaps he knew what had happened. Perhaps he'd remember if he'd killed the person in the parking lot. And perhaps she'd be able to figure out how he'd got involved with the triad and if she'd now be in danger.

And perhaps tomorrow it would rain soup. And cream.

But there were more material considerations, too. Her arm, where Two Dragons—the one who in human form had two dragon tattoos—had got in a glancing bite at the panther's paw. It looked like the tooth had pierced her arm. It wasn't exactly bleeding—just a trickle of blood that increased under the warm shower. She examined the puncture dispassionately. Her memory of the adrenaline-fueled fight had fuzzy edges and she could not remember if the bite had released, or if it had been fully completed before something she did caused the dragon to let go.

If the first, it was probably a narrow, not-too-deep cut. If the second . . . Well, she could easily be looking at a puncture all the way to the bone, at an infection. She couldn't afford that, but neither could she afford to go to the hospital.

Oh, not monetarily. She probably could scrape up the money for a quick visit to the emergency room or one of the twenty-four-hour med centers. What she couldn't afford was for doctors to ask how she got her wound. For them to notice anything at all strange about the shape of the wound. For them to remember her wounds when someone brought the corpse in, certainly with similar wounds. No. Better to trust in Tom and ask him to help her clean her arm and perhaps bandage the wound. Better the devil you know.

There were other wounds too. One on her hip, which she could bandage herself, and then one across her shoulder, at the back, which she didn't think she could take care of without help.

She got out of the shower and dried a little more vigorously than she needed to, to punish herself for her stupidity in getting involved in Tom's affairs. She bandaged her hip and her torso before putting on her robe again.

Frank was going to make her pay for the apron. But at least she still had a job. She'd called while Tom was showering. While Frank had been none too pleased to hear she wouldn't be back the rest of the night, neither had he fired her.

In the kitchen, Tom stood, holding the cup of coffee. The one with the dragon. Kyrie smiled. She hadn't even thought about his reaction. It had come, like most of her dishes, from the Salvation Army thrift store. She picked up the cup left on the counter and poured herself a cup of black coffee. He hadn't thrown a snit at the dragon. He hadn't imagined it was a dig directed at him.

Perhaps he was not quite so touchy and antisocial as she would have thought he was. Or perhaps . . .

Kyrie looked him over. He smelled of soap and her shampoo, and he looked far less dangerous than he had. His black curls were damp from the shower, dripping down his back. His expression was just bewildered enough to make him look younger than he normally did. Even the fact that he was frowning into his coffee cup didn't make him look threatening, just puzzled.

He looked at her, and the frown became less intense, but the eyebrows remained low over the blue eyes, which looked like they were trying to figure out something really difficult. Like the meaning of the universe. "Why?" he said. "I'm dangerous." He shrugged, as if he hadn't said exactly what he meant to say. "I mean, it's dangerous to hang out with me. You saw . . . my apartment." He took a sip of coffee, fast, desperately, as if trying to make up for words that didn't come out quite right. Then choked, coughed, and set the cup down to cover his mouth. "Why did you let me in here?" he asked.

Kyrie could have said many things. That his apartment was one of the reasons. Who would send him out there naked, in a car that looked, clearly, like it had been broken into? Who would send him out into the night with nowhere to stay, no safe place to crash?

But before she spoke, she realized that there would be many people—perhaps most people—who would do that. She'd met them often enough, growing up. The families who took foster children but didn't want them associating with their *real* children; the children at school who shunned you because you lived in a less than savory part of town; the teachers who assumed you were dumb and hopeless because you didn't live with your blood family.

Had she done the same with Tom, in shunning him because of his appearance? His drug habit? But no. She'd been justified in that. Those were things he could and should control. However, this trouble . . . Well, perhaps he'd brought it on himself. Perhaps at the root of it all was a drug deal gone bad, or the theft of something valuable.

She couldn't imagine anyone stealing anything valuable from a triad composed of dragon shape-shifters. She would have to assume Tom was brasher, and perhaps braver, than she. But she didn't know him well enough to rule it out, either.

And again, she had had plenty of experience with his type: the alcoholic foster parents, the doping foster brothers. You gave them chance and chance and chance, and they never improved, never got any better. They just told you more and more lies and got bolder and bolder.

She didn't know what to say and she couldn't guess in which category Tom would fall. So, instead, she stuck to the need at hand. That had always seen her through. When in trouble, stick to the need at hand.

"I need you to help me bandage my arm and disinfect my back," she said. And not sure why his eyes grew so wide at this request, added, "Please?"

He nodded and shrugged. "Of course," he said. His eyes remained wide, as if he were either very surprised or very skeptical. "Where do you keep the first-aid supplies?"

"They're in the bathroom," Kyrie told him. "Behind the mirror."

Tom headed that way. It was a relief to have something to do—to have something to think of. He'd been sitting there, feeling miserable, drinking his coffee, wondering what the best way to leave.

The bathroom was still full of steam—but the smell was indefinably different there. Not just the soap and shampoo he'd used also, but something else . . . Something he could neither define nor explain. It smelled like Kyrie. That was all he could say. It was a familiar smell and he realized he'd smelled it around her even under the layers of odors at the Athens. A hint of cinnamon, an edge of burnt sugar. Only not really, but that was what the smells made him think of. Like . . . What the kitchen smelled like when Mrs. Lopez had been making pastries.

He opened the medicine cabinet and collected bandages, antibiotic cream, small scissors, hydrogen peroxide, and cotton wool. It was the best-stocked home cabinet he'd ever seen. Other than his own. Shape-shifters. You came home cut, scraped, you weren't even sure how.

And Kyrie was one of them. Just like him.

That he was attracted to her didn't make it any easier. He'd been attracted to her from the first moment he'd seen her—giving him the jaundiced once-over when Frank introduced them. But his attraction to women had come to nothing these last five years, ever since he'd found out he was a shape-shifter.

There were too many things to be afraid of—shifting in front of her, for instance. Hurting her while he was shape-shifted. And then the whole thing with the drugs, with which he'd tried—unsuccessfully—to control his shifts. It made him associate with too many shady characters for him to want any girl he even liked involved with. And then, of course, the . . . He shifted his mind forcefully away from even thinking of the object. That. And the triad. This without even thinking of nightmare scenarios: pregnancy. A baby who was born shifted.

And now in one night he'd managed to visit all but the last of these scenarios. He'd shifted in front of Kyrie. He'd probably hurt someone else in front of her. And he'd landed her in the thick of his trouble with the triad. Damn. And all this when he'd just found out she was a shape-shifter too. She was one like him.

Oh, she was not the only one he'd met in his five years of wandering around, homeless and rootless. But she was the first one he'd talked to, the first one he'd had anything to do with. The only female . . . Up to tonight, he would have sworn that only males shifted shape.

And what good did it do him that she too was a shape-shifter—that she would understand him?

Absolutely none. First, he had blown it so far with her that if his hopes were a substance they would be scraping them off the floor and ceiling for months. And second—and second there was the triad.

Tom had been attracted to Kyrie before tonight. Now he liked her. He liked her a lot. He might very well be on his way to falling in love with her. If he had the slightest idea what love was and how one fell in it, he would be able to say for sure. But here the thing was—he cared about her. He cared a lot. An awful lot. He didn't want her dead. As he was bound to be, soon enough, now that the triad had got really serious about finding him.

"It's right there on the shelf," Kyrie's voice said from the doorway. He turned to see her framed in the door, those big, dark eyes looking puzzled.

"Oh, yes, right," he said. "It's actually in my hands." He turned around and lifted the hands filled with first-aid stuff. "I'm sorry. I spaced. I guess I'm tired."

She nodded solemnly. He didn't remember ever seeing her laugh. Smile, sure, a bunch of times, mostly the polite smile you gave customers late at night when they came in looking tired and out of it. But never laugh. Was laughter too far out of control for her? And why did he want to know? It wasn't as if he'd ever find out.

"Right," she said. "Shifting that many times in a row. Staying shifted that long. I've shifted, but not for long tonight, so I'm not—" She yawned and covered her mouth with her hand. "—that tired."

He smiled, despite himself, grateful that she couldn't see it because she had turned her back and was heading back toward the kitchen. Where she sat at the table, pulled the cord on the lamp overhead to turn it on, and rolled up the sleeve of her robe to show a narrow wound with bluish borders, like a bruise.

He sat on the other chair, laid the first-aid materials down on the table. "That looks awful," he said.

She nodded and turned her arm over. On the bottom there was another bruise, another puncture.

"It went all the way—" he started.

She shook her head. "No. The dra— He just bit me. I don't know how deeply. It feels different . . . in the other body." She'd lowered her head to look at her own arm, and her hair had fallen across her face. The temptation to reach over and pull that multicolored curtain back was almost more than he could endure.

"Have you had a tetanus shot?" he asked, going on routine. "Because if you haven't, you should. I don't know how clean . . ." He realized he was about to say he didn't know how clean dragons' teeth were and caught himself in time. He smiled. There was no avoiding it. He was a dragon. She knew he was a dragon. And on that, at least, there was no reason for awkwardness. Hell, she shifted too. He had to keep telling himself that. He had to remember. "I, personally, brush and floss. Use mouthwash, even. But I can't answer to the cleanliness of another dragon's teeth."

That got him a smile. Little more than the polite smile that she gave customers, but a smile nonetheless, and even a teasing sort of reply. "No unified dental hygiene guidelines for dragons?"

"Afraid not," he said. He soaked one of the balls of cotton wool in hydrogen peroxide and gently started to cleanse the area. "Seriously, you really should go to a doctor. I know we shifters heal quickly, but these deep puncture wounds can be dangerous. Only a tiny area exposed to air, see. The space in there can develop an infection very easily. And you could get blood poisoning, something horrible." He looked up and saw her open her mouth. "I know what you're going to say, and I'm not going to tell you that you're wrong. The last thing we need. The very last thing is to call attention to ourselves—particularly with strange animal bites. And I understand how you feel about being in the hospital. I slept under a bridge many a night, rather than going to a shelter when the moon was full and the impulse to shift greater. But, Kyrie, I'm not joking." He pushed as much hydrogen peroxide as he could into the puncture, on both sides, by squeezing the cotton right atop of it. "If you get a fever, the first sign of swelling on your arm, and you must—*must*—see a doctor. It could kill you."

"You know a lot about this stuff."

He nodded, pulling back the cotton wool, tossing it in the kitchen trash in the corner, and waiting while her arm dried. Then he got antibiotic cream and started slathering it on. There was no reason to tell her anything. Or maybe there was. He'd been so desperately alone all these years. "My mom is a doctor," he said.

"Is she . . ." Kyrie swallowed. "Is she . . ."

"She left Dad about ten years ago," he said. "When I was a kid. Went down to Florida with her new husband. I haven't seen her since. But up till I was ten I gave her many reasons to perform first aid on me, and I heard this speech a lot."

Kyrie frowned at him. Then shook her head. "I was going to ask if she was a dragon."

Tom shook his head, then shrugged. "I don't think so. I know Dad isn't. And I don't think Mom is. I've never . . ." He was about to say that he didn't know any older shifters, but then realized he did. He had seen a couple of derelicts shifting while he flew above in the middle of a summer night. It had been further out west, toward New Mexico, and they'd shifted into coyotes and headed for the hills. He remembered because back then, seeing the tattered men shift into ragtag coyotes he'd wondered if he'd end up like that. Old, still a transient, still homeless. It had been part of what led him to steal. . . . "I don't think it's hereditary, or at least not that way. Why? Are your parents shifters?"

She shook her head and shrugged, and her eyes got soft and distant. "I wouldn't know. They left me at the entrance of a church in Charlotte, North Carolina, when I was just a few hours old. I was found by parishioners coming in for the midnight services on Christmas night. There were headlines all over the papers, about it. But I never knew . . ." She shrugged again. "I was raised by foster families."

And perhaps that explained why she held herself under such tight control? Tom wouldn't know. He knew about as much about foster care as he knew about happy family life. A couple of his acquaintances of convenience, while he had been on the streets, had been foster children. They'd told him hair-raising stories about the system. But did it mean that every one was like that? Or only the ones who'd gone seriously to the bad?

He taped the bandages in place over the puncture. "Blood poisoning will make a visible circle, it will start just above the wound, and it will be a red circle that will slowly move upwards if it's not treated. If you see a circle on your arm, you must go to the doctor, immediately."

"Am I to assume personal experience speaks here?" Kyrie asked.

He managed a smile. "My best friend and I." He hadn't thought of Joe in years. Wondered where he was now.

What he was doing. "We had these plastic swords, but you know, they were disappointing because they really couldn't cause enough damage. We could bang on each other all day long with them, they were too light and definitely not sharp. So we improved them by sticking nails in the tip. Rusty nails." He saw her wince. "Yeah. Lucky for us my mom caught the infection in time. Even then I was on antibiotics forever. Now that I think about it, lucky we were both lousy swordsmen, too. We never managed to kill each other, though we tried for a whole day."

He pulled her sleeve down, and started to gather the stuff.

"No," she said. "I want you to look at my back. It feels abraded." As she spoke, she loosened her robe, and edged it down at the back—to reveal a shoulder that had been stripped bare of skin.

"It's more than abraded," Tom said. And because the sight of the robe sliding over the raw flesh of her shoulder made him cringe, he added, "Let me," and pulled the robe down slowly, at the back. In the process, the front fell too, revealing one of her breasts almost to the nipple. Golden skin the color of honey, and it looked velvet soft. His fingers wanted to stray that way, wanted to feel . . .

He concentrated on her back, kneeling so that her back was all he saw. He found the end of the skinned portion where her shoulder blade ended. "This looks awful. How?"

"I think it was a paw swipe," she said. "The claws missed me, but the scales got me."

"Ah," Tom said. He had never thought he was that lethal in his dragon form, and to be honest, he wasn't sure he was. He didn't know how much he looked like the

Chinese dragons. He was aware the tail was different, the paws more massive, but he'd never looked at himself in a mirror while shifted. Or if he had, he hadn't managed to remember it.

He got the antibiotic cream and started applying it in a thin layer to Kyrie's back, trying to touch so lightly that he wouldn't hurt her. She didn't seem to flinch from the touch, so he must be succeeding. There had been a time he wanted to be a doctor. Before . . . all of this.

"When did you shift for the first time?" Kyrie asked.

Tom's hand trembled immediately, as the memories flooded him. Flying over the city. Not the first time, but one of the first. Seeing everything. Then coming home. Breaking the bedroom window. It was devilishly hard to work the paws when you weren't even sure what was happening to you. And then his father. His father, with the gun, ordering him out.

Hell, he didn't even know his father had a gun until then. Until that moment, had anyone asked, he'd have said his father wouldn't have a gun in the house. Tom had heard his father go on and on about gun control quite often. And he was too young to understand hypocrisy.

He took a deep breath and managed to push the memory away. To this day he wasn't sure why his father had ordered him out of the house. He'd shifted back by then. He'd shifted back and grabbed hold of his robe. Which is why he'd ended on the street in his robe and barefoot.

But he controlled the memories, squeezed a dollop of cream from the tube. Kyrie hadn't asked again, so he probably hadn't taken that long to get himself under control. "I was sixteen," he said. "I never had any warning before. I just . . . Shifted. In the moonlight."

In the moonlight, in his room, with its comfortable bed, and all the posters, and the TV, the stereo, the game system. All the things he'd once thought he needed to survive. "I was all excited too," he said. "That first time. I thought it was a cool, superhero thing."

She was silent, and he thought she was thinking about what a fool he'd been. He concentrated on what he was doing. Fingers on the wound on her shoulder, lightly, lightly, spreading a thin, shining layer of antibiotic cream.

"I was fourteen," she said, speaking as from a great distance. "I thought I was dreaming the first few times. And then I thought I was hallucinating. I thought I had . . . I don't know. Seizures or something. I used to imagine that my parents were two mental patients who'd had me and had smuggled me out of the madhouse so I could be raised on the outside."

He laughed despite himself and she turned to look at him, her expression grave. Not offended, just grave.

"I don't think there were any mental hospitals like that in the 1980s," he said. "Where they kept the children of the patients locked up along with the parents. Were there?"

Kyrie shook her head and smiled again, a smile fractionally warmer than the ones she gave the customers. "Not in this country, no, I don't think," she said. "But I was very young. Just a kid. I thought . . ." She shrugged. "Actually at first I thought someone was putting datura in my food or something."

"Datura?" he asked.

"A hallucinogenic. At least, Agatha Christie has a mystery in which someone is putting it in a man's shaving cream to make him dream that he's a werewolf, and I thought—"

"I read Christie too," he said. Often her books were the only thing available in safe homes for at-risk youth or whatnot, where he sought temporary refuge. That and the ever-yellowing pile of *National Geographic*. It was Tom's considered opinion that *National Geographics* were alien artifacts routinely bombarded down onto the Earth. "But isn't datura something Indian, something . . ."

"I didn't tell you I was rational, did I?" Kyrie asked.

He shook his head and reached for the gauze, cutting it to fit the area on her shoulder, and laying it gently atop the wound.

"I thought someone was trying to make me think I was crazy. Perhaps my foster parents. They get more for special-needs kids, you know? And then I read up on it, and I decided I was schizophrenic. I couldn't tell what I did while I was under this condition, so I started hiding. At first I was lucky that no one saw me, and then when I realized what caused it—the full moon, a feeling of anger. Anything. I was damn careful over the next four years. Always slept alone, even if arrangements called for other kids in the room. I'd take a blanket and go sleep on a tree, if needed. It . . . made for interesting times and made me change families even more often. And then I was on my own, and I've been careful. Very careful. But I still thought it was all in my mind. Till tonight."

Tom shook his head as he started taping the gauze in place. He couldn't imagine not knowing the shift was true. But perhaps it was different for dragons. He saw the city from above. He saw things happen. And, of course, within a month of his first shifting, his father had seen him shift and had shouted at him and . . . ordered him out. For shifting. Hard to tell yourself it was all in your mind after that.

"How many of us are there?" Kyrie asked. "I mean—there's you and the triad, but . . . You've known about this more and have been more places. How many shifters have you met?"

She had to talk to keep her mind off what he was doing. He wasn't hurting her. On the contrary. His fingers, touching her skin ever so lightly, were a caress. Or the closest to a caress she could remember.

It had been too long since she'd even let anyone touch her. Certainly not since she'd started shifting. Before that there had been foster siblings who'd got close, some she'd hugged and who'd hugged her. But not since then.

Tom's touch was very delicate, as if he were afraid of breaking her. It felt odd. She didn't want to think of him, back there, being careful not to hurt her.

And she really wanted to know how many shifters he'd seen in the five years since he'd left his house. She hadn't been out much. Well, not out on the street and not out while aware of being in a shape-shifted body. She hadn't been looking for other shifters. But he might have been. Hell, considering his thing with the triad, he probably had been.

He paused at her question. He'd been taping the gauze down over her wound, and he stopped. For a moment she thought she'd offended him.

But he sighed. "I don't know for sure," he said. "I wasn't counting. Including the occasional enforcer for the triad or not?"

"The enforcers for the triad have been trailing you all this time?"

She was sure he'd smiled at that, but she wasn't sure how. His fingers resumed their gentle touch, taping the gauze in place.

"No," he said. "Only a . . . part of a year." He paused again. "Without counting them and . . . and the other triad dragons, of whom there are many, I'd say I've seen about twelve, maybe thirteen shifters. Not . . . not close enough to talk to. I've only talked to a couple. I never went out of my way to talk to them. And sometimes, it was ambiguous, you know. Like, you're walking downtown and you see someone walk in a certain direction and moments later a wolfhound . . . or a wolf . . . comes from the same direction. The only ones I knew for sure were the triad and the orangutan and the coyotes. There seem to be any number of them within the triad. Hundreds. And that might be hereditary. They seem to think they're descended of the Great Sky Dragon. They marry among themselves and they have rites and . . . and stuff."

"So—excluding the triad—a dozen in five years? That doesn't seem like many."

"No. And most of the time it was larger cities than Goldport. Large cities back east. New York and Boston and Atlanta."

"Odd," Kyrie said. "Because just tonight—"

"Yes, you and me and that lion," Tom said, his voice grave, as he finished taping the gauze in place. At least she assumed he'd finished, because he lay the tape back on the table, with the scissors on top of it. And then, ever so gently, he tugged her robe back in place. "I've been thinking the same. Why that many in one night. With the triad here, too, we must be tipping the scales at . . . a lot of shifters. And I wondered why."

Kyrie wondered why too. She'd been living in Goldport for over a year. She remembered the Greyhound bus had stopped here and she'd thought to stay for a night before going on to Denver. But she'd never gone on. Something about Goldport just felt . . . right. Like it was the home she'd been looking for so long. Which was ridiculous, since it was what remained of a gold boom town that had become a university town. And she never had anything to do with either mining or college.

But Goldport had felt . . . not exactly familiar, but more safe. Secure. Home. Like the home she'd never known. She had walked from the Greyhound station to the Athens and seen a sign on the window asking for a server. She'd applied and been hired that night.

But what attraction could the small, odd town have for other shifters. Well . . . Tom had come via the Greyhound too, she supposed. And Frank had offered him a job.

As for the lion . . . She wouldn't think about the lion. "It's probably just a coincidence," she told Tom. And it probably was. Three were not, after all, a great sample. Perhaps they were the only three shifters in town—other than the triad—and had just chanced to bump into each other. The blood had surely helped. She swallowed, remembering what the blood smelled like in the other shape.

Tom came around and started gathering the first-aid supplies.

"What kinds of shifters are there? What kinds did you see? Just big cats? And werewolves? And dragons? Or . . ."

Tom stopped what he was doing. He didn't drop the supplies, just held them where they were. He didn't look at her. "You're going to think I'm an idiot," he said.

"Um . . . no," Kyrie said. She couldn't understand why she would think he was an idiot now. She had a thousand reasons to think him careless, low on self-preservation instincts, and probably a little insane. But . . . an idiot? "Why?"

He sighed. "I swear one of those shifters was a centaur. I know what you're going to tell me, that centaurs don't exist, that I was just seeing a horseman, that—"

"No, I'm not," Kyrie said.

"You're not?"

"Tom, dragons are thought not to exist too."

"Oh." He looked shocked. As if he'd never thought of it that way. Then he grinned. "Well, then I can tell you. Another one of them was an orangutan. Little stooped man, sold roasted chestnuts on the street near . . . near my father's house. And he shifted into an orangutan at night. He was a very nice man, once I got to talking to him. He told me that his wife and his daughters sometimes didn't notice when he shifted." He grinned at that, as he gathered all the first-aid supplies, and headed back to the bathroom.

Kyrie followed him, wondering what to do next. He'd helped her. And, whether his association with the triad was dangerous or not, he, personally, didn't feel dangerous. And they'd lost the triad for the night, hadn't they?

She was reluctant to send him out alone and barefoot into the night. What if he got killed? How would she feel when she heard about it? How would she live with herself?

And besides, having grown up without family, all alone, this was the first time she'd found someone who was genuinely like her. Not family—at least she didn't think so, though he could be a half brother or a cousin. One of the curses of the abandoned child was not to know—but someone who had more in common with her than anyone else she had found. And if he'd gone bad . . . She shook her head.

She didn't know why he'd gone bad. She remembered the smell of blood in that parking lot and the madness in the apartment. Clearly, she too had it in her to commit violence. She would have to control it. Perhaps he was just weaker than her? Perhaps he could not control himself as well.

He put the stuff back in the medicine cabinet, carefully organized, and turned around. "I'll get out of your hair now, okay. Just report your car stolen. You have insurance, right?"

"Yes, but . . ."

"Oh, I'll still pay you for the window," Tom said. "But it might take me a while to be able to get to an ATM. I have some money. Not much. I don't think I'll get my deposit back for the apartment. I thought I'd head out of town, lead the . . . the dragons away from you."

"And leave me stuck in the middle of a murder investigation?"

He opened his hands. "What else can I do? I can't undo what happened." He looked earnest and distraught. "Someone died. And, Kyrie, I wish to all that's holy that I could tell you it wasn't me who killed him. But I can't. He's dead, and I'm . . ."

He opened his hands, denoting his helplessness. "I wish I could tell you I never touched him and that I would never have done that, but my mind is all a blank. I don't even remember being attacked in my apartment, honest. If it weren't for the state it's in . . ."

His hair had fallen in front of his eyes, and he tossed his head back to throw it back. "Look . . . I might very well have done it, and they might find evidence linking me to it. I'm not sure how your DNA works when you're shifted. But if it was . . . If they think I killed him, all you have to say is that I asked you for a ride home, that you had no idea anyone was dead. You could have come out in the parking lot and never seen it, you know? It was behind the vans. I took advantage of your charity and stole your car. No one will hold that against you."

Kyrie bit her lip. There were other things he wasn't even thinking about, she thought. For instance, the paper towels. Properly looked over they'd probably find traces of her hair, dead skin cells, whatever.

But fine, the major evidence would point to him, and she could probably come up with a story that would let her off and get him out of her life forever. So, why didn't she want to? Was it because once he was gone she could go back to imagining that she was just hallucinating the shifts? And she wouldn't have a witness to her shape-shifting.

She put her hands inside the wide sleeves of her robe. "I think that's tiredness talking," she said. "I think if I can come up with an excuse, so can you. You're exhausted from who knows how many hours shifted. And you don't look well." This last was the absolute truth. Tom had started out looking shocked and ill, and he'd progressed to milk-pale, with dark, dark circles under his eyes, bruised enough to look like someone had punched him hard. "You could crash the car out there," she said, and seized upon that. "And I don't want it made inoperable. The insurance never pays you enough to junk it."

He frowned at her, the frown that she had learned to identify as his look of indecision.

"I have a love seat," she said. And to his surprised look added, "In the sunroom at the back. Sleeping porch, really, from when they treated tubercular patients in this region. They thought fresh air was essential, so they had these sunporches. Someone glassed this one in, and there's a love seat in it. Nothing fancy, mind you, but you can have it and a blanket."

She could see him being tempted. He was so tired that, standing in the middle of her little bathroom, he was swaying slightly on his feet. She could see him looking in what he probably thought was the direction of the sunporch, and she could practically hear the thoughts of the love seat and blanket run through his head. She could also see him opening his mouth to tell her thanks but no thanks.

Which was when the doorbell rang.

The noise of the doorbell echoed, seeming to fill the small house.

Kyrie jumped and Tom turned his wrist toward himself, as though checking time on a watch he didn't wear.

She swept her gaze toward the narrow little window in the shower, instead, checking the scant light coming through, blue tinged, announcing the end of blind night, the beginning of barely lit morning.

"It can't be anyone about the . . . It's too early," she said.

And saw Tom pale, saw him start shaking. "Go to the kitchen," she told him, sure that in his mind as in hers was the memory of the bathroom at the Athens, full of bloodied towels, probably tainted with his hair and skin. And hers.

Why, oh, why hadn't she put the used towels in her car? Dumped them somewhere? But where? Outside Tom's apartment? They hadn't exactly had time to stop anywhere and get rid of things.

It was too late for all that, now. All her life, she had faced crises and looked after herself. What else could she do? There hadn't been anyone else to look after her. Now she had to look after Tom too. Not the first time she had this sort of responsibility. Younger kids at foster homes often clung to her, sure that her strength would carry them. And it did, even when she thought she had no strength left.

He was shaking, and she put a hand out to him, and touched his arm. It still felt too cold, even through the sweat suit. "Go to the kitchen. Sit down," she said. "Stay. I'll go see who it is. I'll deal with it."

She walked out through the kitchen and the hallway, to the front room with its curved Seventies vintage sofa that she'd covered in the pretty red sheet, and the table made of plastic cubes where she kept her books and her few prized possessions. It should give her a sense of security, but it didn't. Instead, she wondered what would happen to her books if she were arrested and what would happen to the house if she lost her job. Though it was just a rental, it was the first place she could call hers, the first place where she was not living on someone else's territory and on someone else's terms.

She shook her head. It wouldn't come to that. She wouldn't let it come to that.

The front door was one of the cheap hollow metal ones, but it did have a bull's eye. The neighborhood was quiet enough and the whole city was basically safe, so she supposed it had been put there to allow occupants to avoid Jehovah's Witnesses.

Now she leaned into the door and put her eye to the tiny opening. Out there was . . . a stranger.

He stood on her doorstep, and he was tall, blond. Broad shouldered, she supposed, but with the sort of relaxed posture and laid-back demeanor that made him look more like a surfer than a bodybuilder. Increasing the impression was hair just on this side of long, the bangs overhanging his left eye. He wore a loose white linen suit that seemed to accentuate his relaxed expression. The sunglasses that covered his eyes despite the scant light made him look like one of those artists afraid of being recognized, or else like a man who'd just flown in from a vacation in Bermuda and had not yet fully realized that he was back home.

The sunglasses made his expression unreadable, but he seemed to be looking intently at the door. As Kyrie watched, he raised his hand and rang the doorbell again.

It was what? Four, five in the morning? Surely this was not a casual visit. Casual visitors didn't insist on being answered at this time of night. But then what? A rapist or a robber? What? Ringing the doorbell? Wasn't that sort of unusual? Besides, she could handle herself. Surely she could handle herself.

Kyrie unlocked the door and opened it the length of the chain. The chain was another puzzler. Either the neighborhood had been a lot worse when the security device was installed, or the Jehovah's Witnesses were unusually persistent.

"Ah," he said, when she opened the door, and smiled flashing teeth straight out of a toothpaste commercial. "Ms. Kyrie Smith?"

Before she could answer, there was a faint rustling sound behind her. She turned and saw Tom mouthing soundlessly, "Police?" He raised his eyebrows.

She shrugged. But it if was police, then she really needed to answer. Before he took too close a look at the car. The upholstery was doubtlessly smeared with blood. And, doubtlessly, some of it would be the murder victim's.

Tom nodded at her, as if to tell her to go ahead and open the door. And Kyrie did, about a palm's width further.

The man on the other side got closer. He wore some strong aftershave. No. Not strong, but insinuating. He looked down at her, his eyes unreadable behind the sunglasses. "Ms. Kyrie Grace Smith?"

She nodded. Smith was the name of a foster family she no longer remembered, but it had stuck to her throughout her growing up years.

He reached for a pocket of his linen suit, and brought out a leather wallet, which he opened with a flourish that must have taken years to learn. "Officer Rafiel Trall, Goldport Police Department. May I speak to you for a moment?"

Tom swallowed hard and was sure he'd turned pale at the announcement that the man on the other side of the door was an officer of the law. He'd had run-ins with the police before. He had a record. Oh, he'd never been arrested for more than a night or a couple of nights. And he'd been a minor. And every time his father had bailed him out.

But still, he didn't know what kind of record they kept or if it would have been erased when he turned eighteen. He was sure a couple of times they'd tried to charge him as an adult. Wasn't sure if it had stuck. He hadn't been paying much attention back then. He'd been cocky and full of himself and his family's power and position.

Since he'd left home, he'd done his best not to be caught. He tried to visualize being in jail, and needing to shift. Or shifting without meaning to. He imagined turning into a dragon in confines where privacy didn't exist. He couldn't be arrested. He wouldn't be. He would kill himself first.

Kyrie looked at the ID, then at the man.

"May I come in?" the man asked. "I have a few questions to ask you. Just a few minutes of your time."

Silently, Kyrie opened the door, and the man came in. He didn't look surprised at all at seeing Tom, whom he greeted with a nod. But then why should he look surprised? He couldn't know that Kyrie didn't have a boyfriend, could he?

Tom willed himself to relax, to show no fear. Fear would make the man suspicious and would make him look harder for something that had triggered that reaction.

"Look, this is just a quick visit," the policeman said. "A quick question. You work at the Athens on Fairfax, right?"

Kyrie nodded.

"Mr. Frank Skathari, your boss, said you had left about midnight?"

Had it been midnight? Tom wondered. It seemed like an eternity to his tired body, his dizzy mind. He saw Kyrie nod and wondered if she had any more idea of the time than he did.

"You didn't see any large animal in the parking lot?"

"An . . . animal?" she asked.

"There was a corpse . . . I'm sorry. You might not have noticed," he said. "It was behind some vans. But there was a corpse, and it looked like it died by accident. An attack by some creature with large teeth. We're thinking like a Komodo dragon or something."

Dragon. Tom felt as if the word were directed at him. The policeman looked at him as he spoke. Or at least, his face turned in Tom's direction. It was hard to see what the man was looking at, exactly, with those sunglasses on. "People bring these pets from abroad," he was saying, as Tom focused on him again. "And let them loose. It could be dangerous. I just wanted to know if you'd seen something."

"No," Kyrie said, and sounded amazingly convincing. "I saw nothing strange. I was just concerned with Tom . . ." She made a head gesture toward him. "With getting Tom his medicine."

"Medicine?" the policeman asked, as if this were the clue that would unravel the whole case.

"Migraine," Tom said. It was the first thing to cross his mind. His father, he remembered, had migraines. "Migraine medicine."

"Oh," the policeman said. "I see." He sounded alarmingly as if he did. He looked at one of them and then the other. "So, you won't be able to help me."

"I'm afraid not," Kyrie said.

"That," he said, "is too bad. I was hoping you'd have coffee with me tomorrow." He looked at his watch and nodded. "Well, later today—and discuss if you might have heard something suspicious or . . . found something. Perhaps in the bathroom of the diner. We haven't looked there, yet, you know?"

Tom heard the sound of a train, inside his ears, complete with whistles and growing thuds. He felt as if he would pass out. The bathroom. The damn man had looked in the bathroom and . . . seen the towels. Was he going to use it to blackmail Kyrie? Blackmail Kyrie into what? What had Tom got Kyrie into?

He felt a spasm come over his whole body, and knew he was going to shift. And he didn't have the strength nor the willpower to stop it.

Kyrie gasped. He managed to see her through a fog of preshift trembling, and realized she wasn't looking at him, but at the door she had just closed.

Then she turned around and something—something about him, about the way he looked, made her eyes grow huge and panicky. "No," she said. "No, you idiot. Don't shift."

Her hand grabbed firmly at his arm, and it felt warm and human and real.

Kyrie turned from closing the door on the policeman's smiling face, and saw Tom . . . She couldn't describe it. He was Tom, undeniably Tom, human and bipedal, but there was something very wrong about his shape. His arms were too long, the wrist and quite a bit of green-shaded flesh protruding from the end of the sleeve. His hands were stretched out, too, his fingers elongated and the space between them strangely membranous. And his face, beneath the huge, puzzled blue eyes, looked like it was doing its best to grow a snout.

"No, no, you idiot," she said. "Don't shift. No. Calm down."

He stood on one foot, then the other, his features blank and stupid. His face already half-dragon and unable to show human emotions. His mouth opened, but what came out was half hiss, half growl.

She slapped him. She slapped him hard. "No," she said. "No."

And he shivered. He trembled on the edge of shifting. She realized she had smacked what could be a very large, very angry dragon in a minute. And then she smacked him again on the nose, as if he were a naughty puppy.

She judged how her shifts had left her, tired, witless. He'd shifted twice now. Oh, so had she, but the first time very briefly. How long had he been shifted? What had he done?

"You cannot shift now," she said. And slapped him again.

He blinked. His features blurred and changed. All of a sudden he was Tom, just Tom, standing there, looking like someone had hit him hard with a half brick and stopped just short of braining him. He seemed to be beyond tiredness, to some zombielike state where he could be ordered about.

"Oh, damn," he said, so softly that it was almost a sigh. He looked at her, and his eyes showed a kind of mad despair behind the tiredness. "Oh, damn. I can't be arrested, Kyrie, I can't. I was . . . when I was young and stupid. My father . . . got me out, but sometimes I spent a night in lockup. Kyrie, I couldn't survive it as a dragon. When my dad threw me out, I spent the night in a runaway shelter and . . . it was torture. The dragon . . . The beast wanted to come out. All those people. And being confined. If they take me in on suspicion of murder, if I have to stay . . . Kyrie, I couldn't. I'll kill myself before that."

Suddenly she understood why he'd started to shift, what the words of Officer Trall would sound like to him. She sighed, heavily. "No one is arresting you. At least not yet."

"But he *is* blackmailing us. He's blackmailing you. About the towels in the bathroom. He knows about the blood. And it's all my fault."

"Yes," Kyrie said, wondering if it was blackmail, or what it was, exactly. She remembered the expression in his eyes. Those eyes . . . If it was blackmail, what did he want, exactly? "He knows about the towels because he smelled them."

"Smelled?"

"He found them by the smell of blood, I'd bet. Before any other policemen got to them. He got to them and bagged them and . . . I presume hid them. You were starting to shift, so you probably missed it, but he lowered his glasses and I could see his eyes."

"And?" Tom asked.

"He had the same golden eyes as the lion in the parking lot," she said.

❖   ❖   ❖

"He is . . . like us?" Tom asked, as his mind tried to adjust to the thought. "He is the lion? How can . . ."

"You know the lion was like us," Kyrie said.

He heard the annoyed note in her voice. She had slapped him. Hard. He'd almost gone to pieces in front of her. He felt like an idiot. "But, he's a policeman. He looks . . . he looks well-adjusted. And he traced us . . . And . . . he's in the police?" He swallowed, aware of sounding far less than rational and grown-up.

She nodded. "Yes. I'm very much afraid he's in the police."

"And he's like us . . ." Tom couldn't imagine it. How would he hide his shifts? How would he shift? How would he . . . Did his family know? Or didn't they care? He tried to imagine having parents—a family—who accepted your shifts, who loved you even when you, yourself, weren't sure you were human.

Kyrie shook her head. For just a moment there was empathy in her look. "I can't imagine it either," she said. "I suspect he normally works the night hours, though, just like us. Cops do, too, you know. It's a nocturnal occupation. So we will probably find some of our kind. It's easier to control the shifting if you're awake."

Tom nodded. The whole thing was that even if you didn't shift, if you were a shape-shifter you felt more awake—more aware—at night. It was inescapable. So if you wanted to sleep and actually be able to rest, you did it during the day. And therefore, of necessity, you worked nights.

"Speaking of which," Kyrie said, "sun is coming up soon, and you're practically falling down on your feet."

"You've been yawning," he said accusingly.

She looked at him, puzzled, and he realized he'd said it as if he needed to salvage his manhood. While she'd just been . . . telling the truth.

Looking back, she thought it had all been an elaborate game with herself, to keep herself fooled about the nature of the shifting. After all, if she'd wakened with clothes nearby shredded to bits by large claws, she'd have had to think. She'd have had to admit something else was going on, right?

But in her own home she went to sleep naked, so that when she woke up naked she could pretend nothing at all untoward had happened in the night. Dreams, just dreams. She could tell herself that and believe it.

Only now, she stood naked in the middle of her bedroom and felt . . . well, nude. There was a man in the house. A young, attractive, and not particularly wholesome young man.

Okay, so he was in the back room and frankly, from the way he'd been swaying slightly on his feet, he probably wasn't in any state to be walking around. Not even stumbling around. And there was a locked—she paused and turned the key in the lock—door between them.

But still, she looked at herself in the mirror and she looked distressingly naked. Which meant . . . She blew out a breath, in annoyance at herself, as she scrambled to her dresser, got her loosest T-shirt and a pair of panties, and slipped them on.

What was she thinking? Up till this night she'd never found any reason to like Tom. And what had changed about this night? Well, he might have killed someone. And he was being chased by triads trying to recover something he'd been stupid enough to steal from . . . gangsters.

Yeah. There was a good reason to allow him to sleep in her house. There was a good reason to expose herself to the potential danger of a practically strange—no practically about it; in fact, she knew Tom was strange—man in the house.

She pulled back the covers on the narrow bed pushed up against her wall. The bedroom was barely large enough for the bed and the dresser—both purchased from thrift stores. It would be too small if she had a double bed.

She lay down on the mattress—or more accurately, threw herself down on it with the sort of angry fling of the body that a thin thrift-store mattress couldn't quite take.

She shifted position and flung the covers over herself, refusing to admit she'd bruised something.

There was a reason for Tom to be here. Sure there was. She didn't want to throw him out into the night, barefoot, tired, and confused.

Only, if she'd caught the drift of Tom's story right, he'd been surviving on his own out there for a long time. He was a big man. Well, perhaps on the short side, but definitely well developed and muscular and . . .

No, this was worse than the lion. She turned facedown on the mattress and buried her face in her pillow.

The bedroom was in deep darkness, partly because it was the only room in the entire house that had only one tiny window—very small and high up on the upper corner of the back wall. Now she wondered if the full light of day was near.

What kind of an idiot was she?

Was she now suddenly attracted to hard-luck cases? She'd always laughed at women who came to the diner and, over breakfast with their equally clueless friends, complained about being disappointed by men that, surely, they knew were no good from the beginning. If you picked up with ex-cons, drug addicts, thieves—how could you expect anything good to come of it? Why would they respect you when they'd never respected another human being?

She knew this. So, why would she take this one in? Why? He wasn't even any good at being bad. He was a mess of trembling jelly between bouts of dangerous behavior.

She remembered him in the parking lot, under the moonlight. Pale skin and muscle-sculpted body, and those eyes . . .

Okay, so he was pretty. Since when was pretty worth all this trouble? The world was full of handsome men who weren't her problem. Men who would run the first time she turned into a panther.

And there was the problem, and there she came to and stopped. Because for all else that might be said for Tom, he wouldn't run.

Neither—probably—would Officer Trall. She remembered the disturbing moment when he'd lowered his glasses and fixed her with those recognizable golden eyes that, even in human form, with normal sclera, iris, and pupil, were unmistakable. And he looked just as good in human form.

She threw back the covers.

Again, pretty he might be, but that man was trouble. Pure trouble. He was a shifter, yes, but he was also a police officer. And what did the officer want with her? Why did he want to meet her? She was not so innocent that she didn't notice—of course she did—that he'd mentioned the bathroom, which meant the paper towels. Was it a threat? Was he blackmailing her? Blackmailing her into what?

She remembered the lion in the parking lot of the Athens—virile and energetic and very, very male.

She bit her lip. She wished she could convince herself that it would take a lot of blackmail to get her to what the Victorians called a fate worse than death. But she doubted it. If Tom hadn't been there, if he hadn't pulled her into the car, she very much suspected she would have shifted and . . .

And then there was Tom. His image flickered through her mind, as she tossed her thin blanket and turned first this way, then that. He'd been so gentle, so . . . respectful, when he helped dress her shoulder. Which, by the way, should hurt, shouldn't it?

She sat up in bed and prodded at her bandaged areas, but nothing hurt. Perhaps the antibiotic cream was also an analgesic. She had a bad habit of buying whatever was on sale without reading it too carefully. Well, just as well it didn't hurt. She lay down again, and closed her eyes.

But her thoughts went on behind her closed eyelids.

What was she going to do with Tom? Did she have to do anything with Tom? How far was she responsible for him?

She saw his features close at her comment, she saw his lost expression, all pale face and huge, shocked eyes. She saw him in the parking lot, dragon-form, muzzle bloodstained, and in the bathroom of the Athens, blood all over , his long, dark hair caked with it. She saw him in her living room, half-dragon and mostly man, clearly out of control.

What had he meant to do? Attack the officer? Why? For speaking out of turn?

All right. So, Rafiel Trall might have sounded like he was blackmailing her—blackmailing them. But she wasn't sure he was. There was something to his expression—a softness, a hopefulness . . . that made her doubt that he meant to threaten her. And even if he were, what did Tom mean to do? Eat him? Was he so devoid of any sense of right and wrong? Had no one ever told him you didn't eat people? Ever?

The bed felt too hard, the blanket too hot, the sheet too wrinkled beneath her tossing body.

She was never aware of the moment at which she fell into a dreamless sleep.

Kyrie woke up with the phone ringing.

The phone was on the dresser, across the room from the bed. The ring itself, seeming to run up and down her nerves like fire, carried her halfway there, still asleep, and she woke up fully with the receiver pressed to her ear, while she heard herself say "Hello" in a sleepy voice.

"Ms. Smith?" the voice on the other side was a masculine purr, dripping with sensuousness that caressed the syllables, making the "Ms." sound dangerously like "Miss" and "Smith" sound like a compliment, an indecent proposition.

She knew it was Rafiel Trall without his announcing himself. She could see him at the other side of the phone, relaxed and seductive masculinity, poise and confidence and that something in his eyes, that something in his expression that said he was very bad for her. In the way that chocolate was bad for you. And all the more irresistible for being bad.

"How may I help you, Officer?" she asked, making her voice crispy and official. All business. She had to keep this all business.

"In a lot of ways," he said. "But right now I just want to ask you a favor." She could hear him smile, and she couldn't quite tell how. One of her first jobs, out of high school, had been with a cold-calling telemarketing company. The job hadn't lasted long, though she'd been surprisingly good at it. Perhaps, she thought now, they could hear the harmonics of the panther in the human voice. And bought. And bought. And were very polite with it.

At that job they'd told her to always smile while she was talking because people on the other side could tell. She'd never believed it till now.

The silence lengthened between them, stretched like taffy, feeling sticky and endless, thinner and thinner, but never breaking. "All right," she said, at last. "Ask."

This time there was a very masculine chuckle at the other end.

"I can always say no," she said, tempted beyond endurance by the chuckle.

"You can," he said, gravely. "But I hope you don't. There's a restaurant about . . . oh, two miles from your house. It's the in-house restaurant at Spurs and Lace."

Spurs and Lace was the one good hotel in a Western town plagued with cheap motels and improbable cabin resorts that catered to those families too poor, too numerous, or too shy to stay at the one Holiday Inn. The nineteenth-century hotel was in a completely different class. Once used by moneyed Easterners coming for the benefit of the mineral waters and the dry Western air, it had been renovated to within an inch of its life, furnished with antiques, and updated. It was now the haven of moneyed business travelers and honeymooning couples. An executive resort, Kyrie believed they called it.

"The restaurant is called Sheriff's Star, but despite the name it's good," Trall went on. "They serve brunch, which we're just about in time for."

Again, she said nothing. Oh, she could see where this was going, but she would let him come out and say it.

"I'd like to swing by your house to pick you up in about . . . oh . . . five minutes?"

"Why would you like to pick me up?" Kyrie asked, though her mind, and the recollections of his smell from the day before, gave her pretty good indications.

The chuckle again. "I'd like to feed you, Ms. Smith. Nothing worse than that. And if, during brunch, you should feel like talking to me about the diner, and what you think might have gone on in that parking lot in the dark, I will discuss the other cases we've had with you and—"

"Did you say other cases?" Kyrie asked.

"Indeed."

"Other cases of . . ." She remembered his story the day before. ". . . attacks by Komodo dragons?"

"Possibly. Mysterious attacks, shall we say."

"I see."

"Well, I think if we discuss it, we'll both see better," he said. "So . . . I'll pick you up in a few minutes, if that is acceptable."

"No," Kyrie said, before she even knew she was going to say it. But as soon as the word was out of her lips, she knew why. She knew she had to say it. Stranded at a restaurant with only this relative stranger and no way home on her own? No. She didn't think so. She might have gone stupid last night, but now it was the next day and she wouldn't be stupid anymore. "No. I'll bring my car. I'll meet you there. In twenty minutes."

She could see him hesitate on the other end of the phone. She wasn't sure how, or not exactly. Perhaps the letting out of breath, or perhaps some other sound, too light for ears to consciously discern. But it was there. And it was followed by a hesitant "Your car . . ."

And now it was her turn to smile into the phone "Why, Officer. Would you be embarrassed to be seen with me, because of the condition of my car?"

"What? Of course not. It's just that I thought with the broken window, you have a security liability and—"

"Oh, I wouldn't worry, Officer Trall. After all, it's a good part of town, isn't it?"

After she put the phone down, she thought that it was a good part of town. And that her car might look ever so slightly embarrassing. But probably more so for Officer Trall, whom she doubted ever left the house without wearing a pressed suit.

She refused to be intimidated by him. Or scared by his obvious, open, clear sexuality. To begin with, whether he turned into a lion or not, he was—as she had reason to know, being a female counterpart—only human. Or possibly something less. How much the animal controlled them was something that Kyrie didn't wish to think about. And second, there was very little reason he would be romantically interested in her. She'd guess his suit had cost more than she made in a month.

Chances were he turned on that feline, devil-may-care charm with every female in sight. And meant nothing by it.

Still, she wouldn't look like a charity date. Not at the Sheriff's Star, she wouldn't. Too many times in childhood, she'd found herself dressed in foster sisters'—or brothers'—discards, cowering at the back of a family group, afraid someone would ask why a beggar was let in.

Now she might dress from thrift shops—her salary rarely extended to new clothes, except for underwear and socks—but at a size six that meant she got last year's designer clothes, donated by women so fashion conscious they spent half their time studying trends. That and a bit of flair, and her naturally exotic features, made most people think her beautiful. Or at least handsome.

Before getting in the shower, she checked her wounds under the bandages, and was shocked at finding them completely healed and only a little red. There would be scars, but no wound. Interesting. Very interesting. She must make sure to figure out what that antibiotic cream was. She needed to buy more of it. She always kept a well-stocked first-aid cabinet—part of her trying to be prepared to survive any emergency on her own—but this had been the first time she'd needed it.

She rushed through a shower, dried her hair properly into position, and slipped on a white knit shirt with a mass of soft folds in the front that gave the appearance of a really deeply cut décolletage, but a décolletage so hidden by the swaying material in the front that it was a matter of guessing whether it was really there or not.

Then she put on the wraparound green suede miniskirt. No fishnets, which she occasionally wore to work. There was no reason to look like Officer Trall was having brunch with a hooker either and—with this outfit—fishnets would give that impression. Instead, she put on flesh-tone stockings and slipped her feet into relatively flat shoes.

Fully dressed, she thought of Tom. If she was going to leave him here alone, in the house, without a car, she should leave him a note.

Backtracking to her dresser, she grabbed the notepad and pen she kept in her underwear drawer, and wrote quickly, *I had to go out. There's eggs and bacon in the fridge.* Shape-shifting seemed to come with hunger and, from the way her own stomach was rumbling, Tom would be ravenous. *Don't go anywhere till I come back. We'll discuss what to do.*

She went to the kitchen and was about to put the note on the table when she heard a rustle of fabric from the doorway to the back porch.

Tom stood there, looking only half awake. But his blue eyes were wide open as they stared at her. "Whoa," he said, very softly.

It was, in many ways, the greatest compliment anyone had paid Kyrie in a long time. If nothing else, because it seemed to have been forced from his lips before his mouth could stop it.

Tom awakened with the sound of steps. For a moment, confused, he thought it was his upstairs neighbor walking around in high heels again. But then he realized the steps were nearby. Very nearby.

He woke already sitting up, teeth clenched, hands grabbing . . . the side and seat of a rough, brownish sofa.

He blinked as the world caught up with him—the night before and the events all ran through his mind like a train, overpowering all other thought and leaving him stunned.

And then he realized he could still hear steps nearby. Kyrie. He was in Kyrie's house. She had put him up for the night, though he still couldn't quite understand why. He'd have thought he was the last person in the world she'd want around. But she had given him the sofa to sleep on, and the sweat suit, and . . .

Still half asleep, and with some vague idea of thanking her and getting out of her house and stopping endangering her as soon as possible, he lurched to his feet and stumbled toward the kitchen.

Kyrie stood by the table, her hair impeccably combed, as it usually was when she came to work. The first time Tom had seen her, he'd thought she was wearing a tapestry-pattern scarf. When he'd realized it was her real hair, he'd been so fascinated that he couldn't help staring at her. Until he'd realized she was looking at him with frowning disapproval bordering on hatred. And then he'd learned to look elsewhere.

But this morning, in her own kitchen, she looked far more stunning than she usually did when she came to work. There was this folded down front to her blouse that seemed—at any minute—to threaten to reveal her breasts. He remembered her breasts and his mouth went dry. Beyond that, she wore this tiny suede thing that looked like a scarf doing the turn of a skirt. Below it her legs stretched long and straight to her feet, which were encased in relatively low-heeled but elegant shoes, seemingly made of strips of multicolored leather woven together.

The whole was . . . He heard himself exclaim under his breath and she turned around. He had a moment to think that she was going to disapprove of him again. But instead, she looked surprised, her eyebrows raised.

"I'm sorry," he said. "I'm not used to seeing you dressed up. You look . . . amazing." He just wished her little feather earring hadn't got lost. It would have looked lovely with that outfit.

"Thank you." She smiled, and her cheeks reddened, but for only a second, before the smile was replaced by a worried expression. As if she thought he wouldn't compliment her unless he had ulterior motives. "I was about to leave you a note," she said. "There's eggs and bacon in the fridge."

He realized he was starving. But still, it felt wrong to impose that far. She was being too generous. There was something wrong. "I should go," he said.

"Eat first. And then we'll talk," she said. She spoke as if she had some plan, or at least some intention of having a plan. She threw the note she had written to him into the trash, opened the cupboard above the coffeemaker. "There's cups and coffee beans here," she said. "The coffee grinder is behind the coffee beans. I'm going to go for brunch with . . ." She took a deep breath and faced him. "I'd rather you don't leave because I'm going to go for brunch with the policeman."

Tom felt a surge of panic. "You mean, he might want to arrest me?"

She looked puzzled. "No. I mean I might get some information out of him about what happened and what we can do, or even if there's any danger at all." She waved him into silence. "I know there's still danger from the triad, but I'm hoping there is no danger from the police. If there is, I'll call and let you know, okay?"

He nodded dumbly. Something in him was deeply aggrieved that she had dressed up to go to lunch with the policeman. But of course, there was nothing he could do about that. She wasn't his. He had no chance of her ever even looking at him like less than a dangerous nuisance.

And then for a moment, for just a moment, she looked at him and smiled a little. "Wish me luck," she said.

And she was out the door. And he silently wished her whatever luck meant to her. But he felt bereft as he hadn't in a long time. As he hadn't since that night he'd been thrown out of the only home he'd ever known.

Okay, and on top of everything else, the man is paranoid, Kyrie thought as she got out. *Why would he think I wanted to turn him in to the police?* In the cool light of day, her car looked truly awful, with its smashed driver's side window. She would have to get a square of plastic and tape it over the opening. Fortunately it rarely rained in Colorado, so it wasn't urgent. As for getting money to fix it . . . well . . .

She put the spare key in the broken ignition socket, thinking that would probably be more expensive to repair than the window. And she would make sure Tom paid. Yes, he'd done it to save their lives, but much too thoughtlessly. Clearly he'd either never owned a car, or never owned a car for whose repair he was responsible.

From the look of the sun up in the sky, it was noon and it was a beautiful day, the sidewalks filled with people in shorts and T-shirts, ambling among the small shops that grew increasingly smaller and pricier in the two miles between Kyrie's neighborhood and the hotel.

There were couples with kids and couples with dogs dressed like children, in bandanas and baseball caps. Lone joggers. A couple of businesswomen in suits, out shopping on their lunch hour.

Again Kyrie experienced the twin feelings of envy and confusion at these people. What would they do if they knew? What would they think if they were aware that humans who could take the shape of animals stalked the night? And what wouldn't Kyrie give to change places with one of them? Any one of them. Even the businesswoman with the pinched lips and the eyes narrowed by some emotional pain. At least she knew what she was. *Homo sapiens.*

She pulled into the parking lot of the hotel and, unwilling to brave the disdain of the valets, parked her own car. Wasn't difficult to find a parking space during the week.

Entering the hotel was like going into a different world from her modest house, her tiny car, or even the diner.

The door *whooshed* as it slid aside in front of her, and the cold air reached out to engulf her, drawing her into the tall, broad atrium of the hotel, whose ceiling was lost in the dim space overhead, supported by columns that looked like green marble. The air-conditioning cooled her suddenly, making her feel composed and sophisticated and quite a different person from the sweaty, rumpled woman outside in the Colorado summer.

The smoked glass doors closed behind her. Velvet sofas and potted palms dotted the immense space. Uniformed young men, on who-knew-what errands, circulated between. This hotel was designed to look like an Old West hotel, one of the more upscale ones.

She could all too easily imagine gunslingers swinging from the chandeliers, a bar fight breaking out, and the uniformed receptionists ducking behind their marble counter.

Kyrie hesitated but only for a moment, because she saw the signs to the restaurant and followed them, down into the bowels of the atrium and up in the elevator to the top floor that overlooked most of Goldport. Light flooded the restaurant through windows that lined every wall. Kyrie couldn't tell how big it was, just that the ceiling seemed as far up as the atrium's, but fully visible—a cool whiteness twenty feet up. Soft carpet deadened the sound of steps, and the arrangement of the tables, on different levels and separated by partitions and judiciously placed potted palms, made each table a private space.

A girl about Kyrie's age, blond and cool and wearing what looked like a business suit in pretty salmon pink, gave her the once-over. "May I help you?"

"Yes," Kyrie said. "I'm meeting a Mr. Trall. Rafiel Trall."

The girl's eyes widened slightly. And there was a gratifying look of envy.

What, thinking I can't possibly be in his league, sweetie? Kyrie thought, and reproached herself for her sudden anger and calmed herself forcefully, giving the woman a little smile.

"Mr. Trall is this way," the hostess said and, picking up a menu, led her down a winding corridor amid wood-and-glass partitions and palms. From the recesses around the walkway came the sounds of talk—but not the words, the acoustics of the restaurant being seemingly designed to give tables their privacy—and the smells of food—bacon and ham and sausage, eggs, roast beef. It made her mouth water so much that she was afraid of drooling.

Then the hostess led her around a wooden partition, and stepped back. And there, getting up hastily from his chair, was Rafiel Trall. He was perhaps better dressed than the night before, when his pale suit had betrayed a look of almost retro cool.

Now he was wearing tawny chinos and a khaki-colored shirt. His blond hair still shone, and still fell, unruly, over his golden eyes. The mobile mouth turned upward in what seemed to be a smile of genuine pleasure at seeing her. "Miss Smith," he said, extending a hand. He tossed his head back to free his eyes of hair. There were circles of tiredness around his golden eyes, and creases on his face, as though he too had slept too little and not well.

He shook her hand hard, firmly. The hostess disappeared, silently, walking on the plush carpet as though gliding.

"Sit, sit," Rafiel Trall said. "Relax. I was horribly hungry, so I ordered an appetizer." He waved toward a platter on the table. "Seafood croquettes," he said. "High on protein, though perhaps not the kind . . ." He grinned. The golden eyes seemed to sparkle with mischief of their own.

Kyrie sat down, bonelessly. *What am I doing here?* she asked herself. *What does he want from me?*

And then she knew the answer to the first one. She was here because he had blackmailed her into coming. Regardless of whether a threat had been uttered, regardless of what the threat he might actually mean, Rafiel Trall had mentioned those bloody towels in the bathroom.

Kyrie didn't own a television, but she had watched enough episodes of *CSI* on the diner's television, during slow times of the day, that she knew that on the show, at least, they could tell if someone had wiped someone else's blood off their skin with a paper towel. There would be skin and hair and sweat. . . .

But she remembered Tom and the way Tom had looked. What else could she have done then? Short of ignoring the whole thing and pretending it had nothing to do with her? And then what would have happened to Tom? She wasn't sure what she thought was worse—Tom eating the corpse, or Tom getting killed by ambush in his bedroom.

So she'd used the towels, and now Rafiel Trall held the towels over her head. And Tom's head. Which had brought her here.

But why did Officer Trall want her here? And what was the point of it all? Did he want to blackmail her for favors? No. If he wanted to do that, he would demand she meet him elsewhere, wouldn't he? However secluded the table might be . . . it wasn't *that* private.

Besides—she looked up at Rafiel Trall and refused to believe that he had that much trouble getting dates that he needed to force a girl into bed. Even if she admitted she didn't look like chopped liver.

She became aware that he'd said something and was now sitting, his napkin halfway to being unfolded on his lap, while he looked at her, expectantly.

There was no point lying. "I'm sorry," she said. "I have no idea what you said."

He smiled. "No. You were miles away. I said your outfit is very becoming."

Before she could stop it, she felt heat rise up her cheeks. "Thank you," she said. "But I would like to know why you asked me to come here."

He grinned at her. "I would like to have breakfast with you and to discuss . . . some cases the Goldport police force has encountered recently."

Her expression must have became frozen with worry, because he shook his head. "I do not in any way suspect you, do you understand? I just think you could—literally—help me with my enquiries. And I thought it was best done over a nice meal."

Kyrie nodded and picked up her menu, then put it down again, as the prices dismayed her.

"Ms. Smith—I'm hoping for your help with this. I'll pay for your meal." He smiled, showing very even teeth. "This is a business brunch."

She hesitated. She was aware that whatever he said, breaking bread with someone was an expression of friendship, an expression of familiarity. After all, throughout human history, enemies had refused to dine together.

"Look." He stared at her, across the table, and, for the first time since last night, didn't smile. "I'm sorry I mentioned the bathroom, which I meant to make you think of the paper towels. It was unworthy of me. And stupid. In fact, I . . . got rid of them, okay? I risked my position. But I'm sure . . . Just, I'm sorry I mentioned them. I didn't know any other way to make you help me, and we must talk. About . . . dragons and what's going on."

His voice was low, though Kyrie very much doubted anyone overhearing them would have any idea at all what they were talking about. But his expression was intense and serious.

She nodded, once. Not only was she starving, but she had left Tom in charge of the kitchen, with bacon and eggs at his disposal. Considering how many times he'd shifted the night before and how tired he'd looked, she was sure that he would have eaten all of it and possibly her lunch meat besides, before he could think straight.

Besides, what did Trall mean, *dragons*? He'd mentioned crimes. More than one? What had Tom done? Before she threw her luck in with his, she had to know, didn't she?

"Very well, Officer Trall," she said. "I'll have brunch with you."

He smiled effusively. At that moment, the server reappeared and he informed her they would be having the buffet. He also ordered black coffee, which Kyrie seconded.

The buffet spread was the most sumptuous that Kyrie had ever seen. It stretched over several counters and ranged from steamed crab legs, through prime rib, to desserts of various unlikely colors and shapes.

Kyrie was interested only in the meat. Preferably red and rare. She piled a plate with prime rib, conscious of the shocked glares of a couple of other guests. She didn't care. And at any rate, back at the table, she was glad to notice that Rafiel Trall's plate was even more full—though he'd gone for variety by adding ham and bacon.

They ate for a while in silence, and Rafiel got refills— how long had he been shifted the night before? Could a lion have killed the man?—before he leaned back and looked appraisingly at her. "How long have you known your friend? The . . . dragon?"

Kyrie, busy with a mouthful, swallowed hastily. "About six months," she said. "Frank hired him from the homeless shelter downtown for the night hours. He told me he was hiring him from the homeless shelter and that he thought Tom had a drug problem, so I'm guessing that Frank thought he was doing the world a favor, or was trying to garner a treasure in heaven, or whatever."

Rafiel was frowning. "Six months ago?"

Kyrie's turn to nod. "No, wait. A little more, because it was before Christmas when we were really crunched with all the late shoppers and people going to shows. And the other girl on the night hours had just left town with her boyfriend, so we were in the lurch. Frank got a couple of the day people to fill in, but they don't like it. Most of them are girls who think this part of town is unsavory and don't like being out in it at night. So he said he was doing something for community service, and he went and hired Tom."

Rafiel was still frowning. "And is he? On drugs?"

Kyrie shrugged. She thought of Tom, so defenseless last night, she thought of Tom, looking . . . admiring and confused this morning. And she felt like a weasel, betraying him to this stranger.

But she didn't seem quite able to help herself. Something was making her talk. His smell, masculine, feline, pervasive, seemed to make her want to please him. So she shrugged again. "Not on work time, that I've noticed," she said. She didn't find she needed to mention the track marks. To be honest, they might be scars. She hadn't looked up close. It seemed more indecent than staring at his privates. Which she hadn't done, either. Well, maybe she'd seen them by accident yesterday, but no more than to note he had nothing to be ashamed of.

"His name is Thomas Ormson?" Rafiel asked. "Thomas Edward Ormson?"

Kyrie shrugged again. "I've never known his middle name. I know he's Ormson because he introduced himself as Tom Ormson."

Rafiel made a sound at the back of his throat, as though this proved something. "If you'll excuse me," he said, standing up.

She ate the rest of her roast beef in silence, wondering if, by confirming Tom's name, she had given something essential away and if Tom would now be arrested. But Rafiel simply came back with yet another plate of meat. "How long have you known he was . . . a shifter?" Rafiel asked, cutting a bite of his ham.

"Not . . . not until last night. He was late. I heard a scream and I went to look. And he was . . . shifted." Why couldn't she stop herself talking? Why would she trust this stranger?

"And there was a dead person?" Rafiel asked.

Kyrie nodded.

Rafiel frowned. "Has he been late other nights?"

"No," Kyrie said.

"Are you sure? Not last Thursday? Does he work on Thursdays?"

Kyrie frowned. "He works on Thursdays, and he wasn't late."

"And he's been in town for more than six months?"

She nodded.

Rafiel Trall ate for a while in silence. Kyrie was dying to know what this was all about.

"Why do you ask?" she said. "You said there had been crimes, not one crime."

Rafiel nodded. "What I'm going to tell you is not known much outside the police department. There have been a couple of reported cases, but no one has put two and two together."

Alone in the house, Tom showered. He felt guilty about it, because it was Kyrie's shower. Her water. Her soap. Her shampoo. But at this point he owed her a bunch of money, and he just added to it mentally.

Most of his time on his own, he'd found shelters for runaway kids and, then, when he was older, homeless shelters. He hadn't been homeless as such. He'd just moved from shelter to shelter in between bouts of getting in trouble and running away. He'd only slept outside when the moon was full. Shortly after leaving his father's house—even now his mind flitted away from the circumstances of that leaving—he'd thought it best to abandon New York City altogether. There were too many opportunities, there, for a rampaging dragon to do serious damage. And far too many people who might see him do it.

He'd drifted vaguely south and westward, moving when he thought someone had caught a glimpse of him in shifted form and, once, when a picture of him, as a dragon, in full flight, was published on the front page of the local rag. It had been syndicated to the *National Enquirer*, too. If his father caught a glimpse of it, on a supermarket line, would he have— But Tom shook his head. If he'd not actually given up on his father, he should have. Long ago.

But running or settled for a while in a town, he'd never had an apartment until these last five months. And all showers at these institutions had been rationed and far from private. All the soap had smelled of disinfectant, too.

The last five months, the showers had been heaven. And he'd bought the best soap he could find. His one luxury. But now he was homeless again, adrift. And, with the triad pressing down, he might have to leave.

He only hadn't left already because Kyrie had insisted he stay. And Kyrie was . . . the only one of his kind he'd

ever got close to. Oh, he might also have quite a huge
crush on her. But that didn't count. He'd had crushes
before. He'd moved on. But Kyrie . . . He bit his lower lip,
standing in her tiny bathroom and turning on the water.

Kyrie was something he didn't know what to do about.
He didn't want to leave. He didn't want to lose the only
kindred feeling and fellowship he'd ever known. But with
the triad chasing him, what else could he do?

He showered, enjoying the water, then dried his hair
and put the jogging suit Kyrie had lent him back on. He
didn't own anything else. He didn't even own this.
Nothing but his own skin.

A look outside, through the kitchen window, showed
him a paper in the driveway. He wondered if Kyrie would
mind if the neighbors saw him. But considering she hadn't
told him anything about it, he'd assume she didn't.

He walked out to get the paper. It was noon, or close to
it. The earliest he'd wakened in a long time. The air,
though already suffocatingly hot, felt clear and clean, and
he smelled Kyrie's roses, and the neighbor's profusion of
flowers that spilled over the lawn and around the mailbox,
in an array of pastel colors.

The neighbor, an elderly lady, sat on the porch with a
tall glass of something, her white hair in curlers. She
smiled pointedly at Tom and waved at him. Tom waved
back and found himself grinning ridiculously. Bending to
pick up the paper, he felt as if he were living something
out of a movie. A domestic morning. And he wished
madly that he could live that life and have that kind of
morning. That kind of life. Just be a normal person with a
normal life.

But, who was he kidding? Judging from all the trouble
he'd got into before he'd started transforming into a

dragon, his life wouldn't have been any different had he been perfectly normal. He'd probably still be running from town, a drifter. He probably still would have used. He probably . . .

He put the paper on the table, while he nuked himself a profusion of bacon and fried some eggs in a frying pan on the gas stove. He left half the eggs and bacon in the fridge. He could have eaten them all, easily enough, but he didn't want to do that to Kyrie. Yeah, she'd probably get lunch bought for her today, but what if she shifted again tonight and needed breakfast tomorrow?

Tom knew how much food cost. Over the last five months one of his delights had been learning to cook. He'd bought cookbooks at the same thrift stores at which he shopped for clothes and furniture. Since on a diner's waiter salary it was a challenge to cover everything and put money aside—as he felt he had to—he'd reveled in trying to create quasi-gourmet dishes from meats on special and discounted produce. And he'd eaten a lot of tofu.

Now he cooked quickly, peppering his eggs from a shaker by the stove. His stomach growled at the smell of the utilitarian fare. He knew, from other shifts, that the craving for protein was almost impossible to deny the morning after a shift. Kyrie clearly knew it too.

Kyrie again. Sitting down to eat, he opened the paper. And choked.

Right there, on the front page, the headline above the fold screamed "Murder at Local Diner!" The picture of the Athens in black-and-white made the huge parking lot with the tiny diner beside it look like something out of a film noir.

The story was all too familiar to Tom. They'd found a body in the parking lot—of course anyone reading only the headline would think that they'd found it in the diner proper. Which meant that Frank was probably sizzling. If he was awake. Since he preferred to work nights, perhaps his day manager hadn't found it necessary to wake him and tell him about the paper. Then again, sometimes Tom thought Frank worked around the clock. He always seemed to be at the diner.

Frank's mood might matter or not. Tom hadn't decided yet what he was going to do about work. He needed the job. Wanted it. He'd enjoyed working at the diner more than he cared to think about. It had been his first long-term employment. A real, normal job.

Before this he'd just signed up with the day laborer places. But he'd enjoyed the routine, the regulars, and getting them served quickly, and getting their tips. Smiling just enough at the college girls to get a good tip without their thinking he was coming on to them. The minor feuds with the day staff, the camaraderie with Kyrie and . . . well, he wouldn't call it camaraderie with Frank, but Frank's gruff ways.

He had felt almost . . . human. And now it would all vanish. It all would go as if it meant nothing. Like having a family. Like school. Like a normal adolescence.

He finished eating and cleaned his plate with bread from the red bread box over the fridge, before carefully washing the dishes and putting them away.

Normally he compensated after nights of shifting by grabbing some fried chicken on the way to work the next evening. Or by eating a couple of boiled eggs. Most of what he cooked at home was near vegetarian. So this might be the most protein he'd eaten at one sitting in years.

Oh, he could afford bacon and eggs, but he'd been saving money. He had some idea that he would go to a community college and get a degree. He'd dreamed of settling down.

Now, of course, as soon as he could swing by an ATM, he would have to empty the five hundred in his account to pay Kyrie for the car repairs and the groceries. And at that he'd probably still owe her money. But he would send her money from . . . somewhere.

And on this he stopped, because he hadn't told himself he was going to run. Not yet. But, after all, with the apartment in ruins, and the police investigating a crime around his place of employment, what else could he do? He had to run. Just as soon as he could retrieve . . . *it* from the Athens.

The doorbell rang. Tom thought it would be the police, come to arrest him. But how could they know he was here? Of course, Kyrie might have spoken, but . . .

He tiptoed to the door, trying to keep quiet, and looked through the peephole. Keith Vorpal stood on the doorstep, baseball cap rakishly turned backward and an expression of intense concern on his good-natured face. Since Vorpal didn't usually feel much concern for something not involving shapely females, Tom was surprised and curious. Also curious about how Vorpal had found him.

He opened the door on the chain and looked out.

"Man," Keith said as soon as he saw Tom. "Good to see you're alive. They think someone broke into your place and destroyed it, then tried to set fire to the pieces of furniture. It's all everyone talks about. Did you see anything weird when you were there?" He looked up at the space over the door, probably where the house number was. "I guess you spent the night here?"

Tom opened the door. "Come in," he said.

Keith came in, looking around the room with the curiosity of someone visiting a strange place.

"How did you find me?"

Keith shrugged. "Your boss, at that dive you work in. He said you were staying with the girl, Kyrie? And he gave me the address."

How did Frank know? Perhaps Kyrie had told him. She must have called in sometime after they got back to her place.

"Come on," Tom said. "I'll get you some coffee."

Moments later, they were in the kitchen and Tom had managed to get cups and coffee, and locate the sugar and milk.

"I guess you've been here a lot?" Keith asked.

Tom shrugged, neither willing to lie full-out, nor to destroy this impression of himself as a man in a relationship that Keith seemed to envy.

He wondered why Keith had come over. He seemed to be worried about Tom. But Tom wasn't used to anyone being worried about him. Did this mean the human race wanted him back?

"There have been," Rafiel Trall said, leaning over the table and keeping his voice low, "a series of deaths in town. Well, at least they're classified as deaths, not murders. Bodies have been found . . . bitten in two."

"Bitten?" Kyrie asked, while her thoughts raced. Only one kind of thing could bite a person in two. Well, maybe many kinds of things, but in the middle of a city like Goldport, almost for sure all of those things would be shape-shifters. People like her. Tom had said that there weren't that many out there. But there were the three of them and the triad. Were there more? And if so, what was calling them to Goldport?

"Bitten," Rafiel said, and his teeth clashed as he closed his mouth, as though the words had been distasteful for him to say. And he held his teeth clenched too, visible through his slightly parted lips. "Our forensics have found proteins in the bites that they say are reptilian but not . . . not of any known reptile."

He sat up straight and was silent a moment. "The theories range wildly," he said. "From pet Komodo dragons that escaped and grew to huge proportions, to an alligator, somewhere, to . . ." He shrugged. ". . . an extinct reptile that survived somewhere in the wilderness of Colorado and has just now found its way into town. Though that theory is on the fringes. It's not like we've called a palaeontologist in to look at the bite marks yet. But . . ." He took a deep breath, and it trembled a little as he let it out. "But the teeth size and the marks are definitely . . . They're very large teeth, of a reptile type. I . . ." He shook his head. "You must realize in what position this puts me. Everyone at the police is talking escaped animals and Jurassic revivals. They've stopped just short of positing UFO aliens, but I'm very much afraid that's coming up next."

"And meanwhile none of them guesses the truth," Kyrie said, leaning back.

He nodded. "Or at least what might be the truth," he said. "You see in what kind of a position this puts me. . . ."

She looked at him across the table, and could well imagine that sort of divided loyalty, that confusion of identities. There were many things she wanted to ask. How many other shifters he'd met? Why he suspected Tom specifically? Instead, she heard herself say, "How did you become a police officer?"

He grinned. "Oh, that was easy. Grandad was one. Dad was one." Suddenly the grin expanded, becoming the easy smile of the night before. His hand toyed with his silverware on the side of his plate. "If I hadn't become a police officer, they would think there was something wrong with me. The shifting, they can forgive even if they can't understand. Not being a policeman? Never."

It was a large hand, with square fingers. No rings, except for a large, square class ring, and she scolded herself for looking for rings. Yeah. They could get together and raise a litter of kittens. What was she thinking?

Rafiel shrugged. "So, you see . . ."

"And your . . . shifting . . . when did you start?"

He took a deep breath. "It started when I was about twelve. My parents were aware of it first, as I did it in my sleep. They were a little scared, but I was normal otherwise, and how do you go and tell someone your kid . . . well . . ."

Kyrie nodded. "So . . . they aren't?"

"No. And Dad is retired now, but the first he heard about these corpses he asked if I knew . . ."

"And you think it's Tom?" Kyrie asked, her hands unaccountably clenched on the side of the table, as if this mattered to her personally.

He shrugged. "Just . . . the shape matches, and I've never met another one large enough to actually sever a body in two. But if he was in town that far back, and there were no murders something must have happened three months ago that triggered them. And then you say that he was at work on Wednesday. And on Wednesday we found a body right behind the Three Luck Dragon. Well, actually it was found on Thursday morning, but we think he died around midnight on Wednesday."

Kyrie thought back. As far as she could tell Tom had been at work and had been much as normal.

"Of course," Rafiel said. "The time is never exact. There could be a two-hour difference one way or another. And you see, I don't know any other shifters, any other shape that could just bite a man in half. And how common can a dragon be?"

Kyrie thought of the triad. "There are others . . . like Tom in town."

"Really?" Rafiel asked. He raised his eyebrows. "I've only met, truly met, another one besides you. He was a wolf and was passing through town. Transient. He was brought in for petty theft, and shifted while I was booking him. Fortunately Goldport has a tiny police force. Most officers are part-timers. And I was alone in the room with him at the time. I could . . . cover things up and talk sense to him. But that was the only one I ever talked to. And he was a mess. Drugs, possible mental illness. I've . . . smelled others, but I don't know their shapes."

"Smelled?" Kyrie asked, aware of his smell so close, just across the table, that reek of masculinity and health and vigor—like the distilled scent of self-confidence.

He looked at her, with the look of a man who tries to evaluate whether someone is playing a joke on him. "Smelled—there is a definite scent to those . . . like us. A slightly metallic smell? An edge?"

Kyrie shook her head. She hadn't been aware of ever smelling people before. Perhaps because she hadn't been aware of really shifting shapes before. She thought of people as people, not smells. And yet, as Rafiel mentioned it, she was aware that there was a slight edge in common in his smell and Tom's and perhaps her own. If their smell had been music, the metallic scent would have been a note, subdued but persistent, in the background. She blinked.

"These other . . . dragons," he said, lowering his voice on the last word. "Are they part of . . . the Asian community in town?"

"Why do you ask?" Kyrie said.

"Because all the victims were Asian or part Asian," he said. "That's why I was so surprised when I saw your . . . when I saw Thomas Ormson in his other form. Though thinking about it, he didn't look oriental even as . . . a dragon."

Kyrie shook her head. "Nordic," she said. "Like what they used to carve on the prows of Viking ships." She wondered if the Viking figureheads had been drawn from life. And if they'd really existed, all that time, in the past. "But yes, the other dragons are Asian. Tom said they are members of a triad." She hesitated.

"An organized Chinese crime syndicate?" Rafiel asked. Then added, "I see. Look, I know you feel like you're betraying him or something. But . . . put yourself in my place. The police will never be able to solve this series of deaths. And I know—or at least I think I know— something that could lead them to the truth. But if I speak, I won't be believed. And if I demonstrate it, I don't know . . . I suspect the first few of us who come out to society-at-large face the charming prospect of a life in the laboratory. I don't want that. I don't know anyone who wants that. I'm sure you don't. But at the same time I want to stop the murders. The people being killed . . ."

He shrugged. "They don't deserve to die, and we should put a stop to it. If the killers are like us—and there's a great chance they are—then it's our responsibility to stop it." He looked desperately up at her, his expression very intense and not at all like the relaxed image of the day before. "Do you understand what I'm saying at all?"

Kyrie understood. At least intellectually she understood. And suddenly, in a rush, she felt as if she, the orphan, had been adopted into a family, a family that came with obligations, with requirements. She looked at Rafiel's intense golden eyes, and hoped his smell was not influencing her as she said. "Yes, I see. But you must promise to do nothing against Tom on . . . anything else. Anything beyond the murders. It is not his fault if he is a shifter, and if he weren't a shifter, none of this would come out about him."

Rafiel nodded once and leaned forward. His plate was now empty and he pushed it forward and joined his hands on the place where it had been, his whole attitude one of intense attention to her.

She told him what had happened the night before. Her considerations and thoughts and final decision to take Tom home to his apartment. The condition of the apartment. The attack by the triad members.

She could no more stop herself talking than she could stop herself breathing. Her mind was powerless against his masculine scent.

Rafiel nodded. "That would make sense for the deaths we've been seeing." He pulled a notepad out of his pocket and noted down the description of the triad members.

"Not that we can do anything about it officially," he said. "Because if they catch them then they'll . . . They might very well figure out about us as well, you know."

Kyrie nodded. The rules of this group to which she belonged despite herself were revealing themselves as complex. If they must be hidden—and they must, because revealing one of them would mean revealing all of them—then, surely, surely, they would have to police their own. Like other secretive communities of what had at the time been considered not quite humans all through history, they would have to take care of their own. Slaves, immigrants, serfs—all had policed themselves, to avoid notice from the outside, as far back as there had been humans in the world.

One way or another. She wondered what that meant. She could understand it to mean nicely or by force. And she wondered if Rafiel Trall understood it.

And looked up to find his intelligent golden eyes trained on her. "You know that means we might have to . . . take care of it on our own," he said. "I . . . never met any of *us* till a couple of years ago, and I never thought about it. The possibilities of someone going bad, doing something terrible and how the normals would never be able to take care of it and we'd have to step in. I never thought about it. I thought there might be a half a dozen of us in the world . . ."

Kyrie shook her head. "Tom has seen a dozen or so over five years. Not counting the dragon triad, where he thinks there could be hundreds. I think there's more than half a dozen. I wonder . . ."

"Yes?"

"I wonder how long this has been going on and why no one seems to know about it."

"I don't know," Rafiel said. "When my parents found out, they tried to research. They found legends and stories, poems and songs. And Mom, who reads a lot of scientific stuff, thinks there might be such a thing as . . . migratory genes. People attaching the genes from other species. Going partway there, as it were. But I'll be damned if that explains mythological species, too. Like dragons. Wonder if there are sphinxes and sea serpents, as well." He shook his head. "There seem to be a lot of legends about . . . people like us, until magic stopped being believed and science stepped in. I think we'll have to admit that we are not . . . things of the rational universe. I'm sure Thomas Ormson's shift violates the rules of conservation of matter and energy." He frowned, then suddenly grinned, a boyish grin. "Good thing that's not the sort of law I have to enforce."

Kyrie nodded. Men and their puns. "I've thought the same. But if we exist, if we exist anyway, how come no one has found out? How come one of us hasn't slipped spectacularly in a public place yet, and been found out?"

"Who says we haven't?" Rafiel said. "Have you ever heard of cryptozoology?"

"Bigfoot and the Loch Ness monster?" she asked, unearthing the word from a long-ago spree on the Internet looking up strange stuff.

Rafiel started to shake his head then shrugged and nodded. "For all I know, they're of ours too, yes," he said. "But more than that. Giant panthers in England, the lizard man of Denver, the thylacine in Australia that keeps being seen, years after it's supposedly extinct. And giant tigers and giant black dogs. All of those. And perhaps," he sighed, "Bigfoot and Nessie too." He looked at her. "They're all seen. They're all found. It's just that they're impossible, see. And the human mind is very good at erasing everything that is not possible. I . . . My mother says that the human mind is an engine designed to order reality." He paused and frowned. "You have to meet Mom to understand. But if she's right, then our minds are also designed to reject anything that introduces disorder, anything that goes against the grain."

"Our," she said, before she knew where her mind was headed. "You said the human mind and referred to it as 'our.' You think our minds are human."

"Do you think they aren't?" Rafiel asked. "Why?"

Kyrie shrugged. "Up until last night I thought I was perfectly human," she said. "I had no idea that I shifted shapes. I thought all that was an hallucination. Today I don't know what I think."

Something to the way that Rafiel's expression changed, and to his gaze shifting to a point behind her, made her turn. The server approached to drop off the bill. Rafiel glanced at it and handed it, with a card, back to the server.

"Look, when I went to bed yesterday—well, today at sunrise—we didn't have an ID on the victim yet. I'm scheduled to go and attend the autopsy today."

"Why?"

"Why the autopsy? Because we don't know exactly what killed the man. Our pathologist says the wounds look odd."

"No, why would they have you attend it? I've seen this in cop shows on TV, but I don't understand whey they need a policeman, who's not an expert in anatomy or anything of the sort to be there."

"Oh, that . . ." He shrugged. "Look, I'm the investigating officer. We don't have a murder department. Until these bodies started appearing three months ago, our murder rate was one or two a year and those usually domestic. And the investigating officer has to attend the autopsy. It's . . . That way we're there. They film the autopsy, you know, but a lot of it never makes it onto the film or even the official report. And we need to know everything. Even some casual comment, that the examiner might forget to put in the official report, or that the cameras might not catch. Sometimes, crimes are solved on little suff." He grinned suddenly, disarmingly. "Of course, I'm going on my criminal-science class. As I said, most of the murders here don't involve much solving. The murderer is usually sobbing by the kitchen door, holding the knife. But the classes I took said I should be there. Also, if they find any evidence—dust or hair on the victim's clothing, I'll be there to take it into custody. Chain of custody is very important, should the case ever come to trial."

The victim's clothing. Kyrie remembered the sodden rag of a body the night before, soaked in blood. She hadn't been able to tell if he was wearing clothing, much less what it might be.

She emerged from the reverie in time to hear Rafiel say, "To the morgue?"

"Beg your pardon?"

"I was asking if you'd come with me to the morgue. To watch the autopsy."

"Why?" she asked.

He shrugged. "I don't know. Because though I'm not deputizing you, in a way I am? Because there might be something you see or notice. There might be a hair on the victim's body that is that of a diner regular—"

"I doubt they can find a hair, with all that blood," she said.

"You'd be amazed what's found in autopsy. And I think you can help us. Perhaps help me solve the whole thing." He paused a moment, significantly, playing with his napkin by folding it and unfolding it. "And then we can deal with it." From his expression, he looked about as eager to deal with it as she felt.

"Won't people mind?" Kyrie asked. "Isn't it irregular to have me with you at something like an official autopsy?" She imagined facing the dead body again. All that blood. It was safer during the day, but it would still trigger her desire to shift.

"I'll tell them you work at the diner," he said. "And that you're there because I think you might see or remember something. And if needed I'll tell them you're my girlfriend and you're thinking of studying law enforcement. But it should just be me, and Officer Bob— Bob McDonald. Good man, he usually helps me. He'll be there. But he was my dad's partner when Dad was in the force. Bob won't ask much of anything. He'll trust me. He thinks I'm . . . as he puts it: 'strange but sound.' And no, he doesn't know. At least we never told him. Of course, he's around the house a lot." He shrugged and set the napkin down, neatly folded, by his still half-full water glass. "So, will you come? With me?"

Kyrie sighed. She nodded. It seemed to be her duty to do this. Would it be her duty, also, to kill someone? To . . . execute someone? Until early morning today she'd never even examined her own ideas on the death penalty—she hadn't had any ideas on the death penalty, trusting brighter minds than hers to figure that out. But now she must figure it out. If Tom had killed the man yesterday, did they need to kill him? Was there another way to control him? How much consciousness did he have while killing? And would any considerations of justice or injustice to him have anything to do with it? Or would it all be overruled by the need to keep society safe?

The server dropped off the credit card slip, and Rafiel signed it.

"Your name," Kyrie said. "It's an odd spelling."

"Rafiel? I was named after an Agatha Christie character. Mom is a great fan."

"Jason Rafiel," Kyrie said. "*Nemesis* and *Caribbean Mystery.*"

He smiled. "Mom will love you." Then he seemed to realize how that might sound, and he cleared his throat. "So, will you come with me?"

Kyrie sighed. "I really don't want to," she said. "But—"

"But?"

"But I think I might have to." She felt as if her shoulders were being crushed by the weight of this responsibility she didn't really want to take.

Tom had given Keith coffee and shuffled him to the back room where Tom had spent the night. He felt more at ease there, as if he were intruding less on Kyrie's privacy. She'd let him sleep here. It was a de facto guest room.

"I was just worried about you," Keith said, sitting down on the love seat as Tom motioned toward it. "The paper said a corpse was found behind that diner place where you work. And then with the apartment the way it looked, I thought—"

He had never clearly said what he thought, just frowned and looked worried. And Tom wasn't absolutely sure how to respond. It had been five years since he had actually needed to talk to someone or had a personal connection with anyone. And apparently socialization was reversible, because as far as making small talk—or any talk at all—he might as well have been raised by wolves.

He hadn't been a solitary child. He'd always had his buds, back when he was growing up, all the way from his playgroup in kindergarten to what—he now suspected— had been a rather unsavory group of young thugs in his adolescent years. In fact, it could be said that Tom, growing up, had spent far too little time alone with his own mind and his own thoughts.

But the last five years . . . Well, there had been interactions with other humans, of course, some of which still made him cringe. The man who'd tried to rob him outside his father's house. At least Tom hoped he'd been trying to rob him. Though why a barefoot kid in a robe would have anything worth taking, Tom couldn't understand. All he remembered was feeling suddenly very angry. He remembered shifting, and the dragon. And coming to with a spot of blood in front of him, and no one near him.

And there had been other . . . simpler interactions. But there had been practically no social interaction. Every time he'd talked to another human, or another human had talked to him, one of them had pretty clearly and immediately wanted something of the other.

Now, he couldn't see any signs that Keith wanted something of him. At any rate, there was nothing Tom had—what few possessions he'd owned had been destroyed at the apartment—his changes of clothes, his secondhand furniture, his . . . he realized with a start that his thrift-store black leather jacket would be lost as well, and felt more grief over that than he'd felt over anything else. That jacket had been with him from almost the time he got kicked out of the house. He'd bought it almost new, with the proceeds of his first day as a laborer.

In many ways, that jacket defined him. It had a high enough collar for him to raise and hide his often-too-vulnerable face at moments when he wanted just his tough exterior to show. He'd learned early that looking tough and perhaps just a little crazy saved him from having to do real violence. Which, when anger could literally turn you into a beast, was half the battle.

Tom had lost his home and left without even the clothes on his body. For the second time in his life. And the thought that Keith might want Tom's body made Tom start to laugh—rapidly changed into a cough when Keith looked at him, puzzled. He knew Keith. That was not in the realm of the possible.

Keith, for his part, just seemed to want to reassure himself Tom was okay. Having done that, he now sipped the coffee very slowly. "I guess your girlfriend is out?" he asked.

"Kyrie had an appointment," Tom said.

"She's cute," Keith said. "How long have you guys been together?"

Ah. "Well, we work together," Tom said, edging. "And one thing led to the other."

Keith nodded.

"You? Did the girl see any other dragons last night?"

Keith frowned. "Now that you mention it, yeah. She said she saw four dragons later on. One jumped down to the parking lot, and then three others flew away a while later." He shook his head. "I don't know. Maybe she has a dragon obsession. She's fun and all, but it might be more weirdness than I want to handle." He scratched his head and adjusted his hat. "I have weirdness enough at college."

Tom nodded, not sure what to say. And Keith launched in a detailed description of his college trouble, which involved pigheaded administrators and some complex requirements for graduation that Tom—who'd never been to college—only vaguely understood.

And then in the middle of it—he'd never quite understand it or be able to explain it—there were wings.

Only it wasn't quite like that. There was a powder. A green powder, like a shimmer in the air. Tom had sneezed and was about to say something about it, but it didn't seem to matter. It was as if he were floating a long way above his own body.

And Keith jumped up, dropping the cup that he'd been holding. Tom jumped for it, in the process dropping his own cup. Both cups shattered with a noise that seemed out of proportion to the event, and seemed to go on forever in Tom's mind.

And then he turned, but he seemed to turn in slow motion. For one, his body didn't understand that his legs actually belonged to him. And his legs felt like they were made of loose string, unable to support his weight. He tripped over his feet, and as he plunged toward the floor there were . . . wings over him. Green wings. Dragons. Green. Wings. Had to be dragons.

Suddenly the windows weren't there. Ripped? The screens were ripped from the frames. Glass lay at his feet. And the tip of a green paw came into the room, only it didn't look like a paw, more like a single toe with a claw at the end.

Tom grabbed for the low coffee table in front of the love seat. It was wicker and very unstable, but he struck out with it, hard, at the thing. There was a . . . tooth? fang? coming toward him, and he batted at it with the table. It made a hissing sound, not at all like a dragon sound. And it was dripping. At least Tom didn't think it was a dragon sound. He had no idea what he sounded like when he was shape-shifted.

Keith was kicking something large and green and shimmering.

"Stop," Tom yelled. "You can't kick a dragon. It will blaze you."

Keith looked at him, and Keith's eyes were huge, the pupils so dilated there was almost no iris left. It reminded Tom of something but he couldn't say what.

"Mother ship," Keith said. "The mother ship has landed. They're coming for us. I saw a movie."

"Really," Tom said, reaching out. "You shouldn't kick dragons."

Tom had managed to wrench the wooden leg away from the wicker table, and he had some idea he could stab the dragon with it. But one of the dragons was attacking Keith, while the other was . . . crouching against the glass door. If Tom could attack that one . . .

He started to go for the handle to the patio door, but all of a sudden it wavered and changed, in front of him, and it was the door to the Athens, with all the specials painted on. He pulled at it, but it wouldn't open. So he backed up, and kicked high at it.

The glass shattered with a sound like hail.

The big green body leaning against it shuddered and turned. Toward Tom.

Two toes-with-claws reached for him. A fang probed.

He had time to think, *Oh, shit*. And then he remembered what Keith's eyes looked like. They looked like his own, in the mirror, back when he was using.

The morgue of Goldport was in a low-slung, utilitarian-looking brick building. Someone with misconceived ideas of making it look like Southwestern architecture had put two obviously nonfunctional towers in asymmetrical positions atop the tile roof.

Rafiel Trall parked in front of the building, and Kyrie parked beside him. There were a couple of other cars and a couple of white panel vans parked in front. The street was the sort of little-traveled downtown street connecting quiet residential streets to the industrial areas with their warehouses and factories.

Rafiel put sunglasses on as he came out of the car, and Kyrie wondered for a moment if his golden eyes were unusually sensitive to light. It didn't seem like the most practical eye color to have.

He saw her staring and smiled at her, as if he thought she was admiring him. Kyrie looked away quickly. The man clearly had an ego as large as his shifted shape.

But he was quiet as they walked inside the building. Though it was air-conditioned, it didn't have the same feeling of clean cool as the inside of the hotel. Instead, the cold here felt clammy and clinging and there was a barely discernible smell. If Kyrie had been pressed to define it, she would have said that it smelled like her car a day after she'd lost a package of ground turkey in it, last May. It was the stink of spoiled meat, mixed with a faint tinge of urine and feces—what she'd once heard someone call the odor of mortality—but so faint that she couldn't quite be sure it was there.

"Have you ever been to this type of place?" Rafiel asked.

She shook her head.

"Sensitive stomach?" he asked.

She shrugged. She truly didn't know. She remembered the corpse last night and felt a recoiling—not because she'd been on the edge of losing her lunch over it, but because she remembered all too clearly how appetizing the blood had smelled. Appetizing was far worse than sickening. "I don't think so," she said.

And at that he gave her his bright smile, which seemed to beam rays of warmth through the chilly atmosphere. "Well, anyone of our kind has seen dead bodies, right?"

Kyrie blinked, bereft of an ability to answer. Had she seen dead bodies? Only the one yesterday. What was he telling her? She looked at the bright smile, the calm golden eyes peeking above the sunglasses, and wondered what hid behind it. Oh, she'd guessed—it wasn't that hard given his history—that Tom might have done things he was sorry for. There was that edging and shying away behind his silences. And a man like him who didn't seem totally devoid of interior life and yet ended up on drugs was clearly running away from something.

But until this moment, Kyrie had allowed herself to believe the something had been a few petty thefts, car joyriding, other things that could well fall under juvenile delinquency. Never . . . never murder. She'd never thought of murder, until Rafiel thought that. And now she wondered if the other shifters really had that much trouble controlling themselves in animal form that killing humans was common and accepted. And if it was, what was she doing here? What was the point of murderers investigating murders? If it was normal for shifters to kill humans, how much should the life of a human be worth it to them? How could Rafiel be a policeman? And how could Rafiel talk of it so calmly?

But she couldn't ask him. He'd continued ahead of her, down the cool tiled hallway, and she had followed him, without thinking, by instinct, like a child or a dog. And now he stood near a man who sat at a desk, and said, "Hi Joe. I'm here to see last night's pickup." He removed his sunglasses and pocketed them.

Joe, a middle-aged man, with a greying comb-over and a desk-job paunch, looked pointedly at Kyrie.

Rafiel smiled, that dazzling smile that seemed to hide no shadows and no fears. "Girlfriend," he said. "Kyrie is thinking of joining the force and I told her she should see an autopsy first. Kyrie Smith, this is Joe Martin. You know I've talked to you about him. He practically keeps this place running."

Kyrie, head spinning at being called someone's girlfriend, put her hand forward, to have it squeezed in a massive, square-tipped paw. Joe gave her what he probably thought was a friendly smile, but which was at least three quarters leer, and told her in a tone he surely believed was avuncular, "You take good care of our boy, Ms. Smith. He's been lonely too long. Not that some ladies haven't tried."

And on that auspicious blessing, they walked past Joe and down the hallway, past a row of grey doors with little glass windows.

They all looked similar to Kyrie, and she had no idea what prompted Rafiel to stop in front one of them. But he stopped, and plunged a hand into his pants pocket, handing her a small notebook. She took it without comment, though considering the tightness of Rafiel's pants, she had to wonder what quantum principle allowed him to keep notebooks in there. When he handed her a pen too, from the same provenance, she was even more impressed, because sharp objects there had to hurt.

"Just take notes," Rafiel told her. "And no one in there will ask who you are. They'll assume you're a new officer I'm training. Goldport has one of the smallest full-time forces in the state. To compensate, we have a never-ending stream of part timers, usually either people blowing through town for a few months, or people who took a couple of months of law-enforcement courses and decided it wasn't for them. If they ask, then I'll tell them you work at the diner and I want your opinion, okay?"

Kyrie nodded, feeling marginally better about being an apprentice policeman than about pretending to be Rafiel's girlfriend. A sense of unease about Rafiel built in her mind, even as she nodded and held the notebook and pencil as if she were official. Might as well make some notes, too. Hell. Who knew? She might need them. She was, after all, investigating this herself, wasn't she?

Rafiel opened the door and the smell of spoiled meat leaked out, overwhelmed—fortunately overwhelmed—by the smell of chemicals. She thought she detected rubbing alcohol and formaldehyde among them.

Inside was a small room, with tiled walls and floor, all leading down to a drain in the center of the floor, above which a metallic table was placed and into which something was gurgling. Kyrie knew very well what the something would be, but she refused to look, refused to investigate.

In the full light of day, without the pressure of the moon on her body and mind, it was unlikely that the smell of blood would be appetizing. But she refused to give it a chance, all the same.

The tiled room should have looked cold and sterile and it probably would have, had it been tiled in standard white. However, the walls looked like someone had either gone crazy with artistry or—more likely considering what Kyrie had seen of how the public departments of Goldport, from town hall to schools, operated—they'd received remnant tiles from various public projects.

Be that as it may, bright blue, fierce red, sunny yellow, and the curious terra cotta orange of southwest buildings covered walls and floor.

It all went to make the man who stood in the middle of the room look greyer and more colorless. He would be, Kyrie judged, somewhat past middle age. Colorlessness came not only from his white hair but from a skin that looked like he was never allowed out in the sunlight. He had an aquiline nose that looked broken but probably had just grown like that, and—on either side of it—brightly sparkling blue eyes, rife with amusement.

"Hello there, Rafiel," he said, and grinned. He wore a lab coat, and the sleeves—and his hands, in latex gloves— were stained as colorfully as the tiles that surrounded him. "We were just about to start, but Bob—" He nodded toward the other man in the room, who was somewhat past middle age, with a bald head surrounded in a fringe of grey hair. He wore a bright Hawaiian-style shirt, incongruously patterned with what seemed to be palm trees and camels on a virulently green background. "—Bob said it was proper if you were here, as there should be more than one of you watching."

"I'm sorry," Rafiel said. There was some change that Kyrie couldn't quite define to his tone. "We were having breakfast."

The man in the lab coat—a doctor?—grinned. "Breakfast, before this? Oh, no. You know so much better than that."

"To be honest, Mike," Bob said, "he hasn't tossed his cookies in about a year. Not since that vagrant found at the warehouse that had been there for over three months, last summer, remember?"

Rafiel said nothing, only shook his head and a light red tinge appeared on his cheeks. And Kyrie realized all of a sudden what his tone had been. The sound in his voice had been the sound of a little boy responding to his betters, of a young man convincing the elders of his worthiness.

"This is Kyrie Smith," Rafiel said, gruffly. "She'll be taking notes."

The two older men looked at her as if noticing her presence for the first time. The medical examiner smiled and Bob raised his eyebrows, his eyes twinkling with amusement. She rather suspected that, notebook or not, she'd just been relegated to the girlfriend realm again.

She ducked her head, while the examiner turned to a point in the wall, where a little light flashing and a glint of something seemed to indicate the presence of a camera, and said, "We have washed and set the body, ready for examination." He gestured toward the body on the table.

It looked much better than the night before. Or perhaps much worse. It was all a matter of perspective. The night before, it had looked like a piece of meat wrapped in blood-soaked rags. Now, laid out on the table, it looked definitely human.

"The victim," the medical examiner continued, in that officious voice that people get when talking into recording instruments, "is a Caucasian male, blue-eyed, five foot nine, two hundred and thirty pounds, probably between thirty and forty years old. As far as we can determine, he died of multiple stab wounds, by an instrument to be determined." He gestured toward a large ziploc bag at the corner of the room, against the multicolored wall. It was filled with something that looked black and ragged. "I removed the victim's clothes—T-shirt and slacks—in the presence of Officer McDonald, and bagged them. They will be handed to the custody of Officer McDonald and Officer Trall for further analysis. As reported to me by Officer McDonald, the corpse was not found to have any identification and the police department is waiting for a missing-persons report that might give some clue as to his identity."

"Instrument to be determined, Mike?" Rafiel asked, leaning forward to take a closer look at the very pale corpse crisscrossed by dark gashes.

The medical examiner looked up. "They don't look like knife stab wounds."

"What about . . . I mean, yesterday we thought it might be another of those animal attacks?"

"What animal . . . ? Oh, the victims cut in half?" Mike said. "Not that I can tell. I mean, yeah, the other ones have some marks consistent with perhaps animal teeth, though I would hate to see the animal with teeth that size. But this one . . ." He frowned. "More like he was stabbed multiple times by a weird implement. A nubby sword with a serrated edge, perhaps?"

Rafiel blinked. He looked toward Kyrie and frowned.

Kyrie felt relieved. Well, at least a little relieved. She took a deep breath. A nubby sword with a serrated edge didn't seem like anything that Tom could have been carrying on him. She had seen his teeth—glimmering in the moonlight—and they looked as polished and smooth as the best gourmet knives. So they couldn't be confused with these stabbing implements. And Tom hadn't had anything on him. She remembered him in the bathroom.

Her sense of relief surprised her. Did she care that much if Tom was guilty or not? But then she thought that considering she might be called on to administer justice, and considering she had already hidden him from the law, in a way, yes, she did care.

She made a quick note on the nature of the implements, and looked up to see that the doctor and Rafiel were removing something, with tweezers—from the man's grey hair.

"Looks like the same green powder found on the clothes and the body when we first examined it," Mike said. "We're sending it for analysis."

Rafiel was frowning at a little baggie into which he'd collected what looked like a sprinkle of bright green powder. "Looks like pollen," he said. "Anything flowering about now that's this bright green?" He looked at Bob.

"Not that I know," Bob said. "Label it. We'll hand it over to the lab. Who knows? They might actually figure it out."

He shrugged and Kyrie didn't know if he was being ironic. She also didn't have time to think about it, because Mike had sliced a Y shape on the man's chest and opened the body cavity.

The smell of death and corruption became all encompassing, and the sight of the organs . . . Kyrie swallowed. Even as she swallowed and struggled with nausea, she felt relieved that it wasn't hunger and that she wasn't finding this in any way appetizing. Perhaps panthers only ate fresh meat.

"Are you okay?" Rafiel asked.

She wasn't okay. The smell seemed to be short-circuiting her brain and making her blood rush loudly in her ears. But she nodded and got hold of the considerable willpower she resorted to when she had to prevent herself from shifting. She nodded again. "I'm fine," she said, though her voice echoed tiny and distant.

"Look at that," the doctor said. "That's the stab that killed him. Right through the heart." He pointed at an organ that looked exactly like the others, to Kyrie, all of them an amalgam of red and green, yellow and the sort of greys that really shouldn't exist in nature. "There are several others that reached vital organs, but I'd say that's the one that stopped it. Pretty much ripped the heart to shreds, in fact."

Rafiel and Bob had moved closer, and were looking into the opened body.

"What are those white things?" Rafiel asked.

"Damned if I know," Mike said. "They look like some sort of adipose deposits."

"They look like huge ant eggs to me," Bob said. "You know, the kind you find when you break an anthill open in your garden? Just much bigger."

"They seem to be at all the stab wound sites," Rafiel said.

Kyrie wrote "white things" and "ant eggs" and "wound sites."

"So, some contamination on the blade," Rafiel said. "Can you put some—"

Then as the doctor handed him a bag and said, "You'd best keep it in a cooler, though, since it's not been exposed to the air."

Bob produced a normal picnic cooler from somewhere. It was full of ice. He got the baggy and a couple other baggies of what the doctor thought might be contaminants in the wound, and put them in the cooler.

The autopsy progressed along lines that Kyrie had read about, but never been forced to watch before, and she had to call on all her self-control to continue watching, particularly when they sawed the cranium open to remove the brain. But there didn't seem to be any other surprises.

"I think," the doctor said, "there might be some drug in the blood, so I'd like to get that looked at also."

"Drug?"

"Some hallucinogenic. His pupils were like pie plates when they got him in. I'd say he was high as a kite."

She tried to imagine this man high. He didn't seem the type. Well fed, middling dressed, middle-aged. Oh, Kyrie and everyone in her generation had heard all the platitudes about drug use affecting every class and every type of person. And, as such, they might even be true. But there were two classes it primarily affected—depending on the drug—the very rich and the very poor. And within those, whatever drug was the current drug of choice tended to make people sickly or at least skinny.

This man looked robust and neither too rich nor too poor. And yet, looking at him, something gnawed at the back of Kyrie's mind. She couldn't quite say what.

She took her leave, with Rafiel, and hurried out of the place. Outside, standing in the sun, holding a cooler with whatever samples they got off the body, Rafiel blinked.

His enormous confidence seemed to have vanished and he looked confused and perhaps a little scared.

He looked over his shoulder, but Bob had stayed behind, talking to the examiner. "We have to find who did this, Kyrie. The sooner the better."

"Why?" Kyrie said. There were many things she wanted to ask Rafiel, like why he assumed that one of their kind was bound to have seen corpses before, and why, if that was the case, they should discipline this killer. And why he'd assumed that this too was a death by dragon—other than having seen Tom standing over the body. But she couldn't ask any of those, and anyway, the most important was this—why they particularly and not the police in general should find out what happened to this victim.

Rafiel blinked again. The gesture made him look slow of thought, though it was probably just a reaction to the strong sunshine. "What do you mean why?" he asked.

"Why should we care who did this, if it wasn't a shifter?" Kyrie asked.

Rafiel frowned. "No, but the victim was a shifter. Didn't you smell it?"

Rafiel insisted on following her home. There was nothing for it. "Can't you see?" he said. "I have to. If something is killing shifters . . ."

"How would they even know I'm a shifter?" she asked. "Wouldn't it take knowing the smell? And knowing what we are?"

Rafiel shrugged. "I can't answer that. Perhaps something like your triad friends. Didn't Ormson say that the triad had been shifters for centuries? That it ran in families? That they know what it means and even have a shifter god?"

She looked at him. A monstrous idea was forming. If someone was killing shifters, and if it was another shifter, wouldn't it make sense for it to be someone who . . . oh, worked for the police? Who could keep an eye on people without anyone getting suspicious? He could smell someone—once—and then realize . . .

She shook her head. "Why were you at the diner?" she asked. "Last night?"

Golden eyes widened. "I was coming for a cup of coffee," he said. "I was off work."

"You were coming for a cup of coffee in lion shape?"

He chuckled at that. Audibly chuckled. "No. Of course not. I only shifted when I smelled . . . I was in human form when I first saw you. When I saw you pull Ormson inside. Of course, I knew you were shifters."

"How?"

He looked at her as if she'd taken leave of her senses. "He was a dragon," he said.

"But then why did you shift?" Kyrie asked. "Why wouldn't you just call the crime in?"

"And catch you still shape-shifted?" he said. "I had to make sure you were out of there before I called it in."

"But why shift, then?"

He sighed. Something like a shadow crossed the serene golden eyes and he mumbled something.

"Beg your pardon?" Kyrie said.

"The smell of blood, all right? Combined with the moonlight it caused me to shift and it took effort to get back to my form. Because then . . ." He turned very red. ". . . then I smelled you."

Kyrie thought of the smell of him, rising in the night with all the blatant come-on of a feline-seeking-female ad.

She nodded once. She could believe that. But she still had a question, "Why come to the Athens for coffee? Pardon me, but I know even late at night there are better places open, and dressing as you do, surely you can afford better."

He shrugged. "I don't know, okay? Started going there about a year ago. I like . . . It's homey, okay? Feels homey. And there's you. You're . . . I could smell you were a shifter. And I like looking at you."

Kyrie frowned. "Fine," she said. But she wasn't convinced. For one, she couldn't remember having seen Rafiel at the diner, ever. Of course, considering how busy it got there at times, like the five a.m. rush just before she went off shift, he could have been dancing naked on a table and she would not have noticed.

She looked at him, and, involuntarily, pictured that. No. If he were dancing naked on the table, she would have noticed.

"Fine," she said again. "You can follow me home."

At the back of her mind, she thought that if all else failed, Tom would be there. And Tom could always help defend her against Rafiel. Okay, Tom might not be exactly a superhero. But it would be two against one.

Tom had just kicked the door, and felt something—something giant and pincerlike reach for him when . . .

"What in hell?" came from the direction of the living room in a very male voice. A vaguely familiar male voice. And then there were strides—sounding echoey and

strange through his distorting senses, advancing along,
toward him.

Past the kitchen. He felt more than saw as two pairs of
green wings took flight, from the backyard, into the dark
night sky above.

And he turned in the direction of the steps to see Kyrie
look at him, her mouth open in shock, her eyes wide, her
face suddenly drained of color.

Keith was still doing fake kung-fu moves in the
direction of the utterly broken windows. But Kyrie stood
in the middle of the room, gulping air.

Behind her, stood the policeman lion, golden eyes and
immaculate linen clothes, all in a vague tawny color. And
he looked . . . disgusted.

Tom summoned all his thought, all his ability to speak,
and came out with the best excuse he could craft. "It
wasn't me," he said. "It was the dragons."

Kyrie stood in the middle of her demolished sunroom.
The windows were all broken. As was the sliding door.
And there was Tom—and he looked very odd. Tottery and
. . . just strange. And there was another guy—his neighbor,
she thought, from the apartment.

"I'm sorry," Tom said, again. "It was the dragons." He
pointed at the backyard. "They were attacking."

His voice sounded odd. Normally it was raspy, but now
it sounded like it was coming out through one of those
distorters that kids used to do alien voices. And there had
to be something wrong with him. He was walking
barefoot on shards of glass. It had to hurt. In fact, she

could see little pinpricks of blood on the indifferent beige carpet. But he didn't seem to be in pain.

"Tom, are you all right?" she asked. But by then she was close enough to look in his eyes. His pupils were huge, crowding the blue iris almost completely out of his eyes.

Kyrie took a deep breath. Damn, damn, damn, damn. She knew better, didn't she? Once a junkie always a junkie. And Tom was . . . Hell, she knew what he was. Shifter or not, someone with his upbringing wouldn't have fallen as low as he had without some major work on his part. He had to be totally out of control. He had to be.

But she'd almost believed. She'd almost trusted. She remembered how she'd felt bad about telling Rafiel on him. She remembered how she felt so relieved it wasn't a dragon's teeth on that man's body.

Hell, she still felt happy the man hadn't died by dragon. That meant she didn't have to keep Tom close until she figured out what to do about it. She just didn't have to. She was through with him.

"You're high," she said, and it sounded odd, because she hadn't meant to say it, hadn't meant to call attention to the fact, just in case Rafiel hadn't noticed it. But it didn't matter, did it? If Tom was this out of control, he was going to be arrested, sooner or later.

Tom shook his head, his dark eyebrows knit over his eyes in complete surprise. "Me?" he said. "No. Keith is high. He was talking about the mother ship. I mean, clear as day it was just two dragons."

Kyrie didn't know whether to laugh and cry. All these years she had kept away from dangerous men. She'd laughed at the sort of woman who let herself get head over heels with some bundle of muscles and no brain. And now she'd gotten involved with . . . this. Okay, so not involved, although if she told herself the truth, she had been interested in Tom. Or at least appreciative of his buff and sculpted body. She hadn't done anything even remotely sexual or physical with him, though.

Not that it mattered. She'd let him into her house. She'd let him stay here alone . . . And he'd got his buddy over, hadn't he? And they'd . . . what? Shot up? There didn't seem to be any smell of pot in the air, and besides she doubted that pot would cause this kind of trip. Of course, she knew drugs could also be swallowed or . . . And that wasn't the point. He'd gotten high and destroyed her property.

She looked around at the devastation in her sunroom, and wondered how she was going to pay for this mess. The landlord would demand payment. But she had no more than a couple of hundred in the bank, and that had to last for food and all till the end of the month. And she needed rent.

She took another deep breath. She was going to have to ask Frank for more hours. And even then, she might not make it.

Tom was looking at her, as though trying to interpret her expression, as if it were very hard to read—something he couldn't understand. "Uh," he said. "I'll leave now?"

Part of Kyrie wanted to tell him no. After all, well, he was still barefoot. And bleeding. And he was high. She should tell him to stay. She should . . .

But no, she definitely should not. She'd kept him overnight, so he would be better off leaving in the morning. And now, what? He'd just caused more damage.

"Yes," she said. She heard her voice so cold it could have formed icicles on contact. "Yeah. I think it would be best if you left and took your friend."

Tom nodded, and tugged on the shoulder of the other guy's sweater, even as he started inching past Kyrie, in an oddly skittish movement. It reminded her of a cat, in a house where she'd stayed for a few months. A very skittish cat, who ran away if you so much as looked at her.

As far as Kyrie could tell, no one had ever hurt the cat. But she skidded past people, as though afraid of being kicked.

Now Tom edged past her the same way, while dragging his friend, who looked at Kyrie, blank and confused, and said, "It was aliens, you know. Just like . . . you know. Aliens."

She heard them cross the house, toward the front door. She didn't remember the guy's car on the driveway, but it wasn't her problem if they were on foot. In fact, it might be safer in the state they were. And she didn't care, she told herself, as she listened for the front door to close.

"Kyrie," Rafiel said. He stood by the windows, frowning, puzzled. "Something was here."

✧   ✧   ✧

They'd been walking for a while, aimlessly, down the street, when Tom because aware of three things—first, that he was walking around in a neighborhood he didn't know; second, that he was barefoot; third, that his feet hurt like living hell.

He sat down on the nearest lawn, and looked at his feet, which were cut, all over, by a bunch of glass.

This realization seemed to have hit Keith at the same time, which was weird. As Tom was looking in dismay at the blood covering the soles of his feet, Keith said, "Shit. You're bleeding."

Tom looked up. He remembered seeing Keith's eyes, the pupils dilated and odd. But Keith looked perfectly normal now, even if a little puzzled. "What happened?" he said. And frowned, as if remembering something that didn't make any sense whatsoever. "What happened to us back there? What . . . ?"

Tom shook his head. He knew what Keith's eyes looked like. And Tom had some idea what mind-altering substances could do to your mind and your senses. Hell, for a while there he was shooting everything that came his way. Heroin by choice, but he'd have done drain opener if he had any reason to suspect that it would prevent him from shifting into a dragon. He suspected, in fact, that he had shot up baking soda in solution more than a few times. And who knew what else? It was miraculous enough he'd survived all those years. But nothing, nothing equaled the trip he'd just gone through back there.

He put his face in his hands, and heard himself groan. He'd messed it up for good and all. Not that there had ever been any hope that Kyrie would see him as anything other than a mess. Not considering what he'd done the night before. The . . . corpse. And then his being so totally helpless. There was no way he had a chance with Kyrie. Not any way. But . . .

But now she thought him a drug addict. And the policeman had been with her.

"I'm going to get my car," Keith said. "Do you have any idea which way we came?"

"You have a car?"

"Yeah," Keith said. "I parked just a couple of blocks from . . . your girl's . . ." It seemed to hit him, belatedly, that perhaps Kyrie was no longer Tom's girl. Not after what they'd done to her sunroom. "Do you have any idea which way we came?"

There was something to being a dragon. Perhaps seeing the city from above so many times, Tom had memorized it like one memorizes a map, or a favorite picture. Or perhaps being a dragon came with a sense of direction. Who knew?

But by concentrating, he could just figure out which way Kyrie's house was. He wondered if the policeman would arrest them for even coming near.

Standing up, unsteadily, he said, "Come on." He winced at the pain in his feet. "Come on. It's this way, up the road here two blocks, then up ten blocks, and then to the left another five, and you should see her house."

Keith took a step back. "Whoa, dude," he said. "You've gone all pale, just standing up. Sit down. I'll go get the car. You're sure of the way?"

Tom nodded. He wanted to say he would go with Keith, but he could tell he would only slow Keith down. He sat down on the grass, again, with some relief. "Sure," he said. "Sure. You should see it. If not . . . come back."

He put his face in his hands, again, sitting there. He didn't know how long he and Keith had been fighting the . . . dragons? He was sure they were dragons, but there was a feeling of strangeness, his memory kept giving him images of a big, horned toe. No. A tooth. No . . .

He sighed. He was never going to remember. And he had no idea what had got him so high. And Keith too. For all his attitude with the girls, the one thing Tom had never suspected Keith of doing was getting involved in drugs. In fact, he would bet his neighbor had never got high before.

So . . . How had they got high?

The sugar. It had to be the sugar. He'd drunk nothing but the coffee. No one, absolutely no one would put drugs in eggs or bacon. So, it had to be the sugar. He'd put three spoons in the coffee. Kyrie. Kyrie kept drugs in the house.

He blinked in amazement. Okay, so he'd stolen the— he'd stolen *it*—he forced his mind away from what *it* was—so he could give up drugs. There had been one too many times of waking up choking on his own vomit, struggling for every breath and not sure he was going to make it to the morning. There had also been the ever-present fear of being arrested, of shifting in a jail cell. Of eating a bunch of people.

So, he'd stolen *it* and tried to use it to control his shifts, so that he would stop waking up in the middle of the day dreaming he had eaten someone the night before and not being sure if it was true or not. The drugs weren't working so well for that, anyway. Or to make him stop hurting.

But, even with the . . . object in his possession he hadn't been able to give up on drugs, not entirely, until he'd started working at the diner, and he'd been . . . He'd seen Kyrie, and he'd seen the way she looked at him. And . . . he chuckled to himself. He'd tried to change. He'd really tried to change his ways to impress her. And all the time, all this time, she was doing drugs, too. Perhaps all shifters did them, to control the shift? Or perhaps she disapproved of him for other reasons. But, clearly, a straight arrow she was not.

"Are you okay?" Keith asked. He'd stopped the car—a beat-up golden Toyota of late Eighties vintage—in front of Tom and rolled down the window.

Tom realized he was laughing so hard that there were tears pouring down his face. He controlled with an effort. "Oh, I'm fine. I am perfectly fine."

He had, in fact, been an idiot. But not anymore.

When the office was empty like this, late at night, and Edward Ormson was the only one still at his desk, sometimes he wondered what it would be like to have someone to go home to.

He hadn't remarried because . . . Well, because his marriage had blown up so explosively, and Sylvia had taken herself such a long way away, that he thought there was no point trying again.

No. He was wrong. He was lying to himself again. What had made him give up on family and home wasn't Sylvia. It was Tom.

He looked up from the laptop open on his broad mahogany desk, and past the glass door of his private office at the rest of the office—where normally his secretaries and his clerks worked. This late, it was all gloom, with here and there a faint light where someone's computer had turned on to run the automated processes, or where someone had forgotten a desk lamp on.

He probably should make a complaint about the waste of energy, but the truth was he liked those small lapses. It made the office feel more homey—and the office was practically the only home Ormson had.

The wind whistled behind him, around the corner of the office, where giant panel of window glass met giant panel of window glass. The wind always whistled out here. When you're on the thirtieth floor of an office building there's always a certain amount of wind.

Only it seemed to Ormson that there was an echo of wings unfolding in the wind. He shivered and glowered at the screen, at the message one of his clerks had sent him, with research details for one of his upcoming trials. Even with the screen turned on, he could still see a reflection of himself in it—salt-and-pepper hair that had once been dark, and blue eyes, shaped exactly like Tom's.

He wondered if Tom was still alive and where he was. Damn it. It shouldn't be this difficult. None of this should be so difficult. He'd made partner, he'd gotten married, he'd had a son. By now, Tom was supposed to be in Yale, or if he absolutely had to rebel, in Harvard, working on his law degree. Tom was supposed to be his son. Not the constant annoyance of a thorn in the side, a burr under the saddle.

But Tom had been trouble from the first step he'd taken—when he'd held onto the side table and toppled Sylvia's favorite Ming vase. And it hadn't got any better when it had progressed to petty car theft, to pot smoking, to the school complaining he was sexually harassing girls. It just kept getting harder and harder and harder.

He thought he heard a tinkle of glass far off and stopped breathing, listening. But no sound followed and, through the glass door, he saw no movement in the darkened office. There was nothing. He was imagining things, because he had thought of Tom.

Hell, even Sylvia hadn't wanted Tom. She'd started having an affair with another doctor at the hospital and taken off with her boyfriend to Florida and married him, and set about having a family, and she'd never, ever again even bothered to send Tom a birthday card. Not after that first year. And then Tom . . .

This time the noise was more definite, closer by.

Edward rose from his desk, his fingertips touching the desktop, as if for support. He told himself there were no such things as dragons. He told himself people didn't shift into dragons and back again.

Every time he told himself that. Every time. And it didn't make any difference. There were still . . . Tom had still . . .

No sound from the office, and he drew in a deep breath and started to sit down. He'd turn off the computer, pack up and go . . . well, not home. His condo wasn't a home. But he'd go back to the condo, and have a drink and call one of the suitably long list of arm candy who'd been vying to be Mrs. Ormson for the last few months, and see if she wanted to go to dinner somewhere nice. If he was lucky, he wouldn't have to sleep alone.

"Ormsssson."

His office door had opened, noiselessly, and through it whistled the sort of breeze that hit the thirtieth floor when one of the windows had been broken. It was more of a wind. He could hear paper rustling, tumbling about, a roaring of wind, and a tinkle as someone's lamp or monitor fell over.

And the head pushing through the door was huge, reptilian, armed with many teeth that glimmered even in the scant light. Edward had seen it only once. He'd seen . . . other dragons. Tom not the least of them. But he hadn't seen this dragon. Not more than once. That had been when Edward had been hired to defend a triad member accused—and guilty—of a particularly gruesome and pointless murder.

This creature had appeared, shortly after Edward had gotten his client paroled, and while Edward was trying to convince him to go away for a while and not to pursue a bloody course of revenge that would have torn the triad apart—and, incidentally, got him dead or back in jail.

This dragon—they called it the great something dragon?—had flapped down from the sky and— Edward remembered his client's body falling from a great height, the two pieces of it tumbling down to the asphalt. And the blood. The blood.

He swallowed bile, hastily, and stood fully again. Stood. Ready to run. Which was foolish, because the thing blocked his office door, and its huge, many-fanged head rested on its massive paws. There was nowhere Edward could run.

The dragon blinked huge, gold eyes at him, and, as with a cat's secretly satisfied expression, it gave the impression of smiling. A long forked tongue licked at the lipless mouth. "Ormson," it said, still somehow managing to give the impression that the word was composed mostly of sibilants.

"Yes?" Edward asked, and found his voice wavering and uncertain. "How may I help you?"

"Your whelp has stolen something of mine," the dragon said. Its voice was only part noise. The other part was a feeling, like a scratch at the back of the brain. It made you want to flip up your cranium and scratch.

"My . . .?"

"Your son. Thomas. He's stolen the Pearl of Heaven."

Edward's mouth was dry. He opened it to say this was entirely Tom's business, but he found himself caught in an odd crux. If Tom had stolen something, then Tom was still alive. Still alive five years after being kicked out of the house. Had he learned something? Had he shaped up? He almost had to, hadn't he, or he would be dead by now? No one could continue going the way Tom had been going and still be alive after five years on their own, could they?

He swallowed hard. But Tom had stolen something. This seemed to imply he'd learned nothing. He'd not changed.

He clenched his hands so tightly that his nails bit into his palm. How could Tom still be a problem? How could he? Didn't he know how hard he made it on his father? Didn't he care?

"I don't know what my son has done," he said, and his voice came out creditably firm. "I haven't seen him in more than five years. You cannot hold me responsible for what he has done."

"He has stolen the Pearl of Heaven," the dragon rumbled, its eyes half closed and still giving that look of a secret smile.

"So, he's stolen some jewelry," Edward said. Internally, he felt his heart sink. The Pearl of Heaven was to the dragons as the holy grail to the knights of old. Only they's never lost it. Why did Tom need to muck with something like that? "Get it from him. I don't care."

Did he care? What if they killed Tom? Edward didn't know. He didn't even know if it would grieve him anymore. It wasn't supposed to be this hard. He'd been saying that since Tom was one. And it hadn't got any easier.

"It's not that easy," the dragon said. "The Pearl is . . . dragon magic. Ancient. It was given to us by the Emperor of Heaven. It will not do him any good, but it is the center of our strength. We need it, or we shall fall apart."

Great. Tom would manage to steal some cultic object. Hell, if he found an idol with an eye made of ruby, he'd dig the ruby out just to see what would happen. And Edward remembered all too well the incident in the Met Museum with Tom and the mummy when Tom was five. Other kids just never thought of this kind of trouble to get into.

"So get it. From him. I know nothing of it."

"Ah," the dragon said. And the sound, somehow, managed to convey an impression of disapproval, an impression of denial. "But the child is always the responsibility of the parents, isn't he? Your son has hidden the Pearl of Heaven. It is up to you to find it and give it back to us."

The *or else* remained unspoken, hanging mid-air, more solid, more certain than anything the dragon had said.

"I don't even know where he is," Edward said.

"Goldport, Colorado."

"Fine," Edward said, nodding and trying to look businesslike. He scooped up his laptop, picked up his case from the floor, started pushing the laptop into it. "Fine, fine. I'll call tomorrow. I'll make enquiries. I'll try to figure out where he—"

A many-clawed paw lifted. With unreal, careful precision, it rested atop the briefcase and the laptop and just touched the edge of Edward Ormson's hand. The claw shimmered, like real gold, and ended in an impossibly sharp talon.

"Not tomorrow," the dragon said. "Now."

"Now?" Edward blinked, in confusion, looking down at the talon on his hand, the tip of it pressing just enough to leave a mark, but leaving no doubt that it could press hard enough to skewer the hand through sinew and bone. "But it's what? Nine at night? You can't really book flights at this time of night. Well, not anymore. You can't just show up at the airport and book a flight on a whim. With the security measures that simply doesn't happen anymore."

"No airport," the dragon said, its paw immobile, the pressure of its talon palpable.

"Driving?" Edward asked, and would have sat down, if he weren't so afraid that some stirring, some careless gesture would make the creature stab his hand with that talon. He didn't know what would happen if he did that. He didn't know how Tom had become a dragon, but if the legends were right, then it was through a bite. Or a clawing. "Driving would take much longer. Why don't I book a flight tomorrow? I'll fly out before twenty-four hours. I promise."

"No driving. I'll take you. Now."

"You'll take me?"

The claw withdrew. "Pack your things. Whatever you need to take. I'll take you. Now."

There really wasn't much choice. Less than ten minutes later, Edward was straddling the huge beast's back, holding on tight, while they stood facing the place where the dragon had broken several panels of glass to get in.

There was a moment of fear as the dragon dove through the window, wings closed, and they plunged down toward the busy street.

A scream caught in Edward's throat. Not for the first time, he wondered why no one else saw these creatures. Was he having really vivid hallucinations while locked up in some madhouse?

No. No. He was sure other people saw them. But he was also sure they forgot it as soon as they could. He, himself, tried to forget them every time he saw them. Every time. And then they appeared again.

They plunged dizzily past blind dark offices and fully lit ones, toward the cars on the street below.

At maybe tenth-floor level, the dragon opened his wings, and turned gracefully, gaining height.

Edward was never sure how they flew. He'd always thought thermals . . . But these wings were flapping, vigorously, to gain altitude, and he could feel the back muscles ripple beneath his legs.

He'd put his briefcase's shoulder handle across his chest, bandolier style. And that was good because the dragon's scales were slicker and smoother than they seemed to be, and he had to hold on with both hands to the ridge that ran down the back of the dragon, as the dragon turned almost completely sideways, and gained altitude, flying above the high-rises, above Hudson Bay, circling. Heading out to Colorado. Where Edward was supposed to convince Tom to do something he didn't want to do.

Oh, hell.

❖   ❖   ❖

"What?" Kyrie asked, looking at Rafiel who stood by the windows, frowning at them.

"This window was broken from the outside," he said. "Something ripped the screen aside, and hammered that window down. From the outside."

"How do you know?" she asked. She was looking at her patio door and wondering how she was going to be able to pay for all that glass. Safety glass, at that, she was sure. "How could you tell?"

"The glass fragments are all on the inside," he said. "And scattered pretty far in."

"The glass fragments for this patio door are pretty much inside, too, but there's a bunch of them outside," she said. "I think you're reading too much into it."

"No," Rafiel said. "I'm no expert, of course. I could bring the lab here, and they could tell you for sure. But—see, on the patio door, the glass is kicked all the way out there, almost halfway through your backyard."

"Which isn't very far," Kyrie said.

"Admittedly," Rafiel said. "But see, the door I'm sure was kicked from the inside. But the windows weren't. There's some glass that crumbled and just fell on that side, but most of it got pushed in here, all the way to the middle of the carpet."

Kyrie looked. There were glass pieces all the way through the room, to the foot of the sofa where Tom had slept. There were spots of blood, too, where Tom had walked on the glass, apparently without noticing.

Suddenly, it was too much for Kyrie, and she sat on the end of the sofa where there was no glass. "How could he?" she asked. "What was he high on, anyway? There was glass everywhere. Why couldn't he feel it? What's wrong with him?"

Rafiel looked puzzled and started to say, "Who—?" Then he shook his head. "If you mean Ormson, I think there's a lot more wrong with him than even I could tell you. Though I think I'll do a background check on him tomorrow. His getting that other young punk here worries me. Perhaps he's a dealer? And that guy came by for a hit?"

Kyrie was about to say that she'd never seen any signs that Tom dealt—but what did she have to go on? She had suspected him of it. He'd said he didn't. And, of course, she would trust him because he was a model of virtue and probity. "What is wrong with me?" she asked.

And now Rafiel looked even more puzzled and she almost laughed. Which showed how shocked she was, because there really wasn't anything to laugh about.

The golden eyes gave her the once-over, head to toe. "I don't see anything wrong with you."

For a moment, for just a moment, she could almost smell him, musky and virile like the night before. She got up from the sofa. That was probably what was messing her up. It all came down to pheromones and unconscious reactions and stuff. It was all . . . insane.

She grabbed her right hand with her left, as if afraid what they might do. "Well, that's neither here nor there," she said. "Is it? These windows are going to cost me a fortune, and I will have to work a *bunch* of overtime to pay for it."

"I could talk to my dad. He knows— I could get someone to do the job and you could pay for them on credit."

Kyrie twisted her lips. One thing she had seen, through her growing up years, and that was that families usually went wrong when they started buying things on credit, no matter how necessary it seemed at the time. And since many of the foster families fostered for the money allowance a new kid brought, she had seen a lot of families who had gone financially to the wrong. "No, thank you," she said. "I can take care of myself."

"But this is wide open," he said. "And there's something killing shifters. What if they come for you? How are you going to defend yourself? I have to protect you. We're partners in solving this crime, remember?"

Kyrie remembered. But she also remembered that she wasn't sure what all this meant to Rafiel. And didn't want to know. She'd been a fool for trusting Tom. She'd be damned if she was going to repeat the mistake with Rafiel. What if he had the door fixed in a way that he could, somehow, come in and kill her in the night?

She couldn't figure out any reason why he would want to kill her. But then, she couldn't figure out any reason why anyone would want to go around killing other shape-shifters. It had to be a shifter. Only a shifter would smell them. So, what would he get out of killing his own kind? And who better to do it than a policeman?

"No, thank you," she said, again. "You don't have to take care of me. I can take care of myself. I've been doing it all my life. Pretty successfully, as you see."

"But—"

"No buts, Officer Trall." Without seeming to, she edged around him, and guided him through the doorway from the sunporch into the kitchen. She locked the door to the outside, then grabbed the extra chair and wedged it under the doorknob, the way she'd secured her bedroom in countless foster homes, when she'd been lucky enough to have a room for herself. "You'd best leave now. I need to have something to eat, and then I'll go to the Athens early. The day shift is often a person short, and if I can pitch in at dinnertime, I can work some overtime, and that will help pay for this . . . mess."

As if taken off balance by her sudden forcefulness, he allowed himself to be shepherded all the way out the kitchen door.

"Thank you again," Kyrie said. And almost told him it had been lovely. Which could apply to the brunch, but certainly was a gross overstatement when it came to the autopsy, and just plain silly when applied to what they found back here. Which, admittedly, wasn't his fault.

He was still staring at her, the golden eyes somehow managing to look sheepish, when she closed the door in his face. And locked it.

Alone in the house for the first time in almost twenty-four hours, she rushed to the bedroom. She needed to get out of her skirt and into jeans and a T-shirt. Then she'd eat something—at a guess bread, because she imagined that Tom would have eaten every ounce of protein in the house—and get out of here. The diner had to be safer. More people, more witnesses.

Although it hadn't helped the guy last night, had it?

She shuddered at the thought of that bloodied body on the slab. She would park up front, she decided. On Fairfax Avenue. Within plain sight of everyone.

"Damn," Keith said, after a while of driving in silence.

"What now?" Tom asked. He'd been sitting there, his head in his hands, trying to figure out what he was going to do next. He felt as if his life, over the last six months, was a carefully constructed castle of cards that someone had poked right in the middle and sent tumbling.

If Kyrie was no better than him, then maybe it was something wrong with the nature of shifters. Maybe that was why every one he'd met was a drifter, or . . .

"I forgot to tell you why I came looking for you," Keith said.

"I thought it was to make sure I was all right," Tom said.

"Well." Keith nodded. "That was part of it, only . . . I went to pay the rent today and I got to talking to the building manager about what happened at your apartment and she said . . . The manager got a bunch of your things from the floor. Before she called the police to look at it."

"The police? To look at my things?" Tom asked. He was trying to imagine why the woman would do that. She was a little old lady who looked Italian or Greek and who had always seemed pretty nice to him.

"No, you fool. She got the things before the police came over, because she figured they were your things and you might need them, and the police would just tie them up."

"Oh, what did she get?"

"I don't know. It looked like was some of your clothes, and your boots, and a credit card."

Tom blinked. "I don't have a credit card." Had one of the triad dropped his credit card behind? Tom hadn't been impressed by the collective intelligence of the dragon enforcer trio, but that seemed too stupid even for them.

"Your ATM card, then."

"Oh."

"The manager said it was none of the police's business. She asked me to bring you by for your stuff." Keith looked at Tom. "But maybe I should take you to emergency first. For your feet?"

"No," Tom said. First, because he had enough experience in his own body to know that any wound would heal up seemingly overnight. And second because if he could get some clothes on, and his hand on his ATM card, he was going to find some stuff to buy. Heroin, by choice, but just about anything else would do, short of baking soda. This time he was going to get high and stay high. He would be feeling no pain.

In jeans and a comfortable T-shirt, Kyrie went into the kitchen. She felt naked without the earring she normally wore. She'd found it in a street fair when she was about fourteen and it had been her favorite piece of jewelry since. But there was no point crying over spilt milk or spoiled jewelry. She had lost it somewhere at Tom's house, while becoming a panther. She would have to look out for another one.

Meanwhile she needed to eat something, even if just bread and butter.

She put the kettle on for tea, and opened the fridge to see if perhaps a couple rounds of her lunch meat had survived. And was shocked to find eggs and bacon still sitting on the shelf, where she had left them. Looking at the containers, she determined he'd eaten about a third of her provisions. Which meant she would still have enough for the rest of the week, even if she shifted once or twice.

She'd long ago decided to make breakfast her main protein meal of the day. Even if she ate breakfast at the time other people ate dinner. Eggs and bacon, particularly bought on sale, were far cheaper than meat for other meals.

She got the microwave bacon tray, and noticed Tom had washed it very carefully. She put the pan on for eggs, and again noticed it had been scrubbed with a soft, plastic scrubber, per manufacturer instructions for nonstick pans. Sitting at her little table, washing down the food with a cup of sweet tea—which she preferred to coffee unless she felt a need to wake up suddenly—she felt vaguely guilty about throwing Tom out.

Then she realized the source of her guilt was that he'd actually made an effort to wash the dishes and that, as ravenous as he must have been—she remembered what she'd felt like at the restaurant—he hadn't eaten all of her food. She smiled to herself. So, it was fine if the man were a one-person demolition engine, as long as he had good household habits?

She shook her head. Okay, she clearly was going soft in the head. Perhaps it was the shifter-bond. But if so, couldn't she feel more tenderly toward Rafiel? Was the way to her heart to give as much trouble and cause as much damage as humanly possible?

After washing her dishes, she grabbed her purse and hurried toward the Athens. She'd park up front. With the driver's window in the state it was, she didn't want to leave the car unwatched, anyway. She'd park up front, and keep an eye on it through her work shift.

Hopefully the diner would be short-staffed for the dinner shift, the last few hours of the day staff. Hopefully. They usually were, but then things never went the way one wanted them to, did they? And she'd have to buy another apron from Frank's stock, kept for when a staff member walked out of the job with the apron still on. Another expense.

She checked the chair under the lock between the kitchen and the back porch before leaving the house.

"We were all very worried something dreadful had happened to you." Mrs. Rizzo looked at him, her sparkling black eyes narrowed in what might indeed be worry. Or suspicion. Though that wasn't fair, because she'd never been suspicious of him.

A small woman, so short that she made Tom feel tall, she stood in front of her desk in the little, musty manager's office at the back of the apartment complex. Every possible inch of space on her wall was covered up in pictures—pictures of smiling brides, pictures of babies, and pictures of children looking sticky and sweet in equal measures and displaying mouths with a varying number of teeth in unguarded smiles. A set of pink booties, half knit, lay on her desk, with a gigantic ball of pink yarn and two green plastic knitting needles.

Tom had often wanted to ask her if the pictures were all her children, but he was a little afraid of the answer, and not quite sure if yes or no would be the scarier reply. Instead, he threw back his head to move the hair out from in front of his face—he really needed to find something to tie it soon. A rubber band would do—and smiled at Mrs. Rizzo. "Fortunately I was staying with a friend."

She cocked an eyebrow at him. "A girl?"

"Yes. She works with me."

Mrs. Rizzo grinned, suddenly. "Well, and isn't it about time you found someone to settle down with. Is she a good girl?"

"Yes, a very good girl," Tom said. Or at least he'd thought that until today, and finding out about the sugar. But he wasn't about to discuss that with his apartment manager.

The lady nodded. "Good, maybe you can stay with her until we get your place fixed. It should only be a couple of weeks. Or we could move you to number 35, if you want. I talked to the owner, and he said it would be okay to give it to you. It's a little bigger, but he said you could have it for the same price."

A few hours ago, this would have been an offer for Tom to snatch with both hands. He could have got into the new apartment without paying a deposit, and with no real inconvenience. Oh, his furniture and utensils were gone, but he hadn't had all that much, and he could always replace them in a month or less from thrift shops and garage sales. A sofa first, until he could afford a bed, and a pan and a frying pan would do for cooking in, till he could get more complete utensils. And . . .

But he stopped his own thoughts, forcefully. He would have been very happy to do that a few hours ago. It would have made him nonhomeless again. But a few hours ago, he now realized, he'd still been under the mistaken impression that Kyrie was some sort of ideal woman, something to aspire to. Someone whom, even if he could never have her, he could imitate and hope to be more like. Now . . . "I don't know what I'm doing, yet, Mrs. Rizzo. I'll let you know in a couple of days, if that's all right." Of course he knew perfectly well what he was doing. He was getting the heck out of Dodge before nightfall. He might come back later—if he could—for the . . . object in the water tank of the Athens's bathroom. But he wouldn't come back to live. He wouldn't go back to working there— with Kyrie. No way, no when, no how. And no one could make him.

Mrs. Rizzo sighed. "You're staying with her, right? Well, I hope it works. But if it doesn't, remember we have number 35. I'll hold it for you for another week." She smiled. "It's the one with the bay window." And sounded exactly like someone holding out a sweet to a kid.

Tom nodded. "I'll be in touch. But Keith said you had some of my stuff . . ."

She reached behind the desk and brought out a box that was larger than Tom expected. Protruding out of the top were his boots, and he gave a deep sigh of relief upon seeing them. Then, as he dug through, he found a couple of pairs of jeans, one black and one blue, three black T-shirts, and—carefully folded—his black leather jacket. He felt suddenly weak at the knees. It was like losing half of your identity and then retrieving it again.

At the very bottom of the box was his ATM card, and he found himself taking a deep, relieved breath. He wouldn't need to wait till the banks opened to get out his money before he got out of town. Next to the ATM card was a library book—*The Book of Sand* by Jorge Luis Borges. He could drop that off at the library depot on the way out of town. Good. The library was unlikely to make much of a search for him on the strength of a single hardcover book, but it was best to get out of town with as few things hanging over his head as possible.

Between the book and the ATM card was a red object, which at first he couldn't identify. And then he realized it was Kyrie's red plumed earring.

He should take it back. He should . . . His hand closed around it. Or not. Or not. He couldn't see facing her. He couldn't imagine her reproaching him for getting high and destroying her sunroom. He would have to tell her, then, that the least she could have done was tell him that the sugar wasn't exactly sugar. She must keep the real stuff somewhere. After all, they'd had coffee the night before to no ill effects. So, why didn't she tell him where it was? Tom would much rather have had it.

His hand closed on the plumed earring and he shoved it into the pocket of his jacket.

"You can change in the bathroom," Mrs. Rizzo said, pointing to a little door at the back. "If you want to."

The bathroom was a continuation of the office. Oh, there were no pictures on the walls, which was a very good thing. Tom would have hated to undress completely in front of a mass of staring babies and prim brides. But the hand soap was pink and shaped like a rose, and, on the toilet tank, a much-too-tall crochet angel with a plastic face squatted contentedly over three spare toilet paper rolls, as though hoping they would soon hatch into chickens.

Tom had to watch that, and the mirror, and the vanity, because the bathroom was so small he could barely move in it. He removed Kyrie's jogging suit, folded it carefully, and put it beside the toilet paper angel. Then he put on his jeans and T-shirt with a sense of relief. He wished some of his underwear had been preserved, but if absolutely needed he could do without it a little longer.

Socks were something else—as was the need to put his boots back on. He hadn't felt any pain from his feet recently, but then he'd been . . . busy. He sat down on the closed toilet lid, to look at his feet. And was surprised to find he'd shed most of the glass shards. Only a couple large ones remained, embedded in his skin, but his skin seemed to be . . . He stared at it. Yep. His skin was pushing them out, forcing them out and growing behind them. The other cuts were already closed, though angry red and likely to leave a scar.

This was one of those changes that arrived when he started shifting into a dragon. All of a sudden, he could cut himself or scrape himself and it would heal in a day, or a few hours, depending on the depth of the injury. It was just about the only change that wasn't completely unwelcome.

He washed the bottom of his feet with damp toilet paper, and looked again. Nothing really. Just rapidly healing cuts. He slipped his boots on, wishing he had socks, but it couldn't be helped. With all his belongings still in a box, he went back to Mrs. Rizzo. "I'm sorry to bother you, but could I borrow a plastic bag? It's easier to carry than a box." Meaning, it would actually be possible to carry while he was in dragon form. Which was how he'd kept most of his belongings, while moving all over the country.

She nodded, and bent to get something from behind her desk. Tom wondered what exactly she kept back there, just as she emerged with a backpack, not a plastic bag. The backpack was pale blue and made in the sort of plastic that glistens. "The Michelsons left it behind, when they vacated number 22," Mrs. Rizzo said. "It used to have wheels, but they're broken. They left a bunch of the kids' old clothes, too. Ripped and dirty." She made a face. "When people do that, I wash them and fix them and give them to charities in town. Such a waste. People throw everything away these days. But the backpack I kept, if someone moved in with a school-age kid and needed it."

"It's all right," Tom said. "I only need a plastic bag."

"No, no. It's okay. You can have it. There will be two or three others by September, when school opens. People throw them away."

Well, the backpack was more practical because it closed. Though, in dragon form, he would still have to carry it the same way—by wrapping the straps around his huge ankle—the backpack zipped shut. And there was less chance of losing stuff. "Well, thank you then," he said, reaching for it.

Up close, as he stuffed his remaining belongings—and Kyrie's jogging suit—into it, he realized the full extent of his problem. The backpack had a little orange dragon with stubby wings on the back, and it said underneath, in fiery orange-red letters, "Scorchio." He scowled at it.

"Kids these days like the weirdest things, don't they?" Mrs. Rizzo said.

"Yes," Tom said. And then, with everything in the backpack, he had to say good-bye somehow. Only he'd never said good-bye to anyone or anything, and certainly not to anyone who liked him and whom he liked. "I'll be back," he lied. "In a few days."

"You do that, dear," she said. "I'll hold number 35 for you, okay?"

As he headed out, he caught a glimpse of his reflection in the window of the next-door apartment. Against the dark drapes, he looked like something out of a horror movie—unruly hair, tight black jeans, black leather jacket. Even with the stupid pale blue backpack on, he didn't look like anyone that someone would want to bother.

He stalked off, down Fairfax Avenue, away from the Athens and toward the nearest ATM that way. He had a vague idea that he should go back and pay Kyrie for the mess. He would have done it the day before. But now he told himself there was simply no way. Not any way in hell. She should have told him about the sugar. It was all her fault. Yeah, he probably still owed her for the car—but because of the sugar he was now headed out of town, with nothing but a handful of possessions. He was going to need all his money.

He realized he was holding her responsible for the fact that she wasn't perfect. And that was fine, as far as he was concerned. Wasn't there someone—one person—in the world he could look up to?

"When is your break?" Rafiel asked. He'd been sitting at one of the small tables in the extension room that used to be the sunporch of the Athens and had been enclosed, sometime decades away, to make more space for tables.

Like a sunporch, it was informally furnished. Just plastic tables and chairs, of the type people used outside. On a Friday like this, and when the dinner hour was in full swing, it filled up fast.

A family group or a gaggle of laughing and screaming students surrounded every other table. Only Rafiel sat alone.

She'd smiled at him when first serving him, and the rest of the time she'd avoided looking too closely at him, as she served the noisy groups around him. But now she was pouring a warm-up of coffee into his cup, and he said, "Come on, please? I need to talk to you."

She would believe him a lot more and talk to him with a far clearer conscience if she couldn't detect, as an undertone to his soap and aftershave smell, the lion's spicy-hot scent. She didn't trust herself around that smell. She behaved very stupidly around it. Instead, she made a big show of looking around, as if mentally counting people. "No way for the next hour or so," she said. "I have to keep refills and desserts and all coming. They allowed me to work because they were two people short. There's no way I can take a break."

To her surprise, he smiled. "Okay, then. I'll have the bowl of rice pudding. À la mode." He lowered his voice, "And then I want to talk to you. There's some very odd autopsy results."

❖   ❖   ❖

Stealing a car wasn't hard. Tom walked along the darkened working class neighborhoods first, looking at all the old models of cars parked on the street.

It had to be an old model, because his way of starting a car without a key wouldn't work on the newer models. And in those streets, around Fairfax, with their tiny, decrepit brick houses, the cars spotted with primer on the front, there was a prospect on every corner. He could steal a dozen cars, if he wanted to.

Half a dozen times, he walked up to a sickly looking two-door sedan, a rusted and disreputable pickup and put his hand on the door handle, while he felt in his pocket for the stone he'd picked up from a flower bed near his apartment. The only other piece of equipment necessary to this operation was a screwdriver, which he'd bought from a corner convenience store.

He had everything. So, why didn't he just smash the window, break the ignition housing, start the car, and drive away? Most of these houses looked empty and people were probably still at work or already asleep.

But he'd put his hand on the handle, and reach for the rock, and remember how hard it was to make ends meet from his job at the Athens. How he had never been able to buy a car, but used to read the Sunday paper vehicles-for-sale ads with the relish of a kid looking through a candy-store window.

From those ads, he knew many of these cars would be a few hundred dollars, no more. But a few hundred dollars was all he had in his pocket, and it had emptied his account. And accumulating it had required endless small sacrifices, in what food he ate, in what clothes he wore. Hell, he didn't even shop the thrift stores at full price. It was always at half-price or dollar-day sales.

Oh, he wasn't complaining. He was lucky to have a job, given his past work history and his lack of training. Correction. He'd been lucky to have a job. Now it was over and he'd be lucky to ever have another. What were the owners of these cars employed at? What did they do?

Fuming, he turned away. Damn. This going-straight thing was like some sort of disease. You caught it, and then you had the hardest trouble getting rid of it. They probably didn't sell honesty-be-gone tablets at the local drugstore.

He walked down one of the cracked sidewalks that ran along the front of the pocket-sized lawns, kicking a stray piece of concrete here and there, to vent his anger. Damn. He couldn't walk out of the city on foot. And he wasn't at all sure he could start flying from inside the city. What if someone saw him? What if . . . *they* saw him?

He walked along as a thin rain started trickling down on him from the sky above. The rain felt . . . odd. He'd been living in Colorado for six months and this was the first time he'd seen rain. There was a feeling of strangeness, at first, and then, despite the warmth of the night, discomfort at water seeping everywhere and dripping from his hair onto the back of his neck, running down the back of his jacket.

He walked a long time on his still-tender feet and passed a roped-in car dealership. But it was the sort of car dealership you got in this kind of area—selling fifth- or sixth-hand cars. Of course, he thought, as he walked past, his hand idly touching the rope that marked off the lot, he could probably break into those cars far more easily than into any others. But . . . he stared at the wrecks and semiwrecks under the moonlight. What were the chances that the owner of this lot was living so close to the bone that the theft of a car would really hurt him?

Tom looked at the facade of the dealership proper, and it was a well-known car dealer. Chances were they'd never feel it. His hand weighed the stone in his pocket.

On the other hand . . . On the other hand, the theft of a car—or one more car, as Tom doubted this would be the first—might be what caused the dealership to close doors at this location, to give up on this neighborhood, perhaps to give up on this level of car, at all. And then people in this neighborhood would find it harder to get a car. Perhaps harder to find jobs.

Tom dropped the stone out of his jacket pocket and kicked it violently aside. Then he dropped the screwdriver after it. He walked down the road, his hands shoved deep in his pockets.

He would have to walk, as far as he could out of Goldport. He'd go south, toward New Mexico. Lots of empty space that way, less chance of someone seeing or noticing a dragon flying against the sky. But damn, he could get much, much farther if he could ride. As it was, he'd almost surely get caught by the three dragons. And this time he would have to face them alone.

He realized he was chewing on his lower lip, as he walked down the street where the dilapidated houses gave way to houses in even worse state but divided into apartments, and then to warehouses tagged with the occasional gang graffiti.

He pulled the collar up on his leather jacket. Even with the ridiculous backpack on his back, he didn't think anyone would challenge him. Not for a moment.

Knowing this trip was likely to end in his death, he wished he could buy something to make it easier. Not a lot. Probably nothing to inject. Just some pot to smoke, to ease his nerves. He was going to die, he might as well go easy. Besides, he'd seen there was no point trying to escape the grip of drugs, if even Kyrie did them.

In his six months in the city, he'd seen plenty of drug dealers standing around in shady corners, waiting. This was the type of neighborhood to attract them. But perhaps the rain, unaccustomed in Colorado, had driven them indoors. Tom couldn't see anyone, and certainly not anyone with that pose of alert shiftiness that identified a dealer. He had money. He was willing. But no one was selling.

"Damn dealers," he muttered to himself under his breath. "Just like cops. Never around when you need one."

Wide awake and hopeless, he headed south and west while the sun set and the breeze grew cooler, ruffling at his damp hair, his soaking jeans.

"Frank, do we have rice pudding?" Kyrie asked, coming near the counter.

Frank looked up with a frown, from a talk he'd been having with three customers seated at the part of the counter where you could get food served. His girlfriend wasn't around again, tonight, so he was in a mood. "I just came in and I haven't made any. If there's any, it's leftover from yesterday."

Well, it was all gone, then. But before Kyrie could turn to go give Rafiel the bad news, Frank added, "Is Tom coming in later?"

"Tom?" Kyrie didn't know what to say. She honestly had no idea. And for just a moment was startled that Frank would ask her about Tom. Except that of course, last night she'd taken time off to take medicine to Tom. Or at least that was what she had told Frank. And then she'd told Frank that Tom was in really bad shape and she had to take him home with her and watch him.

"I don't know," she said. "He left my place a few hours ago."

"Do you know where he was going?"

She shook her head. "He was with his friend. The guy who lives downstairs from him," Kyrie said, as she pulled a stray strand of hair behind her ear. And as she did, the customers at the counter looked up. And she froze.

They were the three from the night before. The three dragons. None of them permanently injured, as far as she could tell, though she was sure she'd got the eye of at least one of them in the battle.

But they sat there, at the counter, uninjured, and the middle one even had his hair arranged, as artificially perfect and smooth as before. They all wore tight jeans and satinlike shimmering jackets, with dragons in the back. They looked like something out of a bad karate movie, and Kyrie was so shocked at seeing them here, in . . . well, the glare of the fluorescent lights, that she didn't know what to do.

Two Dragons was the one sitting next to where Kyrie stood. He backed away from her, his eyes wide, and said something in Chinese that sounded like a panic attack.

The middle one said something in return, something she couldn't understand, and put his hand into his pocket, pulling out a sheaf of notes, which he laid on the counter. And then, the three geniuses, in massed disarray, started toward the door. A process only slightly hampered by the fact that not one of them was willing to turn his back on Kyrie. So they moved backward as a group, bumping into tables and booths, snagging on girls' purses and men's coats, and muttering stuff in Chinese that might be apologies or threats.

Clearly, they were rattled enough to forget their English. Clearly, they thought that Kyrie's panther form was too dangerous to anger. Although why they thought she would shift into a panther right then and take them to pieces in front of the diner patrons was beyond her.

Pulling and shoving at each other, they got to the door, then in a tinkling of the bells suspended from it, out of it, tumbling onto the sidewalk where the lights were starting to show, faintly, against the persistent glow of the sunset.

"What was that all about?" Frank asked. "Did those guys know you?"

"I have no clue," Kyrie said, choosing to answer the first question. And this was the absolute truth. She couldn't figure out why they would be scared of her. After all, even if she had been so stupid as to shift here, in the middle of the diner, they could have shifted too, and then they would have had the upper hand. There were three of them, after all.

Unless . . . She smiled faintly at the thought. *Unless the total idiots thought this was a shifter diner and that everyone here would be shifters.* If Tom was right the shifting was ancient, well established in their culture, and perhaps passed on in families. They had a lore and a culture. For people like that it must be utterly bewildering when strangers shifted. *Perhaps they think we too band together.*

Frank was glowering at her, and she realized she was still smiling. He reached for the plates and cups the guys had left on the counter and pulled them down, near the cleaning area, by the dishwasher, glowering all the while and banging the utensils around so much that, if they weren't break-resistant, they would probably have shattered.

"What's wrong?" Kyrie asked.

But he just glowered at her some more, grabbed a dish towel from the counter, and wiped at the serving surface with it. "Oh, nothing. Everything is fine and dandy. You and Tom and . . ." He lifted his hands, upward, as though signifying his inability to understand any of them.

Kyrie skidded back to the sunporch, to give Rafiel the distressing news about the rice pudding.

"There's no rice pudding," she said. "And the three dragons who were at Tom's apartment were just here."

"The dragons?" he said and started to rise. "Here?"

"In human form," she said. "They left." She frowned. "They seemed afraid of me."

He looked at her a long moment, then shook his head. "I don't know what to do. I wonder why they were here."

"Looking for Tom," she said.

"Oh." He looked out the window. "We could follow them, but there's only two of us—"

"And neither of us can fly," Kyrie said. "Besides, there's only one of us. I'm working. But since there's no rice pudding, you're free to follow them."

He just grinned up at her. "Oh, bring me pie à la mode, then. I don't care. I'm in it for the vanilla ice cream." And he winked at her.

"What kind of pie?"

"I told you I don't care," he said. "Just bring me a wedge."

"Green bean pie it is, then," she said, and walked away. To bump into Anthony, the last of the day shift to leave. He was in his street clothes, which in his case were usually elaborate and today consisted of a ruffled button-down white shirt, red vest, and immaculate black pants. "Hey," he said. "What's up with Frank? He's acting like a bear with two heads."

Kyrie shrugged and Anthony sighed. "What that man needs," he said, as if this summed up the wisdom of the ages, "is to get laid. He seriously needs to get laid. His girlfriend hasn't been in for too long." And with that, he twirled on his heels and made for the door. Kyrie had often wondered if in his free time he was a member of some dance troupe. At least that would explain the bizarre clothes.

Kyrie went back to scout out the pie, though the only choices were apple and lemon. She chose lemon, figuring he would like it less, and put two scoops of ice cream on the plate with it. It wasn't so much that she wanted to thwart Rafiel—but a man who ordered with that kind of complacency did deserve green bean pie. Or at least brussels sprouts. Too bad they didn't have any on the menu.

She took the plate of pie in one hand, the carafe in the other, set the pie in front of Rafiel and went off, from table to table, warming up people's coffees.

Despite her best efforts to banish it, the image of Frank getting laid was stuck in her mind. She looked across the diner at Frank, behind the counter, his Neanderthal-like features still knit in a glower. She shuddered. There were things the human mind was not supposed to contemplate.

Edward Ormson's first thought was that they couldn't be in Colorado. Not so fast. Even by airplane it took over three hours. And they couldn't be flying at airplane speeds. Well, they could, but it would have left him frozen as a popsicle sitting astride that dragon.

And he hadn't been frozen, nor gasping for air. The temperature around him had remained even, and he'd felt perfectly comfortable. Only twice, for just a moment, light seemed to vanish from around them. But it was such a brief moment that Edward hadn't had time to think about it. Now he wondered if some magic transfer had taken place at that moment.

Oh, Edward didn't believe in magic. But then he also didn't believe in dragons, he thought and smiled with more irony than joy while the dragon circled down to a parking lot in a street of low-to-the-ground buildings.

They landed softly on the asphalt and the huge wings that had been spread on either side of him, coruscating and sparkling in the light like living fire, closed slowly.

"Down," the dragon said. Or perhaps not said it, because Edward didn't remember sounds. Just the feeling that he should get down. He should get down immediately.

He scrambled off, sliding along scales that felt softer on the skin than they should have.

But once he stood, in the parking lot, holding his briefcase, he realized that the front of his suit had tiny cuts, as though someone had worked it over with very small blades.

He frowned at it, then looked up at the dragon who glowed with some sort of inner fire, in front of him. The beast opened its huge mouth, and all thought of complaining about damages to his clothes fled Ormson's mind.

"Find your son," the dragon said, in that voice that wasn't exactly a voice. "Make him give back what belongs to me."

And, just as suddenly as he'd appeared at Edward Ormson's office, the dragon now stretched its wings, flexed its legs, and was airborne, gaining height.

Alone in the parking lot, Edward became aware that it was raining, a boring, slow rain. Behind him, a little Chinese restaurant called Three Luck Dragon had its open sign out, but there were no cars parked. So either it catered to a local clientele, or it had none.

Did the Great Sky Dragon mean anything by dropping Edward off here? Or was it simply the first convenient place they'd come to?

Edward saw the curtain twitch on the little window, and a face peer out. The lighting and the distance didn't allow him to see features, but he thought it would be the proprietors looking to see if he intended to come in.

Well, today was their lucky day. He'd go in and order something, and get out his cell phone. He would bet now he knew where Tom had last been seen, he would be able to find the boy with half a dozen phone calls.

One way or another, he always ended up cleaning up after his son.

Western towns don't taper off. Or at least that was what Tom had seen, ever since his drifting had brought him west and south to Colorado, New Mexico, and Arizona. You walked down a street, surrounded by five-floor brick warehouses, resounding with the noises of loading and unloading, of packing and making of things resounding within.

And then, a couple of blocks away, you were in the middle of a high prairie, with tumbleweed blowing around. Looking back, you could still see the warehouses, but they were so incongruous that they seemed to be part of another world.

Tom turned to look at the dark edge of the warehouses. He stood on what had abruptly become a country road, its asphalt cracked underfoot. Looking just beyond where he was standing, he saw nothing but an underpass, just ahead. Why there was an underpass was a question he couldn't answer, as it was just two country roads meeting. Perhaps this was what people complained about, with public projects that made no sense.

But right then Tom was grateful of the underpass. In this landscape of brown grass and blowing tumbleweeds, there wasn't much cover, otherwise. He made for the underpass and stripped quickly, shoving all his clothes and boots into the little backpack with the happy dragon on the back. The boots were a tight fit into the small space, but he got them in, and zipped the thing. Then he loosened the back straps to their outmost, and put them around his wrist.

Willing yourself to shift was like willing yourself to die. Because the process of shifting, no matter how easy, always hurt. It took desire to do it, but it needed something else. He got out from under the overpass, and stood—naked in the moonlight, willing his body to shift, willing.

A cough shook him, another, heralding the preliminary spasms that often preceded the shape-shifting. Pain twisted in his limbs, wracked his back, as his body tried to extrude wings from itself. He opened his mouth and let the scream come—something he never did within a city— the scream of pain of his human self, the scream of triumph from the ancient beast once more let forth.

A car drove by, toward the outside of town. One of the tiny SUVs in white. A Kia or a Hyundai or one of those. Tom's confused senses were aware of its turning around and then zooming past again. But no one came out. *Worse comes to worst*, his still rational mind thought, as his body shifted. *They'll just call 911. And good luck with convincing a dispatcher they just saw a dragon.*

In the next moment it no longer mattered. The dragon was him. He was the dragon. His body fully shifted, Tom spread his wings fully, feeling the caress of wind and rain on them. He opened his mouth and roared, this time in triumph. His vision sharpened. He was in a vast noncave. And the dragon knew they should go to ground, they should find a cave.

No, the human part of Tom said. *No. Not to a cave. We're flying west. Deep west, until we come to a town. We'll follow the highway that will take us to Las Vegas, New Mexico, by early morning. Then . . . cave.*

The dragon blinked, confused, because the image in its mind, for a cave, had mattresses and pillows and other things that made sense only to the human. But it had learned, over the years, to trust the ape cowering away at the back of its mind.

It trusted it now, even when it found something wrapped tightly around its front paw. The human mind said they were clothes, and that they shouldn't be discarded.

The dragon harumphed, loudly. Then spread its wings again, sensing the air currents. Half of flying was coasting.

If you needed to beat your wings the whole time, you were going to die of tiredness soon.

He felt the currents. He flapped a little. He gained altitude. He headed out of town.

"Break?" Rafiel asked.

Kyrie was about to shake her head, but stopped. The dinnertime crowd had thinned. Students had left for concerts or movies or whatever it was that college students did with their evenings. And the families, too, had vanished, probably home to their comfy chairs and their TVs.

The only two people in the diner were a man at the back, who seemed to be signing the credit card slip that Kyrie had dropped on his table. And Rafiel.

Kyrie looked at the wall clock. Ten-thirty p.m. That meant there would be a lull till eleven or thereabouts, when the late-night people would start coming in. And she only needed ten minutes.

She backtracked to the counter and put away the carafe she'd just used to give Rafiel a warm-up. "Frank, is it okay if I take ten minutes?" she asked.

Frank turned around. He was still glowering. "Fine. It's fine," he said, as if he were saying that it was all completely wrong.

"Is there a problem?" Kyrie asked taken aback.

"No. I just wish your boyfriend had given us some warning before he decided to disappear."

"He's not due for an hour or so. I came in early," Kyrie said. "And he's not my boyfriend."

But it was hardly worth arguing. And Frank looked to be in a worse mood than she'd ever seen him. "I'll take a break now," she said. "If Tom doesn't come in, it's going to be a hellish shift, and that way I'll be able to stay till five a.m., okay?"

Frank shrugged, which looked like consent. He was grilling a bunch of burgers, though Kyrie had no idea why, given the deserted look of the diner. Perhaps he was precooking them a bit to allow him to cook them faster later on. It wasn't any of her business, in any case.

She backtracked to the enclosed-porch addition. Rafiel must have heard, or watched her conversation. He was standing as she approached. "Ready?"

She nodded. And gestured with her head toward the door at the back of the extension that led to the parking lot. She didn't want to go to the parking lot again. Truly, she didn't. On the other hand, neither did she want to talk to Rafiel in front of Frank. Frank was likely to decide that Rafiel was also her boyfriend and hold her responsible for whatever the policeman did in the future.

She had no idea what had gotten into her boss. He was usually grumpy, but not like this. And then there was Anthony's idea, which made her make a face, as she led Rafiel out the back door and onto the parking lot.

This time the parking lot was deserted, there was no smell of blood, and she took care to stay in the shadow of the building, out of the light of the moon.

Rafiel made a sound that seemed suspiciously close to a purr as he got outside, and he stretched his arms. "Do you feel it?" he asked, giving Kyrie a sidelong glance. "Do you feel the call?"

"No," Kyrie said, as curtly as she could. It was a lie, but only in a way. Yeah, she could feel the call, but she could feel the call every night. And it seemed to her Rafiel was speaking of another call. And there, as if on cue, she noticed his smell again. No, not his smell. His smell was soap and a little aftershave, nothing out of the ordinary. But the smell exuding from him right now was a thick, feline musk that made her think of running through the jungles, of hunting, of . . . "You said you had news that pertained to the corpse?" she said, turning her head away.

"Yeah," he said, and looked away from her, as though her turning her head to get fresh air, slightly less tainted by his musk, were an insult. "Yeah. We got a chemical analysis for the green stuff we found."

She looked at him. He nodded as if she'd asked a question. "The . . . Well, the lab thinks it's of insect origin, although not quite like anything from any insects they know."

"And?" Kyrie asked.

"And those things . . . the white stuff on the lungs?"

"Yeah."

"They think it's eggs."

Kyrie frowned at him and he shook his head, looking impatient and annoyed, as if resenting that she couldn't read his mind. "Not chicken eggs," he said. "They're insect eggs. They don't know what type yet, but they're getting in an entomologist from the Natural History Museum in Denver. He's someone's brother-in-law or brother of a brother-in-law, and he's driving down day after tomorrow. He's supposedly one of those guys who can tell on sight what kind of insect laid eggs where. He's used for investigating crimes by all the local police departments."

"Okay," Kyrie said. "And why did I need to know this right now? Why was this so urgent that I had to take a break to hear it?" His smell was growing stronger. It seemed to fill her nose and her mouth and to populate her mind with odd images and thoughts. She found herself wondering what his hair would feel like to the touch.

"Because I think there was the same powder on your porch last night," he said. "Where those windows were broken."

"My porch? Insects?" she asked. "But Tom said something about dragons and his friend was going on about aliens."

"Well, yeah," Rafiel said, and shrugged. "But I don't think those two were exactly in the state necessary to testify in a court of law. Or for that matter anywhere else."

Kyrie conceded. And yet, she wondered what had happened in the porch while they were gone. Had bugs broken the window? In her mind was an image of masses of bugs crawling out of the loam, pushing on the window, till the sheer weight of their mass broke it. Yuck. Like something out of a bad horror movie. "Any dead bugs, or other pieces of bug in that powder?"

"No," he said. He looked directly at her, as if her face were a puzzle he was hoping to decipher. His eyes were huge and golden, and his lips looked soft. The musky smell of him was everywhere, penetrating her nostrils, her mind.

He leaned in, very close to her, and asked in a voice that should be reserved for indecent proposals, "So, can I come by? After your shift?"

The tone and the closeness startled her enough to wake her from the trance induced by his scent. She stepped back. "No. Why would you? No."

He took a deep breath as though he, too, had been affected by something, and stepped back. "So I can see if you have that powder in your porch or not. And to have it analyzed if you do." He shook his head. "What did you think I meant?"

"All right," she said, reluctantly. "If you want to come. But not when I get off work. Come later, around one or so." She wanted to get some sleep tomorrow. And besides, she was not absolutely sure about Rafiel Trall yet. She'd rather face him in the full light of noon, without the effects of whatever this smell was. "I'd better go back in. Frank is in a mood and I have repairs on the porch to pay off."

Edward Ormson got out of the taxi in front of the diner where he'd been told Tom worked. Finding this information had been a fast job.

He, himself, had found Tom's address on the Web, and his secretary had then called—from New York, that much more impressive—the boy's landlady and asked questions.

Closing the taxi door and waiting till the driver pulled away, Ormson frowned. In fact, in the whole story there was only one thing he didn't understand. And that was that his secretary had told him the landlady seemed fond of Tom.

Oh, it wasn't at all strange that a woman should have some interest in Tom. Even at sixteen, when the boy had left home, there had been to him that roguish charm that attracts a certain class of females. What was odd, though, was that he had reportedly been living within the apartment complex this woman managed for about six months, and she said he'd never been late with the rent, didn't have loud parties, hadn't given the neighbors any cause to complain. He didn't, in fact, seem to have any life

beyond going to work and—according to the woman—
reading out on the steps of the building when the weather
was warm. Reading? Tom? Perhaps it was the wrong
Thomas E. Ormson?

But no. It wasn't that common a name. And besides,
there had been the dragon. Edward swallowed, as he
headed toward the gaudy facade painted all over with the
prices of specials in what appeared to be a full pack of
primary color markers. It wasn't just that "Fresh Rice
Pudding" was scrawled in vivid red that offended
Ormson's sense of aesthetics. It was that above it "Fries
Always Fresh, Never Frozen" was done in at least five
different and mutually clashing colors.

And above the door, something that looked very much
like a pink pig wearing a cook's hat and apron was tossing
a succession of pancakes up in the air. The whole was so
horrendous that it might very well be considered kitschy
chic if it were in the right place. But around the diner,
head shops, used record stores, and closed warehouses
clustered. This was the type of area that would never be
fashionable.

It stood as a bulwark against the fern bars and lofts
proliferating just a few blocks away. Here dingy and
strange would hold the line against quaint and overpriced

Wondering about the hygiene of the place, and if it was
quite safe to go in, he opened the door. A clash of bells
greeted him, and a rough-looking, dark-haired, bearded
man glared at him from behind the counter.

Ormson had intended on approaching the first person
he saw and asking for Tom. But this man didn't look like
the greatest of prospects. His eyebrows were beetled low
over his dark, sunken eyes, and he looked positively

murderous, an impression not improved by the fact that he held a very large knife in his right hand.

Hoping that his hesitation hadn't been noticeable, Edward made for the most distant of the many booths upholstered in dark green vinyl. He was about to slide into it, when the man behind the counter barked, "Hey, you." Edward looked up, not even daring to ask what he'd done wrong.

"That booth is for groups, mister," the dark man said. "Take one of the smaller ones."

Edward obeyed, though wondering why the booth was being held for groups when, clearly, there was no one else in the place. But he really didn't want to argue with the man.

Instead, he slid into the smaller booth and made a big show of picking up the menu and studying it. Normal diner fare, all of it, as far as he could see, with a few Greek dishes thrown in. And though he wasn't sure he wanted to eat here, or even that the food here would be safe to eat, the place didn't smell bad. Greasy, sure. There was an underlying smell of hot oil, as if the place were used, day and night, to fry stuff. Which it probably was. But there were appetizing smells of freshly grilled burgers and fries riding on the sheer greasiness that put a sticky film on every vinyl booth and table. And those were making his stomach clench, and his mouth start to water.

It had been too long since he'd eaten anything. Since lunch the day before. The clock on the wall here showed eleven o'clock, which meant it was one in the morning back home. No wonder he was starving. And he'd eaten in diners when he was in college. To no ill effects. Of course, he'd been younger.

He looked around the still empty diner, hoping that the very angry man behind the counter was not the only person here, hoping that a waitress—or, for a choice, his son—would materialize somewhere, out of the blue.

Not that he had any wish to see Tom. Not really. He had no idea what he would tell the boy, or what the boy's reaction to him would be. Their last parting had been far less than amicable. But if he saw Tom and convinced the stupid boy to give back whatever it was to the dragons—and what kind of an idiot did you need to be to steal from organized criminals?—then he could go back home on the early morning flight. And wash his hands of the boy. And resume his lonely life. Lonely, yes, but at least untroubled by the stream of acts of self-destruction that was Tom's way of living.

He looked around enough, and no one came, and rather than order from the guy behind the counter, Edward thought he would leave. Leave now. The man would probably curse him, as he left, but it was obvious Tom wasn't here. And if Tom was the reason the man behind the counter was so furious, then what would happen if Edward mentioned Tom?

He'd started rising when a couple came in through a side door that seemed to lead to another part of the diner—the covered porch he'd seen from the outside. He first thought of them as a couple—tall, blond man and slightly smaller girl, with multicolored hair. But then he realized the girl was wearing an apron with the logo of the diner, and that the blond man was just following her. In fact, he headed for the door as the girl rushed toward Edward.

"Hi," she said, and smiled. "My name is Kyrie. What can I get for you?"

He thought of asking her for Tom right away, but . . . no. He was hungry, anyway. "I'll have coffee," he said. "And your souvlaki platter, and one of the large Greek salads."

"What dressing on your salad?" she asked.

"Ranch is fine," he said.

She nodded, and went over to the counter. He watched her, from behind as she went. She was quite an attractive girl, probably in her early twenties, with a trim body, hair dyed in an elaborate pattern, and the sort of face that reminded him that America was supposed to be a melting pot. Seen in a certain light, he supposed she could be Greek, or perhaps Italian, or maybe even Native American. . . . Or, he admitted, some other, far more exotic combination. He wondered what the truth was. He also wondered if anything was going on with her and Tom and if that was what had the cook's nose out of joint.

The girl came back in a moment, set a cup in front of him, and put down a container of sugar and another with creamers. She filled the cup and he—ignoring the sugar and the creamers—took a sip.

His surprise at the quality of the coffee must have shown, in raised eyebrows or some change in expression, because the girl smiled at him. And, oh, she had dimples. He grinned back. She wasn't that much younger than him, really, and besides, he went out with girls her age every other week. But was she involved with Tom? Or how did she feel about Tom? He had to ask about Tom, but was it going to ruin everything?

"Excuse me?" he said, before she could turn away. "I don't suppose I could ask you a question?"

She tensed. He saw her tense, as she turned around, even if her face didn't show anything as she said, "Yes?"

"I'm sorry to bother you," he said. "But does Thomas Ormson work here?"

For a moment her face stayed absolutely frozen, and he thought she was going to tell him to go to hell or something. Instead, she put a hand on the table, and it trembled. Oh, no. What was going on here? Was she Tom's girlfriend.

"I thought you looked like him," she said. "But I thought . . ." She swallowed and didn't say what she thought.

"I'm his father," Edward said, low enough that the gorilla behind at the grill wouldn't hear him. "My name is Edward Ormson. Do you know where he is?"

She opened her mouth.

"Kyrie," the gorilla said. And she looked around, as if wakening. People had come in while they were talking, and there were five tables occupied. And she was alone. Also, his dinner was now sitting on the counter, ready. She went to get it.

"I get off at five," she told him. "It might be easier to talk then."

It was night from hell. Or at least night from next door to hell. Nothing bad happened. Kyrie even managed— despite her mounting exhaustion—to not drop any trays full of plates, and not to mix up any orders.

But Tom hadn't shown up. She was of two minds about this. Part of her wanted him to show up. She wanted to . . . Well, for one his father had been at the Athens, and his father was asking about him. That certainly didn't seem like the kind of father who had thrown his son out of the house at sixteen. Then again, she thought—who knew what Tom had done, and how much he could goad people beyond their natural limits?

His father had left after half an hour, and she hadn't given it much thought, until, as she was getting ready to leave, she saw him waiting by the door, looking very proper in his expensive-looking, if somewhat rumpled, business suit.

She nodded to him, and went toward the counter, to tell Frank she was leaving. He glared at her, which was not really a surprise, since he'd been glaring at her—and to be honest at everyone else—all night. Then he motioned with his head toward Tom's father. "Another one?"

She sighed. "I have no idea what you're talking about. He's just . . ." She stopped short of telling Frank this was Tom's father. She wasn't even sure why. Just she didn't want the jokes following on Tom being her boyfriend and his father supposedly visiting her. "He just wants to ask me something," she said.

And anyway, she thought, as she walked toward Mr. Ormson, if Frank couldn't see the resemblance between Tom and his father—same pale skin, same dark hair, same blue eyes—then he didn't want to see it.

They stepped outside the diner, and the morning was lovely, just warm enough to promise heat later at midday, but not warm enough to actually be uncomfortable. Kyrie took a deep breath of the air that seemed much cleaner than it would be later on in the day when Fairfax became clogged with bumper-to-bumper traffic. "I don't know where Tom is," she told his father, quickly. "I saw him last about twelve hours ago. He left with a friend. I don't know where he is. I can give you his address if you want."

"I have his address," his father said. "His landlady said that he worked at the Athens and that she thought his girlfriend worked there too. You wouldn't—"

Kyrie felt herself blush. "No. He doesn't have a girlfriend, that I know." There was no point explaining, and yet she could tell he was looking attentively at her, as though trying to read her expression. Or most probably wondering why she was blushing. Damn her blush, really. For a woman who could and did tan easily enough, she had the most inconvenient blushes. And it really didn't mean anything, except annoyance at Frank thinking she was Tom's girlfriend.

"Can we go somewhere and talk?" Mr. Ormson asked, leaning slightly forward, as if eager to have her answer.

Kyrie shook her head. Her feet hurt, and she felt sticky all over, as she usually did when she'd been working long hours at the Athens. And this time she'd worked ten hours. "I really don't think I have anything else to tell you," she said. "I only know Tom from work." And why was her mind, unbidden, giving her images of his coming out of the shower, his hair still dripping. He'd been perfectly dressed too. Well, almost perfectly. One thing her house didn't have any of was male underwear. "And I really don't know where he could have gone. If you go where he lives, and talk to his downstairs neighbor. I think his name is Keith. He might know where Tom went from there."

"Oh, but I think you might know more without realizing it," he said, and in response to what she was sure was a very annoyed frown, he said, "I'm not underestimating your intelligence, it is just that I know people absorb things about other people, without meaning to. And you might know something about Tom, something that will give me a clue." He hesitated a long time, as if he were not sure a clue to exactly what. "A clue to where to find him."

Kyrie was sure, too, that this was not what he had meant to say. She looked up—Tom's father was considerably taller than him—at Mr. Ormson's chiseled profile, and she wondered what he was trying to find a clue to exactly, and why he'd come looking for his son these many years later. Or had he looked for Tom before? Had Tom refused to see him? Perhaps that was what he wanted a clue for? A clue as to why his son would reject him? Kyrie shouldn't be getting involved with this. She really shouldn't.

"Just a cup of coffee," he said, and looked wildly around, lighting at last at a coffee shop sign a couple of blocks away, the edge of the advance of gentrification of downtown Goldport. "I won't keep you long, I promise. I imagine you must be very tired."

"Yes, but—"

"Please," the man said. "Tom is my only son. If there's any chance I can . . . find him."

Again she had a feeling that what he had been about to say was not "find" but something else—persuade? Reach?

"All right," she said, setting off toward the coffee shop. "But just one cup of coffee." She had to admit to herself at least half the reason for allowing him that one cup of coffee was that she wanted to know what was happening—exactly what was wrong—between those two. Had Tom told her the truth about being thrown out of the house? Or had he run away? What had his father thought of the whole thing? Did his father even know that Tom was a shifter? And did he love him despite that?

Kyrie didn't have any personal interest in the matter, of course. Well, Tom's father seemed nice enough. Possibly too nice to be saddled with Tom as a child. But, really, ultimately, what drove her to walk those blocks to the coffee shop, what convinced her to sit across from him at the little, tottering table, amid the decor that tried too hard to be urban and sophisticated, was curiosity.

She had grown up with many families, but none of them hers. And none of those families had ever shown her much of the tangled feelings between close blood relatives. All she had of it was the understanding drawn from books and movies. She saw family and familial love through a mirror darkly.

So she went with Edward Ormson, and sat at the little table across from him, holding a cappuccino that she knew would have way too much milk, and watching the man sip his espresso grande, or very tall or whatever they were calling the huge cups these days.

"How long has Tom been working at the Athens?" Mr. Ormson asked.

"Six months," Kyrie said. Was everyone going to ask her this question? If Mr. Ormson's next question was about the murders three months ago, she was going to scream.

But he nodded. "And he's . . . he's a good worker?"

"He's responsible," Kyrie said, surprising herself with saying it. "And competent. He always shows up or calls if he's ill. This is the first night he missed work completely." And having said the words, she wondered where he was, what he was doing. She frowned at her cup of foam with very little coffee. She had as good as thrown him out. Of course, he deserved it. Or did he?

Rafiel's talk of an insect-origin powder, his talk of eggs in the wounds of the victim . . . Something was not right, and it seemed certain that high or not, Tom had been fighting something—some creature, possibly the same that had committed murder in the parking lot, just a day ago. But he had been high. And he should not have been high. He should have been more careful in her house.

Somehow this moral high ground was not as satisfying as it should be. She realized that Mr. Ormson was looking attentively at her, and she managed a smile at him, her professional smile that meant very little but seemed to make people feel at ease. "He was better than most servers we get at the Athens."

"Was?" Mr. Ormson said. His blue eyes, so much like Tom's, were filled with a cooly evaluating look that was nothing like Tom's at all.

She shook her head. "He didn't show up today. I'm assuming he gave up the job. I don't know . . ."

But Mr. Ormson continued looking at her, cooly appraising. "Do you . . . I don't quite know how to ask this question, but I need to—do you have any idea if my son might be involved in illegal activities?"

Oh, Lord, the drugs. Yes, she was fairly sure that Tom was involved in illegal activities. But talking about it to this stranger felt like a violation of trust. Stupid to feel that way, she told herself. Stupid. And ridiculous.

He'd broken confidence with her. He'd been a guest in her house and behaved with utter disregard, with utter—

But she thought of the food left on her shelf. She had expected him to eat it all. She wouldn't have held it against him if he had eaten it all. It must have taken a lot of willpower to control himself and not eat all the protein he could. She, herself, and Rafiel too, had binged shamelessly. But Tom hadn't. And if he'd given in to the drugs later, perhaps he hadn't realized what he was doing? Or perhaps he had but had no other choice?

She looked at Mr. Ormson staring at her. No. Tom was, if nothing else, another shifter, a member of this makeshift family in which she'd ended up plunged suddenly. She owed him that much loyalty, if nothing else. Even if he were really guilty of murder; even if she ended up having to fight him or take him out—he was one of hers. And Mr. Ormson, even if his looks were testimony of a genetic relationship to Tom, was not one of them.

She raised her eyebrows at Mr. Ormson, and he laughed, as if she'd said something very funny. Only the laughter echoed bitter and hollow at the edge of it. "Ah. I see," he said, though she clearly did not. "Let me tell you what I know of my son. Let me explain."

"You don't need—"

"No, please let me, then perhaps you'll understand better what I mean, and that I'm not merely fishing for something that will allow me to put my son away or something equally . . . drastic.

"Tom was never an easy child. No, perhaps I lie there. He was a happy baby, chubby and contented. At least, we had a nanny, but when I was home and the nanny brought him to me, he was usually asleep and sometimes he . . . woke up and looked at me, and smiled." He made a face, worried, as if trying to figure out, now, what those smiles might have meant, and suspecting them of some deeper and possibly bad meaning. "But then he started walking. And he started speaking. The first word he learned was no. And he said no very often over the next fourteen or fifteen years. His teachers told us there was nothing wrong with his mind, but his grades were dismal."

He frowned again and took a quick sip of his espresso, as if it could control the flow of words. "I was going to say the first call from the police station, saying he'd been arrested was a shock, but that isn't true. From nursery school onward, we got calls, from Tom's teachers and supervisors. He'd stolen something. Or he'd broken something. His language violated all the rules of every school that ever took children. He had . . . I think they call it appositional deviational disorder. He couldn't obey and he wouldn't submit to any authority."

Ormson's lips compressed into a bitter line. "By the time he became officially a teenager, I'd run out of options. Counselors and boot camps, and whatever I thought might straighten him out, just made him more violent, more unruly. His mother had left by then. She— I think she couldn't understand him. I couldn't understand him, either, but I had my work. She . . . she found someone else and moved to Florida, as far as she could from us and still remain on the East Coast. And Tom and I settled into a routine. As long as he kept his . . . infractions beneath a certain threshold, I could get him out of jail the same day, and no harm done. I thought . . . I thought he would grow out of it."

Kyrie finished her coffee. For some reason, the story was making her feel sorry for Tom. Oh, it was foolish. It was borderline suicidal to feel sorry for someone like Tom. But in his father's descriptions—it seemed to her, from kids she had known in foster care—she read a desperate desire of Tom's to be seen, to be noticed, to be acknowledged. Oh, she didn't think it could all have been solved with a nice talk by the fire. Life tended not to behave like a Disney special, so much more the pity. She suspected that by the time that Tom had learned to walk, learned to say that all-vital *no*, the problem was already intractable. But nonetheless it was possible to feel sorry for the man he might have been.

"There was joyriding," Ormson said. "And drugs. And one or two cases of lewd acts in semipublic places."

Was he watching her face to see if she was shocked? The only thing Tom hadn't told her about was the lewd acts, and she wondered how much of those was showing up naked in public places—something neither he, nor she, could control.

"So." He leaned back. "You can't possibly fear to let me know something he's done. You see, I know."

She inclined her head, in a gesture that might have been a yes, or just curiosity.

He smiled, a tight-lipped smile. "I see," he said. "Well, then I'll ask it outright. Do you have any reason to think my son did something . . . stole something from a . . . an organized crime group?"

She must have trembled, without meaning to. The triad, the three exceedingly dumb dragons at the diner today, all came to her mind, and she must have trembled as she thought about it. She immediately calmed herself down, and forced herself to relax, but there was that look of understanding on Ormson's face.

"You don't have to answer that, but you do have to answer me this. It's very important. Do you know where he's hidden it? The Pearl?"

The Pearl. Ormson wanted the same pearl the Chinese dragons had spoken of. How could he know about it? Clearly Tom hadn't told him about it. He hadn't even seen Tom and wasn't sure where Tom might be. So . . .

She looked at him, and in his intense expression read the same eagerness of the three dragons looking at Tom the night before. The Pearl, they had said. And they'd asked where he hid it.

On her feet, she pushed the chair forward. She remembered to take the cup with her, which was a little strange, in retrospect, and put it on the tray near the other dirty cups.

She headed toward the door at a good clip and got there before Mr. Ormson seemed to realize it, before he got up, before he came after her, with a haste that made everyone in the coffee shop turn to stare at them.

Kyrie was aware of their scrutiny as she ran out, into the still deserted early morning street. She heard him come after her, almost immediately, heard him call, "Ms. Smith. Kyrie. Please, I must explain."

But all she could think was that he—was he really Tom's father?—was working for the dragons. He had no more concern or care for Tom than he did for her. They were shifters, they were alone. They must look after each other.

She ran full tilt back to the Athens, and heard him run behind her, also at full clip. But she was much younger than him, and she ran faster, and was well ahead of him by the time she reached the Athens and headed for the parking lot.

It was only in the parking lot that she realized she hadn't parked there that day. And that was the least of her worries.

Tom was tired. At just that moment, he wasn't absolutely sure how the dragon felt. Though he was still the dragon.

He could feel the dragon's wings, suspended between the earth and the sky, the dragon's front legs tucked upward in flight position, the dragon's tail, serving as a rudder to direct the pattern of flight. But a part of him, a core, looking out through the dragon's eyes, and trying—desperately trying to find a populated place to land—was wholly human, wholly Tom. And tired.

He had to stop soon, he thought as the dragon flew above the spectacular painted desert, the brightly layered mesas of New Mexico. But New Mexico was empty. That was what had made it so attractive. It was a place he could hide, far from human contact. But he needed some humans. He was going to need food and sleep, soon. And he did not want to hunt for wild rabbits, eat them raw and fall asleep on the hard-packed desert dirt.

The dragon's eyes, more far-seeing than any human's, followed a highway and following the highway, a conglomerate of buildings. It wasn't very big. Nothing to compare to the Colorado cities Tom had left behind. It wasn't even as big as Goldport.

Memories from drifting west, through parts of New Mexico, months ago, brought up the name Las Vegas, New Mexico. One of those towns forever being confused with a better known town of the same name in a different state. It was the *only* city large enough to have a hotel in the area within reach of his flying.

He aimed for it and flew in its direction, determinedly, feeling the weight of the backpack reassuring on the dragon's ankle. He had money in there. And clothes. He'd land somewhere outside town, make himself decent for human contact, then slip into town and stop at some truck stop—he seemed to remember an awful lot of them in Las Vegas—for breakfast. And then find a cheap motel room to crash in. Anything, really, so long as it didn't rent by the hour. He wanted to sleep in peace and quiet.

And then he could start looking for something more permanent, and thinking of a way to survive. Some place to hide out for a few months, till the triad either found the Pearl on their own or forgot about him.

And then . . . He had a fleeting thought he could go back to Kyrie then, and maybe . . . But no. That avenue was closed and he knew it.

The human brain in control of the dragon body, guided himself down and down and down, to land between two mesas, on rocky ground, where no one would see him.

He shifted, an effort even greater than shifting into dragon had been the evening before. When it was done, he was weak and pale and trembling, standing naked in between the two rock spires, holding onto the handle of the backpack.

How he managed to get dressed, he didn't know. It involved a lot of starts and stops. Even the times he'd run away from other cities, from other states, he'd never made himself fly eight hours straight, through the night.

Las Vegas could not be more than a mile away. He'd gauged it well when he'd landed. He didn't want to land so close to the populated area that someone would see him shifting. And he was right by the only road into town coming from the direction of Goldport.

He put his backpack on and summoned strength from determination. He must make it to town. It was the only way he was going to get eggs and bacon and a cup of coffee. He could almost taste the cup of coffee. Not to mention the orange juice. Hell, anything wet would do.

With the dry desert air stinging his nostrils and his parched throat, he headed toward Las Vegas.

❖   ❖   ❖

That she'd gone to the parking lot instead of up front where she'd parked her car was the least of Kyrie's worries because in the parking lot there was . . . She swallowed hard, trying to comprehend it and unable to. They were . . .

They were green and huge and glittering like jewels in the full light of day. And they were some sort of Amazonian beetle. At least, Kyrie remembered, vaguely, having seen much smaller versions of these creatures at the Natural History Museum in Denver, pinned solidly through their middle, against a background of black velvet. In a glass case.

But those were small. And dead. The legend had said something about them being used for jewelry, and she could kind of see that, from the way the green carapaces glowed with blue highlights, in the light of the morning.

It would be five-fifteen, she thought, or possibly five-thirty, and soon there would be people coming to breakfast at the Athens, and yet in the parking lot of the building, there were two giant . . . insects dragging something.

She couldn't even look at the something. She didn't need to look at the something. She could smell the symphony of blood sharp and clear as day from where she was standing.

Somewhere in the back of her mind, a steady and very worried voice was intoning, *oh crap, oh crap, oh crap,* almost in the tone of someone praying.

The little voice was prescient. Or more in tune than Kyrie's body and the rest of Kyrie's mind, which stood, amazed and immobilized, staring at the insects.

She didn't know when they first saw her—where were the eyes in those things?—but she noticed a little start and their leaning into each other, communicating—with what?

antennae?—somehow, and then they turned. They advanced on her.

At this moment the little voice that had been intoning *oh crap* grabbed the rest of Kyrie. It turned her around. It sent her running, in broad strides, around the Athens and to her car. She had a vague impression of people inside the diner turning to look at her as she ran by at full speed. Would the beetles follow? Out here, up front? In front of everyone?

They wouldn't if they were shifters, but what if they weren't?

What if, she thought, as she put her hand in through the open window to release the latch, pulled the door open, and, without pause, dove headlong into her car, *they're the result of some nuclear accident? Or some exterminator's bad dream?*

She stuck the key in the ignition, started the car, and headed down the street. It wasn't until she was headed toward home, speeding as much as she dared in this zone, that she realized her moment of frozen panic couldn't have taken much more than a few seconds. It seemed much longer, subjectively, but as she pulled away from the curb, in her car, she saw Edward Ormson on the sidewalk, hands on sides, slightly bent over, in the position of someone who's run too fast, too far.

He had just—almost caught up with her. As for the beetles, they were nowhere in sight. Had she imagined them? She wasn't about to drive around the back of the Athens to find out.

❖   ❖   ❖

Edward Ormson stared at the girl, his mouth hanging open in wonder.

She'd run away from him. She'd looked at him as if he were something profoundly disgusting, and then she'd left without warning. This was not something that happened to him normally, when he was trying to ask someone questions.

Why had she run? What had he said that was so terrible?

Confused, he walked back up in the direction of the coffee shop, where the area was much better. His head ached and he felt very tired. Dragon-lagged, he thought. Whatever magic the dragon had used to get here had left Edward feeling as if he'd been beaten.

So . . . this avenue to find Tom hadn't worked. And he needed to get back to New York as soon as possible. He'd best find a place where he could call his secretary again and get her to call around and ask more questions, find someone who might know where Tom was.

It was eight a.m. in New York and the woman would probably be in the office.

He considered going into the coffee shop, but they'd seen the girl run away from him. At the very least he'd get pitying stares. At worst, they would think he was some sort of pervert and had said something to her that was over the line.

Shaking his head—he still couldn't understand why she had run—he walked past the coffee shop. And came to a sort of little park in the middle of the sidewalk. He sat down on the park bench set in the four feet of lawn amid three dispirited trees.

Tom walked in the shadow as much as he could. Partly because he was thirsty and partly because he realized a guy like him, in black leather, carrying a kid's backpack had to look incongruous. He was holding it by the strap, dangling it from his hand, instead of carrying it on his back.

He hoped anyone seeing him would think he was carrying it for a son or little brother and give it no thought. But you never knew. And he didn't want people to remember his coming through here. He didn't want the triad to be able to find him.

Just before he got to town—he couldn't see it, but he could smell it, a tinge of food and car exhaust in his nostrils—he saw a couple of cars abandoned. Something about the cars tickled his memory, but he couldn't quite say what. Well, at least one of them looked awfully familiar. But it was just a Kia something or other, one of those economy cars that tried to look like SUVs and rarely managed more than looking like a toy patterned on an SUV.

It wasn't Kyrie's car. That was white too, but much smaller. Besides, this one had a driver's side window, Tom thought, and felt very guilty he hadn't sent her the money to have that repaired.

He'd been so furious last night, so furious because she'd failed to live up to his high standards. *His* high standards at that. It took some nerve. Now, he felt mostly tired and vaguely upset at himself, as if he had let himself down.

Fine. He'd eat something, he thought, as he saw, in the distance, the outskirts of town—represented by what looked like an abandoned gas station. He'd eat something, he'd sleep, and then he'd think this whole thing over. If by then he still thought he had done Kyrie an injustice or somehow failed to live up to what should—*yes, indeed, by damn*—be his high standards, he would take as much of the money as he dared and mail it back to Kyrie before he vanished from her life.

He couldn't even tell why he wanted to deal straight with her. It wasn't because she was a shifter. He wasn't feeling particularly charitable toward Mr. Golden Eye Lion police officer. And it wasn't because they'd worked together all this time—because though he'd enjoyed working at the Athens, Kyrie had always looked at him as if he were slightly below subhuman. And it wasn't his attraction for her, because he'd already decided that he had not a snowball's chance in hell.

And then he realized it was how she'd treated him, when she had found him standing over that body. He'd been deranged. He'd been in dragon form. But she hadn't even hesitated. And she didn't even like him. He knew that. But she'd grabbed him, and helped him hide the evidence of his involvement in anything back there.

She'd been there when he needed her the most. Whether she'd disappointed him by keeping funny sugar around or not, she didn't deserve for him to leave her with a huge bill in car repairs. Okay—so that was that. He'd send her some money this evening, send her more when he settled some place and found a job.

The decision put a spring in his step, and he was almost walking normally when he reached the gas station. Which was too bad. Had he been dragging along the road and looking all around in despondency and depression, he might have noticed something about the shadows, something about movement.

As it was, he walked by the squat brick building without a second glance. And didn't know anything was wrong until he felt the impact of something hard on the back of his head. And then he had no time to think about it, as darkness closed around him.

Kyrie was rattled. She didn't know if she had dreamed the beetles, out of being so tired, out of Rafiel's report on there being insect matter in and around the corpse last night.

Normally, Kyrie was very sure of her perceptions. She'd had to trust in them and them alone, as often those who were supposed to look after her or be in charge of her hadn't been very trustworthy at all.

But now? Now she wasn't sure of anything. The last two days had been a carnival of weirdness, a whirling of the very strange. Driving her car along familiar streets and around the castle just before her neighborhood, she thought she wouldn't be at all surprised to wake up in her bed, suddenly, and find that all this, from the moment she'd seen Tom as a dragon, had been a crazy dream. Although if that were true, then her subconscious harbored some very weird thoughts about Tom.

She pulled up at her house, and opened the front door, half expecting to find her house as ransacked as Tom's apartment. But everything inside looked normal and was in its usual place. She locked the door, picked up the mail that the carrier had pushed through the mail slot on the door. Junk, junk, and bills. Which seemed to be the modern corollary of death and taxes.

She went all the way to the kitchen, and saw her chair still under the door to the back porch. Had it really all happened? Had the little porch, which had been her main reason for renting this house, truly been destroyed?

She pulled the chair away, unlocked the door and looked at the broken windows, the glass on the carpet, the . . . mess. Then she turned on the light and walked into the room.

Rafiel had said that there was green powder on this carpet, like there was green powder on yesterday's corpse. She hadn't noticed. But now, by the light of dawn and the overhead light, she could see it—glistening on the carpet. It was even more visible because it must have rained sometime during the night when she wasn't paying attention to the outside—and the rain had puddled it into little rings and patterns on the beige carpet.

She wondered what it all meant, but couldn't even think straight. And she wasn't about to call Rafiel and ask him. Not right now, she wasn't.

Instead, she retreated to the kitchen, locked the door, and slipped the chair underneath. She wished the door were somewhat stronger than the hollow-core, Seventies vintage door it appeared to be. But it couldn't be helped. She was certainly not going to fashion a new door before going to bed. And she needed to go to bed.

She took a hurried shower, with torrents of hot water, and felt as if the heat and the massage on her sore muscles were reviving her. Coming out and drying her hair, she noted that Tom had hung up his towel very neatly on the hook at the back of the door. For some reason she'd expected it tossed on the floor.

As soon as she went into the bedroom, the phone rang. It was a cheap, corded affair and it was plugged in there because it was the only phone plug in the entire house. Possibly because the entire house was not hard to cross in twenty hurried steps.

Normally the only calls she got—at least since she'd got on the telemarketers do-not-call-list—were from Frank, asking if she wanted to come in and work extra hours. And if this were Frank right now, he could go to hell. There was no way Kyrie was about to turn around and go work another shift. Not with those beetles in the parking lot, and she didn't even care whether they were real or a product of her imagination.

But the voice on the other end of the phone wasn't Frank's. It was a voice that purred with masculine self-assurance.

"Kyrie?" it said, though she didn't remember giving Rafiel permission to call her by her given name.

"Yes."

"I have information on the victim."

So, he was going to call her every time he had information? But she bit her tongue and said, "Yes?" because she knew that anything else could start a debate or an argument and that would mean talking on the phone longer and staying awake longer.

"He was Bill Johnson. A roofer by trade. And apparently a coyote in his shifter form."

"A . . . ?" How had Rafiel found that out? It wasn't exactly the sort of thing you could ask people about? Or . . .

"His wife had pictures."

"Pardon me?" Kyrie asked finding this, in some way, stranger than giant beetles in the parking lot of the Athens.

"His wife had pictures of him as a coyote. Lovely lady, I would judge about ten years older than him but looking and acting much older. A grandma type. She pulled out pictures, to show us, of what her husband looked like in his coyote form. She said he got the shape-shifting ability from his Native American ancestors and that he was, like their coyote of legend, a bit of a trickster. And then she said— "

"Showed *us* pictures?" Kyrie asked, as her mouth caught up with her brain in horrified wonder.

"Oh yes. She called him in to missing persons and Officer Bob and I and our one female officer, Cindy, all went along to take her statement and see if she had any pictures of the deceased. Because if it wasn't him, we didn't want to put her through identifying the body. Cindy came along on the principle that the lady might need a female shoulder to cry on."

"And?"

"And she took out the pictures and showed them to us. And the other two looked at each other and then at me as though they thought the poor lady was totally out of her mind with shock and all that. Which she probably was, of course. But still . . ."

"But still, he was a coyote. And she knew. And didn't mind."

"Mind? She was positively gleeful. Very sorry none of their six children inherited the characteristic."

"Children." Kyrie was beyond astonishment. That a shifter could secure all these things that she thought were out of her reach because she was a shifter felt absolutely baffling.

"They live in Arizona," Rafiel said. "Where Bill and his wife lived till about a year ago, when they drove through town and stopped at the Athens for breakfast and all of a sudden realized they'd never felt so at home anywhere. So they decided to sell the place in Arizona and buy a house here. Ever since then, Bill went into the Athens for his morning breakfast after roaming the neighborhood as a coyote."

"Well, at least no one would notice a coyote. Not in Colorado."

"Right. Lions and panthers are something else."

"And dragons."

"Yes."

She could hear him take a deep breath.

"So, we know that the victim was definitely a shifter."

Shifter. Victim. The back of the Athens. The beetles. Kyrie desperately wanted to go to bed, but she felt she should tell Rafiel. After all, he was a police officer. He would know what to do about it, right?

"There is more," she said.

"More about the victim?"

"More . . . another victim."

"What?"

"I was . . . I forgot I parked my car up front," she said. "Because of the broken window. So I went into the parking lot and there were . . . They were beetles. That type of shiny rain forest-type beetle that they make jewelry out of?"

"Someone made jewelry out of beetles?"

"No. It would take a very big person to wear those as jewelry. They were six or seven feet long and at least five feet across, and shiny . . ."

"Are you sure you didn't dream this?"

"No, I absolutely am not sure. But I think they were there. They were huge and green blue and they were dragging something. A corpse. I think it was a corpse because I could smell the blood."

"A corpse? In the parking lot of the Athens? Another corpse?"

"I didn't see it. It was just something—a bundle—they were carrying. And it smelled like blood."

"Are you sure this is not a dream you were having when I woke you up with my phone call?"

"Quite." Kyrie looked toward her still made bed. "Very much so. I haven't gone to bed yet."

"Fine," he sounded, for some reason exasperated. "Fine. This is just fine. I'll go to the Athens and check."

"Take . . . something. They might be dangerous."

"Oh, I wouldn't worry," he said, his voice dripping with sarcasm. "I have my regulation bug spray can."

She had a feeling he didn't believe her, and she couldn't really blame him because she wasn't a hundred percent sure she believed herself. "Right," she said. "And, oh, remember you wanted to know about the dust on the floor of my porch. There is dust. It's bright green."

"Lovely," he said. "I'll be there. Right after I check the parking lot of the Athens."

Tom hurt. That was his first realization, his first awareness that he was alive. The back of his head hurt like someone had tried to saw it open, and the pain radiated around the side of his head and it seemed to him as though it made his teeth vibrate. An effect not improved by a twisted rag, which was inserted between his teeth and tied viciously tight behind his head. His legs and arms were tied too, he realized, as he squirmed around, trying to get into a better position. It felt like there was a band of something around his knees, and one around his ankles. Very tightly tied.

With his eyes closed, trying to remember where he was and why, he smelled old car oil and dust and the mildew of long-unoccupied places. His face rested on concrete, but part of it felt slick.

The gas station. He must be in the gas station he was passing when . . . When someone had hit him on the back of the head. So. Fine. Shaking, he opened his eyes a sliver. And confirmed that he was lying in a vast space, on a concrete floor irregularly stained with oil or other car fluids. This must have been a service station at some point. Light was dim, coming through glass squares atop huge, closed doors that took up the front of the building.

He looked around, but his eyes felt as if they couldn't quite focus. And he wondered if he'd been attacked by some random local hooligans, who had felt an irresistible craving for his leather jacket and the kid's dragon backpack, which no longer appeared to be anywhere near. Or if it was the triad again.

Through the fogs of his mind, he remembered that the white car parked by the road side had been the same make and model as the one that had turned around while he was shifting before. Had they seen him? Had they followed him? Along the highway? If they'd seen him follow the highway, it wouldn't be hard to calculate that he would stop in Las Vegas, New Mexico. It wouldn't have been hard to figure out, either, that he'd land and shift some distance from town.

It couldn't have been hard to find a place to lay in ambush for him.

In the next minute, there was a sound of high censure, in some form of Chinese. Oh, bloody hell. And then, out of a darker corner of the warehouse they came, all three of them. Tom had run into them a couple of times, before the time they'd ambushed him in his apartment.

He'd privately nicknamed them Crest Dragon, Two Dragons, and The Other One. And his opinion that their intelligence and their viciousness were inversely proportional did nothing to make him feel better right now. The only good thing, he thought, as they advanced, speaking fast Chinese at him as though he should understand it, was that they were in human form and not dragons.

As usual Crest Dragon—in his human form a young man with hair so well groomed Tom had wondered if it was a wig—took the lead, walking in front of the other two, who flanked him, left and right. Crest Dragon was waving the backpack around, and shouting something in Chinese.

Truth was, even without having any idea what the complaints in Chinese were, Tom understood the gist of the matter completely. And the gist of the matter was that the Pearl of Heaven hadn't been in the backpack.

Exactly what kind of an idiot did they think he was? He glared at them. And how stupid were they, really? Did they think they would not feel . . . it, if it were in that backpack? Tom remembered holding it, remembered the feeling of power and strength and calm and sanity flowing from it. He could feel it across miles, and he was sure so would they be able to, if he hadn't taken extraordinary precautions in hiding it. And they'd thought he'd carry it in a backpack?

He glared at them, which was harder to do than it should be, because his eyes seemed to want to focus in different directions. How hard had they hit him on the head? And did they realize how hungry he was?

Crest Dragon came closer, waving his arms in theatrical exasperation. Then he flung the backpack—with force—across the building, grabbed Tom by the front of the T-shirt and, lifting him off the ground, punched him hard in the face.

Tom screamed. The pain radiated from his nose to match the pain on the back of his head, but sharper and sudden, edged around with blood and a feeling that his nose had broken. His vision blurred. If not for the rag in his mouth, he'd have bit his tongue.

Another punch came, immediately after. And he screamed again. He tasted blood and didn't know if it was running from the back of his nose, or from his mouth. And it didn't matter. Pain after pain came. He was vaguely aware of being kicked, punched, and hit with something— he wasn't sure what.

On the floor, curling into a tight ball, he endured each sharp pain as it came, and screamed as loud as he could. In the back of his mind, words ran, words so completely calm and composed that he couldn't think they were his. But the thoughts couldn't have belonged to anyone else. And they made sense.

One was: *Scream. Stoicism is for fools.* Another, just as sudden, as complete, was: *Only idiots inflict pain for pain's sake.* And the third, very clear, very sharp, was: *I could shift. I could eat them.*

It was the third thought that caused him to scream louder than the pain. And the word he would scream, if his mouth hadn't been so firmly gagged, would have been, "No."

Oh, he could shift. He could undoubtedly shift. And the binds on his limbs would break away with the force of the shifting, the greater strength and size of the dragon. Of that he had no doubt.

It was even possible that he could defeat all three of them, even if they too shifted. They were not swift of mind and they always had trouble coordinating attacks. But—and this was a huge but—he wasn't absolutely sure he could prevail. Not as tired and weak as he felt.

And then, worse of all, the dragon was very hungry. Starving. Ravenous. The dragon wanted food. Protein. And Tom didn't think he could live with himself if he succeeded in eating another human being. Or even one of these three fools.

A foot—he thought—crashed against his face. It felt like his forehead exploded. Blood flowed down, making him close his eyes.

He screamed "No," as much at the dragon within as at the pain.

Kyrie had just fallen asleep when she heard something. At first it was a little sound. Like . . . something scraping.

The sound, in itself almost imperceptible, intruded into her dreams, where she dreamed of mice, nibbling on cardboard. In her dream, she was in the back hallway of the Athens, and she opened the back door to the parking lot to find thousands of mice nibbling on large piles of cardboard boxes.

As she stood there, paralyzed, the nibbling grew louder, and louder, and then the mice swarmed all over her, thousands of little paws all over her, insinuating themselves under her nightshirt, crawling up her belly, tangling in her hair.

She woke up and sat up in bed. No mice. But she'd been sleeping uncovered, on top of the bed, and there was a breeze coming in around the door to the bedroom, blowing with enough force to ruffle her nightshirt and give her silly dreams.

Kyrie looked at the clock on her dresser. Seven a.m. She should be asleep. She still had time to sleep. Turning her pillow over, she lay back down. And realized she could still hear the sound of mice nibbling on cardboard. She blinked. She was awake. She was sure of that. So why were mice . . . ?

And why did it feel like her head swam? She felt dizzy, as if she were . . . anaesthetized? Drugged? Slow?

She looked at the shaft of light coming from the little window above her bed. Was that green powder dancing in the light? Was she dreaming it? And she still felt dizzy, as if her head wasn't quite attached to her body.

Getting out of bed, as silently as she could manage, she opened her bedroom door. The living room was empty and everything looked undisturbed. Definitely no mice. But she could still hear the crunching, shredding sounds from . . . the kitchen.

Even more cautiously, feeling pretty stupid for moving around her own house as if it were some sort of secret dungeon, she crept down the hallway toward the kitchen. But before she got there, the green glimmer in the air became obvious. It was no more than a glimmer, she thought, a soft shine, like . . . a cloud of green dust. Green dust in the air. Green dust on the corpses. Green dust covering her back porch the day that Tom claimed he had been attacked by dragons.

And she was light-headed and growing dizzy. As if she were being doped.

Had they been dragons? Rafiel had said the powder was of insect origin, but was it? They didn't even know what dragons were—exactly. Other than mythical beasts, of course. And she remembered the beetles in the parking lot of the Athens. It could be those.

She stood there, for a moment, in the hallway of her own house, feeling her head swim. She stared at the green dust, listening to what sounded like an attempt to break through the door—if the thing trying to break through were armed with claws and pincers.

Only, the attempt couldn't be very serious, could it? It was a hollow-core door. How hard could it be to break it down? No, the purpose was to put the green powder into the house first, wasn't it? And why would you do that?

She thought of the victim in the parking lot of the Athens, covered in the green powder. And then she thought of Tom and Keith, clearly high as kites.

Yes, Tom had seemed to do most of the damage she'd found in the sunroom. Yes, their response to the attack hadn't been the most effective. But they had been high as kites. What if they had been high as kites because of the green dust?

What if it that was what was causing her head to swim?

In a moment, she was sure of it. She remembered Tom's casual greeting of Keith when he'd stopped for the key. Friends? Perhaps, of a sort, the friendly acquaintance sort where you trust each other with a key in case you're locked out. Or where you might exchange greetings in the hall. Perhaps the kind where you go in search of your acquaintance when you hear a murder has taken place at their job site. Not the type of friendship, though, where you go to someone's house in order to share a drug with your friend.

Kyrie retraced her steps down the hallway, quickly. Why, oh, why hadn't she allowed herself to be so afraid of bird flu that she bought a couple of surgical masks? In the event, right now, all she could do was improvise.

She opened the door to the linen cupboard and got a washcloth, which she tied over her mouth and nose, careful to cover them as much as possible. Then she retreated further, into the living room where she grabbed the umbrella she had bought for what she thought was a fabulous price when she first moved to Colorado. As her year's worth of letting the umbrella sit by the front door had proven, the price hadn't been quite so fabulous as she then thought. Never mind. It would be of use now.

She grabbed the umbrella by the solid wooden handle that had so impressed her when she bought the thing and wielded it like a samurai sword.

Just in time. From the kitchen came the sound of the door breaking down and then a dry shuffle, shuffle, shuffle, as of chitinous legs moving over the linoleum of the kitchen. She heard her chair being dragged, the table overturned. And she heard the thing shuffle closer, toward the hallway. At the entrance to the hallway it stopped, and, in a series of dry scrapings, it sent forth another cloud of glowing green powder. From the other side of the house came the sound of the door falling down. The front door. Wouldn't the neighbors see it? And who would believe it? They could see it all day long. They'd think they were going crazy and not tell anyone about it.

Kyrie put her back against the hallway wall, as a cloud of green powder came from the living room side, too.

She prepared to sell her life dearly.

❖   ❖   ❖

Tom woke up choking. A taste of blood in his mouth, and his nose felt wholly obstructed. He coughed, and it seemed to help, clearing both mouth and nose. But he was thirsty and he was still lying, twisted, on the floor of the old service station. And his mouth was still gagged.

"Are you going to talk or not?" Crest Dragon asked. He stood directly in front of Tom, hands on hips. "Are you going to tell us where you hid it, or will we have to hurt you again?"

Tom blinked. He opened his mouth, and screamed, because that was all he could do. With a gag in his mouth, it was very hard to tell the idiots he had a gag in his mouth.

Two Dragons screamed something menacing in Chinese in response to his scream, and struck a pseudo-karate position he had probably learned from movies. He came running toward Tom and Tom closed his eyes, fairly sure they were going to hit his nose again.

But before Two Dragons got to him, someone yelled. Other Dragon? Tom opened one eye. It was indeed Other Dragon. The one with the Chinese character tattooed on his forehead. He spoke rapidly, pointing at Tom. And he had one arm in front of Two Dragons, who looked confused. Crest Dragon looked vexed. He turned toward Two Dragons. "You didn't remove the gag? I told you to remove the gag," he said, in rapid English, and threw a punch at Two Dragons who avoided it by ducking under it.

He didn't tell Crest Dragon, obviously the head of this outfit, that he too could easily have seen that Tom was gagged. Instead, he untied the gag at the back of Tom's head, his fingers scraping at Tom's scalp and tangling in Tom's hair as he did it.

As the gag fell away, Tom opened and closed his mouth, hoping his jaw wasn't dislocated. It hurt as if it were, but that was probably only the result of having his mouth open like that for hours.

"Now," Crest Dragon said, and smiled, graciously, looking much like some sort of society hostess. "Now, will you tell us where you hid it?"

Tom judged his chances. What he needed most—what he wanted more than anything—beyond the inner dragon's wish to tear these goons apart and use them as a protein source, was water. Liquid.

He looked at Crest Dragon and, in a voice he didn't need to make any raspier, he managed, "Thirsty. Very. Thirsty."

Crest Dragon looked disgusted, and for just a moment Tom thought they were going to resume beating him. He turned around to the other two.

"You know they said we shouldn't hurt him to where he couldn't talk," Other Dragon said. "You know he has to be thirsty."

How long had it been since he'd been thrown here? It seemed like forever. And he hadn't drunk anything before. Tom closed his eyes, as his captors' argument progressed into whatever form of Chinese they talked, Mandarin or Cantonese or whatever.

Other Dragon had said they shouldn't hurt him to the point where he couldn't talk. Tom had realized, sometime in the last few days, that stealing the Pearl of Heaven had been a grievous mistake. Oh, he remembered it from when he was a kid, in his father's house. He remembered some old Chinese guy showing it to Edward Ormson at his home office.

Hidden around the corner, the then very young Tom had seen the Pearl and felt it. He'd felt the radiance of it penetrating to the core of his being. Since he'd later come to realize that it was a . . . cultic object of dragon shifters, he supposed that the fact that it resonated with him, even then, must mean he'd already been a dragon. It wasn't a late-caught affliction, but something he'd had all his life and only became active in adolescence.

Years later, he'd felt the call of the Pearl and he'd slithered, among those other dragons, so different from himself, to a meeting, where he'd seen the Great Sky Dragon. And the Pearl. He hadn't understood almost anything of the meeting. But he'd seen the guy who had the Pearl shift back into his normal form. And he'd followed him to an unassuming little restaurant. Where he'd stolen the Pearl.

Oh, the reasons he'd stolen it seemed valid at the time. He'd thought since this was used by shifters, since it gave forth a feeling of safety and calm, it must be something that helped control shifts. And perhaps it was. At least, since he'd had it, Tom had been able to stop his drug-taking. Gradually, but he'd stopped it. And the withdrawal effects he'd expected from heroin—all the horrible vomiting and cramps he'd heard about—had never materialized. Or not to any degree worth talking about. It hadn't been much more than a stomach flu. So perhaps the Pearl had helped.

Only then the triad had picked up the scent, and Tom had found that unless the Pearl were kept submerged in water, every dragon within miles of it could follow it.

He didn't even know how many dragons there were around. But he knew that there were enough that they'd ˚acked him. They'd tracked him all the way to Colorado, tracked him to Goldport . . . And he had to leave the Pearl immersed in water, which meant he, himself, couldn't use it.

So, if he couldn't use it, he might as well give it back. Only he couldn't give it back, because he'd seen enough of the dragon triad, enough of the ruthless way in which they disposed of those who crossed them.

They were so mad at him that these—admittedly low-level—thugs had pretended to forget to remove his gag and had proceeded to beat hell out of him. And no, he wasn't so stupid he would believe that they'd actually forgotten to remove it. No. They hated him. They had it in for him. So . . . The minute he told them where the Pearl was, the moment one of them verified it, got his hands on it, and phoned the others back to tell them where it was, he was a dead man.

And Tom didn't want to die. Not yet. So many times over the last few years, he'd thought he would be better off dead.

He didn't know what was different now, to be honest. He still didn't have a chance with Kyrie. Kyrie was probably, even now, snuggling with her lion-policeman.

But, damn it all, Tom felt a sting to his pride, a sting to what he retained as his sense of self, to think that if he died now, Kyrie would only think of him as a fuckup, as a junkie so far out of control that he couldn't keep from getting high in her house—even if he used her drugs for it.

He took a deep breath. He wanted to live. He wanted to know why she kept drugs. He wanted . . . he wanted Kyrie, and a house, roses, and everyday paper delivery.

He wanted the normalcy that had never been his.

A hand lifted him roughly, and he opened his eyes, bracing for a hit. But instead, he found Two Dragons pressing the neck of a water bottle against his lips.

Tom drunk gratefully, as if the water had been the breath of life.

As his mouth and nose became hydrated, the smell of the other three became more obvious. There was some sort of cologne, cheap and probably bought in gallon bottles, and the smell of the masses of product that Crest Dragon had slathered on his hair.

But above it, stronger than all of that, was the smell of living flesh. "No," Tom said. It was all he could tell the inner dragon, who was slavering at the thought of eating these fools.

Edward Ormson walked along the street, too stunned to even hail a cab from the two or three that drove by. This was all very bewildering. He'd called around all day, but couldn't discover anything about Tom. The social workers down at the homeless center remembered him as one of their successes, the landlady liked him, the librarians at the public library down the street gushed over him.

Were they really talking about Tom?

And he still couldn't understand what had made the girl run. In fact, he had no idea at all.

He frowned. It didn't make any sense. What did she know? And who was she, really? She said she barely knew Tom. She said that they'd just worked side by side for about six months.

But there was something else there. Something to the way she talked about him, to the silences, to what she didn't say.

Oh, Edward had always known that Tom could be very charming to women. In fact, it seemed to him that women tended to like rogues and fools and Tom had a strong component of both, so it shouldn't surprise Edward that women liked his errant son. Even when Tom was little, just toddling around the place, the cook, Mrs. Lopez had been quite smitten with him. It was all they could do to keep her from feeding him on cookies and cake constantly. And Tom took advantage of it, of course. He'd been all smiles to the woman, even when he threw tantrums at his parents.

And yet, Kyrie Smith didn't seem to Ormson as the sort of woman who would be attracted to men who were trouble. No. Despite her exotic features and odd hairdo, she'd come across as capable, self-contained, controlled.

So, why did she seem so protective of Tom? Was it possible that for once in his life, just once, Tom had managed to attract someone in more than a superficial way? Was it possible that for once in his life Tom had a real relationship going? Or did she know something about the Pearl of Heaven itself?

For Tom to steal from the triad seemed like the stupidest form of madness, the last loss of his grip on reality that the boy could have come to. But what if this were a cunning plan, hatched by someone with better organizational skills than Tom's? What if Kyrie was behind it? What if she had something in mind for the Pearl?

Edward needed to know more. That's all there was to it. He needed to know more about this whole thing before they could expect him to find Tom and force the boy to give the Pearl back.

He hailed a cab. He'd go back to the restaurant in whose parking lot he'd been let out, and he'd go find out exactly what this was all about. He'd worked for triad members now and then. He was, after all, a criminal defense lawyer.

It had started with pro bono cases, when he'd been asked to represent indigent clients. One of them was associated with the triads somehow, and that had brought him the triad business.

He remembered how shocked he'd been when he'd first realized that some members of the triad of the dragon—the ones he dealt with—were shape-shifters, capable of shifting into dragons. But he had never expected that this would somehow make Tom into a dragon. And he was still not sure how that could have happened. Nor was he sure how Tom could have got involved with the group again after he left his father's house.

But he knew he had to stop it. Somehow. And soon. He had to get back home to New York.

Beetles. Definitely beetles. There was no other name for it. Shiny green carapaces and pincers. Advancing toward Kyrie, one from either end of the hallway. And they hissed. Or at least, it wasn't a proper hiss. Not like a cat's hiss, or anything. More like . . .

More like a kettle left too long on the fire. Or more like the release of hydraulic pressure from a train as it stops. That type of hiss.

One hissed, then the other hissed. They were communicating. They were communicating as they hunted her, as one approached from each side and they contrived to capture her in the middle, Kyrie thought.

This wouldn't do. This couldn't do. If she let them continue to advance, she'd find herself impaled by those two pincer-ended arms that kept advancing toward her, advancing inexorably in front of the shiny blue carapace, even while the creatures behind the pincers hissed at each other.

She imagined the hiss saying, "There she is, we've got her cornered."

Fear and an odd sort of anger mixed in her. This was her house. This was the only house that had ever been truly hers. All those years, growing up, she'd gone from house to house, from foster home to foster home, never having a place of her own, never having a say in even something as little as the color of her bedspread or the positioning of an armchair.

This house, tiny as it was, was the first place that had belonged to her alone. Well, that she'd been sole renter of, at any rate. Where, if she so wished, she could put the armchair on the roof, and it would stay there, because this was her space.

And these things, these . . . creatures . . . had violated it. Worse. They'd come into her house before, and they'd made Tom . . . high. They'd made Tom destroy part of her house. They'd given her an entirely wrong impression about Tom.

Not that they could be the ones who gave her the impression that Tom was an addict—or an ex drug addict. But they, as they were, had given her the impression that Tom didn't care about being a guest in her house, that he'd violated her hospitality. And because of them, she'd let Tom go—no—encouraged Tom to go, out there, somewhere, with no protection.

For all she knew, he was already dead. His own father was looking for him for the dragon triad. And she had kicked him out. Because of these things.

Anger boiled through her, together with a not unreasonable fear that there was no way out of this predicament and that she was going to end up as dead as that corpse they had rolled about in the parking lot of the Athens a few hours ago.

She heard a scream tear through her throat, and it seemed to her that the more advanced beetle—the one coming from the kitchen—stopped.

It seemed to Kyrie too that—though there was nothing on the beetle, anywhere, that could properly be called an expression—the beetle looked like it had just realized it was in deep trouble. Perhaps it was the thing's vague, confused attempt at skittering backward.

And then Kyrie jumped forward. There was no use at all attacking the pincers, so she vaulted over them. She used to be quite good at gymnastics in middle school. In fact, for a brief period of time, she'd thought that she was going to be a gymnast. But the foster family she was with didn't have the time to drive her to the extra practices.

Yet, just enough skill remained to allow her to vault over the pincers, and toward the monstrous head.

Blindly, more by instinct than anything else, Kyrie stabbed at the thing where the head carapace met the body carapace. She stabbed the umbrella down hard and was rewarded with a satisfyingly squishy sound, a spray of liquid upward, and a shriek that was part steam release and part the sound of a car's valves going seriously wrong.

From the other beetle came a sound of high distress, and it advanced. But its companion's body—dead?— blocked its way, and Kyrie jumped down from the carapace, on the other side, ran through her kitchen and out through her ruined back porch.

In her tiny backyard garden, she realized in her human form, she could never get enough of a running standard to jump over the six-foot fence.

But, as a panther . . .

She had never cavalierly shifted. Certainly never during the day. And yet, she was so full of fear and anger, of adrenaline and the need to fight or fly, that it seemed the easiest thing in the world. She willed herself into cat form and, suddenly, a black panther was rearing and taking a jumping leap at the fence. She cleared it with some space, just before she heard a sound behind her. It was an odd hissing, and a sound like . . . wings?

She had an odd feeling that these beetles could fly.

"Will you talk?" Crest Dragon asked.

Tom shook his head. There had been more . . . beatings. At least he supposed they would call it beatings. More accurate would be brutalizing to within an inch of his life.

Tom knew he would heal. The problem was that he suspected so did his captors. And that they were being more unrestrained with him than they would be with practically anyone else.

His defense right now was to look more confused than he felt, to look more tired than he felt. He shook his head and mumbled something that he hoped passed for a creditable wish to speak.

Two Dragons said something in their language that, for all it was unintelligible, was still clearly scathing. Crest Dragon answered curtly and sharply. They both turned to glare at Other Dragon, who shook his head, said something, then shrugged. He disappeared into a corner, where they seemed to have piled up some bags and other effects.

He returned, moments later, with . . . Tom blinked, unable to believe his eyes. But Other Dragon was definitely holding a syringe. A huge syringe. Tom frowned at it. It looked just a little smaller than those sold as basters at stores. He'd once been tempted to buy one for about two minutes until he realized the amount of meat he could actually afford didn't ever require external basting, much less internal.

Now he blinked at the syringe, and looked up at Other Dragon in some puzzlement. What the hell was that? What did they think they were doing? What did they want to put into him? Truth serum? Or marinade? Did they think he would be all the better for a touch of garlic and a bit of vinegar?

Other Dragon seemed rather puzzled as to what he should be doing, too. Twice he turned around to ask something in Chinese. Twice he was told off sharply—or so it seemed—also in Chinese.

At last he sighed, and walked up to Tom, and held the hypodermic in front of Tom's face and shouted something that sounded like a samurai challenge. While Tom blinked, puzzled, Crest Dragon said something from the back. Other Dragon turned. Then looked again at Tom and smiled. A very odd smile, Tom thought. A smile of enticement, of offer that would have made much more sense—as starving as Tom felt—if he'd been holding a rare steak. He leaned in close to Tom and said, "You want this, right?"

The syringe was filled with a colorless liquid. It could be . . . anything. And Tom realized, suddenly, with something like a shock, that he very much did *not* want it, whatever it was. Perhaps it was the Pearl of Heaven that had eased his way up from the pit he'd dug himself into, but he could remember the days he was using. It had seemed so simple then. It had seemed to him that he was sparing himself pain and thought, both.

A life that was too bizarre, too complex—his feelings for the home he'd lost, his wandering existence, and the dragon he could become suddenly, unexpectedly—had been suddenly simplified. He'd sometimes, before the drugs, forgotten what he'd done as a dragon, but when he'd started using, it had made it that much easier. He could either forget or pretend it was all part of a bad trip.

He didn't have to believe—in the unblinking light of day, he didn't have to believe that he had no control over the beast. And he didn't have to see that the beast existed. He didn't even have to be believe himself alone—expelled from the only home he had ever known.

No—the drugs had blurred his mind just enough to make him be able to pretend it was all a dream—just a dream. That he was still sixteen and still at home. That he was not a shape-shifter, a dangerous, uncertain creature.

He'd thought he was fine. He'd . . . He frowned at the syringe, thinking. He'd thought he was doing great. He'd anaesthetized himself into being able to bear his life.

Until he'd woken up choking on his own vomit once too many times. Until he'd woken up, in the morning, naked, under some underpass or beside some shelter, wondering what the dragon had done in the night and why.

And then there were the dreams. Lying asleep in daytime and dreaming of . . . eating someone. Of chasing people down. Of . . . Oh, he was almost sure none of it had ever happened. There would have been talk. News reports. Someone would have noticed. But the dreams were there, and the dreams made him fear one day all control would slip from the dragon and the dreams would become true.

And then there had been the Pearl of Heaven. And the job. And . . . and Kyrie. Who was he to judge her if she too chose to anesthesize herself, sometimes? She had helped him when he needed it most. He wanted to remember that. And he wanted to control the dragon. He wanted to know what he did, to know it was true. He didn't want the slippery dream, again.

"I want to own my own mind," he said, his raspy, low voice startling him. It seemed to come from so far away. And the words were odd, too, formal, stilted, not like himself at all. "I don't want drugs," he said in a still lower voice.

Crest Dragon said something that had the sound of profanity to it. And Other Dragon looked back confused. It was left to Two Dragons, the brash, perhaps younger of them, to step forward and say, "Well, then, if you don't talk, we'll have to give you some."

Which, of course, made perfect sense. But Tom couldn't talk. Because if he talked they would kill him. But if he didn't talk, they would give him this stuff. Which, of course, would make him talk.

He—who just the night before had been looking desperately for a drug dealer—realized if he were going to die, he would rather die sober. He'd rather know whatever there was to know, experience what there was to experience, with a clean perception. But then . . .

But then, and there it was. If he told them they would kill him for sure. Possibly in a painful way. If they gave him the drug . . . perhaps they would leave him alone while they went to verify he'd told them the truth. Okay, it was unlikely they would leave him alone. But with these three geniuses it was possible. At any rate, it would take them longer . . . They would have to get the words from him—and Tom had no idea what this drug was, or if it would make him talk quickly. Or at all. And then they would have to verify.

That would take longer than if he told them the truth up front and they rushed off right away to verify it. Or called someone in Goldport. And that meant there would be more time for something to happen. Something . . .

Two Dragons was waiting. He had his hands on either side of his skinny waist—a dragon tattoo shone on the back of each hand. "Well," he said, with a kind of petulant sneer. "Are you going to tell us where the Pearl of Heaven is?"

Tom grinned. It made his lips hurt, as cracked as they were and with dried blood caked on them, but he grinned anyway. He wished he could gather enough saliva to spit at them, but of course, he couldn't. "Your grandfather's wonton," he said.

And, as they held him down; as the needle went into his arm, he relished the look of surprise—and confusion—on Two Dragon's face.

Paws on concrete. The sidewalk—an alien word from her human mind, forced, unwilling, on the panther, intruded. Sidewalk. People. People walking.

There were screams. Mothers and terrified babies, hurling to the side of the street. A man standing in front of her, gun cocked.

Kyrie's human mind pulled the panther sideways. The bullet whistled by. The panther crouched to leap. Kyrie tugged at the panther.

Trapped. The panther's brain rushed to every nook and cranny, to every possible hiding place, but she was trapped. There was nowhere she could go. No safety. No jungle.

Smell of trees, of green. Smell of moss and undergrowth.

Like a passenger in a lurching car, Kyrie blinked, becoming aware that she was veering off the street and toward the triangular block of land where the castle sat, with its own little forest around it, surrounded by high black metal fence, full of Victorian scrolls and rusting in spots.

Leaf mold on paws. Trees rustling overhead. The pleasing sound of things scurrying along the ground in the soft vegetation. Screams behind her. People pointing through the fence, screaming, yelling.

The panther ran and Kyrie guided it as she could. Through the undergrowth, to the thick clumps of vegetation. She told the panther they were being hunted. That something bigger and meaner was after them. The panther crouched on its belly and crept, belly to the grass, close to the ground, forward, forward, forward, till it found itself all but hidden under the trees.

Kyrie had lost sense of time. She didn't know how long she had been in the panther's mind—a small foci of humanity, of sanity, within the beast. But she knew it had been long, because she could feel pain along the panther's muscles, from holding the position too long.

The panther wanted to climb a tree, to watch from above. It did not like this cowering, this submissive posture. And Kyrie couldn't hear any noise nearby. What remained rational and sane of herself within the panther thought that the people had stayed at the fence, talking, whispering.

They would call the police. Or the zoo. Or animal control. They wouldn't risk their lives on this. No. The panther wanted to climb the nearest tree and Kyrie let it, jumping so quickly up the trunk that Kyrie didn't detect any raised voices, any excitement at seeing her.

The tree was thick, and heavily covered in leaves. And it was around a corner from the front of the house. This way she would see the animal control officers approaching with their darts. Perhaps she could escape.

She wasn't so stupid that she couldn't see the possibility for discovery, for being caught. But she wouldn't think of it. She wouldn't think past trying to escape. She thought, as fast as she could, as hard as she could. And she saw no way out of this. Unless animal control officers missed her. She didn't imagine this happening. She could picture them beating the garden, tree by tree, bush by bush, looking for her.

The other option, of course, was for her to shift. She blinked. It hadn't occurred to her before. Of course, it would be humiliating. But being found naked in a public garden had to be better than to be tranquilized as a panther, and become a woman under sedation. She didn't know if that would happen—but it could.

But . . . But if she were found naked in a public garden, and if her house were examined, wouldn't she be committed? Or in some other way confined? Who would believe she was okay when she'd left her house torn to bits behind and was now here in this garden? At the very least they'd think she was on drugs. It wouldn't do at all.

❖   ❖   ❖

Edward Ormson waited for only one moment, in the shabby entrance of the Chinese restaurant. He'd expected the oriental decor, and it was there, in a round, white paper lantern concealing the light fixture on the ceiling, on the huge fan pinned to the wall behind the cash register, in the dragon statue carved of some improbable green stone or molded from glow-in-the-dark plastic, that stood glowering on the counter by the register.

But the man behind the register, though unmistakably Chinese, wore a grubby flannel shirt and jeans and managed to look as much like the Western rednecks around him as he could. And the TV hanging from the wall was on and blaring, showing the scene of a tractor pull.

He was drinking a beer, straight from the can. To the other side of the elaborate oriental fan hung a calendar with a pinup standing in front of a huge truck. Something about this—the irreverence, the Western intrusions, stopped Edward from his course, which was to ask about the Great Sky Dragon.

Perhaps the creature had only left him in the parking lot because it was convenient. But the name . . . Three Luck Dragon, while not unusual, seemed to speak of dragons, and dragons . . .

He realized he'd been standing there for a while in silence, and probably looking very worried, as the man behind the counter swivelled around to look at him.

"How may I help you?" he asked.

Edward took a deep breath. Come on, if worse came to worst, what would happen? He could always tell the man that Great Sky Dragon was just the name of another restaurant, couldn't he? That he'd got confused?

And besides, if he didn't ask, what would happen? It wasn't as if Edward was going to figure out where Tom was, much less manage to convince Tom on his own. And he had a sneaky suspicion that if he tried to just forget the whole thing and go back to New York, the creature would just come and pluck him out of his office again. Or his house. There was only so much plate glass he was willing to replace.

All this was thought quickly, while the man's dark eyes stared at him betraying just a slight edge of discomfort, as if he were waiting, madly, to go back to his tractor pull on TV.

"I was looking for the Great Sky Dragon," Edward said.

"What?" the man asked, eyes widening.

"I was looking . . . I wondered if you could tell me where to find the Great Sky Dragon," Edward said.

There was a silence, as the man looked at him from head to toe, as if something about Edward's appearance could have reassured him that this was something to do. Slowly, the cashier's hand reached for a remote near the cash register, turned the TV off.

Then he came out from behind the counter and said, "You come with me."

Edward took a deep breath. What had he got into? And what would it mean? Had he just managed to startle a member of the dragon triad who had no idea who he was or what he was doing? And if he had, would he presently be killed by people who didn't even ask him why he wanted the Great Sky Dragon, or what he wanted of him.

He was led all the way through, past a bustling kitchen and, past a set of swinging doors, into a grubby corridor stacked high with boxes.

At the very back of the corridor, a door opened, and the cashier reached in, turned on the light by tugging on a pull chain on the ceiling.

Light flooded a room scarcely larger than a cubicle. There was a folding table, open. An immaculate white cloth covered it. And on the cloth was a mound of peas—some shelled, some still in their pods. On the floor was a bucket, filled with empty pods. Behind the table was a plastic orange chair.

"Wait here," the cashier said. "Just wait."

Hesitantly, afraid of what this might mean, Edward went in. The cashier closed the door after him. Edward could hear the lock clicking home.

"I'll go in and look for it," a voice Kyrie knew said.

"But I wouldn't be too alarmed. It was probably just a large cat. I very much doubt it was a panther. I haven't heard of any panthers having been lost by the zoo. And panthers are not common here, you know," Rafiel Trall's voice went on, as usual radiating self-confidence.

A babble of voices answered him and, from the panther's perch atop the branch, Kyrie gathered that the crowd out there were insulted that Rafiel thought they could confuse a large house cat with a panther.

And yet, the way Rafiel talked, that certainty that exuded from his words, was so convincing that she could also hear the resistence running away. She could almost hear people starting to doubt themselves.

"I'll go in," Rafiel said, "with Officer Bob. Just to be on the safe side, please no one follow us. We'll do a thorough search. If we find it warranted, we will then call animal control. Right now all this commotion is premature."

The panther heard them come into the garden. Wondered how long it would take them to find it. Them. Officer Bob. Kyrie wondered what Officer Bob would think if he found her.

But Officer Bob was looking one way, and Rafiel was looking the other. She could hear them separate. She could hear Officer Bob walking away. She could hear . . . She could hear Rafiel following her trail here.

He followed it so exactly that she started wondering if he was following the trail of broken branches and footprints she'd doubtless left, or following her scent. She remembered he seemed to be able to smell other shifters. To smell them out better than she did, at any rate.

He came all the way to the bottom of the tree, looked up at her, blinked, then smiled. "Kyrie," he said.

His voice was perfectly normal and human, and yet there seemed to be something to it, some kind of harmonics that made the hair stand up at the back of her neck. Not fright. She wasn't scared of him. It was something else.

For just a moment, there was the feeling that the panther might jump down from the tree and roll on him and . . . No.

Kyrie tried to control the panther and had a feeling that the world flickered. And realized she was a naked human, sitting on a branch of a tree in a most unusual position. A position that gave a very interesting view to the man below.

She scrambled to sit on the branch in the human way, and fought a desire to cover herself. She could either hold on to the branch or she could cover herself. Between modesty and a fall, modesty could not win.

"Yes," she said. Heat climbed up to her cheeks and she had a feeling she was blushing from her belly button to her hair roots.

Yes, she was sure she was blushing from the way Rafiel smiled—a broad smile that exuded confidence and amusement.

But when he spoke, it was still in a whisper. "I have this for you," he said, taking it from his pants pocket and handing it up. "I stopped for just a moment when I heard the report on the radio. I told Bob I needed to use the restroom and let him radio we were taking care of it, while I went to a shop and bought this. I'm sorry if it looks horrible, my concern was that it fit in my pocket."

He handed up what looked like a little wrinkled square of fabric. When Kyrie caught it, she realized it was very light silk, the type that is designed to look wrinkled, and that there was a lot more material than seemed to be.

Shaken out, the fabric revealed a sheath dress. Kyrie decided it was safer to climb down from the tree, first, and then put it on. With the dress draped over her shoulders, she climbed down carefully, until, on the ground, she slipped the dress on. Of course, she was still barefoot, but on a warm day, in Colorado, in one of the old residential neighborhoods of Goldport, that was not exactly unheard of.

"Go out at the back," Rafiel said. "From what I could see when we approached, the part where the garden borders on the alley doesn't have any bystanders. If anyone sees you, tell them something about having come in to look for the panther, but the police ordering you out. And now, go." As she started for the path, he pushed her toward another path, the other way. "No, no," he said. "That way. If you go this way you will run into Bob and Bob is likely to have his gun out and be on edge. I don't want you shot. Go. I'll meet you at your house as soon as I can."

Her house. With the bugs. Kyrie shivered. But there was nothing for it. She had to go somewhere. At the very least, she had to go somewhere to get shoes.

Edward didn't wait long. He didn't sit down. He didn't dare sit down. There was only one chair, and it seemed to be in front of the table with the peas on it.

Instead, he stood, uncertainly, till the door opened, and a man came in. He looked . . . Well, he looked like an average middle-aged man, of Asian origin, in Colorado. He wore T-shirt and jeans, had a sprinkling of silver in his black hair, and, in fact, looked so mundane, that Edward was sure there must be a mistake.

He opened his mouth to say so. And stopped. There was something in the man's eyes—the man's serious, dark eyes. They looked like he was doing something very difficult. Something that might be life or death.

"Mr. Ormson?" he said.

Edward Ormson nodded, and his eyes widened. Was this the human form of the dragon he had seen yesterday? He seemed so small, so . . . normal.

But in Edward's mind was the image of that last night before he'd . . . asked Tom to leave. He remembered looking out of the window of his bedroom, next to Tom's room and seeing a green and gold dragon against the sky—majestic against the sky. He remembered seeing the dragon go into Tom's bedroom. And he remembered . . . He remembered running to see it, and finding only Tom, putting on his bathrobe. He remembered the shock.

These creatures could look like normal people. Perhaps . . .

"My name is Lung," the man said, and then, as though catching something in Edward's expression, he smiled. "And no, I am not him. But you could say I . . . ah . . . know him." Lung stepped fully in the room, and seemed to about to sit down in the plastic chair, when he realized that Edward didn't have anywhere to sit.

"They left you standing?" he asked. "I'm so sorry." He opened the door and spoke sharply to someone back there, then stepped fully in. Moments later, a young man, with long lanky hair almost covering his eyes, came in and set down a chair. Another one, swiftly, ducked in the wake of the first, to remove the cloth and all the peas in it. As soon as he'd withdrawn the first one showed up again, to spread another, clean tablecloth on the table. And after that, yet another one set a tray with a teapot and two tea cups on the table.

Lung gestured toward the—blue, plastic—chair they'd brought in. "Please sit," he said. "Might as well be comfortable, as we speak."

Edward sat on the chair, and faced Lung across the table. "Tea?" Lung said, and without waiting for an answer, filled Edward's cup, then his own. "Now . . . may I ask why you were looking for . . . him? His name is not normally spoken so . . . casually."

Edward took a deep breath. "How do you know my name?" he asked.

Lung smiled, again. He picked up his cup, holding it with two hands, as if his palms were cold and had to be warmed on the hot porcelain. "He told us. He told us he brought you to town. That you were to . . . convince your son to speak."

"Ah," Edward said. "I don't know where to find my son," he said, picking up his cup and taking a hurried sip that scalded his tongue. "I haven't seen Tom in . . ."

Lung shook his head. "I don't question his judgments. It wouldn't do to do such," he said. He looked at Edward and raised his eyebrows just a little. "He says you have been . . . useful to us in the past, so you know a little of . . . his ways. And of us. Do you not?"

Edward inclined his head. More than simple acknowledgment, but less than a nod. "I have defended . . . people connected to him, before. I know about . . ." He thought about a way to put it that wouldn't seem too open or too odd. ". . . about the shape-shifting," he said at last.

Lung inclined his head in turn. "But do you know about the other . . . about his other powers?"

Edward raised his eyebrows, said nothing.

Lung smiled. "Ah, I won't bore you with ancient oriental legends."

"Given what I've seen, what I've felt; given that I was brought here by . . . the—"

"Him."

"Him, I don't think I would dismiss it all as just a legend."

"Perhaps not," Lung said. "And yet the legend is just a legend, and, I suspect, as filled with imagination and wild embellishments. What we know is somewhat different. But . . . he is not like us. That we know. Or rather, he is like us, but old, impossibly old."

"How old?"

Lung shrugged. "Thousands of years. Before . . . civilization. From the time of legends. Who knows?" He drank his tea and poured a new cup. "What we do know is this—he has powers. Perhaps because he is old, or perhaps, simply, because he was born with more powers than us. I couldn't tell you which. But whatever powers he has, it is said that he can feel things—sense them. Perhaps it's less premonition than simply having been around a lot and seeing how things tend to work out." He inclined his head and looked into his tea cup as though reading the future in its surface. "If he thought you should be here, then he has his reasons."

"But I can't find my son. I haven't seen my son in years. I didn't even know if he was alive. The— He said that I was responsible for my son, but surely you must see . . . I haven't seen him in years."

Lung looked up, gave Edward an analyzing glance, then nodded. "As is, I think we have it all in hand. We know where your son is. We have . . . Some of our employees have got him. In a nearby city. And they're confident he will eventually tell them what he did with the object he stole. We don't know why *he* thought it necessary to get you, nor why *he* thought you should be here. But he is not someone whose judgments I'd dream of disputing."

A silence, long and fraught, descended, while Edward tried to figure out what he had just been told, in that convoluted way. "Are you telling me I have to stay here, but you're not sure why?" he asked.

The back alley wasn't empty, but it was nearly empty. At least compared to the crowd that surrounded the castle garden in the front. Here at the back, there were only half a dozen people looking in, staring at the lush, green garden, spying, presumably, for movement and fur.

There were two boys and a young girl of maybe fifteen, wearing jeans, a T-shirt, and a ponytail and holding a skateboard under her arm. The other three people looked like transients. Street people. Men, and probably past fifty, though there was no way to tell for sure.

Kyrie, still under cover of thick greenery, wondered at the strange minds of these people who would come and surround a place where they'd seen what they thought was a jungle animal disappear. What kind of idiots, she asked herself, wanted to face a panther, while unarmed and empty-handed? She might be a shape-shifter but at least she wasn't so strange as this.

They were all roughly disposed on either side of a broad gate that seemed to have rusted partly open.

Kyrie could, of course, just walk out and tell them what Rafiel had suggested—that she had felt a sudden and overwhelming desire to look for the panther herself. But she would prefer to find some way past them without having to speak. Remembering a scene from a Western, long ago, she looked at the ground and found a large rock. Picking it up, she weighed it carefully in her hand. Then she pulled back, and flung the rock across greenery, till it fell with a thud at the corner of the property.

Noise like that was bound to make them look. They wouldn't be human if they didn't. In fact, they all turned and stared, and Kyrie took the opportunity to rush forward and out of the enclosure.

They turned back to look at her, when she was in the alley, but she thought none of them would be sure he had seen her in the garden, and started walking away toward the main road and home.

"Hey, miss," a voice said behind her.

Kyrie turned around.

"Are you the one who owns the castle?" one of the homeless men asked.

She shook her head and his friend who stood by him elbowed him on the side. "The woman who owns the castle is much older, Mike."

She didn't stay to hear their argument and instead hurried home as fast as she could. Once out of the immediate vicinity of the castle, everything was normal and no one seemed unduly alarmed by the idea of a panther on the loose. So Kyrie assumed that Rafiel wouldn't have too much of a problem convincing them that it had been a collective hallucination.

Her house looked . . . well, wrecked, the front door open, crooked on its hinges, the door handle and lock missing. Inside, the green powder was everywhere underfoot and, in the hallway, where she had confronted the creature, there was something that looked like sparkling greenish nut shells. Looking closer, she realized they were probably fragments of the beetle—struck off when she'd stabbed it with the umbrella?

The umbrella was still there, leaning against the wall. But the beetles had vanished.

❖   ❖   ❖

Lung nodded, then shrugged at Edward Ormson's question. "I don't pretend to know why *he* wants you here, though I'm sure he has his reasons. However, you don't need to stress too much in search of your son. As I said, he is . . . We have him. And he will talk."

A cold shiver ran up Edward's back at those words. They had Tom? "What do you mean by having him? Do you . . . are you keeping him prisoner?"

Lung seemed puzzled by Edward's question—or perhaps by the disapproval that Edward had tried to keep from his voice, but which was still obvious. "He stole from us," he said. "Some of our men have captured him. They will find out where he put the Pearl of Heaven, one way or another."

One way or another. Edward found his hand trembling. And that was stupid. All these years, he'd gone through without knowing if Tom was dead or alive, or how he was doing. He hadn't worried at all about him. Why should the thought that he was being held prisoner by a dragon triad disturb him so much? Why should he care?

Oh, he could hear in the way Lung said that Tom would tell them the truth eventually that they probably weren't being pleasant with him. He doubted they were treating him very well. But in his mind, with no control from him, was the image of Tom on that last night. Barefoot, in a robe.

Edward had thought . . . well, truth be told, he couldn't even be very sure what he'd thought. He'd seen the triad dragons in action often enough. He knew what they could do. He'd seen them kill humans . . . devour humans. He'd seen the ruthlessness of the beasts. Seeing his son become a dragon, himself, he'd thought . . .

He'd thought it was an infection and that Tom had caught it. He'd thought his worthless, juvenile delinquent of a son had now become a mindless beast, who would devour . . .

His throat closed, remembering what he'd thought then. He didn't know if it was true or not. He assumed not, since Tom wasn't a member of the triad and lacked their protection. If he'd been making his way across the country devouring people, he'd have been discovered by now. He would have been killed by now. So Edward was forced to admit that his son must have some form of self-control. Well. Clearly he had to have some form of self-control if he'd not given in to whatever persuasion they were using to make him talk.

He looked up at Lung, who was staring at him, obviously baffled by his reactions. "What are you doing to him?" he asked. In his mind, he saw Tom, that last night he'd seen him. He saw Tom who looked far more tired and confused than he normally was. He hadn't even attempted to fight it. He'd opened his hands palm up to show he wasn't armed—as if he could be, having just shifted from a dragon. He'd tried to talk, but he didn't make any sense. Something about comic books.

These many years later, Edward frowned, trying to figure out what comic books had to do with the whole thing. Back then he'd found the whole nonsense talk even scarier, as though Tom had lost what little rationality he had with his transformation. And he'd got his gun from his home office desk and ordered Tom out of the house.

Tom had gone, too. And, somewhat to Edward's surprise, he hadn't made any effort to get back in.

"I thought you hadn't seen him for years?" Lung asked. "That you didn't care what happened to him?"

"I don't. Or at least . . ." But Edward had to admit that this last recollection he had of Tom as a sixteen-year-old youth in a white robe, and looking quite lost was an illusion. A sentimental illusion. It was no more real, no more a representation of their relationship than the picture of Tom in the hospital, two days old, with a funny hat on and his legs curled toward each other.

It was a pretty picture and one that, as a father, he should have cherished forever. But Tom had been very far from living up to the picture of the ideal son. And in the same way, at least five years had passed since Tom had been that boy of sixteen, and even if Edward had done him an injustice then—had Edward done him an injustice then?—the man he was now would have only the vaguest resemblance to that boy.

Back then, Tom hadn't known anything but his relatively sheltered existence. And though he'd been popular and had the kind of friends who had got him in all kinds of trouble, his friends were like him, privileged, well taken care of.

Suddenly Edward realized where his uneasiness was coming from about Tom and who Tom was, and what he had assumed about Tom for so many years. "It's his girlfriend, Kyrie," he said.

"Girlfriend?" Lung asked.

"Yes . . . or at least, I think she is. She said they were just coworkers, but there is something more there. She seems to care for him. She was furious at me for . . . I think she realized I was working for you, and she was furious at me."

"The panther girl?" Lung asked.

"I'm sorry?" Edward asked confused.

Lung smiled. "The girl who was with him two nights ago. The one who shifts into a panther."

"She . . ." Edward's mind was filled with the image of the attractive girl shifting, shifting into something dark and feline. He could imagine it all too well. There had been that kind of easy, gliding grace in her steps.

"Oh, you didn't know. Yes, she is a shifter. But I never knew she was his girlfriend."

"I just thought . . ." Perhaps what had bound them was their ability to shift shapes? But what would a dragon want with a panther? The images in Edward's mind were very disturbing and he found himself embarrassed and blushing. "There are other shifter shapes? Other than dragons?"

Lung smiled. "Come, Mr. Ormson, you're not stupid. Your own legends talk about other shifters . . . werewolves, isn't it? And weretigers too? And the legends of other lands speak of many and different animals"

Edward felt his mouth dry. "This has been going on all along? People shift, like that." He made a vague gesture supposed to show the ease of the shifting. "And they . . ." He waved his hand.

"We don't know for sure," Lung said, seriously. "He who brought you here says there have always been shifters, and as you know, he's not the sort of . . . person whose word one should doubt. He is also not, unfortunately, someone one can question or badger for details. He says that there have always been shifters. But that shifters are increasing."

"Increasing?"

"There are more of them."

"How? Is it . . . a bite?" He'd thought that back then. He remembered being afraid that Tom would bite him. He remembered having gone through the entire house, trying to think whether he'd touched anything Tom had touched. Tom's clothes, his toothbrush had all been consigned to the trash at his order.

The man laughed. "No, Mr. Ormson. It is . . . genetic," he pronounced the word as if to display his knowledge of such modern concepts.

Edward felt shocked, not because the man knew the word—he spoke without an accent—but at the idea that such a thing could be genetic. "But there is no one in our family . . ."

Lung shrugged. "In our families, which intermarry with each other quite often, even then only one child in four, if that many, will have the characteristic. In other families, in the world at large, who knows? It could be not one in twenty generations." He frowned. "I have often wondered if it is perhaps that people travel more now, and meet people from other lands, carrying the same rare gene. And if that's the only reason there's been an increase. Although . . ." He frowned. "I don't know that this is entirely natural—or explainable by simple laws of science. We seem to heal quicker than normal people and unless we are killed in certain, particular ways—traditional ways like beheading, or burning, or destroying the heart, or with silver—we're nearly impossible to kill. And we seem to live . . . longer than other people. I don't know how long. Himself is the oldest among our kind. I've never enquired as to those of other kinds and other lands."

Edward swallowed. That gun, that night, wouldn't have killed Tom anyway. Good thing he hadn't fired it. It would be horrible to have to live with Tom after firing on him.

But beyond that, something else was troubling him. The thought that Tom had received that curse from him— and presumably from his mother—and yet, he'd thrown him out. And now . . . "What will you do to Tom, if he tells you where the Pearl is?" he asked.

"He will no longer be . . . a problem," Lung said.

Edward nodded feeling relief. So, they'd let Tom go. "Pardon me if I'm asking too much. You don't need to tell me. I know something of the working of the triads in this country and I know the Dragon Triad is not that very much different, but I must ask . . . Why the Pearl? You're the only ones who have it, right? It was shown to me, years ago, in my apartment, and I remember thinking it was very pretty. But I thought it was a symbol."

Lung smiled, a smile that seemed to have too many teeth and to slide, unpleasantly, over his lips. "It is not a symbol," he said. "Our legend has it that the Pearl was sent down with the Great— with him. The Emperor of Heaven, himself, is supposed to have given it to him."

"Why?" Edward said, asking why the man believed his legend when he had dismissed all others.

But Lung clearly misunderstood him. He shrugged. "Because dragons are by nature bestial, competitive, and brutal. The beast in us overrides the man. We could never band together, much less work together without the Pearl of Heaven. We must find it soon," he said. "Or we will destroy ourselves and each other."

It wasn't until Edward had left and stood outside the restaurant that it occurred to him that saying Tom would no longer be a problem was not a reassurance. On the contrary. Unless it were a reassurance that Tom would soon be dead.

Stopped, in the parking lot, he felt as if ice water were running through his veins. He took a deep, sudden breath and almost went back inside. Almost.

But then he thought it would only get him killed. How could he go up against almost immortal shape-shifters? How could he? He would only get killed. And for Tom?

He needed help. He needed help now.

✧　　✧　　✧

Kyrie locked her front door as best she could, which in this case involved sliding the sofa in front of it, because the beetle had pulled the handle and the lock out of it.

If Kyrie survived all this mess, she would be so far in debt for house repairs that she would be arrested. Or die of trying to pay for it. Or something.

The back door was impossible to close, having splintered in a million pieces. She should have got a solid wood door, after all. And on that thought she got out the phone book, called her bank for her balance, which ran to the middle hundreds. Then she went back to the phone and started calling handymen, finding it somewhat difficult to reconcile her urgency in getting the doors fixed with the price any craftsman would accept for this.

She had just discovered an elderly handyman, who only worked two days a week, who could do both glazing and carpentry, and who thought her situation desperate enough to warrant immediate response when Rafiel came in through the ruined back door.

"Dragons?" he asked her, as she was hanging up the phone.

"No," she said. "As it turned out, beetles. Huge, green and blue and iridescent. If you go to the natural history museum in Denver, you'll find that the much tinier versions of the creatures are used as jewelry by some rain forest tribe or other."

He grabbed blindly for one of the overturned chairs, pulled it upright, and collapsed on it, looking at her. She'd put the kitchen table and the other chair up, and that was where she'd been making her calls. "I've just got hold of a handyman, who will be coming by to fix my porch and my two doors. I gave him the dimensions and he says he has some surplus, older doors he removed from a house and I can have them for nothing. Which only means I'll be broke, not in the red. At this rate I do not dare miss work for six months, but I will probably survive the experience."

But Rafiel only looked at her, the golden eyes dull and uncomprehending. "Beetles?" he said.

She nodded. "Very much so."

"So it wasn't a hallucination in the back of the Athens?" he said.

"Did you find a corpse?" Kyrie asked.

He shook his head slowly. "No. But I found . . . I could smell blood. I didn't want to shift to verify it, but I could smell blood. And death. Fresher than . . . two nights ago. So I'm sure you were telling the truth. Only till this moment I had hoped that you had seen it wrong and that it was actually dragons. Do you mean to tell me we have dragons *and* beetles?"

"It's worse than that. The green powder? I think it has hallucinogenic properties, that it's supposed to make the victim unable to fight. I think that's why I managed to fight them back. I tied a towel over my mouth."

"Ingenious," he said. "I could go back to the Athens tonight in . . . lion form and try to follow the trail of the blood. It's probably fresh enough and because there was no body, I wasn't forced to call out the rest of the force, so the scent won't be diluted." He paused for a moment. "I would have done it then, but I was afraid it would bring too much attention."

He nodded, as if satisfying himself of something. "Then as we were heading for the station, there was the report of a panther. Fortunately it turned out to be a sort of mass hallucination." He cleared his throat. "As you know, these are quite common. Seeing black panthers, I ·an. There's whole counties in England afflicted by it."

He looked at her, and reached for her hand, where it rested on the table. "How did you escape them?"

For a moment, for just a moment, Kyrie had a feeling of misgiving. Was it that Rafiel wanted to know how she'd escaped so that he could warn the beetles? But no. The beetles already knew how she had escaped. He wanted to know. It made sense.

"I stabbed one with my umbrella." She nodded toward the umbrella resting a few feet away against the wall in the hallway. "Between the head and back carapaces. And it was immobilized. Which allowed me to jump over it and escape."

"So, the shift to panther was . . ."

"I thought its mate would chase me."

"It probably would have, except for its being daylight and a busy area." He sighed. "I don't like to think creatures like that have such control. They are shifters, they must be. But what kind of insane nature or magic or evolution could have caused such a thing as shifter beetles?"

Kyrie shrugged. "Whatever it was, it created dragons. Which brings me to Tom."

"Ormson? Must you?" Rafiel looked pained and vaguely put out, as if she were insisting on speaking about a distasteful subject.

"Tom Ormson," she said. "I have reason to believe I did him an injustice. If that powder from the beetles causes hallucinations, I think that might have been all he was high on. On top of that, there is his father."

"Ormson has a father?" Rafiel asked.

"Till this moment you assumed he reproduced by fission?"

"No, I mean he has a father around here, a father who is in some way involved in his life?"

Kyrie shrugged. "I don't think he is. Involved in Tom's life, I mean. I think he came from New York on purpose to find Tom. I think at the request of the triad."

Rafiel's eyebrows rose.

"I think he's a lawyer of some sort," she said. "I . . . vaguely remember Tom telling me that. And I think he is involved with the triads in some way. Well, with the shifter dragon triad, most of all."

"This family just keeps getting better and better," Rafiel said. "I suppose I'll look up the elder Mr. Ormson's background. And his name is?"

"His given name? Edward."

Rafiel nodded. "I'll check him out."

"Wait," Kyrie said. She didn't know she was going to say it, till it came flying out of her mouth. "Wait. I need to ask you a favor. Please. Would you . . . Would you check on Tom?"

"Check on . . . ?"

"I think he's staying with his friend, Keith, who lives in the same building, third floor. Because he left with Keith. Keith would at least know where he was going."

"But why do you want me to check on him? Isn't he a grown-up and able to look after himself?"

Kyrie frowned. She had a sense of deep uneasiness and was quite well aware that a lot of it might be due to her guilt in having misjudged Tom over the drug stuff. "I . . ." She waved at her house and the destruction. "Until today I would have said I was able to look after myself, too, but it's not that easy, as you see. And then he had the triad looking for him too. And apparently his father, working for them." She took a deep breath. "Last night he missed work completely. I'd like to know he's okay."

She stood up. She had some vague idea that the gesture would encourage Rafiel to go. She didn't want to be so rude as to ask him to leave, not when she was asking him for a favor. But the handyman should be here any minute. And as soon as she had locking doors—with a few extra locks—she was going to have to shower and go work. On virtually no sleep.

Rafiel got up too and she was optimistic that he would leave now. But he was still holding the hand he covered with his own when they sat at the table. And now he leaned forward and said, "You don't need to go it alone."

And before she knew what he was doing, he'd covered her lips with his and was pulling her to him.

She'd never been kissed, not even in high school. Any boy smart enough to be interested in her was, presumably, smart enough to realize this was not exactly a safe course of action. Having her lips covered by his, his hands moving to her shoulders was novel enough to stop her from reacting immediately.

His hands were warm on her shoulders, and his body felt warm and firm next to hers. And his tongue was trying to push between her lips.

She put her hands on his shoulders and pushed him back. "I'm sorry," she said. "I'm not . . . I'm not prepared. I don't think . . . Let us get through this first, and figure out what it's all about?"

He started to open his mouth, as if to answer, but at that moment a white-haired man, in impeccable work pants and T-shirt showed at the kitchen door. "Miss Smith? I'm Harold Keener. Ready to start work."

"Well," Rafiel said, looking perfectly composed as if just seconds before he hadn't been attempting to shove his tongue into her mouth. "I'll be going then, and check on Ormson."

Was it Kyrie's imagination, or had he pronounced Tom's family name with particular venom?

And what had Rafiel thought he was doing, she wondered, as she walked the handyman back to the porch to discuss the double-glazed versus single-glazed options and costs. Was he so used to any girl he came on to melting with pleasure that he didn't even bother to check for some signs of interest before jumping the gun? Or had she been giving signs of interest? She doubted that very much, as she wasn't even sure what the signs were.

On the other hand perhaps he just thought with both of them shifting to feline forms, they were perfect for each other? Was this all about creating a litter of kittens? Or was he trying to distract her from something in the conversation? Had he said anything he didn't want her to remember?

Edward Ormson had left the Three Luck Dragon feeling less assured of himself than he was used to feeling. Something in the conversation—perhaps the way these strangers spoke casually of holding Tom prisoner, of interrogating Tom, made Edward feel inadequate and ashamed of himself.

These were not feelings he normally entertained about himself, and he didn't feel right about entertaining them now.

He told himself that Tom had been a difficult child, a delinquent adolescent. But the words of Lung echoed in his mind, telling him that people who shifted into dragons had problems of that sort. That the beast often overruled the human. And if Tom had been born that way, if it was blind genetic accident, then it wouldn't be his fault, would it? He'd been difficult, but then he couldn't have been otherwise. Would parents who were more interested in him and less interested in—what? his career, himself, Tom's mother's devotion to medicine? all of those?—have done better for him? Could anything have prevented getting to this point where a criminal organization composed of shape-shifters was intending to eliminate Edward's son? And Edward could do nothing about it? Except perhaps help them?

The wrongness of it, the wrongness of his having worked for the group that was intending to kill his son, made bitter bile rise in his throat. But why should he care? Where did all this anguish come from? Hadn't he washed his hands of the boy five years ago?

Five years ago. Damn, the boy had only been sixteen. And Edward had ordered him out of the house. At gunpoint.

Edward had been walking along the road leading toward town. Not a pretty road—a place of warehouses and dilapidated motels—and it seemed to be making him think things he'd never thought before. This was all wrong, these unexpected feelings, the sudden guilt over Tom. It was all very wrong. He'd been fine with this for five years. Why should it torment him now?

He was tired. That was all. He was very tired. He hadn't slept at all the night before, and now it was afternoon. He'd hail the first cab that came by. He would ask to be taken to the best hotel in town. He would go to sleep. When he woke up, he would feel much better about this. He would realize that Tom had made his own bed and now should damn well lie in it.

His briefcase was heavy, pulling down on his arm. And no cab came by. Heck, no car came by. He walked on, into the Colorado night.

He should have rented a car, only he didn't think it would take him this long to . . . To what? Make Tom give back whatever he had stolen, like a naughty boy caught with another kid's lunch box?

What did he know of Tom now, really? He would be twenty-one. How he had lived the last five years was beyond his father's knowledge and probably beyond his father's understanding. Who was he, this creature he'd seen growing up till the age of sixteen, and then let go and not seen again?

Tom worked nights in a diner, he could shift shapes into a dragon. And he had the affection—or at least the interest—of that exotic beauty who did not look like the type to be easily rolled by some patter. And Ormson should know that, he thought, with a rueful grin. *I tried.*

He'd walked a few blocks and was near an intersection when, out of the corner of his eye, he caught the yellow glimmer of a taxi.

Waving frantically, he got the cabby's attention, and moments later was sitting on the backseat of an air-conditioned taxi heading downtown.

"Downtown?" he said. "Really."

"Oh, yes," the cabby said. "Spurs and Lace is the best hotel in town."

Edward leaned back against the cool upholstery and hoped they had room. He just needed to sleep. Just . . . sleep. And then all would be well.

✧　✧　✧

"Kyrie," Tom called, and the sound of her name woke him from a nightmare of half-defined shapes and half-formed thoughts in which he'd been, seemingly stumbling without direction.

He didn't know what they had given him. He suspected it was supposed to be some form of truth serum. At least they had expected him to answer questions while under.

He suspected he hadn't. Part of it was because he had the feeling that he'd been touring random recesses of his mind, which, for some reason, featured not only an up-close and personal view of Kyrie's bared breast, but also repeated reruns of Keith's conversation about his problems at college.

And part of it was because, as he became aware of who he was, where he was, and what was happening around him, he heard the three . . . Oh, he must not call them the three stooges, not even mentally. The way he was feeling, it might come flying out of his mouth next thing, and, who knew, they might actually understand the reference. No. He heard the three geniuses arguing loudly in what he presumed was their native tongue. It didn't sound like an argument about which one would go for the Pearl and which one would wait until the order came to cut Tom's throat . . . or however they intended to dispatch him.

With a final scream, Two Dragons ran out the door. The other two shrugged, went to the corner, and came back with sandwiches and drinks.

The smell of food made Tom hungrier than ever. If it weren't for the fact that he was using all his concentration to keep himself from turning into a dragon, he might very well have broken down and told them where to find the Pearl.

The room was acceptable, though it was close to downtown and, from his fifth-floor window, Edward had a view of the area where Tom worked.

Standing there, looking out the window, he wondered if Tom had lived in one of those rectilineal streets that radiated from Fairfax Avenue and which were lined with tiny houses and apartment buildings. Probably, since Edward very much doubted that waiting tables at night in a diner was a job that paid enough for a car. And then he realized he'd thought of Tom in the past tense.

Angry with himself, he took a shower, put his underwear back on, and got in bed. He was asleep before his head touched the pillow.

And he was fully awake, staring at the ceiling a few minutes later, while thoughts that shouldn't be in his head insisted on running through it. Thoughts such as— shouldn't Tom's father do something to save him, no matter how unworthy the boy was?—and really, what had he ever done while living in his father's house that wasn't done by kids of his age and set? He'd gone joyriding. He'd been caught with pot, once. And he'd committed minor acts of vandalism. He'd been naked in public twice, both in his last week at home—after he'd started shifting. Nothing that other kids he ran with didn't do. Kids who were now, for the most part, at Yale and Harvard.

But Edward had kicked Tom out of the house. And never even stirred himself to find out what exactly the boy was doing. Or even if he was alive.

"He was a shape-shifter," he said to the cool air of the room. "He was a dragon."

But the empty room seemed to sneer disdainfully at this excuse, and he sat up in bed, furious at himself. The truth was that since his marriage had broken apart, Tom had been more of a burden than anything else. A hindrance to just living the life of an unattached adult, with a job and a few casual dates and no significant attachments. Because, if Edward hadn't been around for a while, then Tom took it upon himself to get parental attention by getting himself arrested or by—and suddenly Edward smiled remembering exactly what that had looked like—shaving half of his head and dying the rest of his hair bright orange. Why was it that at a distance of eight years that memory seemed funny and endearing?

Fully awake, he dug into his briefcase and brought out his cell phone. He called information in Palmetto, Florida. And then he called Sylvia.

A kid answered the phone, speaking in the endearing lisp of a child whose front teeth are missing and when Edward asked for Sylvia, screamed at the top of his lungs, "Mom."

This was followed by the click of pumps on the floor, and finally Sylvia's voice on the phone. "Hello."

"Hi, Sylvia, this is Edward."

"Who?"

"Edward Ormson."

There was a short silence, followed by "Oh." And, after a longish pause. "How may I help you?"

Exactly like the waitress at an impersonal restaurant, Edward thought, but then they hadn't seen each other in over ten years. She had another family. It was foolish of him to resent it. Well, it was foolish of him to call too, but he felt he had to. She had never even sent Tom a birthday card. Not that Edward had seen.

"I just wanted to know if you've heard from Tom?"

"Who?"

"Thomas. Your son?"

"Oh. Tom?"

Was she not sure who her oldest son was? Edward should have felt revolted, but instead he felt more guilty than ever. What a pair they had made. Poor boy. Poor screwed up boy who'd ended up with them.

She seemed to collect herself, from a long ways away. "Isn't he living with you?" she said.

Edward took a deep breath. "No." And he hung up.

He didn't know what he had expected. That Sylvia was secretly a great mom? After all, she'd turned Tom over to a nanny as soon as she could, and returned to her job before he was one month old.

He walked over to the window and looked out again. No. He knew what he had hoped for. He had hoped that Sylvia would behave like a responsible, caring parent and thereby redeem all his memories of Tom's childhood. Prove to him that the boy had had at least one attentive parent till the divorce. And that if he'd gone wrong it was entirely his fault and his parents couldn't be blamed.

If that could be proved to be true—well, then Edward would feel if not justified at least slightly less guilty in washing his hands of Tom.

But his ex-wife's behavior, his own memories of his behavior only proved to him that Tom had never had a chance. Not even the beginning of one. And yet, he was still alive, five years after being kicked out. And Kyrie Smith liked him. That had to count for something. He couldn't be completely lost to humanity if he'd engaged the interest of an attractive and clearly smart young woman.

Kyrie Smith. She was a panther in her other form, Lung had said. Perhaps she knew other shifters. With their help, perhaps Edward could go up against the triad. Perhaps he could rescue his son.

He wasn't sure he could have Tom move back in. He wasn't sure he could endure Tom for much longer than a few hours. He wasn't even sure that he should ever have had a son, since he seemed to have approached the enterprise with the idea that children were sort of animated dolls.

But he was sure the least he could do was save his son's life. Or not cooperate with his murderers.

Kyrie was not in a good mood. Oh, she was sure most of the reason for her feeling as down as she did was the fact that she really hadn't slept much.

By her calculations, she had slept exactly two hours in the last forty-eight. And even with the best of payment plans—the handyman had allowed her to pay in installments for her new windows and doors—she would not have any spare cash for the next few months.

So she'd been going from table to table, forcing her professional smile and longing—just longing—for the end of the shift. It didn't help that the night was exceptionally hot and the single air-conditioning unit labored, helplessly, against the dry heat that plunged through the windows patrons opened and clung around Kyrie in a vapor of french-fry grease and hamburger smell.

"It doesn't help that Frank is acting like someone did him wrong," Anthony said, as he passed her on the narrow isle between the plastic tables in the addition and gave her a sympathetic scowl. "Couldn't you get your friend Tom to show up?" he said. "I mean, Frank said if I wanted to continue working here, I'd do this shift too."

"I don't know where Tom is," Kyrie said, her voice sounding even more depressed than she felt.

Anthony—tonight resplendent in a ruffled red shirt and his customary tight black pants and colorful vest—looked very aggrieved. "Only, I'm missing my bolero dance group practice." And, at the widening of her eyes that she couldn't control, "Oh, Lord. Why did you think I dressed this way?"

Kyrie just smiled and looked away. There was an answer she had no intention of giving. Instead, she took her tray laden with dirty dishes to behind the counter, scraped them, and loaded them into the dishwasher.

Needless to say the diner was crowded tonight. Probably because people couldn't sleep with the heat—since most houses in Colorado didn't have air-conditioning—and had decided to come here and eat the night away instead. Normally, Kyrie and Tom, after six months of working together, had things down to a routine. Whichever of them went to bus one of their tables did the other's tables too, if they needed doing. They'd worked it out, and it all evened out in the end. When the night was busy, it kept the tables clear so people could sit down as soon as other people left. And that was good. But Anthony, though he was a very nice man, wasn't used to Kyrie's routines.

Kyrie hesitated, alternating between being mad at Tom for not being here, and a sort of formless groping, not quite a prayer, toward some unnamed power to grant his safety. She had as good as kicked him out . . .

No. She wouldn't go there. Of all the useless emotions in the world, the most useless was guilt. She slammed the last dish in the dishwasher, and checked the cell phone she'd slipped into her apron pocket.

Rafiel had said he'd call as soon as he had checked on Tom. He'd call even if he couldn't find Tom. He hadn't called yet. Why hadn't he called?

Kyrie turned from the dishwasher, expecting to see Frank glaring at her for slamming the dish in. But Frank was leaning over the counter, seemingly elated by intimate conference with his girlfriend—or at least the woman he'd been seeing. Kyrie was afraid the staff had decided she was his girlfriend partly as a joke. Which was kind of funny, because the woman was not much to look at.

She had to be fifty if she was a day, with the kind of lined, weathered skin that people got when they'd lived too long outdoors. And she had the sort of features that were normally associated with British women of a horsey kind. Her hair was flyaway, mostly white, and if it could be said to have been styled, she'd been aiming to look like popular pictures of Einstein.

But Frank was leaning forward toward her, to the point where their foreheads almost touched. It revealed his neck, above the T-shirt, and showed a bandage there. Ew. Had his girlfriend given him a hickey?

They'd been seeing each other for a while, but today they seemed cozier than Kyrie had ever seen them.

On the way back to her tables, coffeepot in hand for warm-ups, Kyrie noticed that, despite the woman's weathered features, she wore a very expensive skirt suit. Maybe Frank was interested in her for her money?

"Or maybe he has no taste," she told Anthony, as they met one coming and one going into the addition. "But see, you wished him to get laid and there . . ."

"Don't say it," Anthony said. "Don't even say it. I don't have the money to buy as much mental floss as I'd need to get that image out of my mind." He made a face, as he moved the tray the other way, to clear the doorway. "But it's been going on for a while now, hasn't it? I hear she's the new owner of the castle. And there's talk she's going to renovate it and use it as a bed-and-breakfast. So, perhaps it is just for money." He looked hopeful.

Kyrie gave her warm-ups and then started taking orders. Went back and gave the orders to Frank, whom, she was sure, was ignoring them. Or didn't even notice the new handful of orders spiked through the order wire.

Then she went back again, having caught movement by the corner of her eye, and the impression someone had sat in the enclosure. It wasn't until she was at the corner table, near the outer door, facing the guy who had just sat down, that she recognized Tom's father.

He looked like he'd been dragged through hell. Backward. By his heels. He looked like he hadn't slept in more hours than she'd been awake. His suit was rumpled, his hair looked like he'd washed it and not given it the benefit of a comb—or clergy, since it tossed in all directions, as if possessed of a discordant spirit.

His dark blue eyes stared at her from amid bruised circles. "Don't say it," he said. "I know what you think of me, but don't say anything. I think . . ." He swallowed. "I think that there's reason. Oh, hell. I think they're going to kill Tom. I need help."

That he needed help was a given. That he was so worried about their killing Tom was not. She glared at him. "You didn't seem to be worried about him at all before," she said.

"I . . ." He swallowed again. "I've been thinking and . . . I don't want them to kill him."

Well, and wasn't that big of him? After all, Tom was only his son. She narrowed her eyes at him. The shock, when she'd realized he was working for the people who'd already tried to kill his son once, had turned her stomach. She still didn't feel any better about Mr. Edward Ormson. She'd be less disgusted by a giant beetle. "What will you be eating, sir?"

He looked as surprised as if she'd slapped him. "What . . . what . . . I need to talk. Seriously. They're—"

She took her notebook out of her apron pocket, and tapped the pencil on the page. "I'm at work, Mr. Ormson, and my job is to get people food. What can I get you?"

"I . . . whatever you want . . ."

"We're all out of rat poison," Kyrie said, the words shocking her as they came out of her mouth.

His eyes widened. "Coffee. Coffee and a . . ." He looked at the menu. "Piece of pie."

She wrote it down and walked away. She really, really, really needed to convince Frank to start making brussels sprout pies. Or cod liver oil ones.

✧   ✧   ✧

Tom woke up from a sort of formless dream. He didn't remember falling asleep. His last memory had been of Crest Dragon and Other Dragon having a picnic of sorts in front of him.

Now he opened his eyes to an empty building. He didn't know how long he'd slept, but his nose no longer hurt, and it seemed to him like the pain in his tied arms had eased a little too. Perhaps he'd gotten used to being tied up. Or perhaps his arms had been without circulation so long that he could no longer feel them.

The last should have been alarming, except it wasn't. Everything seemed very distant, as if a great sheet of glass made of indifference separated him from the world and his own predicament.

He lay there, and listened to his own breathing. He would assume he still hadn't talked, though it was—of course—possible he had said something while he was in a half awake state. And if he had . . .

Well, it was possible that the three dragons had gone off to get the Pearl and would presently come back and kill him. Tom could shift now, of course, but what if they were still here? Perhaps just outside? First, as tired as he was, he couldn't fight all three of them at once. Second, what if he ate them?

His mouth felt so dry—his tongue glued to his palate by thirst, that he was sure he would bite them just for the moisture. And yet, there was an off chance. Would he lay here and wait for death? No. He would shift. As difficult as it was, as tiring as it was, he would shift.

Before he could collect his mind enough to concentrate on the shift, though, he heard sounds outside. A couple of cars, a lot of voices. Speaking Chinese. He closed his eyes, and pretended to be asleep.

A group of people came in, babbling in Chinese. Several men, by the sound of it. Tom half opened his eyes, just enough to look through his eyelashes, without anyone realizing that he was actually awake. He forced himself to keep his breathing regular.

And then from the middle of the babble a voice emerged. "Hey. Hey, what's the idea?"

Keith. The voice was Keith's. What was Keith doing here, though?

"You're okay, you're okay," one of the other voices answered, in accented English. "As soon as your friend answers questions, we'll let you go."

And then two men came in, breathing hard, carrying a sack with something very heavy in it. "Where do we put her?" they asked.

"Here," another voice answered. The forest of legs in front of Tom parted enough for him to see, on the ground, a trussed-up human, and the big sack being laid down behind it.

"She's starting to wake up," one of the men said.

"That's fine," another one answered. "With the tranq she'll be weak as a kitten for a while."

A kitten. Tom blinked, trying to focus his gaze. A kitten. The sack—some kind of rough burlap—was large enough to contain a heavy feline. She. Kitten. Kyrie. Not Kyrie.

"Oh, look, he's awake," one of the men who'd come in— and who looked far smarter than the three reverse geniuses—said and grinned. "Yes, that is your girlfriend, but don't worry. So long as you tell us where you hid the Pearl of Heaven, she'll be just fine."

Kyrie. Tom didn't want to shift. If he shifted, he was going to eat someone. But he couldn't tell them where the Pearl of Heaven was, either. Because then they'd just kill him. And Keith. And Kyrie.

He felt his heart speed up and his body spasm. And there was no turning back.

✧ ✧ ✧

There was blood. There was blood and screams and panic. Tom's vision—the dragon's vision, was filled with people. He flamed. There was the smell of fire, and of cloth burning. People with clothes on fire ran to either side of him.

The dragon wanted to feed. To the dragon's nostrils, all flesh was food. The smell of humans, the smell of fodder so close was more than he could endure. The dragon tried to nip left, right . . .

But Tom knew once the dragon started feeding, it wouldn't stop till all humans around it were eaten. He knew from some deep instinctive feeling that having reached the depths of hunger, the dragon would now eat past satiety. And he couldn't let it happen. He couldn't.

If he ate a human, he'd never be able to live with himself. And if he ate Kyrie . . . No.

Tom—what there was of Tom in the huge scaley body with the flapping wings and the tearing claws and the flaming mouth—controlled the body and the wings and the mouth. Forcefully, he walked forward, slashing with his claws at all opposition. Taken by surprise, the others ran out of the way. Tom could hear, to his side, the cough-cough-cough like laughter of a dragon shifting. He would deal with that later.

Before the dragon shifted, before he had to battle others of his kind, he would free Keith. And Kyrie.

Disciplining the dragon, he bent over Keith, and, with a sharp claw, burst the ropes that bound his friend's legs and hands. Keith was looking at Tom with huge eyes and, for a moment, Tom thought he would run away. He remembered that Keith had no idea who the dragon was. But Keith was looking intently at him and said, "Tom?"

Tom nodded, rapidly, and managed to get out, through a mouth not well adapted to speech, "Run."

Then he bent and ripped the burlap bag open. He couldn't see the feline—definitely a feline shape—inside move, though. He felt more than saw movement from it, and then he heard a stumping step from the side, and knew that a dragon had shifted shape near him.

He turned, just in time to find Crest Dragon launching himself at Tom.

Tom jumped aside, enough to avoid Crest Dragon's slashing and then turned around. Then he bent low and slashed across Crest Dragon's belly with a claw.

Bright blood spurted, and there was something like a scream that sounded all too human. The blood made the dragon's thirst worse, but Tom wouldn't let it drink, and, instead, hopped back, to slash at Two Dragons who had shifted shape also, and was trying to sneak up on Tom with all the stealth of an elephant in a very small china shop.

Tom's dragon kicked out at Crest Dragon, who was coming at him again, his back claws leaving red stripes of blood on Crest Dragon's muzzle, even as his muzzle clamped tight on Two Dragon's arm and pulled, ripping it out of its socket.

"Look out, look out, look out," Keith screamed from beside Tom. And he'd grabbed something—Tom couldn't quite see what, but it looked like an ancient and rusted tire iron. Keith was looming with it behind Other Dragon, who had, in turn been sneaking up behind Tom.

Tom clashed jaws at Other Dragon, but Keith hit Other Dragon a sideways blow with whatever the thing was. It must have been a hell of an implement, and heavy enough, because Other Dragon gave a high-pitched scream and fell forward.

But there were other dragons. Too many dragons. A lot of the people who had come in had been severely burned by Tom's original flaming, and lay fallen, some in various stages of shifting shape, but seemingly out of action. But then there were others. Many others.

As a dragon, Tom wasn't particularly good at counting. There was something in the reptilian brain that tended to simplify things down to the level of one, two, many. But the human inside that brain could tell there were at least eight dragons. Maybe more. And Tom was tired. And weak.

He was surrounded by dragons, on all sides, snapping and biting at him. He could feel wounds, even if he couldn't stop. If he stopped, he would die. And though that seemed—eventually—inevitable, he wasn't ready to give up. Not yet.

He circled and nipped. Until his back was to a wall and he was surrounded by dragons. Truth was, he thought, they could already have killed him. They were holding back. They probably just wanted to hurt him enough that he wouldn't be able to resist—he wouldn't be able to stop them from making him answer . . .

But if they didn't want to kill him, that gave him the advantage. He kicked and bit with renewed vigor, and realized that he had allies. On the outer ring, at the edge, Keith was dancing, like a mad monkey—which was exactly how Tom's dragon brain thought of him— repeatedly bashing the dragons at the periphery with whatever heavy implement he'd grabbed.

Oh, they turned, and tried to flame him, but Keith was too quick for them, jumping and running into the darkness, only to appear again somewhere unexpected, and bash another dragon over the head.

And from the other side, another . . . person? Had joined the fray. Only it wasn't in person shape, but as a large feline.

In the semidarkness of the station—was it dark out now?—Tom couldn't see very clearly, but he could see that it was a feline shape. And it was roaring and clawing and biting.

Suddenly, Tom realized he had an open way out of there, to the front door. Awkwardly, his legs streaming blood, Tom ran for it, flaming everything that got in his way. The door had been left open. From carrying the hostages in? Outside in the parking lot there were a lot of cars, and two men who ran at the sight of Tom. Tom flamed the cars. They caught and some exploded. And then, as Tom slowed down, he felt a hand on his front leg. A human hand. Touching him.

He turned ready to flame, and saw Keith, who was physically pulling him forward, toward one of the cars. An undamaged one. "Dude," he said. "You have to change, or you'll have to go on the roof rack."

Tom was already shifting. It was the only way to stop from flaming Keith. He became human, and tired and in pain, in mid-stride, and it was only Keith's determination that pulled him forward, that shoved him into a car—huge car. Like a limo—from the driver's side, and pushed him over to the passenger side.

He threw something on the floor at Tom's feet. Tom was too tired to notice what and just leaned back, breathing hard. Keith waited, his hand on the ignition.

Waited. Waited. And then something—Tom couldn't see very well, he was that tired and in that much pain—heavy hit the backseat.

Kyrie. Tom turned around, even as Keith reached back, grabbed the back door, pulled it shut, then started the car and took off, in a squeal of tires, weaving between the other parked cars on the way to the road, and then down it, at speeds that were probably forbidden in this neighborhood.

The feline looking at Tom from the backseat was not Kyrie. It was a lion. Tawny and definitely male.

As Tom watched, it morphed into police officer Rafiel Trall.

✧   ✧   ✧

Edward Ormson didn't know what to say to this woman. Kyrie brought him back a cup of coffee and a slice of pie, and he actually reached forward and grabbed her wrist, before she could walk away.

"They have him prisoner," he said. "They have him prisoner and you must help him."

"I must help him?" Kyrie asked. She shook her hand, pulling it away from his grasp. "I must help him? How? Aren't you the one who has been trying to catch him, to get him to tell you everything for the benefit of the triad?"

Edward felt exasperated. The woman was beautiful. Her skin was just the tone, her features just exotic enough to make her look some ancient statue of a forgotten civilization—remote and admirable and inhuman. The tapestry-dyed hair only contributed to the impression. But she clearly didn't understand. "You're young," he said. "You haven't got any children. You wouldn't know what—"

"No," she said. And it sounded like an admission, but then she leaned forward on his table, her hands resting on it. "No, I don't have children. But if I did I am sure I wouldn't assume a . . . criminal group was in the right and he in the wrong."

"You don't understand," Edward said. "You don't understand at all. Why would he . . . Why would Tom mess with them? Doesn't he know better? Doesn't he understand? They're dangerous."

"Oh, I'm sure he knows that," she said. "And I'm sure I understand better than you do. I'm sure he had his reasons. They might have been wrong, but I'm sure he had his reasons. I've known Tom too long not to know that he had to have reasons for what he did. He's neither stupid nor crazy, though he is, perhaps, a little too reckless."

Edward snorted at this. "Look, I don't know how good my son is in bed, but—"

The moment the words were out of his mouth, he knew he'd said entirely the wrong thing. She drew herself up. Her face became too impassive, too distant. "Mr. Ormson," she said. "I think you've said enough."

"No, listen, I know he appeals to women, he always has, but he—"

She pushed her lips together and looked at him with an expression that made him feel as though he were something smelly she had just found under her shoe. She opened her mouth. "Mr. Ormson," she said. "I have no idea what you think my relationship with your son is, but—"

At that moment, a phone rang. Kyrie plunged her hand into the pocket of her apron. "Rafiel," she said.

❖   ❖   ❖

"Can I borrow your cell phone?" Rafiel asked, all polite from the backseat.

"My . . . ?" Tom asked. Couldn't the man see Tom was naked? Where did he think Tom kept a cell phone, exactly?

"The cell phone," Rafiel said.

"From your backpack, dude. All your stuff is in there," Keith said, looking aside from his driving, even as he took perilous turns at high speed on the country road. Behind them, in the rearview mirror, Tom could see a blaze going up.

"The other . . . aren't they chasing us?" he asked.

"Nah. You set fire to their cars and the station."

"I did?" Tom asked.

"Yep. As you came out. You were flaming all directions. I grabbed you to prevent you from flaming this car. Don't you remember?"

Tom shook his head. He didn't. But he'd been running on adrenaline.

"And Rafiel stayed behind to keep them in there, until the fire caught. Some must have escaped, but I don't think they're in a state to follow us." He looked at Tom, even as he took a sharp turn onto the highway toward Colorado. "That was awesome," he said, and grinned.

"Your cell phone?" Rafiel asked from the backseat. "If I may."

Tom forced himself to open his backpack. And almost wept at the sight of his black leather jacket, his boots, his meager possessions. He rifled through them, till his hand closed on the cell phone. He passed it to Rafiel, without even asking why or what was so urgent about a phone call.

"You could dress," Keith said. "You know . . ."

And Tom, obediently, without thinking, pulled out his spare T-shirt and pair of jeans and put them on. Then he slipped on his jacket and boots.

Rafiel was talking to someone on the cell phone. "No, damn it, he's fine. Well, he's bleeding, but you know we heal quickly. Don't worry. We'll be there in six hours or so."

"I have to drink something," Tom said. "I have to."

"Um . . . we might stop at a convenience store," he said. He leaned forward, toward Keith, and spoke urgently. "In this area, some of the convenience stores at the rest stops have everything. I could use a pair of shorts and a T-shirt."

Keith looked back, still driving, and grinned. "Yeah, you sure could."

"So," Rafiel said, into the phone. "Don't worry. We'll be there. Yes, I understand. We'll . . . discuss it later."

He turned the phone off and handed it to Tom, then leaned back in his seat.

Tom could only see him from the waist up, of course, but he seemed relatively unscathed by the ordeal. And he was . . . well, everything Tom was not. Much taller, much more self-assured. And a lion. Kyrie was a panther. Tom didn't have a chance.

"So," Keith said, oblivious to his friend's thoughts. "How long have you guys been able to change into animals, and how do I get in on this?"

Kyrie stood, holding the phone, not quite sure what to do or say. Edward Ormson was looking at her, attentively.

"Look," he said. "I know I have said the wrong thing." His expression changed as if he read a response she wasn't aware of expressing in her features. "Okay, many wrong things. But look, however misguided, however wrongheaded, your . . . your reaction to what I was trying to do, to my trying to obtain the Pearl from Tom woke me, made me realize how bizarre all of this was. I haven't seen Tom in five years, and I'll confess I was a horrible father. But I don't want him to die. Can you help me?"

Kyrie looked at him a long time. She'd taken his measure the first time they'd met. Or at least she'd thought so. He was cold and self-centered. A smart man and probably well-educated and definitely good-looking, he was used to having his own way and very little used to or interested in caring for anyone else.

He would have, Kyrie thought, viewed Tom as an accessory to his lifestyle. He'd have the beautiful wife, the lovely home and, oh, yes, the son. Tom—if Tom's personality had always been somewhat as it was now— must have been a hell of a disappointment. They must have clashed constantly—supposing Edward paid enough attention to his son to clash with him.

Weirdly, it was that resentment he felt toward Tom, the fact he talked about Tom as having been insufferable that gave her a feeling that, however hidden, however denied even to himself, the man must care for his son. Because if he didn't truly give a damn about Tom, Tom wouldn't get under his skin so much.

Then she realized she could very well be speaking about herself. She had spent an awful lot of the last six months reassuring herself of how impossibly annoying Tom was.

Of course, he was annoying. Tom was quite capable of sulking through an entire work shift, for reasons she never understood. And he had this way of looking at her, then flinching away as if he'd seen something that displeased him. Particularly on those silent, sulking days. He was also quite capable of doing exactly the opposite of what you asked him to do, if he thought you hadn't asked him nicely enough. But . . .

But Tom was also unexpectedly generous. He would cover for her if she needed it, not complaining about the extra work. He would cover her tables, too, if she was moving slow because she was tired or not feeling well. He would bus a disproportionate number of tables and not call her on it. He had a way of smiling and shrugging and walking away when she offered to give him part of her tips after he'd helped her with the tables. And once when she'd pressed him, he'd said, "Oh, it all evens out, Kyrie." She remembered that.

And he had a way of appreciating the funniest of their diners. Sometimes, while enjoying a particularly funny interaction between a college-age couple, Kyrie would look over and find Tom smiling at them, in silent amusement. And, of course, he was—she remembered him naked, in the parking lot—distractingly handsome. As disturbing as the circumstances had been . . . it couldn't be denied that he was attractive. Despite his height, she'd often seen college girls batting eyes and displaying chests and legs at him.

So, her constant annoyance at him might very well have been a defense.

She realized she was grinning, as well as blushing because Edward Ormson was looking at her as if she had just taken leave of her senses.

"I'm sorry," she said. "I just realized why your son annoys me so much," and was gratified to see him look puzzled at this. "But you don't need to worry about him right now. He is . . . fine now."

"He is?" Edward Ormson started to get up, then sat down. He looked as though someone had cut all his strings, or whatever had been holding him up. He visibly sagged in his chair.

He looked so relieved that she had to smile. She picked up his coffee cup. "Let me get you another coffee. Warmer."

But he got up and handed her a twenty-dollar bill. "No," he said. "No. I don't think I need the coffee. Or the . . . pie. I just need to go to bed. I'm . . ." He rubbed his hand across his forehead. "I find I'm very tired." He pulled something else from his wallet and wrote rapidly in the back of it. "This is my card. There's my cell phone on the front and I put my room number at Spurs and Lace on the back." He handed it to Kyrie. "If Tom should . . ." He swallowed. "If you tell Tom . . ." He shrugged. "I don't want . . . Let him decide."

"I owe you about ten, twelve dollars change," Kyrie said. "Even with tip."

But he waved it away. "I don't want to waste time. I don't care. I'm very tired. I haven't slept in . . . much too long."

Kyrie almost argued, but then she saw him stumble to the door. She put the bill in her apron pocket. She would ring it up later.

She wondered where Tom was and how he really was. And what was happening.

When they stopped at the convenience store, Keith went in first.

"I forgot to ask if he had any money," Rafiel said from the back.

Tom had been dozing. He opened his eyes and looked back at Rafiel, then at the front of the brightly lit store and grinned. "I'd tell you that he probably does, but since we're talking about a man who thinks driving while looking backwards to talk to you is a perfectly safe practice, I can't really be sure."

Rafiel nodded. He looked . . . less than composed and was hiding behind the backseat. Fortunately though even at this time of night the convenience store/rest stop was full of people, Keith had parked in a place with two empty spaces on either side. Of course, the store was brightly lit in front and even with the tinted windows, Rafiel had to feel awfully exposed.

"I don't think anyone can see in," Tom said, in what he hoped was a friendly voice. He was still starving and his mouth felt dry as sandpaper, but the brief doze had made him feel much more human, much more in command of his own faculties. He felt . . . almost like himself. Enough to feel sorry for the guy. Even if the guy had a lot more chance with Kyrie than Tom himself.

Rafiel raised his eyebrows at Tom's comment, and nodded. "I hope not, I would never live down being arrested for indecent exposure. Even if I explained it—somehow—and went free. It's not something police officers are supposed to do, walking around naked."

"Must be a bitch," Tom said, leaning back against the seat and closing his eyes. He wanted to go in and get water and food. All his money was still in the backpack. He'd checked. But he would prefer to go in with one—or preferably—two people who could grab him if he passed out. Or started shifting and tried to eat one of the tourists.

"Yeah," Rafiel said, quietly. "I have clothes hidden all over town." He was silent a minute. "I just never thought I needed them in the neighboring towns too."

Tom smiled in acknowledgment of the joke, and felt a hand on his shoulder.

"I don't think we've been formally introduced," Rafiel said. "My name is Rafiel Trall. I'm a police officer of Goldport."

Tom opened one eye to see a hand extended in his general direction. He shook it, hard. "Thomas Ormson," he said. "Troublemaker. Broadly speaking of Goldport, also."

Rafiel nodded. "I haven't thanked you for saving my life," he said.

"You don't need to," Tom said. "I thought you were someone else."

Rafiel smiled. "At least you had the excuse of darkness. Apparently other . . . dragons have trouble telling a female panther from a male lion. In full light."

"Ah . . . how did . . . ?"

"Kyrie had sent me to check on Keith," Rafiel said, then frowned. "No. To tell you the truth, Kyrie sent me to look for you. She thought Keith might know where you were. So I was at his place when dragons came in. Through the window. So I . . . shifted before I knew what I was doing. And they tranquilized me. With a dart gun."

Tom nodded. "They really weren't very polite," he said, thinking how much preferable a dart gun would be than what they'd done to him. "I think they injected me with marinade."

Rafiel's face went very puzzled, but at that moment, Keith opened the door and threw a bundle at Rafiel. "Shorts, T-shirt, flip-flops. All in the best of taste and the cheapest stuff we could get and still make you decent. Enjoy."

Tom turned back to look at the clothes while Rafiel unfolded them. The T-shirt was white, with a mountain lion on the front and it said "Get Wild In New Mexico." The shorts were plaid and managed to look like a cross between bad golf clothes and a grandpa's underwear. And the flip-flops combined green yellow and a headachy-violet in the minimal possible amount of rubber.

Looking at Rafiel staring aghast at the getup, Tom realized he really liked Keith an awful lot.

But Rafiel recovered quickly. "I'll pay you back, of course," he said.

Keith nodded. Tom, not sure Rafiel meant that as a threat or a promise, raised his eyebrows. Then he said, "Look, I'm dying of thirst. And hunger. I have some money and I want to go inside, but I want one of you to come with me. Or both, preferably."

"Why?" Keith asked.

"Well . . ." Tom shrugged. "I haven't eaten in very long. I also haven't slept much. When I eat I might pass out or . . . as soon as I'm a little stronger, I might try to shift and . . . eat tourists."

Keith's eyes went very wide.

Rafiel, moving frantically and, from the bits visible in the rear-view mirror, dressing, in the backseat, said, "Even in Colorado that seems a bit drastic. And I don't even know if New Mexico's tourists are as annoying as ours." There was a sound of flip-flops being thrown about, and then Rafiel opened the door. "Come on then. We'll escort you to the food and water."

✦   ✦   ✦

Anthony had moved behind the counter and was turning burgers on the grill. That Frank didn't even seem to have realized he was cooking was worrisome.

Anthony turned around, putting plates on the counter for Kyrie to pick up. "Those are your orders," he said. "And would you cover table fifteen for me? And table five?"

Kyrie nodded. She assumed that Frank hadn't responded to Anthony's requests that he cook considering that he normally wouldn't let them behind the counter for more than dishwasher-filling, coffee-pot-grabbing stints. But Frank was still bent over the counter, staring into the eyes of his dowdy girlfriend and whispering who knew what sweet nothings to her.

When had this become so serious? Kyrie had seen the woman around before, but never actually interfering with Frank's work.

They touched a lot, Kyrie noticed. More than they talked. Her hand was on his, her fingers beating a slow tattoo on the back of his hand. And his were on the side of her other arm, also beating some weird rhythm.

Ah, well. Dating for the speech impaired. And sight impaired, Kyrie thought, looking back at Frank's Neanderthal profile, and his girlfriend's faded lack of beauty.

But Anthony was moving the burgers and fries, mixing the salads, and generally cooking like a demon, and she didn't have much time to look at her employer as, over the next few minutes she carried trays back and forth, fulfilling long overdue orders for both her tables and Anthony's.

When she was caught up, she came back to get the carafe and the pitcher of iced tea for refills. Frank's girlfriend had got up and was heading out of the diner via the back hallway. Either that or going to the bathroom, of course.

And Frank had seemed to wake up. "No," he yelled at Anthony. "What are you doing?"

Uh-oh. Now the explosion came, Kyrie thought. But as she approached, she realized Frank wasn't storming over the fact that Anthony had been manning the grill and the deep frier. Instead, he was throwing a fit because there was a little insect on the counter, and Anthony had been about to squish it with a paper towel.

"What?" Anthony said, his hand poised above the little creature—who looked like a beetle of some sort, only too small to be any of the normal ones found in diners. "It's an IPS beetle, man. It lives in pines. It must have come in because the windows are open."

"There's no need to kill it," Frank said, pushing Anthony's hand away and taking the paper towel from it at the same time. With infinite patience, he coaxed the beetle onto the paper towel.

Anthony shrugged and turned the burgers. "It's not like it's endangered or anything, you know? They spray for them up in the mountains. They kill spruce."

But Frank didn't seem to care. He got the beetle all the way into the towel, then walked out back, along the hallway.

Half fascinated, wondering what could have turned Frank, purveyor of burgers to the masses, into a lover of the small and defenseless, Kyrie followed him part of the way. Enough to see him open the back door and put the beetle out, on the ground, close to the dumpster.

Then he waved at his girlfriend, who was walking across the parking lot.

"Is she an animal lover?" Kyrie asked as Frank came back in.

"Debra? No. Why?"

Kyrie wasn't about to explain. Instead, she said, "Is it quite safe for her to walk home alone at night like that?"

He looked at her surprised. And behind the surprise something else. As if he were wondering why she was asking him the question. "Sure. She lives just at the castle. She'll be fine."

It didn't seem to admit further discussion.

"No more hot dogs," Keith told Tom. He handed him a thin pack of something cold. "Sliced ham."

Tom grabbed at it, trying to focus. He was vaguely aware that he'd eaten something like twenty-six hot dogs. And drunk something like four huge cups of something sickly sweet with a flavor vaguely reminiscent of cherries.

Somewhere at the back of his mind was the awareness that he was going to need to use the restroom soon. Even a shifter's bladder couldn't possibly hold that much.

But much closer at hand was a need for protein. Lots of it. He grabbed the pack Keith gave him and was about to bite it as Keith pulled it away.

"Whoa, you need to unwrap it."

Tom was aware of growling. Or rather he was aware of several faces of tourists roaming around turning to him in shock. He was aware of Keith jumping, then shoving the pack—now peeled halfway—back at him.

He shoved the ham into his mouth and ate it, becoming aware, halfway through, that his manners left much to be desired. And that the burning pit of hunger at the center of his being was . . . calmer, if not completely filled.

Rafiel, to whom Tom had handed a hundred dollars to deal with the damage, because he couldn't think and eat at the same time, approached them, carrying a bag of food. Tom could see a block of cheese and a couple of containers of what might be yogurt through the bag.

"Ready?" Rafiel asked. "You seem to have slowed down some."

Tom finished the last crumbs of meat, resisted an urge to lick the package. "I'll use the restroom," he said. "And I'll be right out."

"Good point," Rafiel said. "We grabbed you snacks but no drink. Keith, get us a six-pack of water." He passed Keith some money. "Tom, can I use your cell phone? In the car?"

Tom nodded.

When he got back to the car, Rafiel was behind the wheel and Keith next to him. "You get in the back," Keith said. "We figure you'd want to sleep some."

"There's cheese and cold cuts and stuff in the bag," Rafiel said. "If you're still hungry. And there's water. You can lie down. I drive better than him."

"And there's a bag of baby wipes," Keith said. "Your face is caked with blood. I didn't even think how weird it looked till we went in there."

Tom climbed into the back. He was about to tell them he wasn't that tired, when he stretched out on the broad and comfy backseat. And then his eyes closed. And he didn't know anything more.

❖   ❖   ❖

He woke up with a running conversation up front.

"So, why was he so hungry again?" Keith said.

"The transformation takes . . . I don't know. Strength. Power. It costs us what seems to be parts of ourselves. The muscle needs to recover."

"Would he really have . . . Would he have eaten someone or was he . . . ?"

"I don't know," Rafiel said. "I don't know Mr. Ormson that well. I don't know how many shape-shifts he'd had without replenishing himself. I guess it's . . . I mean . . . I guess it depends. I've never eaten anyone." There was a short silence, and Tom saw Keith look at Rafiel.

"Well, at least not that I remember," Rafiel said. "When you're very hungry or very tired, or scared, or in any other way pressed, the memory of when you're . . . the beast . . . changes. And we smell dead bodies a long distance away. So . . . I found a lot of corpses. Still do. I don't think I've ever eaten anyone, though. And since in my job I deal with unknown deaths and disappearances, I probably would have heard of it. Or, when I was too young to be on the force, my father would have. So . . ." He shrugged.

Tom sat up and rested his chin on the front seat, between the driver and passenger sides. "I might have eaten some of that corpse in the parking lot . . ." he said, and looked at Rafiel, in the rearview mirror. "I don't know if I killed him."

Rafiel shrugged. "As to that, I can reassure you, at least. You didn't. The corpse had no tooth marks, certainly no marks of being killed by a dragon."

"The guy who died?" Keith asked. "In the parking lot?"

Rafiel nodded, at the same time Tom asked, "But you said he was killed by a Komodo."

"Oh, that's right," Rafiel said. "We never told you . . . Kyrie and I, when we came back, you two were high because of the beetle powder. Well, insect powder, but Kyrie says it was beetles."

"Beetles?" Tom and Keith said, at the same time.

"There was green powder all over Kyrie's back porch," Rafiel said. "And it seemed to be of insect origin and . . . well, I have the lab checking for some form of hallucinogenic properties. But the lab seemed to think that corpse at least had some traces of hallucinogenic in his blood. So, we think that the green powder caused both of you to get high and hallucinate."

"Oh," Tom said, and could say no more. Of course. It wasn't Kyrie's sugar. It was the things attacking them. He frowned as he tried to remember. He'd thought they were dragons, but looking back he wondered why. He could remember what seemed to be long, long limbs, with fangs at the end, and he remembered green wings, but they didn't in any way look like dragon wings.

"But you said something about Komodo dragons?"

"Well, yes. There have been a few deaths that seemed to be caused by Komodo dragons. Really large Komodo dragons. Because the victims were all Asian, I suspected it had to do with triad business, and now I'm almost sure of it. I suspect it's the dragon triad. Some way they punish their members. That seems to be totally unrelated to the thing going on with the beetles. You seem to be the only link, Mr. Ormson."

Tom groaned. "My father is Mr. Ormson. I'm Tom. Particularly . . ." He managed a tired smile but couldn't see if Rafiel responded because all he saw of Rafiel in the rearview mirror was his very intent eyes. "Particularly to people who've seen me wolf down two dozen over cooked convenience store hot dogs." He made a face. "They weren't even all that good."

"Oh," said Keith. "There were also two containers of cottage cheese while the man was cooking more hot dogs, and a couple of pepperoni."

"Pepperoni?" Tom asked, and felt a moan break through his lips. "I don't even like pepperoni."

"Well, if you're going to throw up," Rafiel said. "You'd best do it out the window. We're still in Raton and we have about two more hours before we get home."

"I'm not going to throw up," Tom said. "Now, if I had taken Keith's finger when he tried to pull the cold cuts away, then I might have."

"You growled," Keith said.

"Dangerous that," Rafiel said, and though Tom couldn't see his face, he was now quite sure there would be a smile twisting the policeman's lips. "Taking food from a starving dragon. Just so you know, it's not all that safe with a lion, either."

Keith made a sound that might have been a really fake whimper, then perked up and grinned at Rafiel. "Oh, well. Worth the price of admission just to have heard you explain to the cashier that Tom had an eating disorder. I don't know how they thought that related to the fact that his face was covered in blood. Why was your face covered in blood?" he asked, looking back.

"Well . . . I think I took Two Dragons' arm. Front paw. Whatever. But I think there was blood before." Tom touched a snaking pink scar that crossed his forehead. "They broke my skin there. And I think they might have broken my nose, though it looks the normal shape, so maybe they just hit it hard enough to make it bleed and tear the cartilage."

"But . . . How long ago?" Keith said.

"We heal freakishly fast," Rafiel said. "But you might want to use the wipes back there, anyway, Tom. I'd suspect you rubbed some of it off on the seat back there, but you still look like you were in an accident. And if you don't clean up and we stop for any reason . . ."

Tom noted that his first name had been used, as he grabbed the baby wipes and wiped at the mess, using the rearview mirror for guidance.

"And are you undead?" Keith said. "I mean . . . can you be killed, unless it's a silver bullet, or whatever?"

Rafiel shrugged. "I don't know. Tom, have you ever been killed?"

"I thought I was going to be," he said. "Out there, alone with the triad guys. I thought if they didn't kick me to death, they were going to kill me some other way. And if not, I thought I would be killed if I gave them what they wanted."

"And what did they want?" Rafiel said, very softly.

"Well," Tom said. "I brought the conversation around because I thought you deserved to know, but I'm not sure how to explain. Let me start by saying my dad was a lawyer."

"Ah, well, all is clear," Keith said. "No wonder you turn into a dragon."

Tom grinned. "He's a lawyer with a big firm, in New York. Or at least he was five years ago. His firm represented some Asian families that had . . . contracts with the triads. It wasn't so much, I think, that the firm set out to represent a criminal organization. More like they started representing people at the margins of it, and then eventually, they were defending members of the triad in criminal trials. And my dad is a criminal lawyer. So . . ."

Rafiel nodded. "Yeah. I suspect a lot of lawyers end up having contact with less than savory creatures."

"Well, at one point, some people came over to my father's house. There was something that had landed from China, and they wanted him to keep it safe for them till the next day. He was the only person they trusted in New York, one of the very few people they'd had contact with. They came to our condo, which I remember my father was very upset about because he hadn't given them permission.

"I was . . . oh, probably five? My mom was working. My nanny was watching soaps. I was very bored. So I snuck around to hear what my dad was saying. These people were not like the people who normally came to visit, you know—they wore actual Chinese outfits in silk. I was fascinated."

He was quiet a while. He remembered the Pearl unveiling. He remembered . . .

"And then?" Rafiel said.

"And then they explained to my father that this was the Pearl of Heaven. It had been given to the Great Sky Dragon by the Heavenly Emperor. They said that many of their members, though not all, had the ability to shift shapes to become dragons. I didn't believe them, of course. And I could tell my dad didn't. And then they put this felt bag on his desk, and they pulled it down. And the Pearl appeared. It was . . . Imagine something that radiates light, that makes you swim with happiness.

"They said that it was needed to keep peace amid shape-shifters who were dragons part of the time, because the characteristics of the dragons remained in the humans, and there was too much strife otherwise. As a kid—and you realize I never had what could be called a good family life, back then—all I could sense and feel was the warmth and approval of the Pearl. And that's all I remembered."

"And?" Keith asked.

Tom realized he'd been quiet for a long while. "And then at sixteen I started turning into a dragon. I had a little trouble believing it at first, and then I thought that it was very cool. Like a superpower."

"That's what I think," Keith said.

"And then . . . My father caught me coming in as a dragon and transforming. I actually had this down to a science. I could kind of perch on the balcony outside my bedroom, and shift back to human, and then drop into the room through the sliding doors. Anyway, my dad caught me. He must have seen the dragon fly in. And he came to look. I only had time to grab my bathrobe. He thought . . . I don't know what he thought, but he looked terrified. He ordered me out of the house. I thought he was joking. He got a gun."

Tom laughed without humor. "My father who was a member of I don't know how many antigun organizations. He had a gun somewhere in his desk. He ran to grab it. I thought he was joking. I thought he would calm down. He ordered me out of the house at gunpoint and I went."

"Barefoot and in a robe?" Rafiel said. "In New York City. Amazing you survived."

Tom shrugged. "There are organizations for runaways. I wasn't, but I was the right age, the right profile, and all I had to do was say no when they offered to mediate my return home with my father." He shrugged again. "In a year I was lying about my age and getting jobs. But I hated the shift. I hated that it came when I didn't expect it. And because I fought it till the last possible minute, I often couldn't remember what I'd done when I'd shifted. I . . ." He looked at Rafiel. "I tried street drugs."

"Anything in the last six months?" Rafiel asked. "Since you've been in Goldport?"

"Only whatever the triad boys injected into me," Tom said.

"Ah. We don't regulate marinade. The rest is really none of my business. It's all hearsay, anyway. I have no proof. You might just be nuts and think you used and sold drugs."

"I never sold it," Tom said.

"Good. That's harder to give up, sometimes," Rafiel said. "What with connections . . . So, you tried some funny stuff, to control it. Did it?" His interest sounded clinical.

"Not so you could notice. I was using mostly heroin because of its being a depressant. I thought it would stop the shift. Since the shift came with big emotions and such."

Rafiel nodded.

"So I wanted to give it up, but I was scared," Tom said. "The one thing the drugs did was make me forget. And make me calmer when I wasn't a dragon. They . . . simplified my life. I couldn't obsess about being a dragon shape-shifter or about the fact that my own father had kicked me out of the house, or any of that, because I was too worried about getting enough money for the next fix."

Rafiel nodded. "Weirdly, I've heard other addicts say that this was more important for them than the physical effects. The simplification of life and of choices."

"It was for me," Tom said. "And then one day, I was in a small city—I don't even remember where—and I felt . . . I felt the Pearl. And I got the bright idea that if I had the

Pearl I wouldn't need the drugs. So I followed the feeling. And I came to this incredible meeting of dragon shape-shifters. It was dark and the little town was asleep. The parking lot was filled with men . . . and many dragons. And there was . . . the Great Sky Dragon. I don't know how to explain this.

"He's like a dragon god. Not like God, the God above, the one God, but like a god. Like . . . like the Roman gods would be to humans. That's how the Great Sky Dragon was to the rest of us. I could imagine people offering sacrifices and . . . virgins to him. Like in the legends. And he had the Pearl."

Tom heard himself sigh. "I wanted the Pearl. I'm not stupid. Not when I don't want to be. They were all basking in the glow of the Pearl and stuff. And they were all scared of the Great Sky Dragon. I'm not very good at being scared," he said, and watched Rafiel nod.

"I was impressed by the Great Sky Dragon," Tom said. "But not scared as such. So I paid attention to who took the Pearl, and it was another dragon in attendance. He put it in a wicker basket. And I loitered till the dragon shifted shape. He was the owner of a small Chinese restaurant in town. I followed him there. And then . . . I . . . well . . . I waited. And I watched. And I planned. And then I ran in, got the Pearl and got out of there fast."

Tom frowned. "I must have taken them completely by surprise, because they didn't even think to follow me for a while. And meanwhile I found out they couldn't sense or follow the Pearl by sense if it was submerged in water. I couldn't follow it if it was submerged in water. I brought it out West inside an aquarium packed in foam peanuts in a cardboard box, in the luggage hold of various buses."

"Did it help with the addiction?" Rafiel asked.

"It helped with controlling myself, not necessarily the addiction—though perhaps the two are related. When I got it out and looked at it, I felt . . . calm, peaceful, accepted. And then even if I shifted, I didn't feel like it was a terrible thing or that I should be shunned or killed for it. Does it make sense?"

Rafiel nodded. He was frowning. Keith was looking back, and his eyes were wide—and was that pity in them? Tom didn't want Keith's pity.

"Anyway," he said, looking out the window at the mostly deserted landscape they were crossing, "anyway, I kicked the habit. It wasn't as difficult as I thought. Rough moments, but I think that the fact we heal so easily . . ." He shrugged.

Rafiel nodded. "It would help, wouldn't it? The tendency to reassert balance. And Keith, when you asked if we were, I guess, immortal? I don't know, not more than anyone else. It's hard to say. Until you die you don't know, and then it's academic. I try to stay away from people trying to shoot me with silver bullets."

"Or any bullets," Tom said, wryly. "And before you ask, I brought the Pearl with me to Goldport. And it's stashed in water. They want it back. To be honest, I wouldn't mind giving it back, but I can't. Because I think once I give it back to them, they'll kill me."

Rafiel made a face. "There has to be a way of giving it back." He was quiet a while. Then he said, "But I guess it doesn't have anything to do with the beetles, then?"

Tom shrugged. "I didn't know about the beetles till tonight."

"What would you estimate the percentage of shifters in the population is?" Rafiel said. "From your travels?"

"I don't know," Tom said. "Not very high. Considerably less than one percent. Even if we go on legends."

"Even if we go on legends . . ." Rafiel said, as an echo. "But you know, we know three at least, in our immediate sphere, and then there's the beetles, at least two. From their size, there's no way they can be nonshifters. And there's one of their victims who smelled like a shifter— though I only caught a bit of blood. And another that was definitely a shifter. The corpse in the parking lot." He nodded at Tom. "His wife said he was a coyote shifter."

"Lucky bastard," Tom said feelingly. "A coyote would be much easier."

Rafiel laughed and for a moment there was a bond. "Tell me about it," he said. "Here's the thing, though, Tom, why so many of us? And why is all this activity around the Athens?"

Tom shook his head. "I have no idea."

"Except," Keith said, "except maybe there's something like the Pearl of Heaven? Something that calls shifters there? That works on shifters?"

"Perhaps the Pearl?" Rafiel asked.

Tom didn't think Rafiel was working for the triad, but you never knew. "Not the Pearl," he said. "At any rate, where I have the Pearl, it's submerged. So it's not exerting influence on anyone. If the dragons who know what it feels like can't feel it, then neither can anyone else."

"Um . . ."

"Speaking of the triad," Tom said. "How come we're driving their car, and they're not hot on our trail?"

"Well . . . you flamed them pretty thoroughly," Keith said.

"Yeah, but . . . come on? No one has checked? And don't forget they have aerial transportation."

"Well," Rafiel said. "Two things. While you were in the bathroom at the station, I called some friends in New Mexico and told them the old station was a triad hangout and I'd heard from a friend that it had just gone up in flames. At a guess, any of them that got out is in too much trouble to talk, much less count the car wrecks in the parking lot. It's genuinely possible they think you burned."

Tom nodded. "And the other thing?"

Keith chuckled. "We bought three cans of spray paint. While you were in the restroom, we spray painted the top of the car. Just the top. So that aerial surveillance . . ."

"Painted? What color?"

"Mostly bright orange," Rafiel said. "It was what they had. The front is still black. We ran out of paint." He grinned at Keith who was still chuckling. "People did look at us like we were nuts."

"I bet."

"So what do we do now?" Keith asked.

"Well, first we get to Goldport," Rafiel said. "I'd like to change clothes . . ." He frowned down at himself. "And I probably should call in and figure out the news on the case. Also tell them I didn't drop from the face of the world, since I was supposed to be at work a few hours ago."

"And then?" Keith said.

"And then I think Tom and I, and Kyrie should get together and figure out what we're going to do. Both about the Pearl of Heaven and the triad and about the beetles." He looked back at Tom. "They attacked Kyrie's house, you know, after you left."

"Damn. Is she okay?"

"She's fine."

"My fault," Tom said. "I shouldn't have stayed there. They were probably after me."

"Don't be a fool. I think they were after her. She had seen them in the parking lot, dragging a corpse, and it was clear they knew she saw them."

"Hey," Keith said. "Why you and Tom and Kyrie? Why am I being left out of this? What have I done wrong?"

Rafiel frowned. "Well, you're not . . . one of us, are you? I mean . . . we have to police our own and help our own, because if one of us is discovered, the others will be too. But you don't have to help us. You're not . . ."

"Yeah, but I want to help," Keith said. "Can I like be an honorary shape-shifter or something?"

"Why?" Tom asked, puzzled.

"Oh, hell. You guys are cool. It's like SF or a comic book."

"Except you could get hurt. Quickly," Tom said.

"I could get hurt very quickly anyway. Look, they knew you were my friend, they came to my house to get me. Surely that means I'm already not safe. I might as well help."

"Tom, he has a point," Rafiel said. "Kyrie's house is clearly not safe. Your apartment is destroyed. I doubt that Keith's apartment is safe. And I . . ."

"You?"

"I live with my parents," Rafiel said. "They know I'm a shifter. They help me if needed. It's convenient."

"I didn't say anything," Tom said.

Rafiel shrugged. "But I can't bring you guys there. If we're tracked . . . I can't risk them. Dad isn't doing so well these days."

"So you're saying you don't know where we can get together?"

Rafiel nodded. "Drop me off at home first. Then call Kyrie and tell her to meet you somewhere. Then pick me up in her car. We should leave this one in a public park or something. I don't think they'll report it stolen, but you never know." He drummed his fingers on the side of the wheel. "And then we'll figure out where to go. Perhaps a hotel room? A hotel would be good, wouldn't it? It's so public that I don't think even the triad would risk it."

Tom nodded.

"And I'm in? I'm in, right?" Keith asked.

"You're in," Rafiel said.

"There's a distinct possibility you're too addled to be left on your own," Tom said.

"Hey," Keith said, but he was smiling.

Tom felt odd. There was a weird camaraderie. He hadn't had friends in a long time. He hadn't ever had friends, truly. Not real friends.

He only hoped he could keep them all alive by the end of this.

❖ ❖ ❖

Kyrie was standing at the counter, adding up her hours, when her cell phone rang. She dipped into the apron pocket, and brought it out. "Yes?"

"Kyrie?"

It was Tom. Until she felt relief flooding through her, she didn't realize that she couldn't be absolutely sure he was still alive till she heard from him.

She almost called his name, but then realized that Anthony was behind the counter doing something and that she didn't know if Frank was hanging out somewhere. So, instead, she said, "Yes?"

"Thank God it's you," he said. There was a sound like coughing. "You didn't say anything and I wondered if I'd done something wrong and called the police department in New Mexico."

"What?"

"Later. Rafiel said he'd told you that you might need to pick us up."

"Yes."

"Well, can you come? We're in the parking garage for the zoo. We've parked on the third level, and we'll come down to meet you out front. In front of the zoo."

"We?"

"Keith and I. We'll swing by Rafiel's place on the way, okay?"

"Sure."

She hung up and found Anthony staring at her. "Was that Frank?"

"No."

"Damn," Anthony said. "I don't know where he's gone. I'm going to have to stay here and wait for the day-shift people. Will you wait with me?"

"I can't," Kyrie said. "I've got to meet a friend."

"The guy you were talking to?" Anthony asked, gesturing toward the enclosure. "He looks an awful lot like Tom."

"It's his father," Kyrie said, as she headed for the door. She'd parked up front again. She didn't think she could ever park in the parking lot again. Not for all the money in the world.

"Oh," Anthony said, just as she opened the door and went out.

Kyrie realized a little too late that Anthony might think that she was having an affair with Tom's dad. But she didn't think so. Anthony was a rather conventional person, other than the bolero thing, and was more likely to have her engaged to Tom in his mind—and to assume that his father's visit had something to do with finalizing the arrangements.

The drive to the zoo wasn't long. Just a few blocks down Fairfax and then a turn into a tangle of streets named after presidents.

It didn't really matter which you took, since they were all parallel. Either Madison or Jackson took you to a sharp turn at Taylor and then up Wilson where the street namers had run out of presidents and offered, instead, Chrisalys Street, which in turn, exhausted by all these flights of fancy ended in Main Parkway, where the zoo, the library, and the pioneer museum were all located.

Finding Tom and Keith at the entrance wasn't hard either. She simply took a long turn around the parking lot, and—circling by the door—saw the two only people standing there, since the zoo was still closed.

She very much doubted it would have been hard to find them even if there had been crowds streaming by the door, though. Tom looked like he'd been put through a shredder. There was blood on his face, his hair was a mess, and he looked like he was about to fall over from tiredness.

But he smiled when he saw her, and she couldn't help smiling back as she opened the door. For some reason, she expected him to be mad at her for throwing him out—for thinking he'd gotten high. But he didn't look resentful at all. He sat in the passenger seat, while Keith took the backseat. And Tom strapped himself down with the seat belt, too, she noted.

"We have to call Rafiel and go get him," Tom said.

"We do?"

"Yes. He went home to change. His clothes were shredded sometime . . . around the time they captured him." He gave her a quick rundown of everything that had happened and Kyrie listened, eyebrows raised, trying not to show just how harrowing the account was. Particularly the torture.

When he was done she thought how strange he was that he should have endured all that torture and yet have roused himself to action when he thought Keith—and herself—were in trouble. She took a sidelong glance at Tom, who was dialing his cell phone. There was someone there, she thought. Someone salvageable despite whatever his upbringing and his unexpected shifter nature had done to him.

"Rafiel," Tom said into the phone. Followed by raised eyebrows and, "I see." Which was, in turn, followed by, "Sure."

"He wants to know where we're going to be. He says he'll meet us. He's looking up some data on missing people. He says there's a spike over the last two months. He wants to know what the chances are those people are shifters. Something in the family interviews might give it away, he said. And he definitely wants to figure out how many people were headed for the Athens or that vicinity when they disappeared. So he says he'll meet us wherever we're going. And he asks which hotel."

Hotel. Kyrie had been thinking about this. There was an off chance the triad—or the beetles, whoever they were—would decide to call around to hotels for their names. But the hotels they would call around to—if they got around to that—would be in their price range. Not the Spurs and Lace.

"We thought it would be better to meet at a hotel," he said into the phone. "Particularly a large hotel. Lots of guests. No shape-shifter even one not quite in his right mind would want to have that kind of public revelation."

"Where are we going?" he said. "Rafiel says he'll meet us wherever."

"Tom . . . What do you think of your father?"

Tom's eyes widened. His face lost color—which she would have thought impossible before. "Why?" he asked.

"Because he's in town and he—"

"Hang on a second," Tom said into the phone. "I'll call you back in a couple of minutes." He hung up the phone and set it in his lap, then looked at Kyrie. "My father?" he said, not so much as though he were verifying her words, but as though he were in doubt that such a thing as a father existed.

"Your father came to town two days ago and he—"

"Oh, shit," Tom said. "You realize he's probably working for the triad?"

"He was," Kyrie said.

"And? What did he do? Where did he go?"

"He came to me."

Tom's hand clenched so hard on the phone that his knuckles shone white through the pale skin. His face remained impassive. "What did he ask you?"

"Many things. But most of all he seemed to be concerned with where you were, and I couldn't have helped him even if I wanted to."

Tom nodded. "And?"

"And I realized he was working for the triad and I was so shocked that I . . . I left."

"Good," Tom said, and picked up the phone again. "Now, where should we go to that Rafiel can meet us?"

"Tom," Kyrie said, speaking in a low voice because she felt as though Tom were something very unstable on the verge of an explosion. Should not be shaken, stirred, or even looked at cross-eyed, as far as she could tell. "Your father has a hotel room. At the Spurs and Lace."

She expected the silence, and it came, but then she expected a flip remark, and that didn't come. Instead, Tom's face seemed set in stone, his eyebrows slightly pulled together as if he were puzzled, his face expressionless, his eyes giving the impression of being so unreadable that they might as well have a blind pulled down in front of them.

"He said to call him if we needed anything."

"Kyrie," Tom said. It was a slow, even voice. "Are you out of your mind?"

"No." She was prepared to be firm. It was the best solution, and yes, she realized it would disturb Tom, but she was determined to keep them safe. By force if needed. "No. I'm not. He said to call him, and we can meet him at the Spurs and Lace. Our names won't be on the register and I don't think anyone will think that he and you will be under the same roof."

"And there are reasons for that," Tom said, his voice still even. "Kyrie, he's working for the triad."

"No, he's not. He realized that they wanted to . . . kill you. And he came to me. He wanted me to save you."

"No. That might have been what he said. But he was just trying to find me, to—"

"Tom, I am not an idiot," Kyrie said, and saw something flicker in his eyes and for just a moment thought that Tom was going to tell her she was. But he didn't say anything, and she went on. "I saw what he was doing first, but he changed. He said that he didn't want you dead. He came to the Athens in the middle of the night, looking like the walking dead. And he begged me to help him."

"Kyrie. He's a lawyer. Lawyers lie. It's right in the contract."

She shook her head. "He wasn't lying."

"No? How not? What sign did he give you of his amazing turnaround, Kyrie? Tell me. Maybe it will convince me. I know the bastard far better than you do." He left the phone resting on his knees and crossed his arms on his chest, in a clear body-language sign that like hell he'd listen.

"If he shifts into a dragon in the car, I'm jumping out," Keith said, quietly, from the back.

Kyrie ignored Keith. "I know he's changed in his view of it, because he tried to convince me how bad you are."

Tom's eyes widened. "All right, Kyrie. I was the one who was hit on the head, but you seem to be the one affected by it. He's always said how bad I was."

"No," Kyrie said, and shook her head. "Not like this. He stopped just short of saying you botched your spelling bee in third grade. Your father, Tom, realized suddenly that he messed up big with you. And he's trying to justify it to himself by telling someone in increasingly more ridiculous terms how nasty a person you are."

Tom didn't answer. He was biting the corner of his lower lip.

"Look—I—" She stopped short of telling him she had done the same. Just. "I tend to do what he was doing, so I understand the process. Besides, when I told him you were safe, when Rafiel called, he went all slack. I've never seen someone so relieved."

"Okay, so maybe he didn't want me to die. Maybe he was relieved at that. Doesn't mean he won't change his mind again when he actually sees me."

"I don't think so," Kyrie said. "I don't think he will. And Tom, we could use his room. I'm indentured for the next six months, you can't have that much money. We'd have to get Rafiel to pay for it. I'd . . . I'd rather not." The last thing she wanted to tell Tom was that Rafiel had kissed her. Oh, Tom had no reason at all for jealousy, nor did she know if she had any interest in Tom's kissing her—Okay. So, she had to stop lying to herself, she thought again, looking at his face— Yeah, she wanted to kiss him. She just wasn't sure where it would go and *that* she wasn't sure if she wanted. But Tom had no reason for jealousy and she doubted he would have any, but she would still prefer not to tell him about it.

"Kyrie, I don't believe in big turnarounds. I don't believe people change that much."

Oh, she was going to hate to have to say this. "I don't believe it either, Tom, but . . . You're no longer a hard-core drug user who would steal cars for joyrides without a second thought, are you? So there must be change."

Tom's mouth dropped open. For a moment she thought he was going to ask her to stop the car so he could get out. His hand actually moved toward the door handle. And then he seemed to realize she wasn't insulting him. The meaning of her words seemed to actually penetrate through his thick head.

He took a deep breath and held the phone out to her. "You call Daddy Dearest."

It would have been easiest to tell him she was driving and couldn't, but Kyrie was aware of the victory this represented. So, instead, she pulled over into a vacant parking space on the side of Polk Street and grabbed the phone. Pulling Edward's number from her purse, she dialed.

The phone rang, and she asked for the room number from the bored-sounding receptionist. Then his bedroom phone rang. Once, twice, three, four times. She expected the message to come on, when the phone was picked up, and clearly dropped, and picked up again.

"Hello," a sleepy male voice said from the other side.

"Mr. Ormson?" Kyrie said.

"Kyrie." The name came out with force, as though it would be more effort to keep it in. "Tom. Is Tom all right? Anything wrong with—"

"No. Tom is right here. He's fine. We were wondering if we could camp in your hotel room for a few hours."

"Beg your pardon?"

"Tom and I, and a couple of friends. We're . . . in danger from . . . your friends and . . . other people. We wondered if we could hide there till we find a plan of action."

There was a silence from the other side. And then a voice that sounded as if he didn't quite know what he was saying. "Sure, of course. Sure." A small pause. "And Tom is with you?"

"Yes."

"Oh." A deep breath, the sound of it audible even through the phone. "Sure. Of course. Anything you need."

"Thank you," Kyrie said and hung up the phone. She handed the phone to Tom and said, "Call Rafiel."

"Daddy Dearest is even now calling the triad bosses," Tom said. His mouth set in an expression of petulant disdain. "They'll be there when we get there."

"I doubt it," Kyrie said.

"And if they are, we fight them," Keith said, leaning forward.

Okay, so "scared" didn't even begin to describe the state of Tom's emotions as they pulled into the parking lot of the Spurs and Lace.

The problem wasn't being scared. He was used to being scared at this point. In the last three days, he'd been scared so often that he thought he wouldn't actually know what to do if he weren't in fear of someone or something. But this time he didn't even know what he was scared of.

Okay—so, if the triad members were there, Keith was right. They fought. And if Tom had to sacrifice himself so Kyrie and Keith got out of this unscathed, he would do so. He'd been prepared to do it before, in the abandoned gas station. So, why not now?

So . . . that wasn't the big source of his fear. The big source of his fear was that his father would be there, without the triad, and that all would be seemingly nice between them. He couldn't imagine talking to his father as if nothing had happened, as if . . . Worse, he couldn't imagine his father talking to him like that. But he'd been worried about Tom. Tom couldn't understand that either.

He settled for thinking that his father had been exchanged by aliens. It didn't make much sense and it wasn't very likely, but heck, what around here was likely? He'd just think that this was pod-father, and with pod-father, he had no history.

He got out of the car, and followed Kyrie and Keith up to the elevator and up in the elevator to the room, only slightly gratified by the puzzled looks the staff gave him.

Up at the fifth floor, they walked along the cool, carpeted hallway toward room 550.

Tom took in the trays with used dishes at the door to the rooms, and the general atmosphere of quiet. There were no detectable odors in the air. Down the hallway, an ice machine hummed and clunked.

The classiest place he'd been in before this was Motel Six. Oh, he supposed he'd been in hotels as a child. In fact, he had vague memories of a trip to Rome with mother and father and, of course, his nanny, when he was ten. But most of the stuff before he'd left home now seemed to him like scenes from someone else's life.

And perhaps that was the best way to think about it. The Tom who'd been ordered at gunpoint from his childhood home was dead and gone. This new Tom was a stranger to the man in the room.

But when Kyrie knocked, the door was opened by a man who looked far too much like the father Tom remembered for Tom not to take a step back, shocked— even as his father's gaze scanned him indifferently once, before returning, and then his eyes opened wider, and he opened his mouth as if to say something, but closed it again in silence and, instead, stepped aside to let them in.

He was wearing the pants and a shirt for the type of suit that Tom remembered his father wearing—fabric good enough to look expensive without looking ostentatious. But this one looked like hell—or like he'd been sleeping in it. His hair, too, was piled up in a way that suggested a total disregard for combs.

But the strangest thing was that, as he stepped aside, so they could enter the room, Tom's father stared intently at Tom.

Tom let his gaze wander around the room, instead. It was . . . dark red. And opulent. There was a dark red bedspread on the bed and from its sheen it might have been real silk. Someone had pulled it up hastily and a bit crookedly, so Tom's father had probably been in bed when they called, and had tried to make the bed in a hurry. Tom felt a strange satisfaction about this. To his knowledge, it was the first time his father had engaged in housekeeping for Tom's benefit.

Besides the bed, there were a love seat and three armchairs and two chairs, a huge desk, where his father had a laptop, resting. And a lot more empty space than there should be in a room with all that furniture.

Over the bed was an abstract collage that brought the art form completely out of the realm of nutty Seventies fads—a thing in deep textures and gold and bronze colors.

The bathroom, glimpsed as Tom was going past, was all marble and actually two rooms, the first of which contained just a sink with a hair dryer and various other essentials of toiletry. Tom ached for a shower with an almost physical pain, but he went in to the bedroom, quietly.

"Mr. Ormson," Kyrie said. "Thanks for letting us come in at such short notice."

He shook his head. "No problem. Make use of . . . whatever you want. Tom? Are you . . . There's blood on you."

Tom shook his head. "I'm fine." And then, as though betraying that he wasn't, he walked over to the most distant armchair and sat down, as far away from his father as he could get.

His father frowned at him a moment, but didn't say anything.

"I wonder if Rafiel is going to be much longer," Tom said, pretending not to feel the weight of that gaze on him.

Keith sat down on one of the straight-backed chairs, and Kyrie, after some hesitation, took the armchair next to Tom's.

She looked at him, too, but her gaze was not full of disapproving enquiry. Unlike his father's expression, Kyrie's was warm and full of sympathy.

He wanted to smile at her, to pat her hand. But just because the woman didn't want him dead; just because the woman didn't think he was dangerous or a criminal, it didn't mean that she had any interest whatsoever in him.

So instead, he fidgeted in the chair and looked out of the window into the parking lot. But he kept looking at her out of the corner of his eye. She looked good enough to eat—and not in the sense he'd threatened to eat tourists. That cinnamon skin, those heavy-lidded eyes. He looked away. If he allowed himself to contemplate the perfection of her lips, or the way her breasts—one of which he remembered with particular fondness—pushed out her T-shirt, he wouldn't be able to answer for his actions.

Instead, he looked again, at her tapestry-dyed hair, falling in lustrous layers. And he remembered he had something of hers.

Digging frantically in his jacket pocket, he brought it out. He saw her eyes widen, and her smile appear, as he offered her the earring on his palm.

"You found it," she said.

"My landlady did," he said. "And I took it. I was hoping . . . I was hoping I would see you again, to be able to give it to you."

He felt himself blush and felt like a total idiot. But Kyrie put the earring on and was smiling at him. He'd have been willing to go a long way for that. Coming to his father's hotel room seemed like a minor sacrifice.

Even if Daddy Dearest ended up selling them up the river.

The boy looked tense, Edward thought. Only the thing was, he wasn't a boy, anymore, was he? The face looking back at Edward's with such studied lack of expression was covered in dark stubble. And the shoulders had filled out, the arms become knotted with muscle.

Tom was wearing a black leather jacket, ratty jeans, and heavy boots. His father could have passed him a hundred times in the street and never recognized him. Only the eyes were the same he remembered from childhood, the same that looked out of his own mirror at him, every morning. But Tom's eyes showed no expression. They allowed him to look at them, and then they slid away from contact, without revealing anything.

There was blood on him too, and a snaking scar on his forehead. Had the triad done that, or had Tom gone through worse scrapes in the last five years? There were many things Edward wanted to know. Unfortunately, they were the ones he would never dare ask.

He watched Tom for a while, watched him pull out the girl's earring and give it back to her. He wondered if the two young fools had any idea that they were giving each other sick-puppy-dog looks.

But not only wasn't it his place to interfere, he was sure if he tried to tell them, either of them would put him soundly in his place.

"Do you guys want some coffee?" he asked, "I'm making some for myself."

There were sounds that might be agreement from the bedroom, as he set up the coffeemaker. Fortunately the Spurs and Lace went for normal-sized coffeemakers, not the one-cup deals that were normally the rule. And they provided enough coffee and enough cups. He set it to run and thought.

The boy needed a shower. And probably clean clothes. But Edward had a feeling that if he offered either Tom might very well fling out of the room in a fury. He got a feeling that Tom was holding something in, battling something. And that if he let it all blow, none of them would like it.

Of course, if Tom should shift to a dragon . . . Edward peered around the door at the young man and Kyrie, who were now talking to each other, while Tom had closed his eyes and appeared to be dozing.

Neither the young man nor Kyrie looked scared that Tom would shift into a dragon, so it couldn't be that frequent an occurrence.

The coffee was made, and Edward had a sudden flash of inspiration. Everything that he might offer Tom would be refused. But if he handed it to Tom as a matter of fact, there was at least the off chance that Tom wouldn't know how to refuse. He'd looked many things, none of them at ease.

So, testing his theory, Edward poured himself a cup of coffee, and then one for Tom, surprising himself with retrieving, from the mists of memory, how Tom liked his coffee. The boy had only started drinking it when he'd . . . left. But Edward remembered ribbing him about liking three spoons of sugar in it.

He now poured in three packets of sugar and then crossed the room, trying to look completely at ease. For all his appearances in uncertain cases, in courtrooms presided over by hostile judges, this was probably his greatest performance. "Coffee is ready," he told Kyrie and the other young man. "If you wish to help yourselves." Then he walked up to Tom.

The armchair the boy was sitting in was right next to a side table, and on the other side of that was the straight-backed chair normally used at the desk.

Edward put his own coffee cup down on the side table, and leaned over, touching Tom's shoulder, lightly. "Tom, coffee," he said.

Tom woke up immediately, and sat up, fully alert. Edward remembered that he used to sleep late and sometimes miss first period at school. When had he learned to wake up like this, quickly, without complaint? How had he been living that a moment's hesitation between being asleep and full alertness might make a difference?

He couldn't ask. "I put three packets of sugar in. The way you like it."

Tom looked surprised. He reached for the cup, took it to his lips without complaint. And Edward sat at the desk chair, and took a deep draught of his coffee, feeling ridiculously proud of himself. It had worked. If handed things straight off, Tom was too confused to refuse. It was the first time in years . . . No. It was the first time in Tom's lifetime that Edward had set himself to learn how to get around his stubborn son without a confrontation. And it had paid off.

It was all he could do to keep himself from smiling in victory. Fortunately, at that moment, someone knocked at the door and Kyrie opened it.

"Mr. Edward Ormson, this is Rafiel Trall, a police officer for Goldport."

Officer Rafiel Trall was tall and golden-haired, with the sort of demeanor one would expect from a duke or visiting royalty. He shook Edward's hand, but there was a slight hesitation, and Edward wondered what Tom had told him about his father.

But then, as the young people pulled chairs together to talk, Edward slipped out the door, quietly.

He didn't know if they were all shape changers, and he didn't know how they'd react to what he was about to do.

But he knew he had to do it.

❖   ❖   ❖

Tom smiled at seeing Keith immediately assume the role of secretary of the organization. Sometimes people defied all categorization. He'd never expected his wild neighbor, of the late nights and the revolving girlfriends to be this . . . neat.

But Keith grabbed the pad and turned to them. "As far as I can see it," he said, "we're facing two problems. One is the beetles. Kyrie is the only one who's seen the beetles—right?"

"No," Tom said, amused. "We've seen them also. We just didn't remember. I think you thought they were aliens."

Keith looked wounded. "Whatever that powder was . . ."

"Yes," Tom agreed not particularly wanting to go there, ᵗ wanting to explain that he'd thought Kyrie's sugar was drugged. He looked at her out the corner of his eye, and realized that Rafiel was also looking at her with an intent expression. Well, if she had to go to someone else . . . But Tom very much hoped she wouldn't.

"They are blue and green and refractive," Kyrie said. "And they look somewhat like the beetles I've seen in the natural history museum in Denver. I vaguely remember they said they were made into jewelry, and I could believe it because they were so pretty. The little ones in the museum. Not the large ones."

"You don't know what their genus is, do you?" Keith asked, looking up. "Because we could look them up and figure out their habits."

Kyrie shook her head. "I never really thought knowing the name of a beetle would be essential to me," she said.

"Ah, but see, that's where you go wrong," Keith said. Scribbling furiously. "Beetles are always essential. You let them run around unnamed they start music groups and what not." He looked up. "Well, I'll call the museum later, or look it up online. So . . . we have these huge beetles. Are we sure they're shifters?"

"They're the size of that bed," Kyrie said, pointing to the king-size bed behind them. "Or maybe the size of a double bed. Okay, maybe a single bed. But taller. Huge still. Where do you suppose their natural habitat would be? And why wouldn't it have been discovered long ago?"

Keith waved one hand. "Okay, point, point," he said. "But so, we have two shifters. How often is it that shifters get together? Same species shifters? Can you guys like . . . mate in your other form?"

Tom felt a burning heat climb to his cheeks. Without looking he could tell that Rafiel was now staring at Kyrie with a gaze set to smolder. And Kyrie was staring ahead, looking shocked, refusing to look at either of them.

It was funny. Because of course Keith had always assumed that Tom was a player like himself, that he was out there, every night, picking up girls. And of course, Tom's sexual experience, which could be written on the head of a pin, was all in very human form, and had all happened before the age of sixteen.

He threw his head back and laughed. "Keith, you've got the wrong guy, at least where I'm concerned," he said. "The dragons I've known were in the triad. So, I have no idea. Also, the legends are a little quiet on the mating habits of dragons."

"And I had never met another shifter till two days ago," Kyrie said, her voice small and embarrassed. "I suppose it's possible to mate in animal form."

Did she throw a quick look at Rafiel? Tom's heart sank.

"But I wouldn't like to do it," Kyrie said. She sat up straighter in her chair. "For the same reason I wouldn't really like to eat in the shifted form. Even if it's proper food, you know, not . . . people. I like being human. If I'm ever going to have sex, I'd like to be aware of who I'm doing it with and how."

"You've never—" Keith started, then shook his head.

Tom realized he was grinning, and forced his face to become impassive. He hoped Kyrie hadn't noticed.

Rafiel, meanwhile, was shaking his head. "Not in shifted form," he said. "Never. So, I too know nothing about sex between shifters. Though I suppose"—he gave Tom a sly look—"that the sex lives of lions are far better documented than the sex lives of dragons."

But he couldn't touch Tom's self-assurance at that point. Kyrie had just as good as confessed that her experience was not superior to his own. He wondered if she'd done it on purpose.

"You guys are a waste of shifting ability," Keith said, sounding vaguely disgusted. "So, you don't know if two shifters of the same kind, different gender met, if it would lead to . . ."

"Kittens in the basket?" Rafiel said.

"Eggs in the lair," Tom immediately interposed not to be outdone.

"Actually," Keith said. "I was thinking more that some species have truly bizarre mating habits. And if we're dealing with a mating pair, which . . . could we be?"

Kyrie leaned forward, holding her coffee cup in both hands, over her knees. "I think we could be, yes," she said. "I think . . . I got a feeling that was the case."

"So, if we're dealing with a mating couple, you know that insects can get really kinky, right? Like all the biting off of heads of males after mating, or while mating, and all that stuff. Is it possible that the killings are part of a mating ritual? Like where the male has to give the female a gift or something."

"Yes, that's quite possible," Tom said, feeling slightly dumb that this hadn't occurred to him. Possibly because in all he'd read of the mating rituals of beautiful jungle cats, there had never been anything about their requiring the gift of a corpse.

"It might be pertinent," Rafiel said, "that I suspect there have been about two dozen people killed, and that they were all or almost all shifters."

"How could you know that?" Kyrie asked.

"I don't know. I suspect. If you remember, I told you I wanted to wait a little before I came here, because I wanted to find out if there could have been more people who disappeared in that area and whose bodies haven't been found yet?" He took a sip of coffee. "Well, I figured it out. At least partway. There are at least fifteen other people who have been missing, all over the last month or so. And they all disappeared from around the Athens. They were all young and therefore we didn't pay too much attention. Otherwise the pattern would have become obvious. But most of them, the families didn't seem sure they hadn't run away, so we thought we'd give it a little longer . . ." He took another sip of coffee. "We're a small police department. Oh, and most people were either passing through or had just decided to move here. Some interesting things—they all seemed to really like the Athens and had been there more than once. And they all had, the sort of relationship with their families and people around them that . . ." He looked at Tom.

"Say no more," Tom said, and for the first time realized his father was nowhere around. Was he hiding in the bathroom to be out of their hair? Tom didn't think it likely, but then neither had he thought it likely that his father would still remember how Tom took his coffee.

"Well, here's the thing," Keith said. "If these are gifts perhaps they have to be shifters. Do you guys know when someone else is a shifter?"

"Sometimes," Kyrie said. "If you get close enough. There is a definite tang, but I'm not very good at smelling it."

"I can't smell it at all," Tom said.

"I smell it very well, but I have to be near the person and sort of away from everything else."

"And all shifters smell alike?" Keith asked. "Regardless of species?"

Rafiel nodded.

"So, perhaps the gift of the dead corpse has to smell like a shifter?"

"It's possible," Rafiel said. "We don't have enough to go on, but there are definite possibilities. Just the fact that it's a shifter couple is interesting. I'd imagine the odds against it are enormous, and I wonder how long they've been a couple.

"Probably about a month," Tom said. "Since that's when you started noticing the pattern."

"Good job, Mr. Ormson. You might have a future in law enforcement," Rafiel said.

The *Mr. Ormson* was clearly intended to be a teasing remark, and Tom was about to answer in kind, but he thought of his father. If he was in the bathroom, trying to stay out of their way, Tom didn't want to call the others' attention to his absence. Because if he did, and it was nothing, he was just going to sound totally paranoid. On the other hand . . . On the other hand . . . If he didn't call their attention, and his father had gone to the triad . . .

Tom got up, carrying his cup of coffee, as if he were going to get a refill.

"So I think on the matter of the beetles, the best thing really would be to look them up at the natural history museum," Keith said. "See if they have stuff about those beetles habits, then see what helps. And then we have the matter of the Pearl of Heaven."

But Tom had reached the little alcove before the bathroom, the area with the sink and the coffeemaker and cups. Tom frowned at it, because it had no articles of personal hygiene, only one of those kits of horrible toothbrush with toothpaste already on that hotels gave guests who forgot their toiletries. And Tom couldn't believe that his father—of all people—would have forgotten his toiletries.

The door to the bathroom was closed, but not enough for the latch to catch. Tom reached over, and slid it open with his foot, slowly. No one.

There could be a perfectly natural explanation. There should be a perfectly natural explanation. Tom was sure of it. But his heart was beating up near his throat, his mouth felt dry, and his hands shook. He put the coffee cup on the counter, very carefully, and then walked out, feeling light-headed.

Had he really believed his father cared? Had the thing with remembering how Tom liked his coffee been enough to make Tom believe his father gave a damn? He must really be starved for affection, if he'd believe his father could be more than a cold and calculating bastard.

He walked outside to the bedroom, feeling as if his legs would give out under him. His father had gone to the triad. Was probably, even now, making some plan to deliver Tom to the triad. And Tom didn't want to be tortured again. Plus, they would probably be even more upset now, considering he'd just been the cause of death of a number of their affiliates.

"We should just leave it on some public place," Keith said. "Like we left the car. And get the hell out of Dodge. Let the triad feel it and go get it."

Tom tried to shape his mouth to explain that his father had left, that he'd gone to denounce them—to denounce Tom—to the triad. But the betrayal was so monstrous that he couldn't find the words.

And then he heard the key slide into the lock, and he turned, barely staying human, poised on the verge of shifting . . .

And his father came in, alone, carrying two very large bags with the name and the logo of one of the stores in the lobby. And another smaller bag, with the name of another of the lobby stores. One that specialized in candy and snacks.

They faced each other, silently, and his father looked so startled, so shocked, that Tom wondered if he'd started to shift already.

"I'm sorry," his father said. "Was I needed? You guys seemed to be talking about things I didn't understand and I thought I'd get some clothes and a comb, since I left without any of that." He put the larger bags on the bed, then opened the small bag and fished out a red box tied with a gold ribbon. "I thought you might like these, Tom."

Nuts with chocolate and his favorite brand. Okay, this was becoming ridiculous. His father might have kicked him out of the house at sixteen, and he might know next to nothing about Tom's life since then, but, apparently, it was a point of pride that he remembered what Tom liked to eat and drink.

There was really no response for it, though, and Tom, no longer ravenously hungry, still felt peckish of sorts. Besides, this was a hideously expensive brand of chocolates and he hadn't been able to afford it in years.

While he was tearing the ribbon, he saw his father open a bigger assortment of different types and set it on the side table. "For you guys, since none of you look like you've slept enough."

Tom noticed that Kyrie's eyes widened and that her hand went out for a dark chocolate truffle. He would have to remember that. Forget dead bodies. Any female with even a bit of Homo sapiens in her was going to go for the chocolates.

To change subject, and disguise his attention to her every action—and also how scared he'd been at his father's absence—Tom looked at his father and managed to say in a voice almost devoid of hostility, "I wonder if you could talk to us about the triad," he said. "How you came to be here, I mean. And how they got you to come here."

"The Great Sky Dragon kidnaped me from my office," Tom's father said. He dipped into the common box, too, and got a nut chocolate also. It was one of the tastes they shared. "He picked me up and told me that my son was my responsibility and he was going to bring me here, and I could find you and the Pearl, after which he'd take me back to New York. He made it clear I wasn't to return until I'd found them their Pearl. Tom, why did you take it?"

Tom shrugged. He'd tried to explain this before, and was getting tired of explaining. Particularly because the idea seemed really stupid now, and also because he was starting to realize what he'd searched for in the Pearl was what he'd found with Kyrie and even with the guys—acceptance, caring for him, giving a damn if he lived or died.

Instead, he said, "Because hard drugs weren't working for me." And seeing his father look shocked, Tom smiled. "Because the Pearl made me feel loved and accepted and I hadn't felt that since . . . in a long time."

His father had gone slightly red, and was looking at Tom as though evaluating something. "So," he said, "do you still need it?"

Tom shook his head. "No. I told the . . . them." He gestured toward Keith and Rafiel. "I told them that I would give it back, if I could just figure out how to do it. I haven't really been able to do that. Not recently."

"What do you mean?" Edward asked.

"I mean that if I gave it back to them, they'd kill me. They made it very clear they didn't take kindly that I'd stolen it. It's their . . . cultic object or something. They don't like the idea that a stranger grabbed it. I think they'll feel the stranger must be killed. Considering what they did to me when they captured me . . ."

"Okay," Edward said, very calmly. "So, how about I take the Pearl back?"

Rafiel choked on his chocolate. "Not a good thing," he said. "Because if you do that, then I suspect they'll kill you. The whole thing they said about you being responsible for Tom?"

"Okay," Keith said. "I've already said it, but you guys were out of the room. I think the easiest thing is for us to take it somewhere public and leave it. Yeah, they might still come after Tom in search of revenge, but there is at least a chance that after the massive ass-whooping of last night, they would leave him alone as being way too much trouble to discipline."

"Well . . ." Tom said. "Yes, it's possible." It wasn't probable. And it wasn't the plan he would have picked, if he had any other semisane choice. But he didn't think he did, and leaving the Pearl somewhere public and running beat his plan to keep hiding it and running from the triad.

"You could leave it in front of the triad center here in town," Edward Ormson said. "You could put it at the door, in a bucket of water. Wait till the bucket dries. By the time the water dries and they feel it—if we hide it a little—we'll all be out of town."

Tom looked up. "Out of town?"

"You could come back home," his father said, suddenly animated. "Maybe go to college." He looked around at the rest of them. "And I'd arrange for the other two here to go wherever they want to go. College? Move and a business? Just say it. I assume Officer Trall would be safe, by virtue of his position?"

Tom could feel his jaw set. "The only home I've ever known . . ." he said. There was the thought that Kyrie might want to go to college, but he didn't think she wanted to go at his father's charity. *He* didn't want his father's charity. "The only home I've ever known burned a few days ago. I'll have to find some other place to live."

His father looked away and there was a silence from everyone else for a moment. "Anyway," Tom said, "leaving the Pearl somewhere and letting them know later is the best plan I've heard, Keith. Perhaps leave it in a bucket of water and call them though, instead of leaving it in the open and letting them sense it. We don't know if there are other dragons like me around and getting it stolen again would be a pain. They'd only come after me again."

"Yeah," Rafiel said. "So . . . where did you hide the Pearl and how much trouble do we need to go through to retrieve it?"

Tom did a fast calculation in his head. He wasn't sure of Rafiel or his father yet. Though, sadly, he was more sure of Rafiel than his father. Rafiel had at least fought against the triad dragons.

But he'd misjudged his father once. He looked sidelong at his father, and read discomfort and understanding in his eyes, as if he were completely sure Tom wouldn't trust him, and understood it too. As well he should. And yet . . . Tom was going to have to take the risk at some point. Might as well start.

"It's in the toilet tank at the Athens," Tom said. "The ladies' room. It has a huge toilet tank, the old-fashioned kind, so I just put it in there."

Kyrie's eyes grew huge. "What if the tank had stopped?" she asked. "What if —"

He shrugged. "It seemed fairly sturdy. Besides, I wrapped the Pearl in dark cloth, before I put it in. You know the light isn't very good there. If someone looked in there, as ancient as the tank is, they'd just think there was some type of old-fashioned flushing mechanism that they didn't understand."

"And it's been there?" Rafiel asked. "These six months?"

Tom nodded.

"Have you considered," Rafiel said, "that maybe it's the Pearl that's attracting people to the Athens and making them feel at home there?"

"I don't think so," Tom said. "If I can't feel it when it's submerged, if the triad dragons can't feel it while it's submerged, then how should strangers?"

"Besides," Kyrie said, "that feeling was there before. It was there a good six months before that. I felt . . . I know this is going to sound very strange, but I felt almost called to Goldport. Like I had to come here. And once I got here, I had to go to the Athens. Then I saw the wanted sign and I applied."

Rafiel fidgeted. "I developed the habit of going to the Athens for breakfast about a year ago too. And it's not near my house. I just felt . . . called to go there. And I felt okay once I was there."

Tom sighed. "I came to the Athens a few times for meals, before Frank noticed me. He asked if I wanted a job. I didn't want to take a job under false pretenses, so I told him the truth. That I was homeless, that I hadn't had a fixed address for a long time, that I'd never had a full-time job and that I had a drug habit I was working on kicking. He told me as long as I kept clean once he'd hired me, he didn't mind any of those. . . . What's weird is that I'd already stopped in Goldport, and I had no idea why. It was like something in my subconscious had called me here, and to the Athens."

"Aha," Keith said. "Beetles. Mr. Ormson, is your computer connected to the Internet, and can I use it?"

Tom's father nodded. "Sure. Why?"

"I want to search the natural history museum. They have a lot of their collections online now. And they have a bunch of links to other scientific institutions."

"What do you mean by *aha beetles*?" Tom asked.

"Well . . ." Keith blushed. "You see, I like reading weird things."

"You told us," Kyrie said. "Comics and SF."

"Eh. Those are actually the sanest things I read. I also read science books. For fun. As I said, biology is fascinating, particularly insects. I seem to remember that certain beetles can put down pheromones that attract other beetles and their particular type of prey to their environment." He shrugged, blushing to the eyes. "So I think we should find out if the beetle Kyrie says looks like the shifter beetles is one of those."

"Makes sense," Rafiel said.

"Let me help you navigate the computer," Tom's father said, "in just a moment. Meanwhile . . . Tom, I don't mean . . . Well, you have blood on your face and your hair, and I thought . . ." He'd walked to the bed and pulled up one of bags. "I don't think you've changed pants size, and I just got you XL shirts and that. I grabbed you some socks and underwear too. The store here only has designer clothing, but I didn't want to go outside and look for another store."

Clothes? His father had got him clothes? Tom's first impulse was to say no and scowl. But if he was trying to keep his purity from his father's gifts, he was a little late. While the others talked, he'd been happily munching away on his chocolate with nuts. And the box was empty. Besides, he hated wearing jeans without underwear; the leather boots, without socks, were rubbing his feet raw; and if he was to have to go out soon, then he would have to shower.

So instead of his planned heated denial, he said, "Fine. I'll only be a minute. If anyone needs my opinion on anything, call me."

He grabbed the bag from the bed and took it with him to the little alcove before the bedroom. It weighed far more than it should for a pair of jeans and a couple of T-shirts. Opening it, he found it had at least as many clothes as he had owned back in his apartment. Better quality though. And more variety. There were a few pairs of jeans, and chinos, T-shirts, and a couple of polos. And, yes, underwear and socks.

He wasn't sure if he was ready to forgive his father, yet, but he was sure that his feet would thank him.

He went into the bathroom and turned on the shower. Water poured out in torrents. Oh. He might have to take more than a few minutes.

Much to Kyrie's surprise, the museum did have information on its insect collection online. It wasn't complete. All they had was pictures of the insects and their names.

"Is it this one, Kyrie?" Keith asked. And because the three men remaining—while judging from the sounds from the bathroom Tom was doing his best to deplete Colorado's natural water reserves today rather than in the next fifty years—had all crowded together around the computer, behind Keith who was sitting at the desk, they had to part now, to allow her near enough to see.

The picture was very small, and clicking on it didn't make it bigger. But Kyrie was fairly sure it was the same creature. "Yes. I'm almost positive," she said.

"*Cryptosarcodermestus halucigens*," Keith read. "Now a quick Google search."

The sounds from the bathroom had become positively strange. Kyrie had known Tom for six months. She would have sworn he was the last person to ever sing in the shower. And if he had ever sang in the shower, she was sure—absolutely sure—it wouldn't be "The Lion Sleeps Tonight." Although—and she grinned—there was always the possibility that he was trying to tweak Rafiel. And tweaking was definitely in Tom's personality.

She wasn't so stupid that she didn't realize that though the men seemed to get along with each other—fighting triad dragons must have done it—they seemed to have a rivalry going over her. Right now it was composed of mostly stupid things—like how she reacted to something each of them said.

Kyrie wasn't sure she could deal with any of it. She was sure she didn't wish Rafiel to kiss her again. Well, maybe a little. But not if it was going to hurt Tom.

"Aha," Keith said, from the computer. He'd brought up a colorful screen, surmounted by a picture of the beetle.

"Yes, it's that one," Kyrie said. "It definitely is."

"Well, it's our old friend *Sarcodermestus*," Keith said. "And listen to this, guys . . ." He stopped, as they heard the door to the bathroom open and close. "Might as well wait for Tom," he said, under his breath.

Tom, Kyrie thought, as he came toward them, barefoot, walking silently across the carpeted floor, was definitely worth waiting for. At least the man cleaned up well. He'd shaved and tied his hair back. The new clothes, jeans and a white T-shirt, seemed to have been spray-painted on his body. They underlined his broad shoulders, defined his musculature, and made quite a fetching display of his just-rounded-enough-but-clearly-muscular behind. He looked far more indecently naked than he'd been when she'd found him with the corpse in the parking lot. And, as he pressed in close, he smelled of vanilla. Vanilla soap and vanilla shampoo, probably some designer brand used by the Spurs and Lace.

Kyrie swallowed. She wasn't drooling either. And besides, if she were, it would be because it was vanilla. She was almost positive.

He pushed in close, between her and Rafiel—he would—and said, "Listen to what? What have you found, Keith?"

"On the beetles," Keith said. "They rub their wings together to produce clouds of hallucinogenic powder to disable their victims. And the male puts down some sort of hormonal scent. It attracts the female as well as the prey they need to reproduce."

"Prey?" Kyrie said. It was very hard to think next to a vanilla factory. Up till today, she'd always have said she was a chocolate type of girl. But apparently vanilla would to the trick. Provided it was good vanilla.

"They lay eggs in the bodies of freshly killed victims, which have to be of a certain species of beetle. By the time the victims have reached a certain point in the decomposition, the eggs are ready to emerge as larvae." Keith said. "They bury the corpses in shallow graves, so that the larvae can crawl out on their own."

"So, if I were a beetle, which I am not," Tom said, "where would I hide the corpses with the eggs in them?"

"Somewhere safe," Kyrie said.

"The parking lot of the Athens?" Tom said.

"Impossible," Kyrie said, aware of the fact that she might sound more antagonistic than she meant to. "Impossible. After all, it's asphalt. And besides . . ."

"It's public," Rafiel said from Tom's side.

"So, the male lays down a scent to attract the female, does he?" Tom said.

Definitely, Kyrie thought. *And it's vanilla.* Then stopped her thought forcefully.

"Why lay a scent at the Athens?" Tom asked.

"Easy," Rafiel said. "It's a diner. This means they get not only tourists passing through and the workers and students from around there, but also a large transient population. If it's true that shifters aren't all that usual, then it increases their odds of getting shifters—supposing, of course, shifters are the intended population."

"Well, since all the shifters here seem to have some form of the warm fuzzies toward the Athens, I must ask the nonshifters. Keith? Mr. Ormson?"

"It's a dive," Keith said.

"It . . . I only went there because Tom worked there," Edward said. "I wouldn't . . . I don't see any reason to go again."

"So," Rafiel said. "There is a good chance whatever the substance—if there is one—that the male slathered around the Athens attracts shifters only. Which would mean the eggs would need to be laid in shifters. Where around the Athens can one bury freshly killed bodies in shallow graves and not be immediately discovered? It's all parking lots and warehouses around there."

Kyrie had something—some thought making its way up from the back of her subconscious. At least she hoped it was thought, because otherwise it would mean that stories of corpses and weird shifters who lay eggs in corpses turned her on.

"This means that the male has to be a regular at the Athens," Rafiel said. "Or an employee."

"Don't look at me," Tom said. "I already turn into a dragon. Turning into a weird beetle too, that would require overtime. When would I sleep?"

"No," Rafiel said. "I don't think that we can turn into more than one thing. At least I can't and none of the legends mention it. No. But you know, it might be someone on day shift. In fact," he said, warming up to his theory, "someone on day shift or who only works nights very occasionally, would fit the bill. Because then when he's not serving, he could be tripping the light fantastic with his lady . . . er . . . beetle."

Whatever thought had been forming in Kyrie's mind disappeared, replaced with the image of Anthony turning into a beetle but retaining his frilly shirt, his vest. "Anthony," she said. "Perhaps he dresses that way to attract the beetle in human form."

Tom grinned at what he thought was a joke. "He's a member of a bolero group. They meet every night," he said. "He only works nights when Frank twists his arm, poor Anthony."

Okay, so maybe it was a joke, but still . . . "Are we sure he really does dance with this bolero group?" she asked.

Tom grinned wider. "Quite. He gave me tickets once. You wouldn't believe our Anthony was the star of the show, would you? But he was."

"So . . . what can we do?" Rafiel asked. "I can go in and make a note of all the regulars. Or you can point out to me the ones you thought started coming around about a year ago."

"Hard to say," Kyrie said. "I mean, I can easily eliminate those who haven't been there that long. But I can't really tell you if they've been coming for longer than a year, since I've only been there a year."

"It's a start," Rafiel said. "I'll come in tonight. You can point them out to me, and then I can run quick background checks on the computer. Mind you, we don't get the stuff the *CSI* shows get. I keep thinking that they're going to claim to know when the person was conceived. But we get where they live and such."

"There's the poet," Kyrie said.

Tom nodded, then explained to the other's blank looks. "Guy who comes and scribbles on a journal most of the night, every night. Maybe he's writing down 'Plump and tasty. Looks soft enough for grubs.'"

"Or 'Perfectly salvageable with some marinade,'" Rafiel said, looking over Kyrie's head at Tom.

Without looking, Kyrie was sure that the guys had exchanged grins that were part friendly and part simian warning of another male off his territory.

"So, I go into work as normal," Kyrie said.

"And me too," Tom put in. "Well, yeah, I know Frank should have fired me, but I don't think he will. I know how hard it is for him to find help at night."

"Yeah," Kyrie said. "Particularly since he's been weirdly absent-minded." She didn't want to explain about Frank's romance heating up in front of everyone. It was funny, yes, but it was a joke employees could share. Bringing it out in front of strangers just seemed like gratuitous meanness. "Poor Anthony ended up having to cook for most of the night yesterday."

"Which means you were alone at the tables?" Tom said. "I'm sorry."

And this was the type of moment that made Kyrie want to think of things she hated about Tom. Because when he looked at her like this, all soft and nice, it was very hard to resist, unless she could think of something bad he had done. Which, right now, was failing her, because the only bad thing she could think of was stealing the Pearl of Heaven. And he was ready to give it back, wasn't he? "Yeah, well," she said, lamely. "For some reason I'm sure you'd rather be attending to tables than being held prisoner by a triad of dragon shifters. So you're forgiven."

"Thank you," Tom said, and smiled. "So I'll come in tonight, with you, at the normal hour, and I'll . . . we'll watch and see if anyone looks suspicious." The smile became impish and the dimple appeared. "Besides, really, Anthony will thank me. His fiancé is in the bolero group too and by now she probably thinks he's found another one."

"So, that's what we do about the beetles," Keith said. "But what do we do about the triad dragons and the Pearl of Heaven?"

"I'm very glad we made Keith an honorary shifter," Rafiel said. "This guy has a talent for keeping us on target."

"Honorary shifter?" Kyrie asked.

"He wanted to help us. He's jealous of our abilities. So he said we could make him an honorary shifter," Tom said. "I don't think he told us what specifically he would shift into though. I say a bunny."

"A blood-sucking bunny with big sharp teeth," Keith said. "Seriously, how are you going to get the Pearl, Tom, and shouldn't we at least have a tentative plan in place for how to return it?"

"I need to find a container large enough for it," Tom said, showing the approximate size with his hands. It looked to Kyrie like about six inches circumference. "A plastic bucket, maybe. With a lid. Then I can put it in there, in water and carry it without its giving me away. A backpack to carry it in would be good. Not this backpack." He nodded to the thing he'd carried and which he'd let drop in a corner of the room. "Because if I go in with a kid's backpack, Frank will notice and ask questions."

"Right," Rafiel said. "I have a couple of backpacks from army surplus that I use when I'm hiking. I'll go grab one of them before you go in to work."

"Well, this just brings up one question," Keith said, turning his chair around to face them. "And that's how are we going to sleep? Because we all need to be fresh for tonight. Unlikely as it is, we might be able to pinpoint someone and follow them and find the bodies, but we don't want to be stumbling into walls."

"You can stay here," Tom's father said. "There's a few extra pillows and blankets in the closet and I'm sure the bed fits five."

But Tom's father should have known better, Kyrie thought a few minutes later. With Tom and Rafiel in full-blown competition for her attention, chivalry was thick enough in the air that one needed a knife to spread it.

So, despite her heated protests, it ended up with her on the bed, Tom—universally believed to have had the roughest few hours—stretched out on the love seat by the window, Keith curled up on the floor in a corner and Rafiel and Mr. Ormson staking out the floor on either side of the bed. Rafiel lay down between her and the love seat, of course—probably trying to prevent Tom from attempting a stealth move.

Kyrie would have liked to fall asleep immediately, and she thought she was tired enough for it. But she wasn't used to sharing a house—much less a room—with anyone.

She lay there, with her eyes closed, in the semidark caused by closing the curtains almost all the way—leaving only enough light so that they could each maneuver to the bathroom without tripping on other sleepers.

Tom's dad showered. She heard that and the rustle of the paper bag as he fished for clothes. She grinned at the way the older man had neatly outflanked Tom's stubbornness.

Tom was still suspicious of his father, and perhaps he had reason, but Kyrie heard the man lie down on the floor, next to the bed and seconds later, she heard his breath become regular and deep.

She was the only one still awake. She turned and opened her eyes a little. Tom was in the love seat, directly facing the bed. In the half-light, with his eyes closed and something very much resembling a smile on his lips, the sleeping Tom looked ten years younger and very innocent.

A tumble of dark hair had come loose from whatever he'd tied it with, and fell across his forehead. His leg was slightly bent at the knee, and he'd flung his arm above his head, looking like he was about to invoke some superpower and take off flying.

It was all Kyrie could do not to get up and pull the hair off from in front of his face. Forget special hormones laid down by male beetles to attract the females. The way some human males looked while sleeping was the most effective trap nature had ever devised.

Kyrie woke up with a hand on her shoulder. This was rare enough that just that light touch, over her T-shirt, brought her fully bolt upright. She blinked, to see Tom smiling at her and holding a finger to his lips.

He appeared indecently well-rested and, unless it was an effect of the dim light, the scar on his forehead had almost disappeared. He pointed her toward the desk and asked in her ear, breath tickling her, "Do you like steak?"

She looked her confusion and he smiled. "I ordered dinner," he said. "From room service. My father said to do it, since we have to go in before the others."

"Your father?" Kyrie said.

"Don't go there," Tom said, giving her a hand to help her up. "Really, don't."

"No. He was awake?"

"I woke him to tell him I was going to wake you and we'd leave for work. They don't need to be there when we go to work."

Kyrie got up and stepped over the sleeping bodies in the room, to the bathroom. She washed herself, halfheartedly because she didn't have clean clothes to put on. By the sink there were now five little "if you forgot your toiletries" kits— she would love to hear how Edward had explained that to the hotel staff—and half a dozen black combs. Also, a brush.

"I thought you could use the brush," Tom said, putting his head around the doorway. "I got it from downstairs."

She thanked him, pulled the earring from her pocket, where she'd put it for sleeping, and slipped it back on.

The meal was a hurried and odd affair, eating in the dark. But more disturbing than any of it, was looking up from taking a bite and finding Tom watching her.

What did he want her to do? Swoon with the attention? Fall madly in love with him? What would they do together? Both worked entry-level jobs, which was no way to start a family. And if they did start a family, what would it be? Snaky cats?

She glared at him and to excuse the glare said, "Eat. Stop staring. We don't have that much time." And he shouldn't, he really shouldn't smile like that. There was nothing funny.

But she didn't say anything. They finished the trays, left them by the door, and hurried out. "Are you worried about what Frank will say?" Kyrie asked Tom as they got in the car.

Tom still had the goofy smile affixed on his lips, but he nodded. "A little," he said. "Just a little. Frank can be profoundly unpleasant."

"Yeah, and he's been in a mood," Kyrie said.

Tom didn't know whether to be relieved or worried that all Frank said was, "I thought you'd disappeared."

"No," Tom said. "Wasn't feeling well for a while and my dad came to town to look after stuff, so I was with him. I'm sorry I forgot to call."

For some reason, this seemed to alarm Frank. "Your dad? You have— You're in touch with him?"

Tom shrugged. "He heard I wasn't okay and he came to check on me. It's not that rare, parents caring about their kids," he said. Of course, he had no previous experience of this, and he wasn't absolutely sure he trusted his father's newly conciliatory mood. But he'd enjoy it while it was there and not expect it to stay, so he wouldn't be wounded when it disappeared.

Frank looked upset with that. "Well, get on with it. You have tables to attend to."

To Tom it was like returning home. He realized, as he was tying on the apron—"And we'll dock the extra $10 from your paycheck. I can't figure out what you people do with your aprons. Eat them?"—that he'd missed all of this.

The air-conditioner was pumping away ineffectively, too far away from the tables to make any practical difference, which meant that the patrons had opened the windows again, allowing the hot, dry air of Fairfax Avenue, perfumed with car exhaust and the slight scent of hot asphalt, to pour in and mingle with the hot muggy air inside the Athens, perfumed with clam chowder, burgers, and a touch of homemade fries.

It was almost shocking to realize, but he really loved the place. His mind went over the panorama of seasons and imagined the Athens in winter, when it was snowy out and cozy inside and customers would linger for hours at the corner tables—near the heat vents—drinking coffee after coffee. He'd enjoyed coming in from the freezing cold outside and encountering the Athens as though it were an haven of dryness and warmth. He felt happy here. He wondered if it was just whatever pheromones the beetles had laid down around this place talking.

And speaking of pheromones, he got to work, greeting now this customer, now the other, taking orders, refilling coffees. To his surprise people remembered and had missed him.

"Hello, Tom," one of the women who came by before going to work at the warehouses said. "Were you sick?"

"Yeah," Tom said, and smiled at her. She was spectacularly homely—with a square face and grey hair clipped short. But she seemed to treat him with almost maternal warmth, and she always tipped him indecently well. "Touch of something going around."

"You guys should be more careful," she said. "Just because it's warm, doesn't mean that you can't get sick. Working nights, and you probably don't sleep as much as you should. I abused my body like that when I was young too. Trust me, it does send you a bill, though it might come twenty years down the road."

"Well, I'm all right now. What will you have?" He leaned toward her, smiling. And felt a hand pat his bottom lightly.

He believed in being friendly to customers but this was ridiculous. He turned around ready to blast whoever it might be, and saw Kyrie, leaning against him to talk to the customer. "Is this big ape bothering you, ma'am? Should I remove him?"

The customer grinned. "My, you're in a good mood. I guess your boss's hot romance makes things easier, right? He's not on your case so much?"

"Hot romance?" Tom asked.

"Oh, you don't know?" the customer said. "He's been sitting there all the time holding hands with that woman who bought the castle. The one he's been seeing off and on. Now she's here all the time."

"I meant to tell you," Kyrie said. "But I didn't want to talk in front of people. They spent yesterday necking over the counter. It was . . . weird. Poor Anthony had to cook all the meals. Slowed us down to a crawl."

"Well, Anthony is a nice boy," the woman said. "But not like Tom."

"Ah, so you wouldn't want our big ape removal services," Kyrie said, and smiled at the woman, then at Tom, and flitted away to go take the order of the next table.

She left Tom quite stunned. Had Kyrie smiled at him? And had Kyrie really patted his bottom? Forget pheromones. What were they pumping out of those air-conditioners?

"Well, have you asked her out?" the woman said.

"I'm sorry?"

"Oh, don't play stupid. Have you asked Kyrie out?" the woman asked, smiling at him with a definite maternal expression.

He felt his damn all-too-easy blush come on and heat his cheeks. "Oh, I wouldn't have a chance."

The woman pressed her lips together. "Don't be stupid. She might have talked to me, but that entire little display was for your benefit. You do have a chance."

Tom hesitated. He could feel his mouth opening and closing, as he failed to find something appropriate to say, and he was sure, absolutely sure, he looked like a landed guppy. "I don't know," he said. "I'm not anyone's prize catch."

"So?" the woman shrugged. "No one is. You don't make babies start screaming when they see you. You'll do."

He had to get hold of this conversation. And his own unruly emotions. He and Kyrie had things to do. Far more important things. The Pearl had to be returned. They had to stop whatever scary beetles were trying to kill them both. This was no time to go all googly-eyed at the girl. "Yeah, well . . . anyway, what will you be having?"

"The usual. See if you have apple pie. I don't know if Frank baked yesterday, he seemed so distracted with his girlfriend. Apple for preference, but cherry would do. And a coffee, with creamer and sugar on the side."

"Sure," Tom said and beat a hasty retreat around the edge of the booths and back to the counter. There was apple pie in the fridge. He knew the customer enough to put the pie in the microwave for a few seconds' zap to chase the chill away. He got the coffee and the little bowls with cream and sugar and put it all on a tray.

And turned around to see Frank and his girlfriend— and he almost dropped the tray.

There was something odd about Frank and his girlfriend, both, and Tom couldn't quite say what it was.

He'd seen them together before, but usually when she picked Frank up or dropped him off. Now, they were holding hands over the counter, quite lost in each other's eyes. They weren't talking. Only their hands, moving infinitesimally against each other seemed to be communicating interest or affection or something.

With such an intense gaze, you expected . . . talk. And you really didn't expect people their age to be that smitten.

He realized he was staring fixedly at them, but they didn't even seem to have noticed. They continued looking at each other's eyes.

There was other crazy stuff happening there, Tom thought. Because while the woman didn't look like a prize—she looked like she'd been run through the ringer a couple dozen times, and perhaps hit with a mallet for good measure—she dressed well, and she looked like she could do better.

And if she was really the new owner to the castle, she couldn't be all that poor. The property, dilapidated and in need of work as it was, was yet worth at least half a mil, just on location. Where would someone like her meet someone like Frank? And what would attract her to him?

He set the pie and the coffee in front of the customer, who said, "I see you've noticed the lovebirds."

"Yes," Tom said, distracted. "I wonder how they met."

"I don't know," the woman said. "It was at least a month ago. In fact, when I saw them first, a month ago, they were already holding hands like that, so it might have been longer."

A month ago. The cluster of missing people had started a month ago. How would those two facts correlate? Tom wondered. He smiled at the customer and said something, he wasn't sure what, then backtracked to get the carafe to give warm-ups to his tables.

Was he being churlish? After all, he also didn't compare to Kyrie. If he should—by a miracle, and possibly through sudden loss of her mind—manage to convince Kyrie to go out with him, wouldn't people look at them funny like that too, and say that they couldn't believe she would date someone like him?

But he looked at Frank, still holding the woman's hands. And Kyrie had said that the day before he'd been so out of it that he'd let Anthony work the grill. Frank, normally, would not let any of them touch the grill. He said that quality control was his responsibility.

Tom looked at Frank and the woman. He could swear they hadn't moved in half an hour. That just wasn't normal.

He tracked Kyrie through the diner, till he could arrange to meet her—as he went out, his tray laden with salad and soda, to attend to a table, and she was coming back, her tray loaded with dishes—in the middle of the aisle, in the extension where a whole wall of windows separated them from Frank and made it less likely Frank would overhear them.

"Kyrie, those two, that isn't normal."

To his surprise, Kyrie smiled. "Oh, it's cute in a gag-me sort of way."

"No, no. I mean it isn't normal, Kyrie. Normal people don't sit like that perfectly quiet, fluttering fingers at each other."

Kyrie flung around to watch him, eye to eye. "What are you saying?"

"That we're looking for a weird insectlike romance. And I think that's it. The pie-and-coffee lady says that they first met a month ago, at least. I didn't pay any attention when it started, just sort of realized it was going on. I guess the idea of Frank getting some and maybe leaving descendants was so scary I kind of shied away from it. But the pie lady thinks it was already going on a month ago. Though even she says it's getting more intense."

"I haven't given it much attention, either," Kyrie said. "A month at least, or a month?"

"At least a month, I don't know anymore."

Kyrie looked suitably worried. "Okay," she said. "Okay. I'll make enquiries."

Kyrie turned on her rounds, to stop by the poet, and give him a warm-up on his coffee. "We always wonder what you write," she said and smiled. All these months, she'd never actually attempted to talk to the poet, but she figured someone had to. And he was there every night the same hours.

He was the most regular of the regulars. If he had looked at all—and Kyrie had never been absolutely sure of the poet's being fully engaged with the world—he would know, better than anyone, how long Frank's romance had been going on.

The man reached nervous fingers for the ceramic cup with the fresh coffee in it, and fumbled with getting it to his mouth to drink. His pale-blue eyes rested on Kyrie's face for a moment, then away. "I . . . It's just a journal. My therapist said I would be better off for writing a journal."

"A journal," she said. She had a feeling the man wasn't used to much female attention, but if what he wrote was indeed a journal, then he would have all the data there, at his fingertips. "I would never be disciplined enough for a journal."

He grinned, showing her very crooked teeth. Then looked rapidly away and continued, speaking intently to the salt shaker. "Well, it's all a matter of doing it at the same time every day, isn't it? Just being regular and doing it at the same time. After a while it becomes a habit and you could no more go without it than you could go without eating or sleeping."

He looked back at her, just a little, out of the corner of the eye, reminding Kyrie of a squirrel, tempted by nuts on the sidewalk but hesitant about coming out in the open.

She smiled at him. "You must write all sorts of fascinating details about everything that happens in there. I mean, so much better than just memory. My coworker and I were just talking about how long our boss has been in love with that lady there." She gestured with her head. "And we couldn't remember when they started going out."

"Oh." The poet fumbled with his journal, flipping through the pages in a way that seemed to indicate he wasn't absolutely sure how to use fingers. The gesture of a terminally nervous neurotic. "I can tell you the exact day. I have it here, all written down, because it was so amazing. She came in, they looked at each other, and it was like . . . you know, the song, across a crowded room and all that. They looked at each other, their eyes met, and she hurried over there and they held hands." He found the right page and, for once, dared to look up at Kyrie, as he showed it to her. "There, there, you see. Almost exactly a month ago. And they've been like that ever since. Oh, not every night, not that . . . absorbed . . . but at least a few nights a week she walks him in or waits for him when he goes out."

The way he looked at Kyrie, shyly and sort of sideways, seemed to indicate he had his own personal dreams of getting to hold hands with her someday. Kyrie didn't feel that charitable, but smiled at him anyway, and glanced at the page—of which she could understand nothing, since it appeared to have been written by dipping a spider's legs in ink and letting it wander all over the page. "Very nice. Well, now I'll know what you're doing and I can tell the other people when they ask."

She wandered away to check on orders. So far, no one had asked for anything cooked, but it was bound to happen. "Tom, you might need to take over the grill," she said, as she passed him. "As people start coming in who want their early morning dinners."

He looked surprised. "Sure," he said. "I can probably load dishes while I'm up there too, if you want me to."

She didn't tell him anything about Frank and his girlfriend, but she was thinking. What she was thinking, mostly, was that this whole eyes meeting across a crowded room didn't happen to people. Not in real life. But it might very well happen to bugs who were acting on instinct and pheromones.

It turned out not to be as bad as Kyrie expected. The clinch of hands over the bar stopped before the crunch, and Frank took over flipping the burgers and cooking the eggs and what not.

From about ten to midnight they were so busy that Kyrie didn't even notice the other guys had come in— Keith and Rafiel and Tom's dad—until she saw that Tom was serving that table. And then she forgot about them again, as she was kept running off her feet, taking pie to one and a hamburger to another, and a plate of dolmades to a particularly raucous group in a corner.

As the crowd started thinning, past midnight, Kyrie went up to the counter to put the carafe back. And when she turned, Rafiel was standing by the counter. "Can you take a fifteen-minute break?" he said. "Tom says he can handle it till you come back."

"Frank," she said, and realized that Frank had heard them. He waved them away. "Go. If Tom can handle it, I don't care."

On the way to the front door, Kyrie told Tom, "Thank you."

He looked slightly puzzled and then frowned at Rafiel, which did not seem at all like a natural reaction. "Are you sure you asked him?" she asked Rafiel.

"Yes, yes, I asked him." He led her outside, toward his car, parked on the street. "I'm not saying he's incredibly excited about it, but I asked him."

"Rafiel, if he doesn't think he can handle it alone I shouldn't leave him." She started to walk back, but Rafiel came after her and grabbed her arm.

"Seriously," he said. "I don't think he minds the work. He minds you going out with me. Oh, don't look like that," he said, before she was aware of looking like anything at all. "He knows we have to talk. He says there's some stuff you found out."

"Yes," Kyrie said, and sat down on the passenger side of the car. Rafiel had held the door open for her, and closed it as soon as she sat down. He then walked around the car to his side.

"I thought I'd take you for a cup of coffee, so we can talk? There's an all-night coffeehouse down the street."

Kyrie nodded. She had no need for coffee, but she wanted to tell Rafiel about the beetles, and what she thought of the beetles.

❖   ❖   ❖

Edward watched Tom, after Kyrie left. He watched Keith too. Mostly because Keith puzzled him. He sat at the table, taking everything in, seemingly unaffected by the fact that there were not one but two types of shape-shifters that might want him dead.

Dragons and beetles and who knows what, oh my. "You're not scared at all?" he asked Keith, in an undertone.

Keith looked back at him, as though trying to decide exactly how many heads Edward might have. "Well," he said. "It's not so much that I'm not scared. Although . . . I don't think I am, you know?"

"Why not?" Edward asked. He thought of the Great Sky Dragon, flying through the sky and using what seemed to be magic to get from one place to the other without having to cross the space between. He thought of even Tom in his dragon form, of Tom's flying across the New York sky, seeming completely nonhuman.

"I don't know," Keith said. "I told them it was because I read so much science fiction and comic books—and that's probably true." He shrugged. "I mean, you see something very often, even if you know it's fiction, it makes an impression on you after a while and part of you hopes or believes it to be true, right? I mean, even if your mind knows it isn't."

"It's possible," Edward said. To be honest he didn't remember what it was like to be that young anymore. It had been at least twenty-five years since he'd read any fiction. No. More. In college, his fiction reading had just tapered away to nothing. "I suppose it's possible."

"Well, in a way it was like that," Keith said. "I mean, the idea would have probably struck me as much odder, much more impossible if I'd never seen it in stories. But the important thing is, I saw it happen in the worst possible circumstances." He lowered his voice. "They grabbed us and they took us in, and Rafiel was . . . um . . . shifted. And Tom was all tied up, and—"

"He was. Tied?" Edward knew what Lung had told him, and at some level, consciously, he knew that being captured by the triad could be no picnic. But somehow, seeing Tom walk into his hotel room had given him hope that it was all just a big fight. He knew Tom could handle himself in a fight. He wasn't so sure about Tom being helpless.

"Yeah. He was completely tied-up. And he . . . They'd . . . His clothes were caked with blood. They'd taken his jacket and boots off. I think they might have thought to keep them after they . . . you know, got rid of him. Or perhaps they thought that the leather would protect him. And then he . . . shifted. I knew it was still him because of his eyes. And he freed me. And I freed Rafiel, who recovered much faster than they expected. And then we were . . . fighting. And that's the thing you know." He looked at Edward and seemed to realize that Edward was trying very hard to imagine but didn't really know. "I realized they can be taken out with a good tire iron. You don't need to be one of them."

Edward was following his son with his gaze. Tom looked so . . . competent. He'd removed his leather jacket and was wearing a red apron with "Athens" on the chest, and doing a job his father had never, possibly, imagined a son of his doing. But he was doing the job competently.

There had been no complaints. On the contrary. People smiled at him and it was clear that several of the regulars were very fond of him. And he answered back and smiled, and seemed to be a part of this diner. A trusted employee. Which was more than—just five years ago—Edward could have imagined.

To be honest, he couldn't have imagined it two days ago. If he'd thought of Tom at all, he'd thought of Tom as being in jail, or perhaps dead. He would never have believed his son was sane and responsible enough to hold down any job.

"Really," Keith said. "I'd love to be able to shift, because it's cool, but I'm not afraid of them. I mean, the nice ones are nice. The other ones would probably be just as dangerous as normal people."

Edward frowned. That thought too would have been unbelievable five years ago. But he was looking at Tom, and thought Tom was not much different than he would have been if he'd never turned into a dragon. He was just Tom. And, on balance, a much better person than Edward had any right to expect.

Just then, Tom noticed him looking and arched his eyebrows. Edward looked away. He might have thrown Tom out from fear and confusion. Getting him back, however, was going to require a full and rational siege.

If only they managed not to get killed by any other shifters. Edward wished he had Keith's certainty that they could fight against shape changers on equal terms.

❖   ❖   ❖

"We need to talk," Rafiel said. He pulled the chair out for Kyrie, and waited until Kyrie had sat down before going around to his side. He picked up both their orders too, her iced mocha latte and his tall cup of something profoundly foamy.

"Yes, I . . . Tom thinks—"

"Wait," Rafiel said. "We don't need to talk about the . . . creatures." He looked around again, as though afraid someone around them might understand the cryptic comments. "We need to talk about Tom."

"We—uh? What about Tom?"

"Well, he's not as bad as I expected," Rafiel said. "Not nearly. But he is . . . ah . . . Tom has issues."

Kyrie nodded. "Yes, but—" She didn't want to discuss Tom or Tom's issues, nor could she imagine what Tom had to do with any of this. Tom's personality had nothing to do with the predicament they were in.

Sure, it would have been helpful if he could have managed to avoid tangling with the triad dragons. But that was, surely, just a fraction of his problems. The beetles loomed much larger in Kyrie's mind, perhaps because she had experienced them up close and personal. And Tom was not a werebeetle. Of that she was sure.

"No. I just . . ." Rafiel looked flustered, which was a new one for him. "I just am going to say this once and be done, okay? I can't help notice that he's attracted to you, and I think I've seen you . . . I mean, you give the impression of being attracted to him too, sometimes."

"I don't think I am," she said. "It's just that we've been working together for a while and I think I've misjudged him horribly, and I feel guilty about that. So I've been nice to him, but I don't think—"

"Good," Rafiel said. "I mean, really. Tom is not a bad person, but I think he's been through a lot in his life, and I think it makes him . . . well . . . I think he's sometimes not as well-adjusted as he would like to be. And I wouldn't want to wish that on you."

He put his hand across the table, on top of hers. Kyrie withdrew her hand, slowly, not wanting it to seem like a rejection. If she was reading this right, Rafiel had just tried to clear the field of his rival in a most underhanded way, something she thought only women did. Perhaps because she'd seen it between women and girls in her middle and high school years.

Fortunately, she wasn't sure she was interested in either of these men—or in any men. She'd seen too much of marriage and relationships through her time in foster care to think that she would ever take any relationship for granted or view it as a given. On top of that the kinks the shifters' natures would put into any relationship just about had her deciding to remain celibate the rest of her life. The knife-in-the-back approach to friendship and love certainly didn't incline her toward Rafiel.

"Tom thinks that Frank and his girlfriend might be the beetles," Kyrie said, rapidly, before Rafiel could resume his wholly inappropriate talk.

"Frank and his girlfriend?" Rafiel asked. "Why?"

Kyrie told him. She told him about the woman who ordered pie every night and who said that Frank and his girlfriend had held hands a month back, and about the poet and the whole eyes meeting across a crowded room thing.

Rafiel frowned. "Don't you think it's all a bit in the air?" he asked. "I mean, they're just a middle-aged couple, and perhaps they're not so good on the relationship and getting along with each other front. Perhaps they aren't very good at connecting with each other?"

"But . . ." Kyrie said, and seized on the one thing she was sure of. "But his girlfriend first met him around a month ago." And then, with desperate recollection. "And, you know, he had a Band-Aid on his neck the day after I speared the beetle."

Rafiel sighed. "He and how many guys in Goldport? Think. Perhaps he cut himself shaving."

"At the back of his neck?"

"Well, okay, so he scratched himself. Or had a pimple that blew up. It happens. Don't you think if he'd been stuck with an umbrella, even in another shape, it would require more than a Band-Aid?"

"Not necessarily," Kyrie said. "We heal fast."

"I still say this is all in the air," Rafiel said. He sipped at his coffee as if he were angry at it. "You have no proof. There are probably dozen of couples—hundreds—with weird relationships, who started a month ago, and where one of them had some sort of injury on the neck that day."

"I doubt hundreds," Kyrie said. "And besides, you know, there is the fact that she has a very convenient burial ground."

"What?"

"The castle. She bought the castle. You've seen the grounds. She could bury a hundred people there in shallow graves and be fairly assured they wouldn't be found. That's pretty hard in urban Goldport."

"Not really," Rafiel said. "You know, people have backyard lawns."

Kyrie snorted with laughter before she could stop herself. "I suppose you could fit one corpse in my backyard lawn. Two if you put them very close together."

Rafiel was jiggling his leg rapidly up and down. "Yeah, but some people have bigger lawns." He frowned, bringing his brows together. "What do you want me to do about it, anyway? Do you want me to burst into the Athens and arrest them because they hold hands and don't talk?"

Kyrie wasn't used to getting upset at people. Normally, to get along, both as a foster child and as an adult, she'd learned to hide her anger from people. But she couldn't even hide from herself that she thought Rafiel was being unreasonable. That she suspected he was being unreasonable because he felt thwarted in his pursuit of her affections didn't actually make her feel any better.

"I want you to go in there and look around," she said.

His mouth turned down in a dissatisfied little-boy scowl. It was the type of expression she would expect from a five- or six-year-old who had just seen someone else get the bigger piece of candy. "I can't do that," he said.

"For heaven's sake, why not?"

"Because I don't have a warrant." Instead of getting louder, his voice had to lower and lower, until it was low and almost vicious, growling out its protest. "I'm a policeman. I can't go poking around people's property without a warrant. Citizens get all sorts of upset when policemen do that. They would—"

Kyrie didn't think this behavior was more endearing because of its sheer irrationality. She finished her frozen latte, and picked up the cup, which she'd got as a take-out cup, as she'd been afraid of having to finish it on the way back to work. "Officer Trall, if you can hide evidence, lie to other police officers, and suggest that we, as shifters, need to take our law into what passes for our hands, then, yeah, you could and should be able to have a look-see in someone's garden without a warrant. I mean, no one is asking you to go in with a police force. Just go there, shift, and have a good sniff. Death will out, you know?"

He narrowed his eyes at her. "I'm trying to stay on the right side of the law. I'm trying to enforce the law. I'm trying to be a good person, Kyrie, and somehow balance this with being a . . . shifter. I don't think you realize—"

"Oh, I think I realize it perfectly well. I just think you'd be far more energetic in pursuing this if I'd told you that the culprit in this case was Tom Ormson."

"That's underhanded. Tom is a friend. He risked himself to rescue me."

"Oh, and how well you thank him."

"I didn't mean it that way. If you took it that way it's because you chose to. Tom would be very bad for you, and just because—"

"As opposed to yourself? You would be great? What would your mother think of your dragging me home?"

He blinked, genuinely confused. "Mom would love you. I don't understand—"

"I mean, Officer Trall, that your parents might not be so happy that the son they've protected, the son they always thought would need their protection the rest of their lives has a life outside the family."

"That's ridiculous. Did you just call me a mama's boy? I don't think there's anything else I can say to you."

"Well," Kyrie said. She was leaning over the table, and he was leaning from the other side, and they'd been arguing in low vicious tones. Now she straightened. "That is very fortunate, because I don't think I want to discuss anything with you, either."

And with that, she flounced out the door, which—she thought, smiling to herself—the owners of this coffee shop must think was a normal thing for her.

She had gone a good half block before she heard him shout, "Kyrie," behind her, but she didn't slow down, just went on as fast as she could.

This time she didn't go into the parking lot. Didn't even think about it. Instead, she approached at a half run, toward the front door. While she was waiting to cross Pride, the cross street before the Athens, she was vaguely aware of a car squealing tires nearby, and then parking in front of the diner.

She didn't turn to look. Which was too bad, because if she had turned to look, Rafiel's hands on her shoulders spinning her around wouldn't have taken her so much by surprise. And his mouth descending on hers might have been entirely avoided. Or, if not, she might at least have avoided the few seconds of confusion in which her brain told her to get away from the man while parts far more southerly responded to his strength, his virility, and the rather obvious, feline musk assaulting her nostrils with a proclamation of both those qualities.

As it was, she lost self-control just enough to allow him to pull her toward him, to allow herself to relax against him. She lost track of who she was and what she meant to do through the feeling of firm male flesh, and the large hands on her shoulders, both compelling and sheltering her.

He slid his tongue between her lips, hot and searching and forceful.

And in her mind, an image of Tom appeared. Tom smiling at her, with that odd diffident expression when Keith had asked about sex as a shifter.

She pushed Rafiel away. And then she slapped him. Hard.

Tom would probably have missed the kiss, if he hadn't already been watching the door for Kyrie. But he was.

Okay, first of all, and stupid as it was, and as much as he was absolutely sure he didn't actually stand a snowball's— or a snowflake's—chance in hell of getting near her, he'd been indulging himself in quite nasty thoughts about Rafiel.

So, okay, Rafiel needed to discuss the case with her. But couldn't he just have taken her on a quick walk down the block, then back again? Couldn't he have talked to her out there, against that lamppost in front of the Athens? Where Tom could have kept track of them through the big plate-glass window?

And then . . . and then there was everything else. If Frank and his girlfriend were the beetle couple, where did that leave Tom? Truth be told, Tom felt a little guilty for even suspecting Frank of that. Frank had given him a full-time job when no one else would.

Yes, but why had he? Tom wouldn't have hired himself, with his credentials at the time. And then there was his father. He'd told Kyrie not to go there, but it wasn't entirely avoidable. For one, his father was sitting at a corner table, in the extension, getting intermittent warm-ups of coffee and ordering the occasional pastry. He seemed to be discussing comic books with Keith, a scene that, before tonight, Tom thought could only come from his hallucinations.

And his father had already managed to ask Tom if Tom was warm enough—warm enough!—in the Colorado summer, where the temperatures reached the low hundreds in daytime and the buildings gave it back all night. Warm. Enough. It wasn't so much like this man's behavior bore absolutely no resemblance to the father Tom had known growing up. That was somewhat of a problem but, it could be said that any father at all would be an improvement over that man.

On the other hand, this particular father seemed to do parenting by instruments. Like a pilot, flying in a thick fog, might read his instruments to decide his location, how to turn, and where to stop—and if the instruments are faulty might end up somewhere completely different—Tom's father seemed to be trying to mend a relationship that had never existed in ways that didn't apply even to that hypothetical relationship.

Maybe it was that the only relationships Tom's father had ever taken seriously were courting relationships. At least that would explain his trying to win his way back to Tom's heart with chocolates. It didn't explain his thinking that Tom wore the same size pants he'd worn at sixteen though.

On the other hand, these pants were a great advantage, now he thought of it. He would no longer need to worry about siring an inconvenient shifter child—not if he wore them much longer. This, of course, brought his thoughts around to Kyrie again, and to the fact that she was five minutes over her break already.

Oh, he had no intention of telling Frank about it. Even if Frank were perfectly aboveboard and exactly what he claimed to be, there was absolutely no reason to let Frank know this stuff. He'd just get upset.

And so far Tom, moving rapidly from table to table, taking orders, distributing them, warming up coffee, was keeping on top of everything. In a little while, the crowds would drift back in again, and as long as Kyrie was in by then . . .

No. What he hated was the fact that he might be covering up for her necking time with Rafiel. Okay, he was willing to admit that Rafiel might not be exactly the scum of the earth. He could do worse. And she could do worse, too. In fact, any way he looked at it, Kyrie and Rafiel were just about a perfect match.

Despite her upbringing, Kyrie was fairly balanced. And Rafiel, after all, came from such a well-adjusted background that his parents knew about and abetted his shape-shifting. Surely, neither of them had anything in common with Tom, who had been thrown out of his house—at gunpoint no less—by the man who now thought he could heal it all with expensive chocolates and too-tight clothes.

They deserved each other. And neither of them deserved him in any sense. Which didn't mean he had to like it. It didn't even mean he had to accept it, did it?

He seethed, having to control himself to prevent slamming plates and breaking cups. He seethed partly at them, because he was sure they were taking advantage of his covering up for her to go and neck in some shady corner. And he seethed partly at himself, because, who was he to get angry at whatever they wanted to do?

And then, as he turned around, carafe in hand, he saw Kyrie come hurrying toward the door.

Alone. She was alone. He felt his heart give a little leap at this. Not hopeful. Oh, he couldn't have told himself he was hopeful. But . . .

And then he saw Rafiel come up behind her. He grabbed her by the shoulders. He spun her around. His mouth came down to meet hers. She relaxed against him.

The teapot escaped from Tom's grasp and fell, with a resounding crash and a spray of hot coffee onto the nearest bar stools and Tom's feet.

It took him a moment to realize the shattering sound had indeed come from outside his head.

Edward had never seen Tom tremble. He'd held a gun to the boy's head when Tom was only sixteen and he had never seen him shake. But now, he was shaking. Or rather, vibrating, lightly, as if he were a bell that someone had struck.

"I'm sorry I'm late with the warm-up," he said, and his face was pale, and his voice oh, so absolutely polite. "I dropped the carafe and had to brew another one."

"It's okay," Edward said. He'd been enjoying his conversation with Keith, partly because it distracted him from the fact that they might very well all be dead soon. And partly because in the middle of a lot of information about Keith—who apparently had parents and no less than four siblings somewhere in Pennsylvania—there was some comment and anecdote about Tom. Apparently Tom kept Keith's key and usually could be counted on to give it back when Keith came home drunk and confused, having left keys and jacket—and often other clothes—at the last wild party he'd attended.

Keith had engaged in some self-mocking on the subject of the number of times Tom had shown up without a stitch of clothing on, and how Keith had thought that Tom went to even wilder parties than he did. Now, of course, he understood. "He must go through an awful lot of clothes," Keith said. "They all must."

And Edward had nodded. He'd been relaxed. And Tom had looked happy and in his element. Why was he shaking now? Was it just the coffeepot? Was Tom so insecure he'd get that upset over a broken coffeepot?

"It's okay. I really don't need a warm-up," Edward said. "It's excellent coffee, but I've probably already drunk too much. Don't worry."

Tom nodded, and looked aside, as if getting ready to walk away. Then came back and sat down. He put the carafe down, with some care, on one of the coasters and leaned forward. "Father," he said.

It was the first time in five years he'd actually called Edward that. Edward took a deep breath. "Yes?"

"I need you do it for me, the delivery."

"What delivery?" Edward asked, puzzled. They were going to find the beetles, weren't they? What was there to deliver?

"The delivery of the Pearl," Tom said, lowering his voice. "In a few minutes, when I get a chance, I'm going to go into the bathroom and get it, I'll put it in the container before I take it out of the water, then put the container in the backpack. I assume you know where the center for the . . . Where their center is in Goldport, right?"

Edward nodded. "But . . . aren't we going to do that later? I thought we were going to—"

Tom pushed back the strands of his hair that had gotten loose in the course of the evening. "No. I . . . It's me. Look, it's just me. I know there's something wrong with me, but I just can't take it. I can't. I can't be around to watch it. So, you take the . . . delivery to the people looking for it, and I'll go, okay?"

Oh, no. This sounded far more serious than Edward had thought. And he didn't quite know how to handle it. The thing had always been, since Tom was two or so, that if he got something in his mind, no matter how misguided or strange, it was almost impossible to get it out. And if you pushed the wrong way, he only got mad at you and more determined to do whatever he'd set his mind on.

He didn't even want to ask about it in a way that would get Tom's back up. So he spoke as gently as he knew how. "Tom, I don't understand. What can't you take, and why are you going? And where?"

Tom shook his head, as if answering some unspoken question. "Kyrie. And . . . Rafiel. I can't take it. I know this is stupid, okay? I know it's puppy love, okay? But I've never been close to another woman. Well, not since I was sixteen. And I've never even thought about another woman as I think about Kyrie. I know it's stupid. You don't need to tell me—"

"I wasn't going to tell you that—" Edward started.

"But I know it's stupid. I know I never had a chance. Being as I am. Who I am. And I don't just mean the . . . shifting. I mean, just who I am. I know Kyrie deserves much better. I know that Rafiel is better. I've known that since I met him. But I'm too . . . I can't watch. I should be able to because they're both my friends, in a way, so I'm probably immature too, but there it is. I'm immature. I just can't . . . I'd end up getting in a big argument with her or him, or both of them. And I can't do that, because then . . . it would be worse than just leaving. So I'm leaving."

The words had poured in a torrent, drowning out any other attempts at speech, any other attempts at questioning. Now they stopped, and Tom reached for the coffeepot handle, as if to get up and resume his rounds.

"Tom," Edward said. "Where are you going?"

"It doesn't matter. Just . . . somewhere. Somewhere till things cool with the triad and until . . . No, I don't suppose I'll ever forget. I'm not . . . good."

"Perhaps you could consider coming home?" Edward said, and before Tom could correct it, "To my home. You can, you know. I don't mind."

He expected anger, or perhaps a huffing of pain. But instead Tom inclined his head once. "Maybe. After . . . when the triad isn't looking anymore. Perhaps they'll even give up on the idea of revenge, and calm down, and then, maybe."

Edward knew Tom was wrong. He knew Tom was wrong about Kyrie and Rafiel. He'd seen the three of them together and while Rafiel might look a lot at Kyrie, Kyrie looked at Tom. Now, most of the time she looked at Tom with annoyance or borderline irritation.

But that was part of it too, wasn't it? The ones who could annoy you most, the ones who could get under your skin most . . . He remembered what she had told him about how she knew that Edward still liked Tom, still had paternal feelings for him. How it was all about how he fought so hard to counter those feelings.

From what he'd seen, Edward guessed Kyrie had known from experience. She was, at the very least, seriously in lust with Tom. For a moment or two the day before, he'd thought she'd need a drool catcher to avoid staining the carpets of his hotel room. But he would bet there was more there, too. Because Kyrie was not the type to confuse lust with love.

He could let Tom go on believing this, being miserable. Tom would then probably end up in New York again and, knowing his intelligence and his newfound focus, be at Harvard or Yale within the year. And eventually he would find another woman.

But Edward looked at his son's pale face, his set mouth, which looked rigid enough not to tremble. Rigid enough not to betray the desolation within.

"Tom, I've watched her, and I think you're wrong. From her reactions, since I've met her, and from seeing her with him, I've . . . I don't think she's interested in him. And I think she likes *you* a lot."

Tom shook his head. "No, trust me. I had some hope. Not a lot. I mean, I know our different standings. But she was nice to me, and I thought maybe . . . But then I saw them kissing." He gestured with his head. "Up front. I know. I saw." He shook his head. "And I never expected it to affect me so much." He frowned, thunderous eyebrows low over his blue eyes. "I wanted to shift and flame something. Preferably his pants."

Edward almost laughed at this, because it was so much like Tom, to want to flame his rival's manhood right off. But he didn't want to laugh, not while Tom was in pain.

"I just thought you should know. I think you're wrong. But if you still think you must leave, then . . . I hope eventually you'll come back to my home. And before that, call me, okay? Tell me where you are. I'll wire you money. There's no reason for you to be deprived."

It was probably a measure of Tom's state of mind that he didn't protest the offer of money. Instead, he nodded and walked away.

"Man, he has it bad," Keith said. "I didn't realize it was that serious."

"I suspected it," Edward said. "I just didn't know he would take it in his head to run away from it all."

Was that what he'd taught Tom, when he'd thrown him out? To leave difficult situations behind?

Kyrie was shaking. Mostly with repressed rage. That Rafiel would dare grab her like that. That he would dare kiss her. And in front of half the diner too.

She put her apron on, and resumed serving her tables, but felt as if people were staring at her, and found herself blushing. *How could he?*

She suspected Rafiel was the center of attention to his parents, the center of their lives. His "handicap," the fact that he shifted, would make him far more precious to them, and they far more attentive to him. And he'd grown up to be the center of the universe.

Kyrie would bet too that with his body, his easy, self-assured personality, he would have girls falling from his hair and tumbling into his lap. She would just bet. So he probably was not too well aware of the meaning of the word no. Well, she would buy him a thesaurus at the first opportunity.

No, as in never. As in negation. As in I'm not interested. And even if the girl hasn't said it flat out, if she'd given him reason to think she was less than pleased with his interest, then Mr. Rafiel Trall would learn to keep his hands to himself. And his lips too.

She was so mad, that she banged a load of dishes into the dishwasher, after bussing the empty tables. This was the hour when people started leaving before the rush, and she'd bussed her tables, and Tom's too. She banged the plates and cups in, and she gave Frank a dirty look when he glared at her.

The dirty look must have worked, because Frank didn't say anything. Just turned away.

And Frank was, of course, a problem, as was Frank's girlfriend. Kyrie couldn't believe how obtuse and close-minded Rafiel had been. How could he not see that this series of coincidences, here, at the center of the Athens, was far more relevant than no matter how many couples who'd started dating a month ago, no matter how many men with bandaged necks elsewhere?

Damn the man. She couldn't believe someone like that, who was clearly smarter than dryer lint, would attempt to solve crimes using parts of his anatomy that lay below the equator.

She closed the dishwasher and started it, and turned to face Tom. He stood just behind her, his arms full with a tray of dishes.

"Oh, Tom, I'm sorry. That dishwasher is full. Let me open the other one. I'll put the dishes in for you if you want me to."

He shook his head. He was keeping his lips together, as if he were biting them to keep himself from saying something. How weird. It was an expression she'd never seen on his face. "Are you okay?"

"Fine," he said. "Just fine. I'll put the dishes in. You can go." His voice sounded lower and raspier than normal.

She went. She picked up tips, she tallied totals, she filled coffee cups.

On the way back from the addition to the main part of the diner, she saw Tom bussing a table, and thought that was as good a time as any to talk to him.

"I couldn't get Rafiel to listen," she said, in a whisper. "About Frank. He says it's all coincidences, and he refuses to help. What are we going to do?"

For a while, she thought that Tom hadn't heard her. He remained bent over the table, his hand holding a stack of plates to put on the tray, while the other hand held a moist cloth, with which he was poised to wipe where the plates had been. But he didn't move. He just stood there.

"Tom?" she said.

He put the plates on the tray, very slowly. Carefully, he wiped the table. Then he stood up and faced her. His face was stark white. Not the sickly pale it had been in the parking lot the night she'd found him over the corpse, but white—the white of paper, the white of the unblinking heart of a thunderbolt. "I don't know what you want me to do," he said, his voice calm, emotionless. "If you can't get Rafiel to listen to you, I fail to see where I can be of any use. I'm sorry."

"Oh, Tom, don't be an idiot," she said, in an urgent whisper, sure he had to have misunderstood it all. "I want to know what you and I are going to do about it."

Tom shook his head. "No. You don't understand. We're not going to do anything. After tonight, I won't even be here."

"Where are you going?"

He twisted his lips and shrugged. "Somewhere."

She watched him pick up his tray and his cloth and disappear toward the main diner, tray held at waist level.

What on earth was going on? First Rafiel had behaved like a lunatic, and now Tom. What had they been smoking? And why were they not sharing?

"What do you know about this?" she asked Keith and Edward, where they sat in their corner table. "Where's Tom going? What's wrong with him?"

Keith sat back on his chair, looking vaguely scared. "Whoa," he said. "That's one of the few rules of safety I've learned. I don't get in between this kind of stuff."

"What kind of stuff?" Kyrie asked, her temper rising. "What kind of stuff? What is wrong with every male here tonight?"

"I think," Edward said, his voice regretful, his tone slow, "that if I told you what Tom told me I would forfeit whatever trust I've been able to earn back from him. And you must see I can't do that. He might need me. I have to . . . stand by to help him if he needs it. I've got to tell you I hope he comes to his senses, but I don't think my explaining things to you would further this in any way."

"Oh," Kyrie said. "I see. He"—and she pointed at Keith—"makes cryptic remarks, and you make longer cryptic remarks, with far better vocabulary. Whatever. Sure. What is this? Be Stupid Day for males?"

She glared at them a while, daring them to answer. When neither did, she huffed out of there.

They didn't answer because they had no answer. They knew damn well—had to know—that they were acting like idiots. All of them.

Well, she would show them. Rafiel might be more practiced at smelling shifters, but Kyrie would bet that even she, herself, in panther form, could smell a rotting body in a shallow grave. If she knew what she was looking for. Even at the morgue, with all the preserving fluids and embalming whatnots, she had smelled it. She was sure she could smell it undisguised and in the heat of day under a thin layer of earth. The only reason she hadn't smelled it before—if it was there—would have been that she was escaping beetles and cops with guns.

So, when her shift was over, she'd go up to the castle, and she'd shift. She'd sniff around. When she found the corpses, she would shift again, and she would call the police. Take that, Officer Trall. If someone called the corpses in, then Mr. Rafiel Trall would have to do something about it, would he not?

And as for Mr. Tom Ormson, she didn't know exactly what was biting him, but she was in no mood to find out, either. It occurred to her that he might have seen Rafiel kiss her. But if that was what had put his nose so severely out of joint, then Tom needed to take a chill pill, that was what he needed to do.

After all, what fault was hers if an idiot male decided to kiss her? She had slapped him for it, too. Half rocked his head off of his shoulders. And if Tom hadn't stuck around to see that, he was more of a fool than she'd ever thought, and she wouldn't mind if he left and never came back.

She avoided him the rest of the shift.

Edward received the backpack from Tom's hands, and pulled out his wallet to set the bill for the food he and Keith and Rafiel had eaten. He guessed Rafiel wasn't coming back, but he wasn't about to ask Tom. There was absolutely no reason to get the boy even more upset than he already was.

Instead, Edward put the backpack on his back, sure it looked ridiculous with his nice clothes. He got up, and Tom was turning away, putting the bill with the money in his apron pocket. Edward grabbed at his son's shoulder. "Tom." It was as close as he dared come to a hug.

Tom looked back, eyebrows raised.

"I just want you to know," Edward said, "that if you need anything at all . . ." He gave Tom one of his cards. "You probably remember the home address," he said. "But this is the new office address and my cell phone and work phone. Call. Anytime. Day or night, okay?"

Tom nodded, but there was just that look of dubiousness in his eyes that made Edward wonder if he would really call. Or just get into trouble and not tell anyone.

He walked out of the diner, and out into the cooler, exhaust-filled night of Fairfax Avenue. Under the light pole, he noticed that Keith was behind him.

"Can I come with you?" Keith asked. "To deliver that?"

Edward took a deep breath. "I don't think so," he said. "I'm going to deliver it in person, you see, not put it down somewhere and wait for them to find it. I'm afraid they'll go after Tom again if I do that."

"So . . ."

"So the triads are dangerous. And the Great Sky Dragon is not someone—or something—one tangles with for sport. I think I'm fairly safe, because they depend on me for legal representation. But I don't think you'd be safe and I can't allow you to risk yourself."

"But . . ." Keith said. "I can take out dragons. With a tire iron."

Edward couldn't avoid smiling at that. "I know," he said. "And I'm proud to have met you. But I really think this is something I have to do alone."

Keith took a deep breath, and shrugged. Then frowned. "You're not going to allow me to, are you? No matter what I say?"

"I'm afraid not," Edward said. "I'm afraid it wouldn't be safe."

"Okay. Then . . . I'll stay and keep an eye on Kyrie and see in what direction Tom leaves, okay? I'll tell you. When I see you."

Edward nodded, and put out his hand, solemnly. Keith shook it just as solemnly.

Add to the things Tom had accomplished the fact that he seemed to make worthy friends. And that was something that Edward had never expected of Tom. But he was glad. He started walking up the street, to where Fairfax became a little better area. It would make it easier to hail a cab. Once he caught a cab, he would call Lung.

If he didn't give them much time to react, perhaps they wouldn't have time to summon the Great Sky Dragon. Edward wasn't sure he could face that presence.

In fact, he wasn't sure at all he would survive this experience. Despite everything he'd told Keith, he was sure that the triad could buy a replacement lawyer, once they got rid of him.

The funny thing was that he didn't much care if anything happened to him, provided nothing happened to Tom. He'd never got around to changing his will, and if he died, at least Tom would be taken care of. It wasn't like he'd ever been much of a father.

Kyrie hung up her apron and picked up her purse. It hit her, suddenly, and with a certainty she'd never felt before, that whatever happened tonight was decisive.

Because, if she went to the castle and found nothing, she'd have to live in hiding. Perhaps move. Because she couldn't know what the beetles knew or where they were.

On the other hand, if she went up there tonight and found corpses . . . well, it might be the last time she hung her apron on this peg and headed out, at the end of the shift, into the Colorado morning with the sky just turning pink, Fairfax Avenue as deserted as a country lane, and everything clean and still.

She got in her car and drove home, but only opened her front door to throw her purse inside the living room. Then she put her key in her pocket and headed back out.

The way to the castle was quick enough and at this time of morning there wasn't really anyone out. Kyrie could walk unnoticed down the streets. Which was good, because whether Frank and his girlfriend were shifter beetles or not, Kyrie didn't want him to know that she suspected him or his girlfriend. She wanted him to think that she had gone home, normally, and stayed there.

In a way she wished she could. Or that she—at least—had Tom or Rafiel with her. She couldn't believe that both of them had turned on each other at the same time, and she wondered if it was some argument they'd had, of which she was only catching the backlash. Who knew?

The castle looked forbidding and dark, looming in the morning light. Most of the windows were boarded up, except for some right at the front, next to the front door. She supposed that Frank's girlfriend, not needing all the rooms—at least until such a time as she opened a bed-and-breakfast, if those plans were true—had opened only those in which she was living.

Kyrie wondered what Frank's and whatever her name's plans were, if they really were the beetles and if they truly were in the middle of a reproductive frenzy.

Were they intending on having all their sons and daughters help in the bed-and-breakfast? Or simply to take over the castle with their family? Kyrie seemed to remember that beetles were capable of laying a thousand eggs in one reproductive season, so even the castle might prove very tight quarters. And how would they explain it? And would the babies be human most of the time? Or humans all the time till adolescence?

There was no way to tell and Kyrie wondered if other shifters worried about it. She did. But others were, seemingly, in a headlong rush to reproduce, regardless of what it might mean. She thought of Rafiel and scowled.

As she approached the front entrance to the garden, Kyrie saw a woman in a well-cut skirt suit and flyaway grey hair walking away from the alley where the back entrance opened. She was walking away from the castle, toward Fairfax. Maybe she was going to pick Frank up from work.

Which would mean, Kyrie supposed, that they weren't guilty and were just an older couple in dire need of social skills.

But it would also mean it was safe to go into the castle gardens. Kyrie ran in.

The gardens were thick and green in the early morning light. There was dew on the plants, and some of it dripped from the overhead trees. Above, somewhere, two birds engaged in a singing competition. She started toward the thicker part of the vegetation, where she could undress and shift. She didn't think that the woman living here now had any domestic help, but if she did, Kyrie didn't want some maid or housekeeper to scream that there was a girl undressing in the garden. Embarrassing, that.

Avoiding a couple of spiders building elaborate webs in the early morning sunlight, Kyrie made it all the way to the center of the garden, somewhere between the path that circled the house, and the outside fence.

There were ferns almost as tall as she was and she felt as if she'd stepped back into another geologic age when the area was covered in rain forest. She removed her clothes quickly and with practiced gestures. Shirt, jeans, shoes, all of it neatly folded and set aside. And then she stood, in the greenery, and willed herself to change.

It came more easily than she expected. The panther liked green jungles and dark places. It craved running through the heavy vegetation and climbing trees.

Kyrie forced it, instead, to stand very still and smell. It didn't take long. The smell was quite unmistakable.

❖   ❖   ❖

"Hello," Edward said into his cell phone in the back of the car. "May I speak with Mr. Lung?"

There was no answer, but a clunking sound as though the phone had been dropped onto a hard surface. From the background, Edward could hear the enthusiastic voice of a monster-truck rally narrator. Then, as if from very far off, the shutting of a door echoed.

Edward hoped this meant that someone was calling Mr. Lung. It was, of course, possible that once it had been determined that Edward hadn't called to order an order of moo goo gai pan with fried rice on the side, the cashier had simply left. Or gone to the kitchen to pinch an egg roll or his girlfriend's bottom.

It took a long time, but at long last, Edward thought he heard, very faintly, approaching footsteps. And then—finally—the sounds of a phone being moved around on a counter.

"Mr. Ormson?" Lung's voice asked.

"Yes. I have what you . . . I have the object you require. I'm heading to the restaurant to return it."

"You are? And your son?"

"We'll leave my son out of this," Edward said.

"I see. Will we?"

"Yes."

"Your son caused much damage and death to our . . . organization."

Edward said nothing. What was he supposed to say?

After a long while, Lung sighed. "I see. But you are returning the object in dispute."

"Yes."

"Well, then I shall wait anxiously. I will see you in how long?"

"About ten minutes," Edward said, and hung up the phone. He looked at the light growing brighter and brighter in east, every minute. If he was very lucky, then they wouldn't summon the Great Sky Dragon this close to dawn. Or if they did, he wouldn't make it here.

If he was very lucky.

He felt he could stand just about everything short of facing that huge, enigmatic presence once again.

The panther scented the corpses right away. Fortunately, they were a little past ripe, even for its tastes. Kyrie was grateful for this.

Locked at the back of the huge feline mind, she could feel the huge paws tread carefully through the undergrowth, and she could feel the big feline head swaying, while it tasted the air. Death. Death nearby.

The death smelled enough like what the animal recognized as its own mortality to slow down its steps, and it only continued forward because Kyrie forced it to.

But it continued. Around the lushest part of the vegetation and toward a little clearing of sorts, in the midst of it all.

The vegetation that had once grown here had been torn out, unceremoniously, by the roots, rose bush and fern, weed and bulb, all of it had been pulled up and tossed, unceremoniously, in a huge pile beside the clearing.

What there was of the earth there had then been turned. Graves. Kyrie could smell them, or rather the panther could.

Kyrie was sure the smell would be imperceptible to her human nose, but her feline nose could smell it, welting up through the imperfectly compacted earth—the smell of decay, of death, of that thing that inevitably all living things became.

Only this death had the peculiar metallic scent that Kyrie had learned to recognize as the smell of shifters. The people laid to rest here had been shifters. Her kind. She looked at the ground with the feline eyes, and forced the feline paw to make a scratching motion on the loose earth.

It didn't take long. The hand wasn't much more than fifteen inches down. The panther wanted to run away and to forget this, to pretend it had never existed.

But Kyrie forced it to walk, slowly, ponderously, to where Kyrie had left her clothes. Kyrie would shift. And then she would call the police.

But before she got to where her clothes lay, she found herself enveloped by a cloud of green dust. It shimmered in the morning air, raining down on her.

Pollen. It had to be pollen. Just pollen. She wished it to be pollen. But she could feel the panther's head go light, and indistinct forms take shape before her shifted eyes. Game, predators, small fluffy creatures and large ones, all teeth and claws, formed in front of the panther's eyes, coming directly from her brain.

Kyrie could feel the huge feline body leap and recoil, as if the things it were seeing were normal.

And then . . . And then she saw the beetle. It was coming through the vegetation, blue-green carapace shining under the morning light.

Not quite sure what she was doing, Kyrie forced the panther throat to make a sound it had never been designed for. She screamed.

The Chinese restaurant looked dismal grey in the morning light, as Edward got out of the cab in front of it.

As he was paying the fare, the cabby gave him an odd look. "They're closed, you know," he said. "They only open for lunch and that's not for seven hours."

"I know," Edward said, giving the man a generous tip and handing the credit card slip back. When you're not sure you're going to live, you can be very generous. "I'm meeting someone."

The cabby frowned. And older man, with Anglo-Saxon features, he was one of those men whose expressions are slow and seemingly painful, as though their faces had been designed for absolute immobility. "Only," he said, "they've found corpses in this parking lot, all the time. I've read about it in the paper. Are you sure you want . . . ?"

Edward nodded. He wanted to explain he was doing it for his son, but that made it sound way too much like expected a medal for doing what any decent father would do. Brave death to keep his son safe. Only . . . he supposed he hadn't been a decent father. Or not long enough for it to be unremarkable.

"I'm sure," he said. "I'll call you for the trip back," he said. "Your name is on the receipt, right?"

"Right," the cabby said, but dubiously, as though he couldn't really believe there would be a trip back.

The truth was neither did Edward. As he walked away from the cab—already peeling rubber out of the parking lot—and toward the silent door of the Three Luck Dragon, with the closed sign on the window, he would have given anything to run away.

But instead he fumbled off the backpack as the door opened a crack and Lung's face appeared in the opening. "Ah, Mr. Ormson," he said. Then he stepped aside and opened the door further. "Come in."

"There is no need," Edward said. "I have what you want, here. Take it and I—"

But the door opened fully. And inside the room were a group of young men, all glaring at him. They all looked . . . dangerous. In the sort of danger that comes from having absolutely no preconceived notions about the sanctity of the human life.

"I said, come in," Lung said.

It wasn't the sort of invitation that Edward could refuse. For one, he was sure if he did those dark-haired young men glaring at him out of the shadows would chase him down and drag him back. The only question was whether they would shift into dragon form first.

Edward suspected they would.

Walking away from Goldport by the shortest route did not require going near Kyrie's house. However, walking away from Goldport and not heading out of town via the route to New Mexico did lead Tom down Fairfax Avenue, in the general direction of the castle and Kyrie's neighborhood. Though those were a few blocks north from his path.

Kyrie. The name kept turning up in Tom's mind with the same regularity that a sufferer's tongue will seek out a hole in a decaying tooth. It hurt, but it was the sort of hurt t reassured him he was still alive.

Kyrie. The problem was that he'd actually had hope. He'd seen her look at him. She'd patted his behind. She'd smiled at him. He'd had hope, however foolish that hope might have been. If he'd never hoped for anything, he wouldn't have been so shocked and wounded at seeing her with Rafiel.

And, yes, he was aware that the fact he couldn't bear to see them together was a character failing of his, not of theirs. He was also aware she hadn't betrayed him. Looks and even pats on the bottom are not promises. They certainly are not a relationship. They are just . . . lust.

Perhaps, he thought, as he walked in front of closed-up store doors and dismal-looking storefronts in the grey morning daylight, *perhaps she lusts after me—though who knows why—but when it comes to love, when it comes to a relationship, she's a smart girl. If she were interested in me, it would only be proof of either stupidity or insanity.*

But . . . but if it wasn't her fault, why was he punishing her?

He scowled at his own thought. He wasn't punishing her. If anything, he was keeping himself from being punished daily by the sight of her with Rafiel.

It hurt. No, it wasn't rational, but it hurt. Badly. And Tom didn't do well with hurt. He wasn't punishing Kyrie. He'd go out of town, through Colorado Springs. Probably buy a bus ticket there. Maybe go to Kansas for a while. It had been a long time since he'd been in Kansas.

But, the relentless accusing voice went on in his mind, if he wasn't trying to punish her, why was he leaving Kyrie to face the beetles alone? Why was he leaving her when she couldn't even sleep in her house?

Because it wasn't his problem. Because she wasn't his to worry about. She could always bunk up with Rafiel, couldn't she? And she was sure he'd keep her safe. She wasn't Tom's to keep safe.

If she had been, he would have given up his life for her, happily enough.

But what kind of love was that? He minded seeing her with Rafiel? He minded her being happy? But he didn't mind leaving town while she was in danger?

No wonder she'd picked Rafiel. Tom's love was starting to sound a lot like hate.

As the last few thoughts ran through his mind, Tom's steps had slowed down, and now he stopped completely in front of the closed door of a little quilting shop, just one crossroad past where he would have turned up to go to Kyrie's place.

Maybe he should go and check on her. See if she was home. See if she was well . . . Then, if she told him she was fine and that Rafiel would take care of her, he could leave town with a clear conscience and never worry.

He turned around, in front of the shop—the window screaming at him in pretty red cursive that summer was the ideal time to quilt—and headed back toward the crossroad. He'd just turned upward on it, when he saw, ahead of him, just scurrying out of sight on a bend of the road, a giant beetle, its blue carapace shining in the sun.

Kyrie, Tom thought. He knew there were other places they could be headed. But right then he thought of Kyrie. He thought only of Kyrie.

And then the scream came. It was all Kyrie and yet not human—a warbling mix of terror coming from a feline throat designed only for roaring and hissing.

Without even noticing what he was doing, he broke into a run. He made the turn ahead in the street in time to see the beetle creep into the greenery-choked garden of the castle.

And the scream came again.

Kyrie was hallucinating. Or rather, the panther was. In front of the feline eyes arose a hundred little animals that needed hunting, or rearing predators.

And yet, at the back of the panther's mind, Kyrie managed to remain lucid, or almost lucid. There was a beetle. She must not loose track of that. A beetle with shimmering blue-green carapace. And it was trying to kill Kyrie. And lay eggs in her corpse.

This certainty firmly in mind, Kyrie aimed at anything green-blue that she caught amid the snatches of illusion clogging the panther's vision. The panther's claws danced over the extended limbs with what looked like a poison injector at the end but might merely have been a lethal claw of some sort. She careened over the bug's back, and scrambled halfway away before the beetle caught up.

They were right over the graves, and the funky smell of them disturbed the panther, even through the hallucinations.

And at the back of the panther's mind, Kyrie knew soon she would be dead and buried in this shallow grave.

Tom had run full tilt into the garden of the castle, before he realized what he was doing. He was only lucky the beetles were too busy to realize he was running after them.

Of course, what they were too busy with was Kyrie. And once they noticed Tom they would start pumping the green stuff, and make Tom high as a kite and his fighting totally ineffective.

Twenty yards from them, seeing the huge black feline leap and dance ahead, in mad attack, Tom stopped. He pulled his jacket off, and tossed it in the direction of a tree, making a note where it was. He would come back for it. Then he peeled off the white T-shirt and, wrapping it around his head, tied it in a knot at the back. Its double thickness of fabric made it hard to breathe, and he could wish for better clothes to fight in than the pants that were slowly castrating him.

But he didn't get his choice. And it didn't matter. He must fight for Kyrie.

He grabbed a tree branch and plunged forward into the battle swinging it at any beetle limbs within his reach.

Clouds of green stuff emanated, turning the air green and shimmering.

Tom realized the smaller beetle—the one he'd followed?—was immobile and rubbing its wings to emit cloud after cloud of green powder. Meanwhile the one fighting Kyrie—and so far not losing, though also not managing to get any hits in—was not emitting green powder.

Interesting. So, they could only make people hallucinate when they weren't actively fighting, was that it?

Well, he thought, jumping back and landing atop the beetle, with a huge tree branch in hand. *Well. He was about to take the fight to the enemy.*

❖   ❖   ❖

And now Kyrie was sure that she, personally, was hallucinating. On top of the panther-conjured images of scared little furry things, there was . . . Tom. Oh, not just Tom, but Tom in gloriously tight jeans, with his shirt removed, and his muscular chest bare in the morning sunlight.

Of course, the shirt he'd taken off was tied around his face, which seemed a really odd hallucination for her to have. And she would think she would dream of his grabbing her and kissing her, rather than of his hitting some very hard blows on the beetle with a huge tree trunk—far too big to be a branch—he'd got from nowhere.

And yet, she thought as she tried to concentrate on hitting any green-blue bits of bug that she could see through the panther's addled eyes. And yet the sight of him fighting the bug was far more distracting than the sight of the small furry things could be for the panther.

She bit and snarled and clawed at bits of bug, but in her mind she was admiring the way Tom leapt, the way he could turn on a dime, the force he put into the swing of that tree branch in his hand. From his movements, he too must have taken gymnastics or dance, or something.

Absorbed between her fight and disturbing glimpses of half-naked Tom, she could barely think. She heard the squeal of brakes toward the back entrance of the garden, but she paid it no attention.

Which is why she was so shocked to see Rafiel running toward them, gun drawn, blond hair flying in the wind and his expression quite the most distraught Kyrie had ever seen. He was screaming something as he ran, and it seemed to Kyrie—through the panther's distorted senses—that one of the words was "die." The other words, though, were "gravy" and "pick." She wasn't sure what gravy had to do with it.

Rafiel let out shots as he ran, aimed at the beetles, and from the high-pitched whining of the one that Tom was beating, Kyrie would guess at least one of the bullets had found beetle flesh. Whether that meant it had also found any lethal points was something else again.

Behind Rafiel, Keith came, running up, with what looked like a hoe in his hand. Where had he found the hoe?

Tom heard a bullet whistle by and looked up to see Rafiel running into the garden firing wildly. Still beating on the beetle—smacking it repeatedly on the head seemed to make it too confused to either fight, flee, or put out green powder—Tom wondered if he was the intended victim or the beetle.

But the next bullet lodged itself solidly in the beetle's— Frank's?—flesh, and the creature emitted a high-pitch whine. And then it went berserk, limbs failing up toward Tom, trying to dislodge him, trying to stab at him.

Tom hit at the limbs, wildly. Keith was running up, behind Rafiel, and as Rafiel leapt toward Kyrie's beetle and shifted shapes mid-leap, his clothes falling in shreds away from the lion body, Keith grabbed the falling gun and aimed it at Tom's beetle.

Kyrie was grateful when Rafiel, now in lion form, joined the fight, but—though the panther was having trouble seeing clearly—she could see enough to see Keith grab the gun and point it in the general direction of Tom.

She didn't think that Keith would hurt Tom. Or not on purpose. But from the way Keith was holding the gun, she could tell there was no way in hell he could hit the broadside of a barn.

Unfortunately, he wasn't aiming at the broadside of a barn. He was aiming at a general area where Tom was a prominent feature. Without thinking she leapt, hitting the still human Tom with her weight and bringing him rolling off the bug and onto the ground, with Kyrie just by his side.

Just in time, as the bullet whistled through the space where he'd been.

❖   ❖   ❖

Kyrie was attacking him, Tom thought, as he hit hard on the ground, just barely managing to tuck in his head enough that he wouldn't end up unconscious. Why was she?

And then he realized that Keith had a gun and clearly had no idea what to do with it, as several erratically fired bullets flew over the beetle's carapace. Just where Tom would have been.

Still stunned by his fall on the ground, Tom put out a hesitant hand toward the huge mound of fur beside him. "Kyrie?" he said.

A tongue came out and touched his hand. Just touched, which was good, because it felt just like a cat tongue, all sharp bits and hooks.

A nonfeline hissing sound, a scraping, and Tom saw the beetle was turning around and was aiming sharp clawlike things at Kyrie.

Before he could think, he knew he was going to shift. He had just the time to kick off his leather boots as his body twisted and bent. And he was standing, as a dragon, facing the bug. He did what a dragon does. He flamed.

First, Kyrie thought, flames weren't particularly effective in these circumstances. Tom's flame seemed to glance over the beetle's carapace, without harming it. And second, if Tom continued flaming, he would hit a tree and roast them all alive.

But before Kyrie could change shape and yell this at Tom, who was clearly addled by adrenaline and change, Keith came flying out from behind them, hoe in hand. He had dropped his gun. Which was good. But Kyrie wasn't sure that a hoe was the most effective of weapons.

Only she couldn't do anything, except shift, in a hurry and scream, "Don't flame, Tom," as Keith landed on top of the beetle and started digging into the joint between the neck and the back carapace. Digging, as if he were digging into soil, making big chunks of beetle fly all over.

The beetle went berserk.

Sometimes the only way to stop a flame that is doing its best to erupt from a dragon's throat is for the dragon to force himself to become human. This Tom did, forcing his mind to twist his body into human shape. Just in time to avoid burning Keith to a crisp atop the beetle. Which was good, because Keith seemed to have hit on something that worked. He was digging up large chunks of beetle flesh, throwing them all around in a shower of beetle and ichor.

And the beetle was stabbing at him, fortunately pretty erratically. The beetle's arms weren't meant to bend that way. Not upward and toward something on its back. Only, even an erratic blow was bound to hit, eventually. Unless . . .

Tom grabbed the tree branch he'd let drop, and started beating at beetle limbs. From the other side, Kyrie was doing the same.

Kyrie was back to her human form, and Tom couldn't look at her with more than the corner of his eye. Not if he wanted to continue fighting in any rational manner at all.

But, damn, that woman could swing the tree branch with the best of them.

As the beetle stopped moving, and its high-pitched scream grew, Tom became aware of another sound behind him. A feline protest of pain. He turned, in time to see the beetle get a claw into Rafiel between shoulder and front leg.

For a moment, for just a moment, Tom thought, *Good. He deserves it.*

But an immense feeling of shame swept over him. Why did Rafiel deserve to die? Because he'd bested Tom in winning the affections of a woman?

Hell, by that criteria there would hardly be any males left alive in the world.

Shame made Tom jump forward, toward Rafiel, tree branch in hand, beating at the beetle. Just in time, as Rafiel was crawling away, bleeding.

And now Keith scrambled up on the back of this beetle. He looked like nothing on Earth and certainly no longer like the hard-partying college student. His clothes were a mess, he seemed to have bathed in greenish-brown ichor, and he'd lost his cap somewhere.

But he had an insane grin on his face, as he started digging up chunks of this beetle. And Tom concentrated on keeping the beetle from stabbing his friend, by beating the beetle's limbs away. Kyrie joined in on the other side.

Soon the beetle had stopped moving.

But from behind them there was still a high-pitched sound, like the beetle's scream.

Tom turned around, expecting to face yet another beetle. Instead, he saw Rafiel desperately clutching his shoulder and struggling to get up while pale, white, giant worms swarmed over him.

Tom didn't understand where the worms came from, but they had big, sharp teeth and were biting at Rafiel.

Tom ran toward Rafiel and started grabbing at the worms trying to eat Rafiel, while Kyrie ran up to smash the ones that were merely around Rafiel.

A second later, Keith and his hoe joined in.

❖   ❖   ❖

Grubs, Kyrie thought. The more advanced grubs on the corpses beneath the thin layer of soil had come alive at the smell of Rafiel's blood, and were swarming him.

She saw Tom jump ahead and start to pull the grubs off Rafiel. As mad as she was at Rafiel, she didn't want him eaten alive by would-be insects. And besides, Rafiel had got in this trouble by trying to help her in the first place.

She jumped into the fray, gleefully smashing at the grubs with her heavy branch.

And Tom had got the last grub off Rafiel—who seemed more stunned than hurt, and was swinging the huge piece of tree he carried, likewise beating down the bugs. Keith joined in with his hoe.

There were a lot of grubs, more and more—pale and white and writhing—pushing up out of the soil, as soon as they smashed a dozen or a hundred.

So absorbed in what she was doing, her arms hurting, while she kicked away to keep the grubs from climbing her legs, Kyrie didn't keep track of Rafiel.

Until she smelled gasoline and realized that Rafiel had got a huge container of gasoline from somewhere and was liberally dousing the clearing and the surrounding vegetation.

❖ ❖ ❖

Tom had just realized what the worms were. They were grubs. Babies. It seemed odd to be killing babies who were acting only on instinct.

But . . . were the babies human? He couldn't tell. They looked like white grubs, featureless, except for large mouths with sharp teeth. With which they'd probably been feeding on decaying human flesh.

Would they ever be human? How could Tom know? Except that, of course, their parents had been human. At least part of the time.

He swung the tree branch and smashed little beetle grubs while wondering if with time they would learn to be human babies and human toddlers. But . . . would they? And even if they did, when adolescence came, when most people started shifting, would they be able to control their urges to shift? And their urges to kill people so they could lay eggs in the corpses?

He just decided that he'd hit all of them who attacked him, but he would not, could not, kill any that might still be asleep beneath the soil. They should take those, and see if they became human babies as they developed. If they did, chances were they wouldn't shift again till their teen years. And meanwhile, they could see that they got a good education, and didn't believe they could kill people for their sexual gratification.

If shifters would look after punishing their own criminals, then they had to look after educating their own young, didn't they?

He'd just thought this when he smelled gasoline, and, looking up, saw Rafiel spreading gasoline over the entire area and the surrounding vegetation.

Tom had to stop him. He had to. He was going to kill all the babies. And themselves with them, probably.

As tired as he was, he didn't realize he'd shifted and flamed until he saw fire spark on the gasoline-doused tree on the other side of the clearing.

Oh, shit.

"Run," Kyrie screamed, managing to grab at Keith's arm, and making an ineffective grab at Tom's wing, as she scrambled ahead of them toward the back entrance of the garden—the nearest one.

If she thought for a minute she could go over the fence, she would have done it. She couldn't pull Tom, though, and he seemed dazed, staying behind, staring at the flames.

"Tom, run," she yelled, but there were sheets of flames where they'd been, and she couldn't stop, but ran. Ran all the way out the gate. Where she collapsed in a heap on the beaten-dirt of the alley, a few steps from Rafiel's car.

Rafiel was facedown in the alley, but he was clearly alive, taking deep breaths that shook his whole body.

Kyrie heard Keith ask, "Are you all right, man?"

And realized Rafiel was on all fours, throwing up.

Tom ran out of the gate, fell, then scrambled up, holding on to the eight-foot-tall metal fence of the castle to pull himself upright.

And Kyrie couldn't help smiling when she realized he was wearing a jacket and a pair of leather boots. And nothing else. So, that was why he had delayed? Tom and his jacket and boots.

He dropped something at her feet. "I tripped on these."

Her clothes. As she shook them out, even her earring dropped out.

But he had his back to her, and was still clutching the fence posts, while he stared at the roaring inferno growing inside the garden.

"We have to go," Kyrie said. "We have to get out of here. The fire department will be here in no time."

"But . . ." Tom said. "The babies."

"You mean the grubs? Tom, those weren't human. They tried to eat Rafiel."

Tom made a sound half growl. "We don't know if they were babies. Do we know what we were during gestation? Perhaps they would have shifted when they were fully grown, and only a few of them would ever shift again and not for years."

"Tom," Rafiel said. His voice sounded shaky. "I understand the feelings, but we had to kill them. We couldn't afford for the corpses to be found with those larvae. They would be taken to labs. Do you want them to figure out shape-shifting? They might very well come after us and kill us all, if faced with a dangerous example like that."

"So, you killed them to save your life? Is that right? Do you have the right to kill things just because there's a remote chance it would eventually lead to your death?"

"Hell, yes," Rafiel said.

"It's not moral," Tom protested.

"If I'm dead, morality doesn't matter to me anymore. Tom. Look, they bit me." He showed round bite marks, as if from a hundred little mouths equipped with sharp teeth. "They were dangerous. They would have bit other people. Killed other people. Besides," Rafiel shrugged. "Technically *we* killed them. You flamed them."

"Only because I was trying to prevent you from killing them," Tom said, and realized how stupid that sounded.

"Tom," Kyrie said. "It was self-defense. The heat of battle. And they were probably dangerous. Please calm down. We need to get out of here before those fire trucks get here. Hear them?"

Tom heard them, the wailing in the distance, getting near.

"We can go to my house," Kyrie said. "Take showers. I'll make something for us."

Just then, Tom's phone rang in his jacket pocket. "What now?" he said, grabbing the phone and taking it to his ear.

"Mr. Ormson," a cool voice on the other side said.

"Yes."

"We have your father," the voice said.

Oh, shit. The dragons. "But you have the Pearl of Heaven too," Tom said.

"Yes. But . . . There is someone who wishes for more than the return of the Pearl." The voice on the other side was slick and uncaring and inhuman. "He says there must be punishment."

"What punishment?" Tom said, feeling like he'd been punished enough this last hour.

"Severe punishment," the voice said. "One of you will be punished. Either you or your father. We're at Three Luck Dragon, on Ore Road on the other side of town. If you're not here in half an hour, we'll punish your father. The Great Sky Dragon is tired of waiting."

The phone line went dead and Tom thought, *So, let them punish my father. He deserves it. He's the one who got involved with the triad.*

But Tom was the one who had stolen the Pearl of Heaven. Worse, Tom was the one who had asked his father to return it. And his father had gone, without complaint. Even though, knowing even more about the triad than Tom did, he must have realized this was the kiss of death.

Tom didn't realize he had made a decision until he was running down the alley.

"Where is he going?" Rafiel asked Kyrie, as Tom started running.

Kyrie shrugged, but Keith said, "Something must have gone wrong with his father taking the Pearl out to the triad."

"What?" Rafiel said.

"Whatever happened to we'll leave the Pearl somewhere?" Kyrie said. "And let them find it?"

"I guess that wasn't practical," Keith said. "Since Tom was heading out of town."

"He was? Why?"

"I don't know," Keith said. "But he'd seen the two of you kissing and he said he couldn't stand to stay around."

"Oh no," Kyrie said.

"He's not going to get very far dressed like that, before someone arrests him for indecent exposure," Rafiel said, as Tom hit the end of the garden, and turned onto Fairfax. And then he jumped, and opened the door of his car. Getting into the driver's seat, he yelled, "Get in now."

Kyrie had barely the time to scramble in, beside Keith on the backseat, before Rafiel tore out of the parking lot in a squeal of tires and a smell of burning rubber.

He pulled onto the curb just ahead of the running Tom, leaned sideways and opened the passenger door. Then before Tom could swerve to avoid it, he yelled out the door, "Get in now, Tom. Get in."

"I don't want to get in," Tom said, stopping.

"That you might not, but you're naked. Someone will arrest you long before you get where you're supposed to go," Rafiel said, way too reasonably.

Tom looked down. Yeah. He supposed a leather jacket and a pair of leather boots didn't constitute decent clothing. And he had to get to the restaurant without being arrested.

He flung into the passenger seat of the car. "I need to go to Three Luck Dragon on Ore Road on the south side."

"I know where it is," Rafiel said, starting the car up. "Wonderful Peking duck." Then, as though realizing that Tom's driving motive wasn't a wish for food. "Your father?"

"Yes," Tom said, and covered his face with his hands. "I should never have sent him to them. Hell, I can't do anything right. Damn."

He felt a hand on his shoulder, from the back, and heard Kyrie's voice. "If you were planning to go out of town, you did the only thing you could do," she said. "And your father, did he protest?"

"No," Keith said. "He knew there was a danger. He wouldn't let me go with him. But he, himself, went willingly. Tom. Your father is an adult. He made his own decision."

"Doesn't mean we'll leave him to die," Tom said.

"Right," Rafiel said. "Which is why I'll get us there as soon as possible. Meanwhile, there are clothes under the front seat, Kyrie, if you could get them. There should be at least two changes of clothes. And there should be a pair of pants and a T-shirt Tom could use. They'll be large as hell, but they should make him decent."

Before Tom could protest, he found Kyrie handing him a T-shirt and a pair of sweatpants. Removing his jacket and boots and putting clothes on was difficult in the tight confines of the car. And Tom wasn't absolutely sure if the dragons cared if he had any clothes on.

But he understood there would be a psychological advantage to being fully dressed when he got there and tried to negotiate his father's release with the dragons. If he were naked, he'd be embarrassed, and that would put him at a strong disadvantage. No. He had to be dressed. And he had to get his dad out of this.

He should never have involved his dad in this.

Before they got to the restaurant Kyrie could smell the shifter scent in the air. She wondered how many of them were there.

Speeding down the—at this time—deserted Ore Road, lined by warehouses and dilapidated motels, they made one last turn . . . And then she saw it. At least she imagined that was it. She couldn't imagine any other reason why the parking lot in front of a low-slung building ornamented with an unlikely fluorescent green dragon on the roof would be crammed—literally crammed with men.

No, she thought, as she got closer. Men and dragons.

And at the head of it all, golden and brilliant in the morning light, was a huge dragon. Ten times bigger than Tom in his dragon form. And even bigger than that in presence. He *felt* a hundred times larger than his already immense size.

In his front paw, raised high above the assembly, he held Edward Ormson.

Kyrie wasn't close enough to see Edward's expression. But she could see his arms moving. He was alive.

Rafiel stopped the car in front of the parking lot. Impossible to turn into it. And besides, Tom was already struggling with the latch, trying to jump out.

Kyrie opened the door, too, as soon as the car stopped. And was hit by the silence of the hundreds of beings in the parking lot.

It was the silence of suspended breath.

Tom had *never* been so scared. Not even when he'd been sixteen and his father had thrown him out of the house at gunpoint. Not even in the wild days and terrifying nights afterward, while he tried to learn to live on the street while not dying of sheer stupidity.

It wasn't only his terror, he realized. It was the terror and awe of all those around him. He could hear it in their silence, see it in their absolute immobility. And he could feel it rolling in waves over him whenever he looked at the great golden dragon who stood in front of the multitude. Holding Tom's father.

Right.

There were moments, Tom had learned, when fear was the best thing. Fear of the street thug kept you from saying something that would have made him kill you. Fear of the poisonous snake kept you too far away from it to be bitten. And fear of some animals would make you stand absolutely still, so that their eyes, adapted to movement, couldn't see you.

And there were moments when fear had to be ignored. His fear was perfectly rational. He could sense the menace of the Great Sky Dragon and the fear that infected those around him, crowding the parking lot. He could feel it, and it made him struggle to draw breath. It made him have to fight his every instinct to be able to step forward into the crowd, which parted to allow him through.

His fear was the most natural thing in the world and it came from the fact that he did not wish to die. And it didn't take a genius to know that was the most likely outcome of this situation.

And yet . . . And yet, of course Tom didn't want to die.
There had been enough ambiguity in the exchanges in the
car that he thought he just might still have a chance with
Kyrie. And who, thinking of Kyrie—particularly when
she'd smiled at him—could want to die and not even try
for something more with her?

But all of that was irrelevant, for the same reason that it
was irrelevant whether or not Tom could or wanted to eat
some human beings on occasion. It was irrelevant because
if Tom did it and succeeded he wouldn't be able to live
with himself afterward.

As he wouldn't be able to live with himself if he walked
away now and let them kill his father. His father had
walked into this at Tom's request. It was Tom's doing, and
it was high time Tom dealt with his own mistakes.

He walked forward through the crowd, which parted
for him, leaving him a wide aisle to walk through.

He could hear his friends walk behind him, but he
didn't turn to look. That would only make what he needed
to do harder to accomplish.

Edward wasn't really scared until Tom showed up.
Before the Great Sky Dragon arrived, even, while Lung
and his minions had kept him prisoner in the entrance
area of the restaurant—where the TV blared endlessly
about round-the-clock monster truck rallies—he'd
realized what was going to happen and he was prepared to
take it.

Funny how, just days ago, when the Great Sky Dragon
had told him that he held him responsible for Tom's

actions, Edward had bridled at the idea and tried to deny it. Now it seemed absolutely self-evident.

Tom was something that Edward had made. Not only by inadvertently passing on some long-forgotten gene that had caused the boy to turn into a dragon—no. Of that guilt he could have easily absolved himself, because . . . who can be sure of what he's passing on to his sons? And who can control what his children inherit?

But these days with the other shifters—getting acquainted with Kyrie and even the policeman—Edward had realized that he'd done something else, something drastically wrong with Tom. Because the other shifters weren't as troubled and hadn't gone through so much to get to a place of balance. And hadn't made mistakes nearly as bad as the ones Tom had achieved.

Which must mean that shifters weren't inherently unstable. Of course, Edward had tried to tell himself that Tom was inherently unstable; that there had been something wrong with the boy from the beginning. But he'd seen Tom at the diner—Tom holding down a job and establishing contact with other human beings all around him.

There was nothing wrong with Tom. If he'd gone around the bend, it had to be his father's doing.

And so, Edward was ready to pay for his crimes and for the fact that he had been a truly horrible father. So he'd been perfectly calm, in the Great Sky Dragon's grasp, while the dragon lifted him above the crowd. Even though he'd been held there, immobile, for half an hour, he didn't feel scared or upset.

He devoted his time to a vague dream that Tom would come back; would figure things out with Kyrie; that sometime in their future they would have children. Even if

Edward would never get to see his grandchildren, he could imagine them vividly. And it was worth it to him to sacrifice himself for them.

And then the car stopped. And Tom showed up. The four of them—the four children, as Edward couldn't help thinking—walked through the massed triad crowd toward the Great Sky Dragon.

Tom was at the front, looking pale and drawn and absolutely determined.

"Tom, no," Edward shouted. "It's not worth it. Leave."

But Tom shook his head, black curls tossing in the light of the morning. He frowned. He walked all the way to the front of the Great Sky Dragon and stood, feet planted apart, arms crossed on his chest. "I've come," he said.

Edward had the impression the giant creature holding him laughed, though there was no sound. "It is good that you come," it said. "And now, what do you want to do?"

"I want you to let my father go," Tom said, casting his voice so that, normally low as it was, it could be heard all over the vast parking lot.

"Or?" the Great Sky Dragon asked.

"I don't think there's any or," Tom said. "You're much bigger than I am, and we're surrounded by all your minions. I'll fight you, if you want me to, but I don't think there would be any contest."

"No," the Great Sky Dragon said. "There wouldn't."

"So, I'm here. You do whatever you have to do, but you let my father go first."

"Tom, no," Edward said. "Don't do this. I don't want you to sacrifice yourself for me. I was a horrible father."

At that something like amusement flickered over Tom's face, which, from where Edward was looking at it, looked like a terrible, pale mask incapable of human movement.

For just a moment, Tom blinked, and looked up at his father, and his eyelids fluttered, and his lips pinched upward in an almost smile, "No shit, Sherlock. Did you have to consult many experts to come to this conclusion?" He shook his head. "But it doesn't matter, because I've always been an even worse son, and—" As Edward opened his mouth, Tom held up a hand to silence him. "What's more, I brought this final situation on by my own actions. I'm not stupid. I wasn't a baby when I stole the Pearl of Heaven. Nor were my impulses uncontrollable. I knew what I was doing. I knew whom I was messing with. And I did it anyway. So, you see, it's my doing, and who but I should suffer for it?"

Tom looked away from his father. "Let my father go," he told the dragon. "And promise me that all my friends will be able to leave safely. And then do whatever you think you have to do to even the score."

Edward felt himself being lowered, slowly, until his feet touched the pavement. He put out a hand and grabbed at Tom's shoulder. "Tom, no. Please. I can't live knowing—"

But the dragon flicked a toe at Edward's back. Just, flicked it. And Edward went flying, backward, head over heels, to land bruised and stunned at Kyrie's and Keith's feet.

❖   ❖   ❖

Tom watched the dragon flick his father out of the way and send him flying. A look back over his shoulder showed him that his father was alive and well. He turned back to the dragon.

Having no illusions about how long—or how little—remained for him to live seemed to make everything around him very bright and sharp. The dragon glittering in the light of the morning was a thing of beauty, golden and scintillating. And the sun coming up over the Three Luck Dragon painted the sky a delicate pink like the inside of certain roses when they're just opening to the light of morning.

As for the morning air, it smelled of flowers and it felt cool to the skin, with only a hint of warmth to indicate the scorcher the day would later become.

I'll never see another sunrise, Tom thought. *Yesterday was my last sunset. That meal eaten with Kyrie, hastily, in my father's hotel room, was my last meal. Worse, I'll never kiss a girl, beyond the halfhearted kisses and gropes I got back before I knew I was a dragon. I'll never kiss Kyrie.*

Weirdly, none of this seemed startling. It was as though all his life he'd been hastening toward this. Or rather, as if all his life he'd been worried about how he was going to die and what would put an end to his life. Now he need worry no more. He knew exactly where he would end and how.

A brief thought of whether there was anything after flickered through his mind. His parents were Catholic—or at least Catholic of the sort that didn't believe in God but believed that Mary was His mother. They went to mass sometimes. Certainly for big occasions and momentous parties, like weddings and baptisms and funerals. And Tom had attended catechism lessons in the faraway days of his childhood. Well, at least he'd been present while dreaming up ways to trip up the catechist, or look up her skirt.

He had no objections to the idea of an afterlife. But he also couldn't believe in it. Not really believe. If there was anything on the other side of this, he sensed it would be so different that who he was and what he thought on this side would make no difference at all. For all intents and purposes, Tom Ormson would stop existing.

He wanted—desperately wanted—to look over his shoulder at Kyrie. He heard her back there, her voice muffled, as though someone held a hand over her mouth. She was yelling, "Tom, no."

But he didn't dare look. If he saw her. If he actually saw her, he knew his courage would fail him. Instead, he stood, legs slightly apart for balance, letting his arms uncross from his chest and fall alongside his body. In a position that didn't look quite so threatening.

He looked up at the huge, inhuman eye of the Great Sky Dragon.

"Ready?" the creature said.

"Ready," Tom said.

The creature lowered its head to be level with Tom's and said—in a voice that was little more than a modulated hiss, "You have great courage, little one."

And for a moment, for a brief, intense moment, Tom had hope.

Then he saw the glimmering claw slice through the air. It caught him just above the pubic bone. Tom saw it penetrate, before the pain hit. It ripped upward, swiftly, disemboweling him from pubic bone to throat.

Looking down, Tom saw his own innards spill, saw blood fountain out.

I'm dead, he thought, and blinked with the sort of blank stupidity that comes from not believing your own eyes.

And then the pain hit, burning, unbearable. He screamed, or attempted to scream but nothing came out except a burble of blood that stopped up his throat, filled his mouth, poured out of his nose.

He dropped to the ground and for a second, for an agonizing second, struggled to breathe. His rapidly fading brain told him it was impossible. He was dead. But he tried to breathe, against pain and horrible cold and fear.

He inhaled blood and heard Kyrie call his name. He thought he felt her grab his hand, but his hand was as distant and cold as the other side of the moon.

And then there was nothing.

"Tom."

Kyrie had struggled against Rafiel and Keith, as they held her back, struggled and kicked and tried to yell at Tom not to do this. It wasn't worth his sacrifice. It just wasn't.

They could fight the dragons. They could.

"No, we can't," Rafiel told her. "He's giving himself up so that the rest of us can get away in peace. If he doesn't do that, all of us will die."

"There's hundreds of them and five of us, Kyrie," Keith said. "We'll all die."

"Then we'll all die," she yelled. "Can you live with the idea you calmly allowed him to sacrifice himself for us?"

"I can't," Edward said. But he was gathering himself up from the ground, and he looked bruised and tired and hurt. He didn't look like he would lead any charges against any dragons.

So Kyrie yelled, "Tom, don't do it," and tried to struggle free, to go grab him. If they ran. If they ran very fast . . .

But Keith and Rafiel both grabbed her and held onto her arms, and covered her mouth.

She was twisting against them, writhing . . .

And it all happened too fast. That claw rising and falling, in the morning sunlight, catching Tom and ripping . . .

Kyrie saw blood fountain at the same time that the men, startled, let go of her. She careened forward, under the power of her own repressed attempts at movement, and the burst got her to Tom just as he was falling, his face contorted in pain.

She didn't even—couldn't even—look down to where his body had been ripped open. His insides were hanging out, and he was twisting, and his face looked like he was suffering pain she couldn't imagine.

His wide-open eyes fixed on her, but she didn't know if he could see her. She fell to her knees, and grabbed his hand, which felt too cold and was flexing in what seemed to be a spasmodic movement.

"They can still save you," she said. "They can still save you. The wonders of modern medicine."

But blood was pouring out of his mouth, blood was bubbling out of his nose, and, as she watched, his eyes went totally blank, in the morning light. Blank and upward turned, and wide open.

She couldn't tell if his heart was still beating and, since it was probably in the mass of organs exposed in the front of his body, she couldn't check. And she didn't need to. She knew he was dead.

She stood up, shaking slightly. And then she lost it.

She never knew the exact moment when she lost it. When she realized she was doing something stupid, she had already flung herself forward, at the Great Sky Dragon, arms and legs flying, mouth poised to bite.

"You bastard," she said. "You bastard." Only it wasn't so much a word as a formless growl, and she kicked at the golden foot and tore with her nails at the golden scales.

She felt more than saw as several of the human spectators, the triad members, plunged forward to grab at her, and she didn't care because she could take them all. All of them.

Only the Great Sky Dragon grabbed her in its talons, one of them still stained red by Tom's blood, and brought her up to his face, to look at her intently with his impassive eyes. "Pure fire," the voice that wasn't a voice said. "I wonder if he knows what he holds."

And then she was tumbling down, and hitting the ground hard.

As she struggled to sit up again, she could see the Great Sky Dragon already high in the sky, flapping his wings— vanishing.

Around them, the other men—or mostly dragons— were disappearing. Some flying and some just . . . scurrying away.

Aching, Kyrie looked over at Tom's corpse. He was still staring blankly at the sky. What did she expect? That he would get up and say it was all a joke? Corpses rarely moved.

She swallowed hard. Grief felt like a huge, insoluble lump in her throat.

But the madness was gone. She knew she couldn't avenge herself on the dragons. Or on any of them. She knew as she knew she was alive and that Tom was dead that there was no remedy for this.

She scooted forward and took hold of Tom's hand. "I'm sorry," she said. She knew he couldn't hear her, and she'd never devoted any thought to the possibility of life after this one. But if there was anything, and if he could hear her . . . "I'm sorry. This is not how I meant for this to go. I didn't even realize . . . I didn't know myself until just now." She squeezed the cold hand, knowing it was beyond comfort.

"Kyrie, you have to get up," Rafiel said. "I'm going to call the police. You have to get up from there."

She shook her head. "No. I'll stay with him. I'll go with him. We can't leave him alone here." She saw a fly try to alight on Tom's wide-open eyes, and she waved it away with her free hand. Oh, she knew he was dead and he couldn't feel it, but it seemed . . . indecent.

"Kyrie, he's going to the morgue. You can't go with him. You don't want to. Let me help you up," Rafiel said.

She felt him tear her fingers away from Tom's hand. As if from somewhere, far away, she heard her own thoughts tell her that she was in shock. And she believed them. It just didn't change anything, did it?

There were sounds of someone throwing up behind her. She thought it was Keith, but she didn't turn to look. It had to be Keith, anyway, since there were only the five of them . . . the four of them here. And it couldn't be Edward because he was crying, somewhere to her right side. He was crying, loudly and immoderately. And she thought that was weird because she didn't know lawyers could cry.

Rafiel threw something warm—a jacket?—over her shoulders. "You're trembling, Kyrie. You need something warm," he said.

"Tom's jacket," she said.

"What about it?"

"It will be ruined," she said. "All the blood. He's going to be very upset." And then she realized what she'd said was nonsense, but she couldn't seem to think her way out of that puzzle.

She felt Rafiel lead her very gently. And then there were lights, and noise, and a siren, and someone was asking her something, and she heard Rafiel's voice say, "She really can't talk now. She's in shock. I'm sorry. Perhaps later. We were walking across the parking lot to see when the restaurant opened, and this giant Komodo dragon came running out of nowhere, and it attacked Tom. I'm not really sure of the details. It all happened so fast."

Kyrie felt Keith shove her into a car. She didn't care whose car, nor where she was going.

❖　❖　❖

And then life went on, somehow. It all seemed very odd to Kyrie that life could go on after something like that. She'd seen someone die—no. She'd seen Tom die. She'd seen Tom die so that the rest of them would be allowed to go free.

It all seemed very strange, and she thought about it very deeply. She thought about it so deeply that the rest of life seemed inconsequential.

It all seemed a great mystery. One minute Tom had been alive and well and afraid, and making wisecracks and being himself. And the next minute—no, the next second, he was so much flesh, on the ground. No life, no spirit, no breath.

It was very odd that such a great change could be effected so quickly and that it could never be reversed.

There should be, she thought, and realized she was in her kitchen, sitting at the table and staring down at the pattern of the table—whirls of fake marble engraved on the Formica—*there should be a rewind button on life. So that you could press the button and life would be again as it was before. And the horrible things wouldn't have happened.*

Someone was knocking at the door. At the kitchen door. Tom. But no. Tom would come no more.

But someone was knocking on her kitchen door. And she was sitting at her table in her robe and—she looked—yup, a long T-shirt. She was decent. And someone was knocking, so she guessed she'd better let whomever it was in.

She stood up, opened the door. Keith was there, on the doorstep, wearing his ridiculous backward hat. Only it had to be a new one, because the other one had burned with the castle, had it not? She seemed to remember . . .

He had her newspapers under one arm, and was staring at her, in utter dismay. "Kyrie," he said. "Have you slept? Eaten anything?"

"I don't . . ." She frowned. "I don't remember."

"You don't remember?" Keith asked. He looked scared. "Kyrie, it's been two days."

Two days? Since Tom had died?

"I just realized I'm . . . in my robe. In my home . . ."

"We brought you back. Mr. Ormson . . . Edward put you to bed."

He had? For some reason the idea of a strange male—of a strange older male—undressing her didn't embarrass her. Not even a little. It didn't matter.

She became aware that Keith had dumped the papers on the table, and was bustling around, setting a teapot on, opening the fridge, letting out with exclamations of dismay, if at her housekeeping or the lack of food in her fridge, she didn't know.

It seemed like all of a sudden, he was putting a cup of tea, a plate of toast with jam, and a peeled boiled egg in front of her.

"I'm not the best of cooks, Kyrie, I'm sorry," he said. "This is about all I can cook. But will you eat? A little. For me?"

He was looking pleadingly at her, and he looked far younger than she thought he was, and she thought if she didn't eat he might very well cry.

The toast and the egg tasted like straw to her, but she forced herself to eat them. The tea, at least, was sweet and warm, and she swallowed cup after cup, while Keith poured.

"Have you talked to Rafiel?" Keith asked.

Kyrie had to concentrate to remember Rafiel. It all seemed such a long way away and vague. After a while she shook her head.

"Well, they found journals. Apparently Frank kept journals. He'd managed to keep the beetle under control until just a few years ago and then . . . biological clock or what not and he went insane and started . . . laying down pheromones bait, to attract females and victims. He wrote all about it in his diary. He started laying the pheromones over a year ago. As if he were trying to reassure himself he wasn't crazy. Though most of the killings were the female's doing. He just helped drag the corpses to the castle, afterward."

She nodded, though what Keith was saying only made sense in a very distant and impersonal sort of way, as if he were talking about people who had been dead for centuries and whom nothing could affect.

"He was intending to make Tom the fall guy for it all, you know. That's why he hired someone from the homeless shelter with a history of drug abuse. The idea was to make all corpses disappear, except a couple, which would be found near Tom's apartment, and it would be thought that Tom had killed them all, that he had gone over the edge. The beetle's hallucinogenic powder would have helped. That's why they attacked us here. They wanted you to throw him out. They didn't want anyone to be around him, or to know him that well."

Well, and that had worked. And had led by degrees to everything else. But Kyrie felt too numb to even feel guilt. None of it mattered. She put her empty cup forward, and Keith filled it again.

"Kyrie, can you take a sleeping tablet? I bought some over-the-counter ones. I couldn't . . . I couldn't sleep without having nightmares. I have one. Can you take them? Or will they cause you any problems?"

"I can take them," she said, her voice sounding pasty and altogether like a stranger's.

He put the small yellow tablet in her hand. She swallowed it with a gulp of tea. Presently she felt as if the world around her were becoming blurry.

She was only vaguely aware of Keith's leading her to her bed, and tucking her in. For such a young kid—though he might be her age in chronological years—he had an oddly maternal touch as he tucked the blanket around her.

"Sleep," he said. "I'll take a key. I'll come check on you."

❖   ❖   ❖

"This too shall pass," Kyrie said, and startled herself with saying it. Keith had come and checked on her and forced her to eat and sleep for the last two days.

This morning she'd woken up realizing that she couldn't go on like this.

Life would go on, even when there didn't seem to be any point to it. And it wasn't as though she could say, "Please just stop my subscription, I don't want to play anymore." Nor did it seem to matter. Not that way.

A wedge of sanity was forcing itself into her shock and grief. She'd liked Tom. She'd liked Tom a lot. Although at least part of the feeling was probably lust. She remembered his sprayed-on clothes, and she could smile, in distant appreciation.

She got up out of bed. It was eight a.m. Keith had been dropping by every morning at ten, after early classes. She didn't want him to catch her naked. And she really should stop being a burden to the poor young man. It was time she got herself together.

A glimpse in the mirror showed her how fully horrible she looked, with her unwashed hair matted and falling in tangles in front of her face. Witch of the Rainbow Hairdo, she thought and smiled, an odd smile, from pale, cracked lips.

She opened her dresser and got out jeans and a dark T-shirt, and underwear. She lugged everything to the bathroom, where she realized she still had her red feather earring on. She couldn't remember preserving it through the fight at the castle, but she must have, because she was wearing it.

She took it off and laid it, reverently, on the vanity. Tom had saved that for her.

Under the hot, full shower, she washed rapidly. Shampoo. Twice to get rid of all the grease she'd allowed her hair to accumulate in the last . . . three? four days? And then conditioner. And then soap her body, slowly, bit by bit, making sure every bit got properly scrubbed.

She doubted she had washed . . . since. There was green-red ichor on her legs. And her arms and hands were stained the dark—almost black—red of dried blood. Tom's blood. She watched it wash down the drain, in the water.

Damn. It wasn't only that she'd liked him. It wasn't only that she lusted after him and she'd never had a chance to do anything about it. It was that she'd only realized what he was made of as he was dying.

Oh, not just because he stepped up and offered himself in exchange for his father—and safety for all of them—but because he'd done it without complaint. And as a matter of course. Even the creature . . . the dragon, had told him he had courage.

Why you'd say that to someone who was about to die was beyond Kyrie. Maybe the dragon believed in an afterlife. Maybe he'd thought it would make things easier . . .

She finished showering and dried. Tom's towel was still there, hanging from the hook at the back of the door. She resisted a wild impulse to smell it, to bury her face in it and see if any of his scent remained on the fibers.

But no. That way lay madness. That way lay people who kept the rooms of dead people just the way they'd been when the person died. That way lay widows who slept with their husband's used clothes under their pillows. And it wasn't as if she had the right, even. He wasn't her husband. He wasn't even her boyfriend. Until a few days ago, she would have told people she didn't like him.

She dressed herself, combed her hair, carefully put her earring in.

The face that looked at her from the mirror was still too pale, and she looked like she'd lost weight too. Her cheekbones poked out too far. But there was really nothing for it, was there? Life went on.

She'd got to the kitchen and put on the kettle, when someone knocked at the kitchen door. She thought it was Keith. He'd taken a key—what did he think she was going to do? Try to kill herself? Did he think he'd need the key to get in and save her?—but he still knocked before getting in.

"Come in," she said.

"I can't," a muffled voice said. "It's locked."

She reached over and unlocked the door. And . . . Edward Ormson came in.

He stood just inside the door, as if uncertain what he was going to do or say, or why he'd come here at all.

Kyrie turned from the small pan in which she'd just put an egg to boil. Keith must have brought eggs one of these days, because there were two cartons in the fridge. "Do you want an egg?" she asked.

"No, thank you," he said. His skin looked ashen. His eyes, so much like Tom's, were sunken in dark rings. "I've . . . eaten."

She got a feeling that what he was really saying was that he never wanted to eat again. Ever.

"I . . ." He hesitated. He was wearing cargo pants and a T-shirt and looked ruffled and uncertain and a long way from the smooth lawyer who'd landed in town however many days ago. "I would like to talk to you."

"Sit," Kyrie said. "As long as you don't mind if I eat while you talk."

As a matter of fact, though, she got two cups down from the cupboard, and grabbed the sugar bowl, which she put between them. She poured a cup for Edward and said, "Put sugar in it. Even if you normally don't. It seems to help. Keith has been making me drink it."

"Keith . . ." Edward said.

And Kyrie thought that he was going to accuse her of having an affair with Keith right after Tom had died, as if she'd made Tom any promises. And besides, she wasn't. Having an affair with Keith. She'd barely been aware of him here, to be honest, except for his making her eat and drink. And she thought he'd done the dishes once, because everything was out of place in the cupboard.

But Edward grimaced, and ran his hand back through his hair, just like Tom used to do. "Yeah, Keith has been coming to my hotel room every morning, too. And making me eat. He wrangled a key from the front desk somehow. I have no idea what the front desk people think is going on, and I'm afraid to ask." His grimace became an almost smile. "But he's kept me alive, I think. It didn't seem . . . to matter for a while."

"I'd have thought you'd be back in New York," Kyrie said. "With your family."

He shrugged. "There is no family. There was Tom. And I couldn't leave . . . yet. They're going to give me back the body tomorrow. I'll be flying it back with me for burial. Our family has a plot in Connecticut." He hesitated. "There will be a funeral. Probably closed-casket funeral. I wouldn't want . . ." He shook his head. "I thought you might want to come. I . . . you don't have to but if you want to I'll pay your fare. I've asked Keith, too. Other than that it will just be me and my business associates. I think . . . some of Tom's friends should be there."

Kyrie contemplated this. She wasn't sure. On the one hand it might offer . . . closure. On the other hand, she just wasn't sure. After all—she knew he was dead. Did she need to see him buried too?

And yet, it did seem right that he should have friends there with him, didn't it? He shouldn't go into the ground watched only by people who thought he'd gone bad. Poor Edward's son who'd gone to the wrong.

"I'll try," she said. "Yes. I think I would like to go."

"Good," he said. "And that brings me to what I wanted to talk to you about. You know the Athens is closed. From what I understand it is about to be foreclosed on. Not only had . . . the owner no living relatives that anyone can find, but he hadn't paid the mortgage in about three months. Apparently whatever frenzy . . . well . . . He wasn't taking care of business."

She nodded, not sure what he meant.

"I wanted to offer you . . . I wanted to . . . I know you're unemployed now."

Kyrie shook her head. "Waiting jobs aren't hard to come by," she said. "Particularly late-night ones. People offer them to you for being alive and breathing."

"I know," Edward said. "But I would like . . ." He took a deep breath, as if steeling himself to brave a dragon in full rampage. "Tom liked you an awful lot."

She nodded, then shrugged. It didn't seem to matter.

"I'd like to offer you college money," Edward said. "And however much money you need to live while you're in college. You can study whatever you want to." He swallowed, as if something in her expression intimidated him further. "I can't help you much in most professions, but if you take law, I can see to it that our firm hires you, and if you're half as smart as you seem to be, I can probably nudge you up to partner before you're thirty."

She heard herself laugh and then, in horror, she heard abuse pouring from her lips. She called him every dirty word she could think of. And some she wasn't sure existed.

His eyes widened. "Why . . . why?"

"You're trying to make reparations," she said, and the sane person at the back of the mind of the raving lunatic she seemed to have become noted that she sounded quite wild. "As if Tom were responsible for my being without a job. Tom isn't, you know. It was not his fault that the beetles ran wild. It was not his fault—"

And then the tears came, for the first time since all this had started. Tears chased each other down her cheeks, and there was a great sense of release. As though whatever she'd kept bottled up all this time had finally been allowed to flow.

She became aware of Edward's hand, gently, patting her hair. "You have it all wrong," he said. "I'm not trying to make up for anything Tom did. It's just that without Tom, I really have no family. And besides, I owe him a debt. Whoever started it—and it can be argued I did—right there in the end, he gave his life to end it, so that I could go free. That's a debt. I'm trying to look after the people he cared for. Don't deny me that. I've offered the same thing to Keith. Anything I can do to help, in his studies or his career . . . I'm a fairly useless person. Most of what I can offer is money. But that's yours, if you need it."

As suddenly as they'd started, the tears stopped. Kyrie wiped at her face, and swallowed and nodded. "I don't know, yet," she said. "I just don't know. I'll . . . I'll come to the funeral. And then we'll see."

❖   ❖   ❖

"There are jobs with the police force, if you should want them," Rafiel said.

He stood by her kitchen door, looking, for the first time since she'd known him, stiff and ill at ease.

Kyrie sat at her kitchen table. She'd been going through all the newspapers, one by one. The one from after Tom's death talked about the two horrible tragedies in town— the group of people who seemed to have died in the garden at the castle. And Tom's death. The headline screamed "A Tragic Night In Goldport."

She looked up at Rafiel. "Surely the CSIs could tell that the bodies had been dead a while and buried," she said.

Rafiel seemed to take this as encouragement to come further into the house. "Yes and no," he said. "They could see . . . sort of, that things weren't exactly textbook. But the thing is that the fire got really hot there, at the center of the garden, and they couldn't say much for sure about each of the corpses, except identify them through dental records."

"The . . . beetles . . ."

"They must have reverted, in death or in burning, because they found skeletons." He sat down at the table, across from her. "They identified Frank and the woman who owned the castle. The castle itself survived, by the way. There's talk of someone buying it to make a school for deaf and blind kids."

Kyrie nodded, and flipped through the other papers. There were pictures of all the other dead. Even Frank, with his Neanderthal brow, graced the front pages of all newspapers. All of them smiled from posed photos or looked out from poses obviously clipped from candid snapshots. All except Tom.

"There are no pictures of Tom," she said.

Rafiel shook his head. "No," he said. "His father's picture of Tom, in his wallet, is from when Tom was six. We didn't think it was appropriate. And while his father thinks there are mug shots from his juvenile arrests, he didn't think those were appropriate either. And no one has tracked them down, possibly because the record is sealed."

Kyrie felt bereft. She couldn't explain it to herself, but she felt like she needed to see Tom's face, just once more. She was afraid of forgetting him. She was afraid his features would slip from her mind, irrecoverable.

While she'd come to accept that she'd live on past this, that she might very well live on to find someone and marry, maybe, sometime—her shifter handicap being accounted for—she couldn't bear the thought of forgetting Tom. "It's just . . . I would very much like to remember his face," she said.

Rafiel looked at her, intently. He was wiggling his leg again, this time side to side, very fast. "About what I said about Tom, the day . . . I was an ass, Kyrie. I could tell you were interested in him, and I was afraid. You . . . are very special to me, Kyrie."

She didn't know what to say to that, and just looked at him, with what she was sure was a vacant look.

He laughed, a short laugh, more like a bark. "And I'm being an ass again, aren't I? I can't give you a picture of him. Unless you want the one from when he was six and I don't suppose . . ." He sighed. "Would you like to come to the morgue? To see him? He's being given back to his father tonight, so if you want to see him, it has to be now."

Kyrie thought of Tom's face contorted in pain, as she'd last seen it. She wasn't sure that was the memory she wanted.

"He doesn't look like he did, you know. In death . . . His face has relaxed. They . . . the coroner closed him up. He doesn't look gross at all. More like he's sleeping."

"You were there?" Kyrie asked. "For the autopsy?" She thought of what she'd seen done to the corpse from the parking lot—the body opened, the brain sawed out of its cavity.

"There was no autopsy. It didn't seem needed. We supposedly saw death, you know, attack by wild animal. They found a couple of scales on his body. They're not exactly Komodo dragon scales." He frowned. "To be honest, they were in his boots and were probably . . . his . . . but they analyzed as reptile scales and the paper is printing something about the danger of exotic pets. They love to preach. And his father didn't want him autopsied, so he wasn't. He really looks . . . very natural."

Kyrie wasn't sure. The morgue had scared her. But perhaps seeing Tom without that expression of agony on his face was all she needed.

She nodded. In the bathroom, she caught herself putting on lip gloss and combing her hair. As if Tom could see her.

Feeling very silly, she headed out the door with Rafiel.

The morgue was . . . as it had been before. The guy at the desk didn't even make much fuss over Kyrie coming back. Just tipped his hat at her, as if she were a known person here.

Rafiel led her down the cool, faintly smelly corridors, to a door at the end. He opened the door and turned on a very bright fluorescent light, which glared off tiled walls. In this room, the tiles were white, and it made the whole thing look like an antiseptic cell. Or the inside of an ice cube.

It wasn't an autopsy room. Just a small room, with a collapsible metal table set up against one wall. On the table was something—no, someone—covered with a sheet. The room was just this side of freezing.

"We don't have drawers," Rafiel said. "Just ten of these rooms. If needed we can cram three people per room, but I don't think we've ever needed to. The closest we came were the bones, from the castle, and those we just put all together in one room, while we sorted out who was who and identified victims by dental records and DNA."

She nodded. She didn't remember walking up to the table, but she was standing right next to it, now. She couldn't quite bring herself to reach out her hand and pull the sheet back.

Rafiel reached past her, and pulled the sheet back. Just enough to reveal Tom's face and neck.

He was right, Tom didn't look as he had at the time of his death. He also didn't look as other dead people that Kyrie had seen. She expected wax-dummy pallor. She expected the feeling she'd had when she'd seen other dead people—even when she'd seen Tom dead, in the parking lot. That feeling that all that mattered had fled the body and the only thing left there was . . . meat.

But there wasn't that sense. Instead, there was as much color as she'd seen on Tom when he was pale. Not the paper-white pallor of his anger, and not the sickly pale of the parking lot, when they'd discovered the corpse. Just, even, ivory white. His lips even had a faint color—pale pink. And his eyelids were closed, his quite indecently long eyelashes—how come she never had noticed?— resting against the white of his skin and giving the impression that at any minute his eyes would flutter open and he'd wake up.

She looked up to ask Rafiel if embalmers had worked on Tom, but Rafiel had left. Very decent of him. Giving her time alone with Tom.

She ran a hand down Tom's cheek. It felt . . . warm to the touch. She didn't know embalmers could do that. She caught at a bit of his hair. It felt silky soft in her hand. Clearly, they'd cleaned the body of blood.

Bending over him, she caught herself and thought this was insane. She couldn't, seriously, be meaning to kiss a dead man? But he didn't look dead. He didn't *feel* dead, and it wasn't as though she meant to French him. Just a quick peck on the lips. A good-bye.

She bent down all the way, and set her lips on him for a quick peck.

His lips were warm—warmer than she would expect, even from someone alive who was lying down in a refrigerated room—and she would swear they moved under hers.

And then she heard him draw a breath. She felt breath against her own lips. His eyes flew open. He looked very shocked. Then he smiled, under her lips. He wrapped his arms around her shoulders. He pulled her down onto him.

And he kissed her very thoroughly.

It should have been scary, but it was not. It was just . . . Tom. And his mouth tasted, a little, of blood, but it wasn't unpleasant. As soon as he allowed her to pull up, she said, "You're alive."

He frowned. "It would seem so. Shouldn't I be?"

She shook her head. "We're at the morgue."

He raised his eyebrows, but the mild curiosity didn't stop him from pulling her face down toward him, and kissing her again.

"Oh, hell," a voice said, startling them both; sending Kyrie flying back from Tom; and making Tom sit up and the sheet that covered him fall.

He pulled it back up, to make himself decent, but left his chest exposed, and Kyrie blinked, because where she was sure there had been a torso-long rip that exposed his insides, there was now only a very faint scar, as though he had only had a superficial cut.

They turned to the person who'd said, "Oh, hell."

It was Rafiel, and he was leaning against the wall, by the door, looking at them with wide-open eyes. "Shit," he said very softly. "It's nice to see you well, Tom, but how the hell do I explain to the coroner that his corpse with massive trauma is going to walk out of here?"

"Tell him reports of my death were greatly exaggerated?" Tom asked, raising an eyebrow and smiling.

"But we need to get him out of here soon," Kyrie said. "And get him some clothes. He's going to catch his death of cold."

"I doubt it," Rafiel said. "I very much doubt it. Unless cold is a silver bullet."

And life went on even when the best that could possibly happen had happened. The day that Tom was let out of the morgue—though the coroner had insisted he go to the hospital for X-rays and a full checkup before admitting that Tom might, just possibly, be alive—they'd bought a daybed and a dresser for the back room.

They'd been quite prepared to use the rest of Tom's money and get it from the Salvation Army, but Edward had insisted, and so Tom had a matching daybed and dresser in Southwestern style, as well as a bookcase and a bunch of books his father had bought him to replace the ones that had been destroyed in his apartment.

The back room was now his, and for the use of it, the kitchen and the other common areas, he would pay half of Kyrie's rent, and half the utilities. Kyrie's bathroom had acquired a bottle of something called Mane and Tail, which she'd told Tom seemed more appropriate for Rafiel, and shouldn't Tom's shampoo be Wing and Scale?

But they weren't living together. Not exactly. They were roommates, not lovers. They hadn't slept together, didn't know if it would ever happen.

For now there were kisses, now and then, and the occasional holding of hands. Tom had explained what he wanted with disarming frankness. "I'd like to date," he'd told her the night he'd gotten out of the morgue—was it only two weeks ago?—over dinner. "I've never dated, you know? Not even high school dating. I groped a few girls in school." He'd grinned. "They all complained. And I think I suck at relationships. Of any sort. I need practice. I'd like to date. Well . . . go together, as if we were kids. And then work up to the rest, if it works out."

The decision to share a house seemed odd in light of that, but it wasn't. Between two shifters, one of them should be able to watch out for the other. And also, they'd both realized that they'd been awfully lonely. And whether they were ever anything else again, they were friends.

They were also partners. Not in a romantic sense, but in a business sense.

Kyrie remembered a whole afternoon of shouting between Tom and his father. Both men assured her they'd never raised their voices, but she remembered sitting on the sofa in her living room while they glowered at each other and shouted, both of their expressions very much alike, and both far more intense than the argument warranted.

The gist of it was that Edward wanted to give Tom the moon, the stars, and happiness on a plate—or at least the only form of it Edward could give him. He wanted Tom to go back to school. He wanted to pay Tom's expenses while he did. He still wanted to pay Kyrie's too. Both studies and expenses.

Tom . . . wanted something completely different. He wanted the Athens. He would accept enough money to go to cooking school. Not chef's school. Far too fancy. Tom wanted to learn enough to be the cook of the Athens. And he wanted Kyrie to have part ownership of it.

Which brought them to this evening, two weeks later, standing outside what used to be the Athens. There was a new sign, up front, and Keith, perched up on a ladder, was finishing painting it. It said, in fancy old-English script "The George" and, in case someone missed the reference, there was a cartoonish drawing of Saint George, spearing a flaming dragon.

It was all very baffling to Kyrie, but Tom had insisted. And when Keith came down from his ladder, to much applause from the four of them—Kyrie, Tom, Rafiel, and Edward—and took a bow at his artistry, and Tom led them inside, the bafflement continued.

Tom had found somewhere, in the bowels of the Salvation Army—while he was trying to find replacements for some of his personal effects behind his father's back— an old, possibly antique, and definitely disgusting painting. It showed Saint George on a horse putting a lance through the chest of a dragon, who fountained quantities of blood. He now proceeded to hang it over the big booth at the back, the only one that could sit ten people.

"I hope you realize it's in extremely poor taste," Kyrie said.

"Yeah," Rafiel said. "That would kill you. That was the difference between you and the other corpses. The Great Sky Dragon didn't get your heart."

"I wonder if it was on purpose," Keith said.

"I'm sure it was," Tom said, finishing nailing his picture and jumping down from the vinyl seat, and backing up to admire the effect. "I suspect he considered it the equivalent of turning me over his knee."

"Has the coroner recovered yet?" Kyrie asked. "From having one of his corpses walk out?"

"Well . . ." Rafiel said. "He's now talking about how Tom was in comatose shock from the injury. In another five days he'll have convinced himself that he never pronounced Tom dead. I mean, if he told the truth, people would wonder if he'd been drinking his own formaldehyde. *He's* probably wondering if he's been drinking his own formaldehyde. People hate doubting their own sanity. He'll make . . . adjustments."

"But could the Great Sky Dragon know that?" Keith asked. "Wouldn't he have feared Tom's coming back would hit the papers and blow the whole shifter thing sky-high?"

"I doubt it," Tom said. He turned around, a frown making a vertical wrinkle between his eyebrows. "I very much doubt it. He's been around a lot. He knows people."

"What I want to know," Rafiel said softly, "is if the great triad presence in town was because of the Pearl of Heaven and if they'll now thin out, or if we're stuck with them for good. We don't have the police force to deal with an international criminal organization. . . ."

"I wonder if they'll leave us alone," Kyrie said. "They strike me as people with notoriously little sense of humor—whatever the Great Sky Dragon has. And they're bound to be a little . . . miffed at us." She looked out the corner of her eye at Edward, who had already declared his intention to leave the firm that worked so much for the triads. He'd start again on his own. He'd made some noises about maybe moving to Denver. She wondered if any of these intentions would survive once he got back to New York.

But Edward didn't notice her look. He was still staring at the picture of Saint George, wide-eyed. "Good Lord, Tom," he said. "It will put customers off their food."

"I very much doubt it," Kyrie said. "Tom has been hiding talents. He can actually cook."

"And college students will eat anything," Keith said.

"There is that," Kyrie admitted. Then she looked at Tom, who was looking at her with a little smile. When he looked like that, it was very hard not to kiss him, and she'd been trying very hard not to kiss him in public. It only gave people ideas. Besides, they were at The George. They were supposed to behave as business partners. "So, what's the symbolism, Tom?"

"Can't you tell?" he asked softly. "I thought you'd get it." Smiling, he looked around at the still empty tables. The door was closed, the Closed sign firmly in place. In a minute, Keith—who wanted to work for them part-time, at night, even while going to college—was going to go out and hang the "Grand Opening" and "Under New Management" signs out there. But for now everything was quiet.

"The pheromones that Frank laid down will take years to wear out," Tom said. "Rafiel," he looked at the policeman, "has had them analyzed, and they are very potent. It's not unusual for little beetles to lay down chemical signs that attract mates and prey from miles away. These ones might very well act on the whole country. And they're specific for shifters. We'll have shifters coming out of our ears for years to come. Chances are," he said, looking at Rafiel, "that we'll have to keep order in our own little strange community. So many occasions for people to go over the edge. And we can't afford for the more out-of-control of us to expose us all to danger. So . . ." He waved expansively toward the picture on the wall. "We get to be both the beast, and the dragon slayer. It's perfect."

"If you say so," Kyrie said.

"There's people milling around out there," Keith said.

"Those aren't people, darling," Kyrie said, turning around, and surely surprising poor Keith with the playful appellation. "That's the poet and pie lady. They just want to come and loiter all night, eating too little food." She grinned at him. "Go open the door."

"And I suppose I'd better eat something," Edward said. "I'm taking the last flight to New York." He looked at the menu. New menus, freshly laminated. "Good Lord," he said. "What are these?"

"It's old diner lingo. Tom insisted. There's a translation in front of each item."

"You really have to learn to start saying no to that boy," Edward said, smiling. "He has entirely too many crazy ideas for his own good."

"Oh, trust me," Kyrie said. "I say no enough." And had Tom's father blushed?

He looked away from her and backed, to sit at a table facing the counter. Keith was opening the door. Behind the counter, Tom had put his—blue, emblazoned in gold—apron on. Yesterday he'd spent the whole day scrubbing the counter and kitchen area till it glimmered. And they'd interviewed and hired the staff. Anthony. And a couple of the day girls. And Keith, and half a dozen other new faces.

They, themselves, would have to work twelve hours or more a day, everyday. It didn't matter. That it was their place made all the difference.

Keith was writing stuff on the glass window. Most of it incomprehensible to the normal—or even abnormal—mind because it was taken from Tom's research of old diner lingo. There was for instance "Moo with Haystacks," which she thought was supposed to be burger and fries, for $5. She was going to have a talk with Keith and get him to write stuff everyone understood.

But for now, it was the first night, and she didn't mind if only the regulars came in.

Edward looked up from his menu. "I think I'll try the hash," he said.

"Really?" Kyrie asked.

"Really. I haven't had it in years, and since my own son is cooking, the chances are low he'll poison me. They're there, but low."

"All right," Kyrie said, and glanced in the menu to see the fancy name that Tom wanted hash called. Getting back to the counter, she looked over it at Tom.

He'd tied his hair back and tied a scarf over it, pirate style, to keep hair from the grill. Which just meant that he wasn't in the spirit of cooking in a diner yet. And he smiled at her, which made all thoughts flee her mind for a while.

It took her a few seconds to remember Edward's order, and to relay it in the new-menu-speak. "Gentleman will take a chance," she told Tom.

His features crinkled up in a smile. "Oh, yes. I am quite sure he will."

IF YOU LIKE...
YOU SHOULD TRY...

DAVID DRAKE
David Weber

DAVID WEBER
John Ringo

JOHN RINGO
Michael Z. Williamson
Tom Kratman

ANNE MCCAFFREY
Mercedes Lackey

MERCEDES LACKEY
Wen Spencer, Andre Norton
Andre Norton
James H. Schmitz

LARRY NIVEN
James P. Hogan
Travis S. Taylor

ROBERT A. HEINLEIN
Jerry Pournelle
Lois McMaster Bujold
Michael Z. Williamson

HEINLEIN'S "JUVENILES"
Rats, Bats & Vats series by Eric Flint & Dave Freer

HORATIO HORNBLOWER OR PATRICK O'BRIAN
David Weber's Honor Harrington series
David Drake's RCN series

HARRY POTTER
Mercedes Lackey's Urban Fantasy series

THE LORD OF THE RINGS
Elizabeth Moon's *The Deed of Paksenarrion*

H.P. LOVECRAFT
Princess of Wands by John Ringo

GEORGETTE HEYER
Lois McMaster Bujold
Catherine Asaro

GREEK MYTHOLOGY
Pyramid Scheme by Eric Flint & Dave Freer
Forge of the Titans by Steve White
Blood of the Heroes by Steve White

NORSE MYTHOLOGY
Northworld Trilogy by David Drake
A Mankind Witch by Dave Freer

ARTHURIAN LEGEND
Steve White's "Legacy" series
The Dragon Lord by David Drake

SCA/HISTORICAL REENACTMENT
John Ringo's "After the Fall" series
Harald by David D. Friedman

SCIENCE FACT
Kicking the Sacred Cow by James P. Hogan

CATS
Larry Niven's Man-Kzin Wars series

PUNS
Rick Cook
Spider Robinson
Wm. Mark Simmons

VAMPIRES
Wm. Mark Simmons